'A life-changing book for young Deaf and disabled people…
of personal growth and pride – demonstrating the importance
of the #OwnVoices movement.' CARLY FINDLAY, OAM

'Asphyxia's work is brilliant: a deep, original insight, and
a book that everyone should read.' JACKIE FRENCH, AM

'Brilliantly imaginative, totally immersive – Asphyxia tilts the
world sideways and invites you to see what was always there.
Don't miss this book.' AMIE KAUFMAN

'*Future Girl* takes me back to my own… transformation
into loving myself as I am: a signing Deaf woman with
a place in both the Deaf and hearing worlds.'
DRISANA LEVITZKE-GRAY

'Beautiful, immersive… a sensory feast.' JACLYN MORIARTY

'I really enjoyed this gorgeous book and related
to so many things. That is rare. I can't wait for the
world to read *Future Girl*.' ANNA SEYMOUR

'*Future Girl* confronts the challenges ahead of us and will
open minds and hearts to the possibility of other worlds.'
SEAN WILLIAMS

Australian Government | Australia Council for the Arts

This project has been assisted by the Australian Government through the Australia Council, its arts funding and advisory body.

First published by Allen & Unwin in 2020

Copyright © Text and Illustrations, Asphyxia 2020

Thanks to Deaf reader Anna Seymour, and Auslan interpreter Belinda Diggins, for double-checking the Deaf cultural content in the story.

Allen & Unwin
83 Alexander Street
Crows Nest NSW 2065
Australia
Phone: (61 2) 8425 0100
Email: info@allenandunwin.com
Web: www.allenandunwin.com

A catalogue record for this book is available from the National Library of Australia

ISBN 978 1 76029 437 3

For teaching resources, explore www.allenandunwin.com/resources/for-teachers

Illustration technique: acrylic and watercolour paint, ink, collage, encaustic, plaster, spray-paint, rubber stamp, Photoshop and Procreate

Thanks to Elise Jones for editorial support
Cover design by Asphyxia, Sandra Nobes & Jenine Davidson
Text design by Sandra Nobes & Jenine Davidson
Set in 11.5 pt Sabon by Sandra Nobes
Printed by C&C Offset Printing Co. Ltd, China

10 9 8 7 6 5 4 3 2

MIX
Paper from responsible sources
FSC® C008047

www.asphyxia.com.au

FUTURE
GIRL

by ASPHYXIA

ALLEN&UNWIN
SYDNEY • MELBOURNE • AUCKLAND • LONDON

This book belongs to

Piper McBride

PRIVATE! (Do not read.)

WEDNESDAY 17 JUNE

My pencil scratches over the plastic sheet, outlining a red cylinder. With a white pen I add tiny hairs, a floating tail. Not bad. It's luminous, glowing. Taylor nudges me, points to the time on her visi-screen. She means, *Stop faffing around with that drawing, focus on your visi, and get on with the assignment.*

I add a caption to the bottom: *E coli.*

'That's E coli?' Taylor types. 'I thought you were inventing recon lollies. Something new for your mum to make.'

'This is a dangerous missile,' I type back. 'It lurks in wild food, waiting to kill you. Don't be deceived by its pretty face. And anyway, Mum doesn't do food design. She just researches the nutrition to include.'

Taylor scowls and smooths her fringe with her palm. She only cut it last week – it still looks weird on her. My hair is long and straight and dark and has been that way forever.

'I know that,' Taylor types. 'Are you gonna help write this thing up? We'll get dismal marks if you leave it to me.'

She's done as I asked, drafted an outline. I sigh and punch 'food poisoning' into Cesspool. It spits out a long list of feeds about people who ate wild food and died. In a perverse kind of a way, Mum loves this stuff. Every time another story comes out, recon sales jump. One of these days, everyone will be eating recon and wild food will be a distant memory.

1.

My head throbs and the insides of my ears itch. I'm sick of sitting under fluorescent lights, lined up in rows with a hundred other girls wearing blue-and-white uniforms, staring at our transparent plastic desk-mounted visi-screens. But that's Mary Magdalene Ladies' College for you. I rub my ear moulds so they scratch at my ears, but it's not enough. I can't take out my hearing aids yet, though; not until class finishes.

Taylor nudges me again and gestures with her head towards Madison, Alyssa and Briony. Something's going on. They're crowding around Madison's visi-screen, a matching set with their new fringes. A buzz ripples through the classroom as a bunch of other girls notice and wander over to join them. Soon enough, they're all talking emphatically... and they keep glancing over at me.

I check our teacher, Lisa. She throws me a glance before typing something into Cesspool and bringing up whatever it is on her own visi. She's supposed to be controlling our behaviour! Why isn't she telling everyone to shut up and focus on food poisoning? And what does whatever's going on have to do with me?

I strain my eyes, trying to catch my classmates' words on their lips, but everywhere I look I see faces obscured by long locks of shiny hair. My hearing aids are no good for stuff happening on the other side of the room.

I stare anyway and notice a rim of inflamed red skin around Madison's wristlet. She's had it implanted! Wow. No wristband required, and no need to recharge it anymore. Forgetting your wristlet because it's charging has been the worst – no tram check-ins, no access to your money at shops, no way to prove your ID – since the government rolled out Cesspool (sorry, *QuestTool*) two years ago. I just wish I was better at one-handed typing, but despite the new school subject they introduced to help us adjust, I'm as hopeless as everyone else. Except for Briony, who has lightning fingers.

Taylor taps her visi and brings up News Melbourne. Mum comes into focus, speaking to the camera. Oh. Everyone knows I'm Irene McBride's daughter. Taylor taps again, and the text version rolls down the screen.

N NEWSMELBOURNE

Recon Rally Unfounded

Parents of unwell children are rallying at Federation Square, expressing concerns recon could be causing the recent rises in rhinitis, asthma and Energy Deficiency Syndrome, particularly in vulnerable people such as the young and elderly. However, Organicore's leading scientist, Irene McBride, provides reassurance that recon is not the cause: 'Increasing pollution, declining air quality, and problems with water due to desalination plant issues are all likely culprits for health issues. We at Organicore are committed to finding solutions, not creating problems. The common cold, cancer and obesity are now history, thanks to our research team, and we are working on detoxification boosters to include in recon to address these current problems.'

Onscreen, Mum looks poised. The image cuts to Fed Square, where angry parents are clutching pale, wheezy-looking children. One placard says *Don't drug our kids*, which seems a bit harsh.

I remember when Mum added the fat-destroyers, cancer-zappers and virus-killers to Nutrium Sustate, the nutrition powder she developed. At first the idea of mass medication in our food was controversial, but that changed once Karen Kildare was elected prime minister and News Melbourne started publishing the stats each week so that we could all see the health benefits for ourselves.

I massage my temples and try to ignore the stares. So what? It's just news. But I can't help myself from sliding News Melbourne into view; despite Mum's apparent confidence, I know this will be stressing her out.

A new feed has replaced the one about recon, though. Mum's already history. Instead, there's a photo of Organicore's biggest competitor: people are crowding through the doors of an outlet of the Allstar supermarket chain.

NNEWSMELBOURNE

Consumers Swarm Supermarkets

This week's oil price jump has affected incoming shipments of food and consumer goods, resulting in a shortage on supermarket shelves. Desperate consumers are stockpiling basics, leaving with trolleys piled high, while others meet sparsely stocked shelves with disappointment. It's a tough week for consumers, with electricity and gas prices also on the rise and petrol already beyond the average household budget.

I yawn. I'm sick of this oil thing already. I don't get why it's such a big deal: with a recon subscription, we don't need to queue at the supermarket, and it's not like recon is unaffordable. Maybe Allstar will be unable to meet consumer demand and will go out of business. Now *that* would make Mum happy.

Taylor pokes me and eyeballs her visi. She's written me a message: 'Come to a party with me and Beau on Sat night? It's in Fitzroy, not far from you.'

Beau's the guy she's been hanging around with. Things must have escalated if she's going to a party with him. I haven't met him yet, but according to Taylor he's older, tall and magnetising.

I type back, 'Good to see you putting in a solid effort on our assignment.'

She kicks me under our desk. I nod and give her the thumbs up. *Yeah, I'll come.*

Piper McBride

**FRIDAY
19 JUNE**

My hand flies, the pacer pencil I'm holding scribbling grey lines loose and fast across the plastic sheet. I glance in the mirror. My picture needs to be darker around the eyes. I work back and forth around the eyelids, my face coming into focus. It doesn't look much like me, I don't think, but I've finally done a face with the right proportions!

Now, how to capture my skin? It's pale, with a few freckles. When I try to draw the freckles, they look just that: drawn on. I ignore my school uniform and sketch in my favourite top instead. I'll add red paint later. My nose isn't quite right, so I check the mirror again and nearly jump out of my skin. Mum's right behind me.

'Hey,' I say, though I can't hear my own voice.

She gestures for me to put my hearing aids in. Sigh. The desperate must-get-a-cotton-bud-now itch has only just worn off my ears. Not that a cotton bud ever satisfies that itch. Reluctantly I plug them back in and turn to Mum. 'I didn't realise you were home.'

'Piper, you should be wearing your hearing aids. What if there's a fire? How will you hear the alarm? What if someone comes to the door?'

My eyes throb. Mum's easy for me to understand, but the headache is arcing up again anyway. Right now, I just want to be left alone, to fix the nose in my picture, figure out freckles. I couldn't care less if someone comes to the door and I ignore them. The only person who ever visits me is Taylor, and she always messages me so that my wristlet vibrates when she arrives.

'Nice to see you too, Mum. How was your day?'

She shakes her head, and I check her face more closely. Something's not right. Her eyes are tight, the lines around them sharply etched. Her shoulders are heavy and her hair's not straight. She keeps it dyed, in a neat (usually) black bob, like an older version of Karen Kildare. The top buttons of Mum's jacket are open, exposing the high neck of her ruffled shirt, and even that is slightly askew.

'What's up?' I set aside my drawing and follow her into the kitchen. It's bright after the bathroom. The huge expanse of bench, which we never use for cooking now that we only eat recon, is piled with my art stuff – it's the best and brightest space to work at in our house, when I'm not in need of the bathroom mirror. The dining table is covered with folders from Mum's work, so we mostly use the breakfast nook in front of the bay window when we eat together – a cosy spot with a soft blue velvet chair for each of us and a round marble table. There's a framed painting of the ocean on the wall, which I did in Year 7. I'd do it better now, adding shading beneath the waves to give them more texture. Mum selected the blue velvet chairs specially to match my painting, though, and they make the room look classy and the amateurishness of the painting look deliberate.

'Can I get you a glass of wine?' I ask. That always soothes her. I pour one and hand it to her. 'Out with it.'

Mum sighs, removes her jacket, kicks off her office shoes, and curls up in her velvet chair. She looks pretty and comfortable. I'm glad I inherited her fine bones. I should paint her, with the dying sunlight through the bay window catching her hair from behind. Though I'd add plants blurred through the glass instead of the shed Mum optimistically calls *the guesthouse*. She's been meaning to fix it up since we moved here but, surprise surprise, work's always got in the way. At least she did up the house: it's beautiful everywhere, not just in the breakfast nook, with velvet curtains, thick lush carpet, and our favourite pieces of furniture from Grandma's house. Mum let me pick the artworks and frames for each room, and about half of them are pieces I've done over the years.

'Every day someone on the board calls me, telling me again to get on top of these eth rooms,' Mum says. 'To fix the problems with recon. But I can't figure out what's going on, or how to fix it.'

'Get on top of what?'

Mum enunciates clearly: 'HEALTH RUMOURS.' She tips some wine down her throat.

'I thought you said the other day that you were making detoxification boosters?'

'No. I don't actually know how to stop people from getting asthma or EDS – otherwise I'd have put that into recon when it was first released!'

EDS? Oh, Energy Deficiency Syndrome. '*Is* recon to blame?'

Mum shrugs. 'It doesn't make any sense – none of the original tests suggested anything of the sort. But…some of our longer-term lab rats we feed recon to have developed the same timtims.'

I presume she means *symptoms*.

'Mum! You lied on the news!'

'I was just buying us more time. A mass scare would create

chaos. We have about sixty-five per cent of the population eating recon now, and if they suddenly reject it, we'll go under. Imagine the consequences if that happened. Piper, we eradicated *cancer*! I'll fix this, I know it. I just need more time. But the latest experiment I tried hasn't worked out, and the board's getting impatient. *And* there's a may problem—'

'A what problem?' I massage little circles around my eyes. I wish I had something like wine to relax me. Sometimes I take painkillers for my headaches, but they upset my stomach, so I try not to use them too often.

'MON-EY.' Mum drains her wine. 'My monthly pay didn't come through last week; I'm still trying to sort that out. And filling the car with petrol cleaned out my account. How can they charge forty-seven dollars fifty per litre? And now there's an electricity bill that's just ridiculous!'

I wouldn't have a clue what petrol costs normally, but going by her face, the news isn't good. 'You could get the tram to work?' I say. I've been at Mum for ages to ditch the car and take up public transport. Save the world and all that.

'I'm going to have to. Petrol costs threquas of what I earn in a week!'

'Three-quarters?'

'Yes.'

I blink. I didn't expect her to say yes. Or to share any of this information with me, for that matter; we don't usually talk about this sort of stuff. Maybe I should capitalise on her agreeable mood! 'Mum, do you reckon I could get an implant?'

'Piper, didn't you hear anything I just said? We have no money, and until Organicore fixes up whatever is going on with their payroll, I'm not buying anything!'

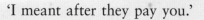

'I meant after they pay you.'

'After they pay me, the first thing I'll be focusing on is paying my overdue electricity bill.'

Wow. This really is quite bad. I've never heard Mum complain about money before.

'You could pay for the implant from the Europe account,' I say. Next year we're going to Europe. We'll see the Louvre and the Tate and the Van Gogh Museum. Mum's taking a whole month off work. Mum, me and all the famous art of the world. I can't wait. We were supposed to go this year, but Mum got caught up at work and we had to postpone.

'The savings for our trip to Europe are all in shares. They'd have to be sold. I'm not touching them until it's time to buy our airfares.'

Mum gets up and opens this week's recon cupboard, which we always keep where the fridge used to be, perusing the choices. I follow her over and stare at the rows of boxes neatly lined up in their slots.

'Clopa foos padta we cheeps,' she says, taking one out. I read the box label to understand her. *Global Fusion: Pad Thai with Chips*. 'I think Organicore has gone a bit far this time.'

Organicore has a whole team of meal designers. They take the Nutrium Sustate powder from Mum's team, mix it with BioSpore, which is just a calorific spongey mass, and then add flavours, colours and texturisers. When it comes out of the mould, you can barely tell it's not really fish, porridge or baked beans.

I hold out my hand. 'Let me have it. Experimentation is good for the psyche.'

'SY-KEE, Piper.'

'Huh?'

'You say SY-KEE, not SIKE.'

Oh. It's pretty hard to know how to say stuff the right way when you don't get to hear it being said. I take the box and go to press *heat*, but Mum snatches it back.

'You can't have that one; it has my name on it.' I roll my eyes as Mum finds me my own Global Fusion and puts her one back, picking herself out Smoked Trout with Salad instead. She's a stickler for ensuring we eat the recon tailored specially for us – our body weights and medical statuses – I suppose because she invented it. I don't tell her that Taylor and I swap meals all the time.

While we wait, Mum says, 'Did you do the vocation tutorial at school?'

My headache intensifies. My lack of ambition is the bane of Mum's life. 'I entered all my interests and it suggested nursing. Can you see me as a *nurse*? The doctor would tell me to administer eight millilitres of morphine to the patient in bed fourteen, and I'd go to bed forty and administer eighty.'

Mum sighs. 'Yes, that might not be appreciated.' She pours herself a second glass of wine and takes a big mouthful. 'Science, Piper. There are always jobs in research. And depending on the role, maybe your deafness wouldn't matter.'

'*Boredom*, Mum! I can barely keep my eyes open during science. How do you expect me to survive fifty years in the field? I'll be in a coma by the time I'm twenty.' I rub my hearing aids. My ears are itching again. 'So that leaves one option: art!'

Mum rolls her eyes. 'No one except Picasso ever made any money from art, and he was probably dead before the dollars started rolling in. Think of your dad.' She reaches for her recon box and I see the light's gone off. I never hear the beep.

I open mine. It smells delicious; I love pad thai. 'Dad could be a famous artist by now.'

Neither of us would know it if he was. He left when I was a baby and we haven't heard from him since. Mum doesn't seem too cut up about it, and I can't say I miss him given that I never really knew him.

'That reminds me,' Mum says. 'A certain package from Spain arrived today.'

I jump to my feet. '*Mum!* Where is it? How could you forget?'

She gestures towards the hall and I tear down to the table by the front door. Yep, there's a plastic box there with my name on it. I rip open the packaging, and there it is: my long-awaited *real paper* journal. The cover is plain, bound with tape. I'll paint something to stick over it. I open the journal and finger the pages. The texture is lush, nothing like plastic. It's smooth but not slick, creamy but still white. Everything, *everything* I draw and paint looks better on real paper.

I bring the journal to the kitchen and throw my arms around Mum. 'Thank you, thank you, thank you!'

She smiles. She does love to indulge me, I'll say that. 'Happy sixteenth birthday, Piper.'

My birthday was two months ago. It took this package ages to arrive. But it's here now. *Real paper!* I'll keep it with me always, and make myself a little kit to keep with it: a pencil case with a few colours of paint, my favourite pens, scissors, an eraser, a set of graphite pencils … and I can't forget a glue stick …

I rush to my room, flick on the light, and open my desk drawers. Which paint colours? Definitely red. And I love black.

But not too many or it will be too much to lug around. I'll include my tin of watercolours for sure. And a few brushes...Maybe I can fill a little bottle of water to keep with me. I grab my largest pencil case and begin collecting supplies.

The light flicks off, plunging the room into dullness. Mum is standing in the doorway. 'Guv the letriss situation, we're going to have to conserve it until my pay comes through. One lie at a time. And I'm turning off the heating. And the hot water too, unless you stick to threemy showers once a day.'

It's hard to lipread her when it's so dim, so it takes me a moment to figure out what she's said. 'Electricity? One light at a time?'

Mum nods.

Threemy? Oh! 'Did you say I can only have three-minute showers?'

'That's right. You'll have to learn to wash your hair faster.'

Whoa. I can't believe Mum's serious. At this rate, she'll single-handedly save the world after all.

She holds out my dinner. 'You forgot this.'

But who cares about pad thai and chips, or electricity for that matter, when I have a portable art studio to set up? 'Do you think you could bring your dinner in here, Mum? So we can have the light on in my room instead of in the kitchen?'

Mum obliges, and once the room is bright again and she's settled on my bed, eating, she says, 'You know, there are plenty of jobs with QuestTool, and they probably wouldn't rely much on hearing. You could start at the bottom, approving content, and work your way up.'

'Mum! Not now!' I turn back to my drawer and fish out an 8B pencil. I'll need a rag, too, to wipe my brushes on.

I follow Taylor into a lounge room. The house is dark, but the party's not exactly rocking: there are maybe ten people sitting on mismatched old couches and armchairs set around a table littered with half-finished beers, vodka and cherrygrog. Incense is burning, ash spilling onto the table. I hope it won't melt the plastic. The smoke is cloying. Music blares and the beat thumps in me, but the rest is a jumble of random sounds. I want to rip my hearing aids out, but figure I'd better leave them in to be sociable.

A tall, skinny guy with dirty-blond hair and a tattoo of a menacing crow on his forehead peels himself off the couch and greets Taylor, pulling her into his arms. Is this Beau? He's wearing a thick shirt with a high ruffled neck, and neat trousers with zips in the legs going up to his knees.

Now I see why Taylor's all dressed up. She's pulled her hair into two buns on top of her head, and suddenly her fringe looks chic instead of weird. Heavy black eyeliner rims her eyes and the effect is tragi-glam. She's wearing a short blue dress made of some kind of fake wool, with long sleeves, ruffles at the wrist, and a high white faux-fur collar. Despite the warm dress and some platform boots, her solid legs are bare. I've never seen this outfit before. I didn't think Taylor had the money for new clothes.

I glance around the room and see that the other girls are dressed similarly, with upswept hair, dramatic make-up and gorgeous dresses. I feel underdressed with my bare skin, flat hair, jeans and thick jacket. I look more like one of the guys, only not as clean and sharp.

Taylor grabs my arm and introduces me. I was right, this is Beau. He takes my hand and leans in to kiss me perfunctorily on the cheek, assaulting me with an intense cloud of perfume. I resist the urge to step back, giving him my best smile instead.

'How are you?' I ask. If Taylor likes him, he must be nice.

He says something back that I don't catch. It's too dark for me to have a hope of lipreading.

I glance up at Taylor. 'Drink,' she mouths, miming herself downing a cup.

'Thanks, that'd be sweet.'

Beau disappears, and Taylor finds a spot for us on one of the couches. I squash up against a beefy guy who's leaning back against the cushions and looks half asleep. He eyes me lazily and says something.

I don't think I'll hear him if I ask for a repeat, so I just smile. Taylor turns to a girl on her other side and starts having an animated conversation.

The beefy guy speaks to me again and I glance at Taylor, nervous, but all I can see is her back. I smile, nod and give him the thumbs up. That seems to satisfy him for the moment. I hope no one else speaks to me.

I wait for the guy to look away and then surreptitiously slip my hearing aids out of my ears and zip them into my jacket pocket. The world goes quiet, save for the rhythmic thump of the beat, which I feel more than hear. That's better.

Opposite me on another couch, three guys and two girls are immersed in conversation. I can see them shouting to be heard, laughing. I think the blonde girl is flirting with one of the guys. Two of them have implanted wristlets.

Next to them in a chair is a couple making out, and that guy has a wristlet implant too. The girl's kneeling on his lap and he's holding her butt cheeks while they tongue each other. I watch, curious and mortified. Sweet sixteen and never been kissed, that's me. I can't picture any guy wanting to kiss me, and while I like the idea of being kissed, I'm not sure I'd want to have my arse groped in public like that. It seems undignified.

Beau reappears and hands me an opened can of cherrygrog. His wristlet is implanted too. He leans down and says something into my ear.

I lean back, turn my head, and strain to see his mouth. 'What did you say?'

He tries again to access my ear and we do this weird dance, with me trying to keep my eyes on his face. I win. He repeats himself, confused, but it's hopeless. I shrug.

'I can't hear you over the music,' I shout. I can't bring myself to admit I'm deaf. I just want to fit in, be like everyone else, despite the fact that my outfit is all wrong. Why didn't Taylor tell me? Though if she had, what would I have worn? It's not like I own platform boots or a short dress. Taylor and I always wear jeans when we hang out. Maybe I need to go shopping.

Beau tries again and gestures to the other people in the room.

'Cool place…' I say.

He nods and gives up on me, probably thinking I'm too inane to have a real conversation with. He reaches past me for

Taylor, pulling her to her feet. Then he wraps his arms around her and they dance. It seems that things have progressed in the Beau department.

I sip the cherrygrog. It's sickly sweet and burns my throat, like cough medicine. The air starts to take on a surreal texture, the faces opposite me seeming to move almost in slow motion, luminous against the shadows. I take a deep breath, try to clear my head, but the incense smoke catches in my throat and I cough.

I wish I'd brought my journal.

I can't do this.

The couple making out are practically lying sideways in the armchair now, and the guy's hand slides up the girl's leg.

The beefy guy shifts. He's waving his hand slowly near my face, a patronising gesture: *Earth to plain girl.* I realise he's been speaking to me and I've been ignoring him.

'Sorry. What did you say?' I ditch the cherrygrog on the table. I've tried Mum's wine before and never liked it. I don't like this stuff either.

He leans towards me, and I feel his breath on my face as he speaks. But I can't catch even a single word. His mouth barely moves. I smile and nod, my fallback, but it doesn't satisfy him, and I realise he's asking me a question.

'What? Sorry, I still didn't hear you.'

More breath on my face. I try to guess the possibilities. *How do you know Beau? What do you think of this party? Where do you go to school?* But nothing I can think of matches the shapes his mouth makes. I throw him an uneasy smile, shrug and stand up. I've got to get away. This is not working.

Taylor is still dancing with Beau. She's smiling a flirty smile, but I can tell she's not quite comfortable. After a moment,

I see why. Beau has dipped down and is sliding his hand up her leg, all sexy-like. Taylor flinches slightly and spins out of reach, dodging him, but he does it again, and this time she lets him. Only her head is ducked forward, and when Taylor does that it means she's thinking about what to do next.

When his hand disappears up her dress, Taylor's head tips back and she laughs. She's decided to go with it. But I know he's moving too fast for her. Can't he read her body language?

I tap her shoulder and she turns to me, eyebrows raised. Beau says something and they both laugh, their faces friendly and warm towards me. I have no idea what's so funny, but it seems mean to stand there with a stony face and I really do want to make a good impression on Beau, so I laugh too. Beau makes another comment and we all laugh a bit more.

Finally, I grab Taylor's hand. 'I'm sorry, but I have to go.'

She turns from Beau, who stops dancing and reaches for another drink. She makes sure she's facing the light and mouths clearly: 'Why? What's wrong?'

'Can we go outside for a minute?' I ask.

I take her hand and Taylor traipses after me. The air outside is cold and crisp, clearing my head instantly. I inhale deeply. We stand under the verandah light, Taylor facing it so I can lipread her. I put my hearing aids back in.

'Don't let him do anything you don't want him to do,' I say.

'I know. But it's exciting being with him. He's kind of bad. Know what I mean?'

I shrug. 'I don't think I've felt that.'

'I can handle him. Why are you leaving?' Taylor rubs her legs.

'I can't lipread in the dark. Aren't you cold?'

Taylor nods. 'But it's worth it. Gotta suffer for beauty.'

'I guess that's why I'll never be beautiful. Not prepared to suffer.' I gesture to my boring clothes.

'You're always beautiful, Piper,' she says. 'Me, I need a funky dress and make-up to pull it off.'

'Where'd you get the dress? It's gorgeous.'

'Lollies and Dirt.'

My eyes widen. 'It must have cost a fortune!'

Taylor laughs. She's shivering.

'You're cold. Go back inside. It looks like Beau fancies you as much as you like him.'

'Maybe tonight's going to be my night. Will you be okay to get home without me? I'd come, but…'

But she might have sex with Beau. 'I'll be fine. Go.'

As soon as I'm alone I pull my hearing aids out of my ears again. I walk slowly to Smith Street and hail a tram. It's crowded even though it's late. There are hardly any cars on the road. When I wave my wristlet past the tram's check-in point, it vibrates.

Insufficient funds.

What? I had plenty of money in my account! I should get off the tram, but I don't. I cast my eye around for inspectors but don't see anyone official. Bringing my bank account up on my wristlet, I see that I have exactly fifteen dollars left. That should be plenty.

Then I see the last transaction: me checking in on the tram to go to the party. Eighty-five dollars at 9.12 pm. *Eighty-five dollars?!*

I hope Mum's pay has been sorted out. I'm going to need some more pocket money. The guy in front of me gets off at Clifton Hill and I see a row of new ads above the windows.

We apologise for an unavoidable fare rise due to increased fuel costs. Please check updated fares before travelling.

It's a bit late for that. Have they increased fare evasion fines too?

I think of what I'll paint in my journal tomorrow: A page of deep blues and greens. Lots of layers and texture. A tiny sliver of grey sky at the top.

You've NOT drowning. Just swimming DEEP.
I'm not sure I can do this teenager thing.
Perhaps I'm doomed to stay a child
                    FOREVER

TUESDAY 23 JUNE

Three days later I'm on the tram again, on my way home from school, and an inspector climbs on, scanner ready. I push urgently through the throng and manage to dive off just before the doors close. About ten other people dismount with me. Are we all travelling without checking in? I don't know how else to get home.

Organicore still hasn't paid Mum, and she didn't give me this week's pocket money. We haven't talked about the fact that I can't pay my tram fare. I wonder whether she can't either; she ditched the car this week as promised. Thanks to the lack of heating and light, we've both basically been spending as much of our time at home as possible in bed.

I shake my head, trying to push the worry away. I'm only in Church Street, so it's a long, long walk home, with the wind whipping my hair. I switch off my hearing aids but leave them in my ears for warmth.

The roads are quieter than usual. The streets and sky are grey. I miss trees, and green, and I curse the tree vandals who stole them all, leaving only stumps behind. If only wood never became so valuable. I sigh. There are some shrubs behind garden fences, but they're dry and listless thanks to the water restrictions.

I jump as a guy races past me on a bike, grazing my arm. Couldn't he have given me a little space – like, ridden *around* me? He probably rang his bell, presumed I'd move out of his way. I wish the *possibility* that I can't hear would occur to people. Taylor has reported this to me before: the swearing and yelling as I walk calmly on, 'ignoring' cyclists and their bells.

Over an hour later, I trudge into my street and it's the same: grey, grey, grey. There's a wide island down the middle of the road sprinkled with dead grass – thank you, drought – and no one in sight but me and an old guy trudging along slowly. I've seen him before, working his way up and down, up and down the street, going nowhere; it seems lonely. Organicore has delivered – there are recon cupboards inside the gates of about half the houses, including ours. Even the cupboards are grey.

My feet ache. I push the cupboard aside, knowing I should bring it inside, but wondering instead whether my old bike might be in the guesthouse with the rest of the stuff we don't use anymore. Taylor and I used to mess around on our bikes together, but after I crashed mine the handlebar was twisted and it felt weird. I haven't ridden it since.

I drop my schoolbag by the back door and head for the guesthouse. The smell of damp and dust assaults me as I flick on the light, illuminating piles of crap Mum and I haven't dealt with in years. I move a box out of my way and it shoots up a puff of white powder when I plonk it down, so I check out the packet inside – plaster! Wow. I reckon I could use that in my journal.

I find the bike and fiddle with it, wondering if I can fix the wonky handlebar, or maybe learn to ride with one hand further forward than the other to compensate. Then I take it for a test ride. It's in pretty bad shape. I think there's a repair place in High Street.

Leaving the bike out the back, I take the plaster inside. In the kitchen, I mix it with some water and spread it over some pages in my journal. It doesn't take long to dry, and the texture is amazing, like an old wall. I turn a page and it feels substantial, heavy. The plaster cracks a bit, and even that looks good.

I decide I'll add layers…collage some stuff over it. I take a sheet of plastic and paint it yellow. Then, using black, I add stripes. I tear the sheet into strips and glue it down randomly onto empty pages. The effect is strangely appealing. I dig out my sewing kit and stitch a plastic pocket inside the journal's front cover, then slip in the leftover part of the striped sheet to use later.

Thud. The house vibrates. Surely it's too early for Mum to be home?

But I put my head into the hallway and it *is* Mum. She's standing at the hall table by the front door, face red, mouth working furiously, hair wild. She always talks – okay, shouts – to herself when she's angry.

'Mum?' I say tentatively. 'What happened?' I need my hearing aids.

She turns to me, furious, her mouth going a mile a minute, and thumps her fist on the table. The hall reverberates. This is bad.

I hold up a finger and retreat into my bedroom. When I put in my hearing aids, I'm slammed with the noise of Mum shouting, the sounds random and incoherent. My head throbs. How to calm her down?

I go back to the hallway, but she's charging towards the kitchen. I follow and find her glaring at her work notes on the dining table.

'Do you want some wine?' I ask.

Instead of answering me, she swipes at the table and her notes fly to the floor, spilling across the kitchen. A chair topples with them, causing a crash I feel through my feet.

'*MUM!*' I shout, grabbing her. She deflates, sagging against the table, breathing hard. I'm standing on her notes. 'What happened?'

'I lost my job.'

What?! No. That's impossible.

'What did you say?'

'I. LOST. MY. JOB.'

'You can't lose your job!'

Mum's been with Organicore since the beginning. She *is* Organicore – she's their scientific foundation. Organicore is *us*, too – the core of our lives. This doesn't make sense. Why would they fire her? I know she's been struggling with solutions to the health problems, but it took her way longer than this to come up with Nutrium Sustate in the first place.

I check the cupboard under the bench for some wine, but it's empty. Huh? Mum never runs out. I fill a glass of water instead and hand it to her. She takes a sip.

'Theyfa hips of peep. Bob Forsy too.'

My headache tightens. Making sense of lip patterns exhausts me. Sometimes I understand Mum perfectly for hours at a stretch. Every now and again, I don't. But now I have it: *They fired heaps of people. Bob Forsyth too.*

Bob Forsyth is Mum's colleague, but also her biggest competitor. She's always only one step ahead of him. Her worst nightmare would be for him to step into her job.

'Speak clearly, Mum. Why did they fire Bob Forsyth? No, scrap that. Why did they fire *you*?'

'They said it was because I'm making no progress, but that's crap.' This time Mum enunciates clearly, and I hear her as well as lipreading her.

'Well, obviously.' I stare at Mum with my eyebrows raised. 'What's the real reason?'

'Olprees.'

'What?'

'Oil prices.'

'What's that got to do with your job?'

Mum takes a long drink of water and scowls at the glass. Then she sighs. 'Picking up the BioSpore from the farmers and getting it to the warehouse, delivering recon to subscribers, it's all costing too much. So they've cut every department they can, including their research division. Even marketing is gone. You can't run a company without investing in its future!'

'That's ridiculous.'

'I know. I think Organicore may not *have* much of a future, Piper, and I think they know it.'

That's impossible too. A company that feeds sixty-five per cent of the population will always earn enough to run.

'At least now they'll have to pay the money they owe you,' I say weakly.

Mum looks down, her hair falling over her mouth as she says something. It sounds like *train of monk monk*.

'What did you say?'

'They'll pay me when they can.'

'Which means never?'

Mum shrugs.

Maybe I'm going to have to get a job. But who's going to employ a deaf person? Maybe Cesspool, like Mum suggested the other day, since they hire lots of people to make sure there's no pornography or other inappropriate stuff being published. I'd be no good with the videos, but I could vet the text? The thought sits heavily inside me.

I pick up the chair, set it back on its feet. 'Early dinner?' I suggest. Given there's no wine, maybe food will put Mum in a better mood. Recon is delivered every second Tuesday, so we'll have plenty of new stuff to choose from today.

I can't tell if Mum replies, because she's looking down again. I take it as a yes, head out the front, and wheel in this week's cupboard. Pressing my thumb over the scanner, I feel the click as it unlocks. But only half the slots are filled.

I show Mum, who doesn't seem surprised.

'I hope they charged half for this!' I say.

'They charged double. I had to sell some shares to pay for it.'

At this rate, it might be a while before we get to Europe. 'Will they deliver the other half next Tuesday?' I ask.

'I doubt it. Because it's so expensive to pick up BioSpore, they're only getting it from the closer farms. So now there's a shortage. We're going to have to ration this, Piper. From now on, we each get one recon for dinner, but only half a recon to eat through the day. At least until we see what happens next Tuesday.'

This is surreal – like stepping into a movie. Mum and I each pick our recon and shuffle through the mess on the kitchen floor to the breakfast nook.

'What've you got?' Mum asks.

I hold up the box. 'Minestrone.'

'You say MINNA-STROANY, not MIYN-STROAN.'

Even with civilisation collapsing around us, Mum can't stop fretting about my pronunciation.

'MINNA-STROANY,' I repeat back to her. 'So much for those silent es.'

Mum taps her wristlet and our big visi-screen lights up. Lately she's restricted our use of it to one hour a day. She picks the first half-hour, which is always news, then I get to pick the second.

Mum's face, enormous, looms in front of us. They're showing old footage I've seen before, of her leaving some conference hosted by Organicore. She looks poised, calm and elegant. Mum taps again and the subtitles appear.

'...has left Organicore. It is unclear why she and Organicore have parted ways. Could this be related to rising concerns that recon may be affecting the health of some consumers? Organicore spokesperson, Lily Jones, says the decision is part of the new, streamlined Organicore, poised to beat distribution issues...'*

My wristlet vibrates. It's Taylor. I tap and she comes into focus on the tiny screen. She's on a visi, sitting at a table I don't recognise, looking happy and vibrant – the opposite of the mood going down in our house – though there are dark circles under her eyes.

'Beau and me and a bunch of others are going to tunks tonight,' she says. 'Want to come?'

'Going where?'

Taylor makes the shape of a pipe with her hands, then crosses her wrists over in a giant X. 'TUN-NEL X,' she enunciates clearly.

I rub my temples. I can't think of anything worse: Trying to lipread in a dark nightclub, making like I'm not awkward as hell. Fake smiles, laughter, and nodding at incomprehensible words. And anyway, it's Tuesday. How come Taylor is allowed to go out on a Tuesday night all of a sudden?

'Uhm…it's not a good time for me. Mum just lost her job.'

Taylor covers her mouth with her hand and I catch a glimpse of bright-red skin around her wristlet. Her hand disappears so I can lipread her, and in the background Beau walks past, greeting someone offscreen.

'That's terrible!' she says. 'I thought your mum was the *core* of Organicore.'

'Tay, what have you done? Did you get the implant?!'

She holds up her wrist and grins. Sure enough, the flat screen is embedded in her skin.

'Did it hurt?'

'Like getting a blood test. There was a prick from the needle. Then I watched them slice into my skin with a knife but couldn't feel anything. It was bizarre. After the anaesthetic wore off it started to hurt, but I took painkillers. It's not too bad.'

'I can't believe you *watched*!' I say. Then Mum grabs my arm and I jump. 'What?' I ask her.

She gestures to the big screen, on which a plane is landing.

'…Dow Index plunged another whopping twenty-three per cent, with some companies entirely underwater, including Air Australia, Tel-Event and Wealthco. Australians are panicking…'

Oh god, our shares. Our trip to Europe. Mum's entire savings.

'Tay, I'm sorry, I can't talk now. I'll see you tomorrow.'

Concern fills her face. 'Are you okay?'

Mum's fingers are still digging into my arm. 'I'm fine. I'll talk tomorrow.'

I disconnect and look at Mum. She's white, eyes wide.

'I hope you sold a lot of shares,' I say.

'Just a few.'

'Have you got enough money for me to get my bike fixed? I'll get caught if I keep taking the tram without checking in.'

'I can give you sixty dollars. I don't have more than that.'

'Mum, we need to make a plan.'

She sags in her chair, and for the first time, she seems small to me. Her fingers drum on the armrest, and eventually she says, 'There is one asset we still own outright: this house. If we move into the guesthouse we could rent it out until I get a new job.'

'The guesthouse is hideous!' I exclaim, then I shut my mouth abruptly. I sound like a brat.

'You have a better idea, Piper?'

But I don't.

'There's a sink,' Mum says, more to herself than me. 'But no hot tap, only cold. If only I'd renovated it when I did the rest of the house – but at least I put the toilet in. Why, oh why, didn't I add a shower at the same time?!'

To compensate for my previous comment, I say, 'Plenty of those new cheap apartments don't have kitchens these days either. We'll hardly be the only ones.'

Mum throws me a weak smile. I can see she appreciates the effort.

But inside I feel sick. *The guesthouse?* It's just a grotty shed crammed with stuff. And where would we *wash*?

'I'll need to work out my morning coffee,' Mum says. 'The coffee machine uses too much electricity so I've been heating water on the stove for it.'

'Oh right. But wait, don't we have a camping cooker? From when we went to Wilsons Prom?'

That was *years* ago. Mum hasn't had time for camping in forever.

'Somewhere. But we'd need gas for that. I'll see if I can get some.'

'Maybe Karen Kildare can give you another job?' I ask hopefully. One of the perks of Mum's job is that she works so closely with our prime minister.

'I'll call her tomorrow,' Mum says, and I feel a little better.

I wheel my bike all the way up High Street in search of the repair place. There are people everywhere, and it's weird because now there are really hardly any cars around – just the occasional electric car. Instead, pedestrians have filled the roadway, trudging wearily, carrying heavy-looking backpacks. Bikes weave among the people, and every now and again the road vibrates as a tram chugs past, overloaded with passengers.

The shops are dark, too. I miss the bright sparkle of their window displays all lined up in a cheery row. I check a camping store, and the large hardware chain, but all their solar panels have sold out. So have their gas bottles.

My favourite café is closed, with a huge orange sticker over its doorframe: *Health violation – no entry until approved.* Damn. They should've just stuck with recon, instead of insisting on also selling wild food. I peer through the window at the front bar where they sell their recon edible art. What will their artists do for work now they can't create meals that look like bizarre retro objects? And where will all the local high school kids go to try to compete with each other to find the weirdest after-school snacks? I'm still not over how jealous Taylor was the time I scored a Frozen Charlotte doll that tasted of hot chips and cream.

When I reach Thornbury at last and find the bike shop, one ad among a tonne of them in its dusty window catches my eye instantly – because it's written by hand, on actual paper! *Food shortages? Learn to grow your own. A Transition Towns Workshop.*

Mum's voice echoes in my head.

Without Nutrium Sustate, your body doesn't get what it needs.

Recon won't give you food poisoning; stick to the safe stuff.

Remember all those colds you had when you were little?

But it's only been four days of recon rations and I'm feeling kind of hungry all the time. Right now, I just want a big meal – who cares if it isn't perfectly nutritionally balanced. And surely a pack and a half of recon a day's still enough to protect us from getting sick.

Despite all the horror stories about wild food, even *Mum* braved the crowd at Allstar this week trying to get us some – not that it did much good. The shelves had been picked bare during the shopping riot last week, and apparently since then new deliveries have been sparse, with people snapping everything up as soon as it arrives.

I take a photo of the ad with my wristlet. We don't have much of a garden: just a tiny patch of grass out the front, and a concrete courtyard between the house and guesthouse. But still, maybe I could squeeze in some food? Grow something in pots?

I wheel my bike inside the shop and squint into the gloom. Strung up on the wall, hanging from the ceiling, and lined up on the uneven concrete floor is a motley collection of old, mismatched and cobbled-together bikes. Some have two wheels, but lots have three, or trailers, or huge crates attached to them. The paint on most of them has rusted off, and nothing looks clean. The floor could do with a sweep.

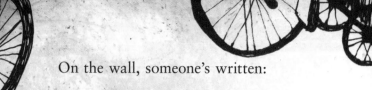

On the wall, someone's written:

Imagine: if the GDP was replaced with a contentment index.

What's the GDP again? Something to do with money?

I turn and find myself face to face with a shop guy, who's mid-sentence, gesticulating emphatically at me with his hands. Only he's not saying anything I expect, like *Can I help you?* or *How are you today?* Maybe it's something about the photo I snapped of the ad out front? About my bike? Or is the shop closing?

If Mum was here, she'd jump in quickly: *She's not ignoring you on purpose. She's deaf.* Her elbow would be in my side, and she'd be hissing to me: *You have to look at the shop assistants to see if they're talking.*

'I'm sorry?' I say. Usually if I'm not wearing my hearing aids – and right now I'm not – I can't be bothered trying to lipread shop assistants. All that effort, and for what – small talk? Though I do wish I had my hearing aids on in this particular case. This guy is hot. But it'd be undignified to grab them from my pocket and plug them into my ears in front of a stranger.

He points to my pocket, to my ears, makes a few other hand gestures, and says, 'Uh herry erds er wisting.' I understand him perfectly:

I could die. My face hot, I grab my hearing aids and shove them into my ears after all, slamming myself with a blare of white noise: trams; people talking or shouting; background music, maybe; other sounds I can't identify.

'Sorry,' I say, and he says something back but I can't hear him at all over the noise. I shrug.

'Ordef,' he says, bringing his fingers from his ear to his chin. *You're deaf.*

Now I get it: he's gesticulating because he's using sign language. I've never actually *seen* sign language before.

'I'm good at lipreading – I don't need to sign,' I say hastily. I don't want people seeing I'm deaf – because then they'll assume I must be stupid as well, which is what always happens when they see my hearing aids before they talk to me.

The guy drops his hands. 'Oh. Okay. Fair enough.' He seems disappointed. His eyes, half hidden by his hair, are warm and sparkly bright. His jeans are scruffy, and there's a hole in the elbow of his jumper, but his skin is perfect – smooth, gold and glowing.

'How did you know it was my hearing aids whistling? No one ever recognises that sound.'

He grins. 'I'm a…' I don't catch the last part. 'Mamamsdif.'

My mum's… what? *Diff?* No, *deaf* – that fits my question. It's so much harder to lipread strangers than people I know well, like Mum and Taylor.

'You're a what?' I ask.

Automatically, he lifts his fingers and starts making a word with them, but halfway through he realises it's pointless. 'Oocat feegaspell canoo?' he asks instead.

You can't…fingerspell? (Is that a sign language term?) *Can you?*

I shake my head.

'Coda,' he says, and his hands are moving again.

Cola? 'What's that?' I ask.

'Child of Deaf Adult,' he replies.

Is that really what he just said? What *CODA* stands for? It's so…stating the obvious. I nod, trying not to look too uncertain.

He gestures to the front window and says, 'Et larses run by my may, Essgoo.'

If he's talking about the workshop then I figure *et larses* must mean *that class is*. It takes a moment, but then I have it: *That class is run by my mate. It's good.*

'Yeah, I'm not sure I'll go.'

'Youshoo. Wall neeta know about foo, ispishna.'

You should. We all need to know about food… but what is *ispishna*? He's still talking.

'Annees a great teacher, aproms.'

And he's a great teacher, I promise.

Now I know what isphisna means: *especially now.*

'Well, maybe I will.' I glance at my bike. 'Do you do repairs?'

'Shoo, wassap?'

He's nodding, so I figure that's a yes. I show him how the handlebar is askew.

He straddles the bike, steadying the front wheel between his feet, then wrenches the handlebar to the left. I tried that, but it didn't budge for me the way it does for him. He examines it carefully from above and evidently decides he wrenched it too far, because he yanks it back in the other direction slightly. Then he's satisfied.

His hair falls over his shoulder and I resist an impulse to touch it. Ummmmm...

He reaches down and checks the tyres, then turns to me and says, 'Daneepa.'

I nod, assuming he's telling me they need pumping up. Sometimes I can't be bothered decoding everything.

He must see the uncertainty in my eyes, because he points to the tyres and makes a pumping motion with his hand. He gestures for me to follow him, and we traipse to the back of the shop. It's darker here. And dirtier.

I watch him pump the tyres and tweak the wheel cover and drizzle some oil over the chain. The hairs on his forearms are white against his skin, and a black streak of grease is smeared along his left arm. Finally, he turns to me with a nod.

'What do I owe you?' I ask.

He shakes his head. 'Nothing.' He's waving his hands around in the air again. Then he grins at me and winks.

He's *flirting*! And he knows that I'm deaf. How is this possible?

I'm so shocked that I twirl the tip of my hair between my fingers for a moment before I remember my manners. 'Thank you. I appreciate it.' I hold out my hand.

He laughs and shakes it, then he says what I assume is his name since he's pointing to himself, but I don't catch it. His palm is warm and dry, his fingers dirty from my bike.

'Piper,' I say, with as much confidence as I can muster.

He motions me to the counter. Is he going to make me pay after all? But no, he pulls out a slip of paper (yes, more actual paper!) and leans forward to write: _____

Marley.

He knew that I didn't understand him. I flush, he winks at me again, and somehow it's all fine.

'Well, Marley, it's nice to meet you. Nice shop you have here. Though I don't know how you make any money.'

God, why did I say that? I sound inane! And maybe now he'll charge me. Stupid. I grab my bike and make my exit before I can put my foot in it further.

Riding home I feel bright, energised, my fingers strangely warm, like the bite has washed out of the winter cold. Even my hunger has faded to a background gnaw.

Marley. No one's ever seen through me quite so efficiently. Well, maybe Taylor has, but never some guy. Not someone I've just met in a bike shop. I roll down the hill, wind whipping my hair back, and think about how I'll draw him. He'll be all colour, warm and vibrant, the bikes surrounding him, a pattern of black silhouettes.

I shove my hearing aids into my ears before I unlock the front door. Now that Mum's always at home I don't even get those few quiet hours after school to unravel my headache before dinner. I wonder if we can eat early, because I'm starving.

I stop abruptly. Something's not right. The hall table's gone. So's my painting at the far end of the hall. The house feels hollow, empty. I rush to my bedroom, and my bed and desk are gone, though my wardrobe still spills my clothes onto the floor and the shelves are still crammed with old toys, things I've made, and photos of me, Taylor and Mum. What the hell?

The lounge looks bare too, without its huge visi-screen and floor rug. A shadow flashes over me and I turn as Mum bursts through the back door, wearing old clothes and rubber gloves.

'*Mum!* Where's my art stuff? What have you done?'

'Relax, Piper. I'm just setting up the guesthouse. Come see.'

She leads me out the back door and through the little concrete courtyard. She's bristling with energy.

My heart starts beating like crazy. The piles of junk are gone. The dust, cobwebs and dirt have gone too, though not the yellowing water stains on the wall, nor the cracks in the ceiling and windows. In the far corner is my bed, neatly made. My desk is beside it, with my art stuff stacked on top, and the amateurish painting I did of the ocean has been nailed to the wall above. I can see through the doorway next to my desk that the tiny toilet room has been cleared of boxes. Mum's bed is in the corner to my left. There's barely enough space to stand between the foot of her bed and the foot of mine.

I can see Mum's worked really hard, but the effect is...dingy. It's the bare lightbulb and naked aluminium windows, and the pitted concrete showing around the edges of the rug from the lounge.

'We have space for the dining table and chairs, or the armchairs and table from the breakfast nook. Which do you think?' Mum asks.

'Definitely the breakfast nook stuff.'

I try to sound normal, but a huge vice is crushing my chest, squeezing out all the air, and my head throbs wildly. Surely we're not going to *live* here? There's no bench. I won't have anywhere to spread out my art. My desk is too small to count. But the blue velvet chairs might help this space feel cosier.

'Can we bring the curtains too?' I ask.

Mum shakes her head. 'The people who rent our house will need to be able to close them for privacy. Otherwise we'll be able to see straight in from the courtyard.'

I swallow, hard. *Keep it together, Piper.*

'I need you to help me bring in the armchairs,' Mum says. 'Then you can go through your stuff and pick what to keep. You have your desk drawers and the space under your bed – everything has to fit there. We'll need to ditch the rest.'

'Where's everything else? What did you do with the visi?'

'I sold it.' I stare at her, aghast. 'We need the cash, Piper. That reminds me. Do you have any change left over from fixing your bike? I need it to put towards your school fees.'

I bring up my wristlet and transfer the sixty dollars back to her. Now there's nothing in my account.

Mum touches my arm. 'I know this is tough. But look what I found when I was cleaning out all the junk – it was Grandma's.'

She points to a crate she's tucked under my bed. I pull it out and there are cans of spray-paint, an old yellowing receipt book that's mostly empty, a couple of notepads, some sewing paper, a roll of old-fashioned stickytape, and even some paperclips. Who knew we had a paper goldmine out here? Wow.

I shake one of the cans, which emits a satisfying rattle. Pulling off the lid, I spray a bit onto my fingers – it works!

Mum grabs me. 'Piper, not in here – that stuff stinks!'

So it does. But I don't care. I'll make stencils! They'll look grungy and incredible sprayed onto those plastered pages in my journal.

I cast my eye around for my journal, but Mum's onto me. 'You can play with that *after* you've dealt with your stuff.'

'Can't we eat first?'

'After.'

Organicore didn't deliver the other half of our order yesterday, so it's just as well Mum forced us to ration the last batch. But I'm still not used to the reduced amount of food during the daytimes.

I do what Mum says. It makes me feel sick, condensing my life into a handful of boxes and three drawers. I distract myself by picturing Marley, the guy from the bike shop, here in my space. (Ha, as if!) Suddenly I don't mind ditching the more embarrassing relics of my childhood quite so much.

In the end I keep most of my art stuff and get rid of almost everything sentimental I've ever owned, save for the photos, which I tack to the wall by my bed. I'm so lightheaded from hunger by this stage that this feels surreal, like a movie of someone else's life.

The guesthouse is crammed tight now. Mum's still hammering nails into the wall, so I sit on my bed and pick listlessly through Grandma's papers. Wind blows through a gap between the window and its frame and I shiver.

Some of Mum's stuff has got mixed up with Grandma's papers – scientific notes and the like from Organicore. One catches my eye because it's from Karen Kildare. I still find it amazing that Mum has a personal relationship with our prime minister.

From: **Karen Kildare**
To: **Irene McBride**
Date: 10 June

Irene,

I need to respond to today's rally. I know we're spinning it that the problem is pollution, not recon, but can you give me any scientific evidence to back this up? Or do the protestors have a valid point? I am genuinely concerned that they might…

You know that if it was up to me, I'd never have approved the recon rollout in the first place, not before the longer-term testing was complete. Irene, if you're not certain that recon is safe, demand that the board orders a recall and pauses the program until you work it out. If anyone can convince them of this, it will be you.

Karen

I blink and read it again. What does she mean, *if it was up to me*? Karen Kildare *chose* to roll out recon as part of her welfare program. She's Prime Minister of Australia! Why doesn't *she* tell the board to pause the program?

Something large and soft hits me on the side of my face – Mum's jumper. She's always throwing things at me to get my attention. I scowl. 'What?'

'You can start heating dinner.'

I put Mum's jumper on over my own, but I'm still cold. 'Not until you tell me about *this*,' I say, waving the email in the air.

As soon as Mum sees what I have, she lunges across the room and snatches it from me. 'Piper! You did *not* see this.'

'But I—'

'Piper. NO. *Dinner.*'

I glare at her, but do as she says. The recon cupboard fills the little space between my desk and the door to the toilet. Organicore didn't deliver my usual choices last Tuesday, and now there's a bunch of stuff left that I'm not too sure about, such as Steak Tartare. I select it dubiously and pick Spaghetti Bolognaise for Mum.

Weirdly, my meal doesn't need heating, but Mum's does. Mum is furiously avoiding eye contact, so I heave the loudest sigh manageable, pull out a thick plastic sheet, and start cutting a stencil of a starburst while I wait. Then I take it outside, set it against a random page in my journal, and spray black paint over everything. The moment of reveal is amazing: everything's black until I peel off the stencil and the shape comes into view, retro and regal with crisp lines and soft overspray here and there where tiny speckles of paint have snuck in when they weren't supposed to. I could so get addicted to this.

It's *so* weird to sit in our blue velvet chairs around our tiny marble table in the dingy, freezing guesthouse. I open my recon box to discover a strange lump of mashed raw meat inside – not steak at all.

'Huh?' I ask, holding it out to Mum.

'It's a French delicacy. Oort kwazeen.'

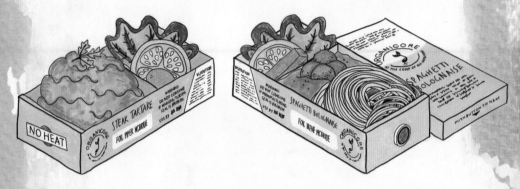

'What did you say?'

Mum repeats it about five times, but I still don't get it, so finally she types it into her wristlet. *Haute cuisine.* Apparently it means cooking of a very high standard. But they seem to have missed the cooking step here.

I remind myself there's no actual meat in this dish, just BioSpore, though why anyone would choose to imitate uncooked flesh is beyond me. I shovel some into my mouth anyway... and it's weirdly good.

'But *Mum*,' I say with my mouth still full. 'Why on earth can't Karen Kildare just tell the board what to do?!'

Mum clamps her mouth shut and shakes her head.

I stare at her, hard.

'This is none of your business.'

'It *is* my business. I'm an Australia citizen. If you don't tell me, I'm going to ask my teacher.'

That sorts it. 'Piper, you have to absolutely zip it. This is confidena stuff.'

Confidential stuff.

She glares at me, and I nod earnestly.

'Karen can't tell the board what to do, because the board hires her.'

'What do you mean? She's the prime minister, so she's hired by the people of Australia.'

Mum chews slowly for a while. She gets up and goes to her bed, pulls off the doona and spreads it over her lap. It's huge, and she offers me the other end. I pull it over my knees.

At first I think she isn't going to answer me, but eventually she says, 'Five years ago, the board was thinking about how to get recon accepted into every household in Australia. They had a new investor with plenty of money, and the elecans were coming up. So, they decided to hire someone to front a politicer party that would run for government. If that party got elected, then the government would primate recon, provide it for welfare, and so on. It was the perfect way to get recon out there. They picked Karen Kildare, who was the Face of Australia at the time – remember that? She was good at public speaking, a young pretty model, everyone liked her. You were only eleven, I suppose.'

It takes me a moment to digest this. It's not easy decoding the odd weird word when the words keep flowing.

'So, you're telling me that while we voted for Karen Kildare, the real prime minister is the board of Organicore?'

'Well, effectively, yes. But this is strictly insider information. You can't tell a soul. Not even Taylor.'

'But why did Karen Kildare agree to all of this?'

'Because she saw her chance to do so many good things,

Piper. Like shutting down all that terrible crime on the internet, reducing homelessness, creating equal access for all to the school creekum...'

'Well, so long as those things happened, who cares if they were recommended by the board or by Karen Kildare herself... I guess?' I say uncertainly.

Mum starts to say something, then abruptly closes her mouth. 'Yes, true. But make sure you zip it.'

'Mum, you've said that a hundred times! My mouth is zipped. But what about the testing?'

'Karen Kildare was elected before we'd completed long-term testing on recon, and the board didn't want to wait, so they had her set up the welfare program right away. All the results were great at that point, and the benefits were just so huge. But now, as you know, some of the slightly longer-term results are coming back as... less than optimal.'

Mum massages her temples.

'Maybe the board really *should* recall recon,' she goes on. 'I didn't think so. The health risks we've solved far outweigh these potential new ones – and I was *sure* that I could work things out. But now they've fired me, there's no one in there fixing the problems.' She smiles bitterly.

'Just come clean, Mum! Go to News Melbourne and tell them the truth!'

'And sabotage any prospect I have of getting my job back, and sorting this all out? Organicore will come knocking, you just wait, Piper. There's no one else who can fix this.'

'I thought you said they were going under?'

'Well...I don't know for sure. They might make it through till they work out another mode of transport.'

I scoff down my last mouthful of steak
tartare. I could eat another whole meal.
'Should we stop eating recon, if it's not safe?'

Mum shakes her head. 'It's the only thing
we have to eat at the moment, unless we're
prepared to queue at Allstars at six in the
morning and take food from people there
who don't have recon subscriptions. Besides,
we've been eating it this long… We'll keep an
eye out for side-effects, of course. I suspect
it *could* be a tolerance thing – some do well,
others don't. I think we'll be fine, Piper. This
isn't a permanent situation – things are going
to get better.'

After dinner I pull off my hearing
aids and lie on my bed with my journal,
my head spinning in the sudden silence,
cold air whispering at my cheek. I
think of Marley. Of Karen Kildare,
Organicore. The guesthouse as *home*.
It's all too much.

I dump the contents of my
brain onto a page in my diary – a
grid, a symbol for each thing
bothering me, wresting order from
the chaos – working fast, messy,
smearing layers of paint upon paint,
until slowly everything settles.
Finally, I'm calm enough to sleep.

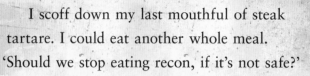

Welcome to your
new implant!

$$

TUESDAY 7 JULY

We're supposed to be putting the finishing touches on our food-poisoning assignment. I've done my part, and Taylor needs to write the conclusion, but she's not at school.

Where is she?

Should I write it for her – get it out of the way?

It suddenly strikes me that the assignment is part of the government's curriculum. Organicore's curriculum. It seems rather self-serving. Is wild food really as bad as we've been taught that it is...? It never occurred to me to question this before now.

It's not even lunchtime and already my headache is settling in. I wish I could take out my hearing aids. I wish I could eat! I'm sick of being naggingly hungry all the time – it messes with my head, makes it hard to concentrate. I already ate my half-a-recon on the way to school, which was dumb but I hate missing breakfast. I don't even care that it becomes weirdly rubbery thanks to having to heat it a second time. Our Organicore delivery is due today and they'd better deliver a full cupboard this time!

I'm not going to write Taylor's part of the assignment. She can do it herself. I type 'How to grow wild food' into Cesspool but it just churns out a list of feeds about pathogens. I've decided I'm definitely going to the food-growing workshop this weekend.

I bring up the job application questionnaire I started yesterday. I stare at the visi, feeling as dull as the screen, which is on low-power mode. *I find making friends a breeze.* I'm to indicate how strongly I agree or disagree with this statement. What does this have to do with approving Cesspool content? My finger hovers over *strongly disagree*, but then I think of when I met Marley and tap *neutral* instead.

When I next glance up, everyone in class is staring at me. Like, *everyone.* What the hell? I focus on the girl next to me, Brianna, and a rally-like chant I've been blocking out takes shape on her lips: 'Pi-per, Pi-per, Pi-per...'

They're all chanting it. Heat suffuses my face and my skull pulses. Where's Taylor when I need her?

'What?'

They laugh. At me, not with me.

Brianna says something and gestures towards the teacher. Lisa, too, is staring at me. Her lips move, but the only word I catch is *presentation.*

Couldn't someone have tapped my shoulder to let me know it was my turn? Am I really so revolting that no one save Taylor can bear to touch me? Even the teacher?

I can't do this. I simply cannot do school without Taylor. Where is she?

Tears threaten, but I blink and stand up, tall as I can. 'Sure, I don't mind going first.'

Nonchalant and casual, I walk to the front and aim my wristlet at the large visi on the wall to bring up the first image from my talk. We wrote these a month ago; my mind races as I try to remember what I'd planned to say. The tall spires of Organicore fill the screen.

I swallow, hard. 'Okay, so my hero is Adhya Vasi, Australia's biggest success story. She was only a uni student when she had the vision for Organicore.'

Will they all think it's ridiculous I'm presenting about Organicore, knowing that Mum doesn't work there anymore?

'She started Organicore, and then sold it for billions of dollars once it became a worldwide phenomenon. She was furious that almost two decades into the twenty-first century, women were still assigned most of the domestic load – so she decided that if men wouldn't do their share, nobody should, and made it her mission to do away with shopping, cooking and washing up! She was an environmental visionary, too – it was her who first came up with the idea of companies collecting and reusing their own rubbish. The result was recon. And that's how Adhya Vasi came to be known as the Future Girl – for her forward-thinking ideas.'

I change the image to a close-up of Organicore's most popular meal, the ice-cream burger. Suddenly everyone turns to Alyssa – she must have said something, because scorn spreads across the room. I check Lisa's face, which is stern. She addresses Alyssa, but the only words I catch are 'Piper' and 'health'. She nods at me to continue.

'At first,' I go on, louder than before, 'Nutrium Sustate was mixed with wheat or rice, but it was too complicated to create perfectly balanced meals that way. So they developed BioSpore. The second generation of recon, with preventative medicines, wasn't released until Adhya had sold the company.'

Now everyone's stopped paying me any attention at all – even Lisa, who's fiddling with her wristlet. I suppress a sudden urge to shout what Mum told me about Karen Kildare to them all. That'd get their attention.

The bell saves me. I might not hear the class chanting, but I always hear the bell – a devastating, whirling sound that obliterates all else.

I check the battery on my wristlet – still only half full. I've been trying for quick top-ups at the desk charger in as many classes as I can. At least school is good for something.

It's dark outside in the hallway without the lights. I stand against the wall to avoid being crushed by throngs of Mary Magdalene's 'ladies' and call Taylor. She appears on my wristlet screen standing in a field of brown grass. Huh?

'Where are you, Tay? You coming to school?'

She shakes her head and says something I can't make out.

'What? It's loud here.'

She bites her lip and I watch her type with one hand. 'In Seymour. Not coming.'

'What are you doing in *Seymour*? How did you get there?' I hold the wristlet close to my mouth when I speak.

'Train,' she types back.

'But it's so *expensive*!'

'Beau can afford.' She's always abrupt when she has to type.

'Is his family super-rich?' I ask.

But Taylor's looking away, talking to someone offscreen. Something dodgy is going on.

When she looks back at me, I ask, 'Did Beau pay for your implant? How did you get your parents to agree?'

She laughs and types: 'He paid. Not shown parents yet.'

'Tay, *what*?' If her parents didn't authorise the implant then it's totally illegal. And if they haven't seen it yet, she mustn't have been home in ages. 'Are you living with him now?! You'll end up in trouble!'

'Do I look like I'm in trouble?' She moves her wristlet down and I see she's wearing another new outfit – a gorgeous black velvet jacket and soft white shirt with a high ruffled neck. Then she says, 'Gotta go,' and disappears from the screen.

'What about the conclusion for our assignment?' I message to her, but she doesn't answer. I was going to ask if she wanted to come to the food-growing workshop, but there doesn't seem to be much point.

I hate lunchtime without Taylor – I never know what to do with myself, and it's even worse now I don't even have any lunch to eat. I trudge past the art room and glance inside longingly. Alice, my art teacher, is in there. She gives a friendly wave and gestures for me to come in, so I do.

'Yanno yacacami do arta lish times, if you'd like.'

Lish? Nope. *Yanno*? Maybe *you know*?

'What did you say?' I ask.

She faces me more squarely and speaks again, slowly and clearly this time: 'You know you can come in and do art at lunchtimes, if you want.' It's a bit too slow and embarrasses me – I'm not stupid! But at least I understand her this time.

Art at lunchtimes? I thought we all had to go outside! I help her clear away the mess from the previous class. 'What are they for?' I ask, pointing my head at a bunch of tiny knives of assorted sizes, some with odd-shaped blades that form little *V*s and *U*s.

'Rubbastum.' She holds out a thick sheet of rubber.

'Rubber stamps?'

She nods.

'Wow. Cool. How do you make them?'

Alice draws a circle on the rubber and shows me how to carve around it, first with a little *V* tool and then with a bigger *V*. I'm to clear away excess rubber with the *U* and trim the edges with a small normal-shaped knife. I picture my journal filled with images from rubber stamps. I could make all sorts of textures, shapes...maybe some flowers?

Alice hands me a fresh sheet of rubber and motions for me to have a go. I draw in a diamond pattern – it's simple, but I think it will look great in my journal. Alice goes off to the staffroom, and I flip out my hearing aids and carve, and while my hunger doesn't disappear, my headache does. I start to feel better inside.

Buying processed and health-checked wild food is one thing, but growing it is another thing entirely, so I tell Mum I'm going for a walk up High Street rather than admit I'm off to a food-growing workshop. I'll ease her into it, once I know what I'm doing. We only received half a cupboard of recon again, and I'm over it.

'If you see gas, message me and I'll send you the money to buy some,' Mum instructs.

We don't have tenants in our house yet, so she goes in every morning to make her coffee. I tell her we should move our stuff back in and live there until she finds someone to rent it – or at the very least go in there to *shower* – but she's showing people through every day and says it has to be ready to rent at the drop of a hat. And she turned the hot water off last Wednesday when she shifted us into the shed.

So, I haven't washed for a week and a half. This morning I finally heated a pot on the stove and gave myself a sponge bath in the kitchen. I need to be clean in case I bump into Marley today. At least Mum still lets us use the kitchen stove inside.

I wheel my bike up the driveway, staring longingly at our empty house. Who will sleep in my bedroom? I push the thought away and pedal hard, all the way up the hill to

Preston. I imagine Marley riding beside me, our eyes meeting now and then with little knowing smiles, as if we share some secret.

On my way, I pass three separate people with their heads under their car bonnets, retrieving engine parts. Will they sell them, or repurpose them somehow?

I thought the workshop venue would turn out to be a School of Horticulture or similar, but when I arrive, warm and breathless, it's just a private house – one of those old brown brick ones that Greek people used to build when they first arrived in Australia. A woman at the gate waves me inside.

I pick my way down a path to the side of the house through a horde of people – way more than I was expecting. I guess they're all hungry and worried too. My stomach rumbles as if on cue and I force myself to ignore it. I can't help scanning the crowd for Marley. *Is* he here? He said the teacher was his mate. But maybe he already knows how to grow food. Would he even recognise me? Should I remind him, if he doesn't?

I near the end of the path and the crowd isn't moving. All I can see is the back of a tall guy in front of me and the woman in front of him – no teacher. I wait, polite. If class has started, I can't tell.

This is pointless. If I'm going to learn anything I need to be more assertive. I ease myself forward through the crowd, whispering, 'Excuse me, excuse me,' until I'm in the backyard and can see the teacher, who's standing on a plastic crate. He's maybe twenty-five or so, Greek, and he talks fast, his hands emphasising his words.

I attempt to tune in, but lipreading when you start in the middle is just about impossible. He could be saying anything.

He gestures to a garden bed behind us and I catch the words 'tomato' and 'we need' and 'important'. I turn the volume of my hearing aids to full, but it doesn't make any difference. His voice booms in, but the words don't.

My eyes drift around the garden. Marley isn't anywhere to be seen. I swallow hard to squash my disappointment. There are plants – a great tangled mess of them, leaves and vines everywhere – but whether they actually equate to food is beyond me. What does wild food look like on a plant? I think of pictures I've seen of fat red apples bulging from trees, but there's nothing like that here. I can't imagine a meal of leaves being very appetising.

What about water? How do they get enough water, with the restrictions and it being so expensive and all that?

Girl! Concentrate! The guy is excited now, talking passionately: 'Compost eeda funday a fillily.'

I repeat the sounds to myself, but nothing besides *compost* comes to me.

'Dessata guffa eedebe compost,' he says.

He reminds me of Marley, but I can't quite think why. I glance around again and notice a green corrugated plastic water tank against the house. I think you're allowed to use as much water as you want if it comes from a tank – but it's hardly rained this year, thanks to El Niño. Have they still collected enough water in their tank to sustain this garden?

I check out the crowd. There's such a mix of people, like you'd never find at school. I don't see anyone with an implant. I guess these people are more into doing things naturally. There are older people who look conservative, with heavy faces and crossed arms, plus lots and lots of people in their twenties, who mostly look more alternative. One girl, who's wearing a long, scruffy skirt with another skirt over the top of it, stands like she owns the world: feet apart, confident, relaxed. Her skin is clear and her eyes are bright. She's beautiful. I wish I was like that. I feel small and awkward next to her.

Come on! Focus! → This is important.
→ No more distractions.

'I allus lika make sure I write…'

Always like to make sure I write… But now I've missed his next words.

'Laree seeds that are gooquan an supplant yourself…'

Supplant? Transplant? I'm going in overdrive here, but nothing makes sense.

A lump swells in my throat. I swallow hard. If I'm not careful, I could cry. But no, this is all wrong. I accept being deaf. I know it's my lot in life. It doesn't bother me. I'd rather be deaf than perpetually ill or academically slow or allergic to recon or whatever. So…why the hell am I sniffing like mad, tears snaking down my cheeks?

I rub furiously at my eyes, willing my chilled-out attitude to return. But it doesn't. This matters too much. I abandon my lipreading efforts and channel all my energy into holding back the wave of desperation threatening to consume me.

And then it does. Right here, in front of everyone. I'm bawling – and I must be making noise because people are turning to me, concern on their faces. I push them away, shoving through the crowd until I finally stumble out the gate. I grab my bike, but the numbers on the lock are a blur through my tears. I hunch over it, sobbing.

Why, why, oh WHY can't I just
take it all in like everyone else?
Why does it have to be
So DIFFICULT?

It's not just about being deaf. I mean, it *is*.
But it's also about being hungry and cold and living in a
horrible, dingy shed instead of at home, and Taylor not
coming to school for days, and me not knowing who she
is anymore now that she wears fancy clothes and has a
boyfriend and hangs out in *Seymour*, of all places.

I finally get my lock undone and I pedal furiously,
the world lurching blurrily through my tears.

Art class is the only time at school that I don't wish I was someplace else. Right now, I don't even care that it's been a week and Taylor's *still* not here. I dab a bit of red paint onto the lips of the girl in my painting and stand back to look at it critically. Not bad. I like the messy effect – but somehow it's still a bit prissy.

Someone touches my shoulder and I turn. It's Alice.

'I said, youcoo go furth wathi, Piper,' she says. 'More lays, more texta, build up depth.'

I think she's telling me to go further with this. *More layers, more texture.*

I nod. That might help with the prissiness.

'Remember you told me your favourite at woks were the ones that have been dirtied and dammy?' Alice asks.

This is art class, so I presume she means *artworks*. Dammy? Maybe *damaged*?

She's still talking. 'Don't be afraid to' – I've missed something – 'carve into them, scratch them up, add paint so that underneath layers are party hidna hevasutty to them.'

'So that underneath layers are what?'

'PART-I-ALLY HID-DEN and have a SUB-TLE-TY to them.'

I'm mortified that she has to over-enunciate these words for me to get them. 'Do you think she looks prissy?' I ask.

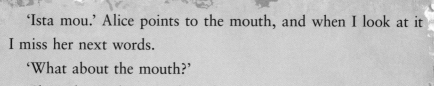

'Ista mou.' Alice points to the mouth, and when I look at it I miss her next words.

'What about the mouth?'

She indicates her own face, fingers framing her lips. 'It needs to be wider.'

Yes, I see it now.

The end-of-day bell blares, ending our conversation. I take my time packing up, smearing some leftover paint on empty pages in my journal. Then I flip to random pages and add dots and stripes.

Eventually Alice touches my arm again. 'Sorry, Piper, but I havtaloggap.' She's holding the key.

I quickly wash my brushes and put them away while she waits. She locks the door behind us, then turns to me and says something. But it's noisy and dark in the hallway and I don't catch a single word.

'What did you say?' I ask.

She repeats it again, practically shouting, but I still have no luck. I tell her not to worry, but she's determined. Eventually she types on her wristlet: 'You are starting to find your style.'

I smile, thank her, and bolt before she can say anything else that will require a hundred excruciating repeats. I'm still raw from my meltdown at the food-growing workshop. This stuff is getting to me in a way that it didn't used to.

I'm carried outside in a throng of other girls, and as soon as I hit daylight hunger slams me again, this time in the form of a desperate craving for apple pie and cream – sweet, rich, heavy. I rip my hearing aids out of my ears and poke my fingers into my ears to scratch them, but they don't reach far enough. I can never, *ever* satisfy the itch my hearing aids create. At least my headache isn't too bad today – just a dull throb.

I make my way to the bike rack, only...where's my bike? I cast my eyes around, but I don't see it. *Where's my bike?!*

I locked it here this morning. I know I did. No!

Could I have locked it at the other rack? But I didn't.

I check anyway. No bike.

No bike no bike no bike.
I [NEED] my Bike!

I know I should tell a teacher, but it's home time and the thought of wasting time searching offices for someone who's still here, explaining to them what's happened, waiting for them to get the cops here, explaining myself again...I just don't want to do it. I decide I'll report it to the police directly and update the school tomorrow. I check my wristlet for the nearest police station.

Luckily there's one only a few blocks out of my way, but when I get there it's crowded, the queue stretching well out the front door. I take my place and wait. And wait. And wait.

It's freezing now that I'm not walking. I stomp my feet to keep warm, and message Taylor: 'Hello, remember me? That strange girl you used to know back in the days when you attended school? Guess what, my bike's been stolen!! Do police ever recover bikes? Where are you?'

She doesn't reply. Again. I flip back through my other messages, checking to see if there's anything I've forgotten to answer, but there's just the one Mum sent me yesterday saying tenants have applied to live in our house. She's jubilant. I'm not. I delete it and tuck my fingers under my armpits to warm them up.

My wristlet vibrates and it's a message from Cesspool. 'Congratulations, you have been shortlisted!'

It directs me to another test, and yet more details that I need to supply to them. I spend an hour answering their pointless questions in ways that hopefully don't reflect the true, pathetic nature of my personality, and looking up results from my last three medical check-ups. Is this all really necessary?

A bunch of people ahead of me suddenly separate from the queue and leave. What's going on? I look around but there's no clue, and the thought of trying to communicate with a stranger in the queue is too much. I turn back to my wristlet.

Eventually I make it to the front and the officer behind the window glares at me when I tell her I'm here to report a bike theft. She says something dismissively, looking down, and waves me away.

I don't leave. 'What did you say?'

She mumbles again, and when I ask again for a repeat she finally looks at me.

'My bike's been stolen,' I tell her, loud and clear.

This angers her. I don't catch a single word of what she says, but clearly it's a telling-off. She waves me aside again and stares pointedly at the person behind me, who comes to stand beside me. This new man and the police officer get talking, and the officer isn't dismissive of him.

Confused, I swallow hard and turn to go. On my way out, an older woman wearing a hijab grabs me. She speaks slowly, clearly, and gestures to my ears. I gather that she saw my hearing aids and figured out I'm deaf.

'They made an announcement,' she says, looking at me expectantly.

'Yes?'

'They don't have the reasus to pross petty crimes.'

Reasus – reason, rhesus … maybe resources?

Pross – procedure? Process? A shortened version of prosecute?

They don't have the resources to process petty crimes.

'Are you telling me that they won't look into bike theft?' I ask.

She nods. I miss a few words but catch what I think might be 'too many bikes stolen...' Then something 'major problem...' She's speaking slowly, clearly, looking intently into my eyes.

'Everyone's bikes are getting stolen now?'

'Yes. So the police...' something something.

'They don't care?'

'They can't. Busy.'

I get it. I thank her.

'I hope you find your bike,' she says, clear and slow, before I turn and leave.

It's not until I've walked two blocks that I realise I was working so hard to understand her that I forgot to show appreciation for her kindness. And since she was still in the queue, she must have been there to report something more serious than a petty crime. God, I must have seemed so self-absorbed.

An hour later, when I'm halfway home, I suddenly realise that I now have the perfect excuse to return to the bike shop and see Marley again. I wonder what those rusty old mismatched bikes cost? Will Mum be able to afford one when the new tenants pay their rent?

I tell Mum there is absolutely no way I am going to school. My feet are killing me after yesterday. She agrees to report the theft to school for me, and I sardine myself onto a tram, watching warily for inspectors, and spill out near the bike shop.

I check the noticeboard in the window, my stomach doing flipflops. The ad for the food-growing workshop has disappeared.

Marley emerges from the gloom of the shop, his blue eyes glitzing as brightly as last time. 'Piper! Howza washup?'

He remembered my name! Well, I remembered his, didn't I? But that's hardly surprising since I've flicked past it in my journal every day since I met him. I pull my hearing aids out of my pockets and plug them in. I don't want him to tell me they're whistling.

'Yall set ta platta garden now?' His hands move swiftly.

I shake my head. 'I still don't know how.'

There's chemistry here – I feel it. He's leaning casually in the shop doorway, hair falling into his eyes, but there's an intensity to his gaze that catches me right in the throat.

'Angelo din inspa you?'

Didn't inspire you?

I swallow. 'He was fine. I think. I couldn't hear a word.'

'Oh.' Marley frowns, concern in his eyes, and embarrassment flashes through me. I should've just told him it was good.

'How do you normally get by?' he asks. 'I mean, yado sigh. How do you know wasgoan?'

'Sorry?'

But he's only halfway through repeating it when I understand. *You don't sign. How do you know what's going on?*

I let him finish speaking before I reply. 'Cesspool helps a lot. All our classes are online now. Easy.'

'There's not much about foogron on Cesspool.'

'I know. I tried looking it up already.'

'Angelo tried tasup an infacen, but his application was rejected.'

To set up an info-centre.

Marley's going slow and clear. How does he do this so seamlessly? His speech isn't exaggerated, like when Alice talks – it's casual, comfortable.

'They said it was safe and they can't be responsible forkaragee thisacoo lead to food poisoning.'

'Did you say they said it *wasn't* safe?'

Marley nods.

'Well, they have a point there,' I say, but I'm thinking of Karen Kildare being handpicked by the Organicore board, and the fact that only approved news can be shown on Cesspool, effectively meaning Organicore gets to decide what is reported.

Marley raises an eyebrow. 'We've been eaten reefoo for all of mantee. We've evoll teat it. It's better fus than that plaster stuffee box.'

I blink. *Reefoo* must be *real food*. *Evoll* is probably *evolved*. So, going by the same word-group, I'm guessing *mantee* could be *humanity*. But plaster? Why's he talking about plaster? This is not commonly spoken of. And the word's on my brain because I've been using it lately. Must be something else. What? *Plastic*? Yes, probably. Okay, so... *We've been eating real food for all of humanity. We've evolved to eat it. It's better for us than that plastic stuff in a box.* I presume he means recon.

My desire to escape convoluted conversation battles with my desire to talk with a gorgeous guy who may, just *may*, be attracted to me. The gorgeous-guy factor wins.

'There hasn't been a single recorded case of food poisoning from recon, though,' I counter.

'No, but now we have kids having engy deficy sdrome, reenus, all that.'

It seems Cesspool hasn't done a good job of keeping this out of the news. But I remember the gentle, reassuring way the article I saw at school made out that it was just the worries of a bunch of obsessive parents.

'How come you wan lernta grofoo if you're a recon subscriber?'

'Shortages. Organicore only delivers half these days. I'd rather have enough to eat.'

'Fairnuff. Youshoo meet my mum. Really. She's deaf, ansha's never eaten recon ina life. She coo teach you to grow foo.'

'But your mum uses sign language, right? I can't sign. Or does she speak too?'

'She *can* spee but she won't. But everone understas my mum. She's a ver clear communicator. If you're sta, I can interpre.'

If you're stuck, I can interpret.

I stare at him. Why would he bother and why does he care? But I know the answer already: he feels that electric charge between us too. The thought of going to his house gives me a thrill. I like his energy. I want to be around that.

But as soon as I say yes, he backpedals. 'I ber actually ask her, check she's happyta meet you.'

I give him my Cesspool address and gesture towards the shop. 'I'm wondering how much your bikes cost. The cheapest ones? Nothing fancy.'

We go inside and Marley asks, 'Wha bout your bike? Tha working okay?'

'It was stolen.'

Marley shakes his head and throws up his arms in sympathetic exasperation on my behalf. 'I shoulda tolyou tha lock was strong enough.'

'My lock *wasn't* strong enough?'

He nods. 'You nee one lie this.' He leads me to the counter and pulls out a hefty steel bolt in plastic packaging. The price label says *$249*.

I sigh. 'I can't afford that.'

'Wha can you affor?'

'In truth…nothing. My mum lost her job and we're living on the hair of a possum until she gets some money. I just thought maybe some of these would be cheap?'

I gesture around the shop. There's a bike with a leather bag with straps. I missed that bag the first time. I'll go back to my drawing of Marley in the bike shop and add it in. I mentally grab some other details to draw, then turn back to Marley.

'These are for sale.' But he's shaking his head and his tone tells me they *aren't* for sale. 'They're for rent. I haven ableta get new bikes in for weeks. Tha newens a sollout.'

The new ones are sold out.

'Why do people rent a bike?'

'Fa moven big stuff. Moven house, tha kinda thing. Satimes

I elp em move too.' He hasn't finished. He's thinking, drumming his fingers. 'Lea it wimmee. I have an ide. I'll messy you.' He gestures typing with one hand on his wristlet.

I don't want to go. I point to the words painted on the wall:

Imagine: If the GDP was replaced with a contentment index.

'GDP, that's the government measure of money, right? Is a contentment index a real thing?'

'Not asfa asa know. Mafren Kilsy wrote that. She reckons success shoo be measured by how happy we er. Not by money.'

'I like it.'

I can't think of anything else to say so I shake Marley's hand and rush off. I shove my hearing aids back in my pocket and walk home, thinking of the contentment index. Does Karen Kildare measure success by money? The Organicore board certainly does, and perhaps that's the same thing. Maybe they need a health index. Recon could score eight points for eradicating obesity, cancer and colds, and lose how many for the health problems that have come up in their place?

I turn down a side street. The shop on the corner has a big white wall. Glancing around me, I see no one's looking. I pull a fat texta out of my bag and write in large block letters: 'IMAGINE IF OUR PRIME MINISTER WAS INDEPENDENT.'

Heart pounding, I shove the texta into my pocket and hurry away. I've never done that before. But I don't feel guilty – I feel excited. Like I've finally found a voice. A tiny voice, but one that will be heard, at least, by anyone who walks past this wall.

The tenants are moving into our house. I sit in a sliver of early-morning sun in the courtyard at the bottom of the drive, sketching rubber-stamp designs, trying not to notice. Alice lent me a set of little carving knives. But the tenants are distracting.

At the top of the drive is a small boy of around five with white-blond shoulder-length hair and a stocky little body. He eyes me warily, ducking behind his father, who's thin with matching wavy hair in brown and a beard. His posture's slightly stooped, as if he lacks confidence. His manner with the boy is gentle; he hands him a few small things to carry into the house (my house!), while he himself struggles under a pile of boxes.

A woman gets out of the car and efficiently stacks the remaining boxes at the top of the driveway, then leaves again in the car. This is their second load. The petrol they're using must be outrageously expensive, and I wonder how far away they're coming from.

My wristlet buzzes. It's Marley! My heart skips a beat. 'My mum says yes – come over on Sunday.'

'Can't wait,' I fire back.

Was that too enthusiastic?

I'm going to have to wash again! On Sunday it'll have been over a week since my sponge bath. But now we're stuck in the freezing guesthouse for real, and the thought of removing all my clothes at once and adding cold water does *not* appeal.

'Same,' Marley messages back, and I feel a bit better. 'What are you doing?'

'Carving rubber stamps. You?'

'House move by bike.'

I picture a house loaded onto the back of one of Marley's cargo bikes. The image is irresistible. I sketch it out quickly and snap a photo. 'Like this?'

'Ha! We're just moving the contents.'

Well, of course! But that wouldn't make such a good drawing. I glance up at the tenants' plastic boxes. Boring. If I took some artistic licence, though…maybe turn the boxes into cute packages tied with string? Old-fashioned suitcases? I sketch out my ideas. These would make adorable stamps. I transfer the drawings to the rubber and begin carving. It's soft, and the rhythm of the work is meditative. My mind goes into freefall.

My grandparents had suitcases like these. I miss being with them at their farm in Kinglake – all those long weekends with Mum, plus summer holidays while she worked. When Grandpa died of coronavirus and we barely had time to blink before Grandma succumbed too, Mum said at least they were together. I get that she was trying to reassure me, but I believe death is an endless black, dreamless sleep, no feelings involved. I know Mum had to sell the farm to pay off our house, but it still hurts. Our house that strangers are now moving into.

My wristlet buzzes again. This time it's Taylor calling, so I put my hearing aids in.

'Sorry I've been a terrible friend,' she blurts. 'Did you get your bike back?'

She's in a brightly lit room with black-and-white chequered tiled walls behind her, sitting on a cool retro orange stool facing

the visi. She's wearing yet another new top, with a high pink lace collar, and her hair is styled into a complicated pile of plaits. She looks beautiful, but there are still shadows under her eyes.

I shake my head. 'It's gone. Where are you? Are you okay?'

'I'm fine! I'm good.' But she says it too fast to be convincing.

'What's happening, Tay? Is there something dodgy going on?'

'No!' Taylor laughs, but there's no crinkle in her eyes.

And just like that, the screen on my wristlet goes black – I'm out of power. *Damn it*. I can't charge it when I don't go to school. Will Mum notice if I plug it in briefly while she's out?

But scrap that, because here's Mum home now, no doubt from yet another unsuccessful gas hunt. She stops at the top of the drive to talk to the man, then gestures for me to join them. I drag my feet. I can't believe how distant Taylor's become – since when doesn't she tell me what's going on in her life?

'This is my daughter, Piper,' Mum says, then to me, clearly: 'ARCHIE. His partner, Erin, will be back any minute now.'

'Nice to meet you,' I say obediently. Though it's not.

'His son is Tayger,' says Mum.

'Tiger? That's a cool name.'

But Mum shakes her head. 'T-A-G-G-E-R-T.'

I nod, and check with Mum if I can escape. With her eyes, she lets me. But when she's finished with Archie, she's in the courtyard, back on my case. 'Why are you not at school, Piper?'

'Because I don't have a bike or money for the tram.'

'You have a pair of perfectly good legs.'

'Mum! It's two hours to walk there.'

'Kids have been walking a long way to school for all of time. You can take the rest of today off, but tomorrow you're going.'

I scowl and hunch over my stamp.

▶ To: Taylor
Okay stranger, if you can't make it to school, let's hang out this weekend instead? Come over Saturday?

▶ From: Marley
Got busy yesterday. Wanted to ask if you'll show me your rubber stamps.

▶ To: Marley

▶ From: Marley
You're a girl of many surprises. Meet me at the bike shop
3pm Sunday?

*This sounds kind of like a date.
Umm, with his mum...*

*But he's messaged me 2 days in a row.
Is he just being NICE??*

▶ To: Taylor
Or hell...just call me?

▶ From: QuestTool – Content Approval Administration
Office
Congratulations! You are invited to attend an interview
at QuestTool Headquarters on 24 July at 2pm. Please tap
below to accept, and fill in the following questionnaire
ahead of your interview.

I copy Mum's technique for washing, standing on a towel by the sink and sticking my head under the tap to wash my hair while I'm still dressed, then stripping and using a soapy washcloth for the rest of me. The water chills me to the bone, but at least now I'm fresh and clean.

I think longingly of our shower. If the new tenants can afford petrol, I bet they've turned the hot water back on. They shut the living room curtains that first evening and haven't opened them since – I guess they don't want a constant reminder that we're living in 'their' backyard – but I've seen plenty of light peeking through the cracks.

All we have is one power point with a little meter Mum plugged into it to track our usage, so we can calculate our share of the electricity bill. She watches the numbers like a hawk, and if I so much as plug in my wristlet for five minutes she has a fit. She's even forbidden us from using the overhead light, and plugs a tiny reading lamp in once it's pitch dark outside instead, so we can track that usage too.

I get changed three times, then give up and just wear my warmest clothes – jeans and my thick jacket – because what's the point of looking gorgeous if your teeth are chattering?

By the time I've walked to the bike shop, my heart's pounding and I'm sick with nerves. What if we don't have anything to say to each other? What if I can't understand a thing? What if...

But I needn't have worried, because as soon as I push in my hearing aids and step through the doorway, Marley grins and holds up a finger. He's lying beneath a weird three-wheeled trike, a spanner in his hand. He finishes whatever he's doing to it and sits up, wiping his hands on his jeans, then gestures to an ordinary two-wheeled bike nearby that's been built from pieces of various other bikes of all different colours.

'I made you a bike.'

I panic. I don't have any money! I didn't clear a bike purchase with Mum. I was just enquiring as to how much they were last time.

'What does it cost?' I ask.

'No, no, don't worry about that. You can boat. Keep it for as long as you need.'

His eyes sparkle. He's *into me*. He wouldn't do this if his interest was just casual.

'Did you say *borrow it*?'

Marley nods. 'I know it's nothing special. But my plays a bit far to walk.'

We ride along the Merri Creek bike path, me concentrating hard and trying to ignore the rumbling in my stomach, Marley cruising casually in front of me, hands behind his back. He's so beautiful. I picture myself dinking with him on his bike. I'd sit behind him, wrap my hands around his waist and rest my head against his back.

I haven't been here in ages. The river is fast and dirty, with old recon boxes, plastic crates and clothing caught in the current. I remember trees here when I was little, but they've all been stolen – stumps are all that's left, plus low spindly shrubs and lots of weeds and vines.

Eventually we leave the path, and just as I lose track of where we are Marley parks his bike in front of a tall brick fence. The barbed wire strung along the top makes me uneasy. I hope he isn't kidnapping me. Maybe I should have told Mum where I was going. She was out when I left, and I didn't leave a note; I figured she wouldn't be up for me going to the home of some male stranger I've just met, even if his mum is supposed to be here.

'Why all the security?' I ask.

'Tree vandals.' Marley unlocks a door set into the wall, and when I hang back, nervous, he hands me the key. 'There. You can leave any time you want.'

Our fingers touch and hot electricity jolts through me. I look away – his gaze is intense.

We step inside and it's like emerging into paradise: lush, green, wild and tall. There are trees with leaves and trees without, and one without is covered in round orange fruit. Vines twist around trunks and clamber up the wall. Plants are tied to tall wooden stakes (wood!) and there are patches of earth, only the soil is black and moist, not brown and dusty like in my street.

Marley gestures for me to follow him; for a moment I think he's going to take my hand, but he doesn't. We enter a new area gridded with boxes of plants, which feels orderly and neat after the chaos of the entrance. It's bordered by trees and bushes, and when we push past them we're in yet another space: a large pond with seats around it and an arbour above. A plant curls its way up through the arbour, but perhaps it's dead since it has no leaves.

This is a garden full of rooms, each with its own mood.

And then there's a house, a tiny cottage covered with clambering plants, only it's turned inside out, with the kitchen on the deck. It's impossibly old-fashioned, like stepping into a rendition of 'Hansel and Gretel', yet modern too: the roof is lined with solar panels, and a wind turbine pokes into the sky.

I fall in [LOVE.]

I want to stop, call everything into slow motion, pause in each garden-room to absorb all each one has to offer: the energy, the beauty. But Marley is oblivious, searching for his mum. He abandons the deck and leads me through yet more garden spaces: a pen full of chickens; a wall stacked with rabbit hutches.

Who knew you could fit so much into one block? It's like a compressed farm, with all the animals in miniature – rabbits instead of horses, chickens instead of cows. How peculiar that from the street it looks like just any ordinary house block, albeit a big one. I don't think they carve up the land out here as much as they do in Northcote.

Against a wall lined with metre-wide, open-fronted wooden cubicles that look full of random garden debris, there's a person. I don't notice her until she moves, because her green coat is camouflaged. She doesn't look like Marley, but her smile exudes the same warmth. She's small – smaller even than me – with quite heavily lined skin and brown-and-grey hair pulled messily off her face in a bun.

I stand entranced as she and Marley flash their fingers at each other, hands a blur, faces strangely animated but unintelligible, lips moving but not in patterns I know.

Ripped off! Marley said everyone could understand his

mother! But I'm too exhilarated to care. My senses are overloaded. Even my hunger is forgotten.

She turns to me and holds out her hand, withdraws it, wipes some dirt onto her jacket, then extends it again with a self-deprecating grin. I smile and shake it.

She scans me, curious. Does Marley bring home strange girls all the time? What did he tell her about me? She points to her chest and makes shapes with her fingers. I glance at Marley. His cheeks are pink. He seems … slightly sheepish? Is he embarrassed to introduce me to his mum?

'She's fingerspelling,' he says clearly. 'She says her name's Robbie.'

I point to myself and match Marley's clear way of speaking. 'Piper.'

Robbie doesn't need Marley's translation. She just nods, makes more shapes with her hands and lips, and this time I lipread her perfectly, though there is no sound: 'Pleased to meet you.' With the word *you*, she points at me.

She gestures at the garden, and points to me again. She mimes planting a seed and a plant growing; stares at me expectantly.

I nod and turn to Marley. 'Can you tell her, *Yes, I do want to learn to grow things.*'

'It's all right, just talk directly to her, and if she doesn't understand you, I'll fill in the gaps.'

I point to myself, copy her mime, and nod. Then I add with my voice: 'But I don't know anything about plants, or how they translate into food. Your garden is beautiful.'

Marley's fingers flash and Robbie smiles with pleasure, lifts her hand to her chin, and gestures towards me. 'Thank you,' I lipread simultaneously, though again there's no sound.

I commit the sign to memory. *Thank you.*

Robbie indicates for us to follow her, and we're having a tour. She fingers leaves, mimes chewing them, and I understand she's telling me they're edible, even though this time she's not mouthing any words. She gestures to her body and gives me the thumbs up.

Marley translates: 'This one is particularly good for your eth.' *Health.*

She snaps off a handful of larger leaves. She's wearing a leather tool-belt apron thing over the top of her skirt, with a small garden fork hanging against her hip. There's a wide pocket across the front, and she tucks the dark-green crinkled leaves inside.

In the box-room, she points to a thicket of fine feathery plants, mimes uprooting them, and points to me. Uncertain, I look at Marley.

'Pull them up.'

He winks at me and I throw him a small smile. My confidence is growing: much of Robbie's communication is about acting and mime, and I *can* read her.

I grasp a plant, pull hard, and am astonished to see a carrot emerge from the earth. It's dirty and a bit crooked, but unmistakably a carrot. I imagine sinking my teeth into it. My hunger is back. Robbie indicates for me to pull up some more.

Next she has me snap off a fistful of a very fragrant plant with thin spiky leaves – some kind of herb – which she makes me rub between my fingers and inhale deeply. We saw off a round ball of leaves, which is apparently a cabbage.

We dig around in the ground until we find some dirty knobs – potatoes! Then Robbie points to the leafless tree with the orange fruit. She makes a small theatre of this one: mimes cutting a fruit open, taking a bite, and discovering one is in heaven.

'They're pessimmys,' Marley adds.

'What did you say?'

'PER-SIM-MONS.'

I have to ask for two repeats, because I've never heard of this fruit.

Robbie touches Marley's elbow, makes a gesture that looks like her right hand climbing her left arm, and points to Marley. Next she holds up three fingers.

Obediently, he scales the tree, effortlessly swinging into its branches and hanging by one hand as he plucks each piece of fruit. He drops them into my palm one by one, and when we have three I hand them to Robbie, who tucks them into her leather pocket, now fat with food.

She asks a question which I don't get. Marley nudges me, his fingers warm against my skin. 'What do you want to eat for dinner? Fish, chicken or rabbit?'

I'm staying for dinner? My eyes widen. I thought we were picking all this food as a demonstration. I dared not think I'd get to *taste* it! Though suddenly I feel a little worried, too, because the only vegetables I've really found recognisable have been the carrots. I like potato chips, but how those brown knobbly stone things will turn into a plate of glistening gold strips is anybody's guess. I haven't seen a whole cabbage since I was a kid, and the fruit and herb are a total mystery to me.

'Or are you fesadar?' Marley asks.

'Am I what?'

'VEG-E-TAR-I-AN.'

'Oh. Umm, no, it's okay, I eat meat.'

I flounder. I mean, I eat meat-flavoured recon but there's no actual meat involved, which certainly helped Organicore get lots of animal rights and climate change activists on board. So, actually, I suddenly realise that I have kind of been vegetarian these last few years. Also, when Robbie said *fish, chicken or rabbit*, surely she didn't mean…

I think of the enormous white chickens in the pen we walked through, and the soft furry bunnies in their hutches, their red eyes fixed on me. Are we going to kill one? Is that part of the demonstration?

'Fish,' I say hastily, figuring that will have to be recon, since there are no fish left in the ocean.

But Marley and Robbie lead me to the pond beneath the arbour, and when I kneel down and peer into dark water, I discover fish flicking through its murky depths! Marley and Robbie disappear, returning with a fishing net and a large rubber hammer.

I eye the hammer in alarm, and Marley, seeing my wariness, points to himself, turns one hand into a wriggling fish, and brings the other hand down on it in a death blow. So, he will do the killing. Which doesn't really settle my alarm at all.

I point to myself and bury my face briefly in my hands. Robbie laughs, gives me the thumbs up, and we are all agreed. Marley will kill; I won't be watching.

Robbie puts the net into my hands and I scoop up two silver fish the size of my forearm, which are flipping around wildly. Marley reaches into the net, grabs one and tosses it back.

I hand him the net, and my hunger turns to queasiness and then outright nausea as I turn my back. I don't hide my face in my hands, though. I stare upwards, at the trees, at the sky, at the abundance of nature and plants before me. I see a spider and some insects I can't identify.

Then it's over, and we're traipsing back to the inside-out kitchen with the dead fish and a leather apron full of vegetables.

Robbie sets me in front of a basin of water with a stiff-bristled brush, and my job is to scrub the vegetables clean. I scrub and scrub, paranoid at the thought of eating dirt and dying from it, until eventually Robbie gets impatient and grabs the potatoes from me, slicing them up with a knife at remarkable speed. Marley's disappeared.

There's a short square stack of blackened bricks, hollow in the middle, sitting atop a concrete bench. Robbie pokes twigs into an opening at the bottom and sets them on fire. When she places a large pan on top, over the hollow part, I understand that this is a stove.

Suddenly I'm very interested indeed. There are some unused bricks behind the guesthouse at home. Could I build such a thing? There's no mortar holding these bricks together; when one of the bricks gets nudged out of place, Robbie just pokes it back with a stick. But where would I find twigs to burn? There are those bushes along the river…

I surreptitiously take a photo with my wristlet and Robbie springs me. I flush with embarrassment, but she doesn't seem to mind. She disappears into the house and returns with a scrap of paper. Again – *paper*. She starts writing on it, at which point I realise with a jolt that she's not wearing a wristlet, so has nothing to type into.

> It's called a rocket stove. Clever design: channels the heat precisely, so uses very little fuel. Most people don't know about these, but they're easy to build.

I point to myself, and mime building bricks in a similar pile, to tell her I will make one.

She grins, gives me the thumbs up, and points to the opening at the bottom where the twigs go in, which is above the first layer of bricks. There's a thin strip of wire mesh I hadn't noticed before slotted horizontally between the bottom two bricks; the burning twigs rest on top of this metal.

> Very important. The wood sits on top, and oxygen flows underneath.

Well, that's a bit of a letdown because I have no idea where to get a bit of metal like that.

Robbie starts cooking – with vegies, fish, sizzling butter and herbs – and I follow her instructions, all given through mime.

Stir.

Add twigs to the fire.

Ease them in slowly so they won't make too much smoke.

It's impressive how she can make herself so clear without a sound.

With a mix of mime and lipreading and words scribbled on the paper, I ask where Marley's gone, why he's not helping, and Robbie explains that she grows and cooks the food and Marley does other stuff to contribute to the household – something about bread and bikes, though I'm not too sure how that fits into the scheme of things.

Before I can clarify this, we have a bit of an emergency with the rocket stove when the flame gets too high and threatens to burn our dinner. The smell sets my mouth on fire, and I long to steal a taste from the pan but force myself to resist.

Robbie whips the pan off the heat and adds a spoonful of thick golden honey from a glass jar. The smell is sweet and heady now. Once the food is back on the stove and the flame is safely low again, Robbie holds up the honey jar and indicates a path leading down the far side of the house.

I shrug, not comprehending, and reluctantly peel myself away from the pan of food to follow her. We come to a box on legs with a steady stream of insects flying in and out, and suddenly I understand – they're bees!

Robbie and I serve up the food and carry the plates inside. The house isn't exactly warm, but it's snug after the biting cold outdoors. Robbie reaches for a light switch at the bottom of the stairs, flicking it on and off in quick succession. No light turns on so far as I can see, but next thing I know Marley appears. We settle at the table in front of our plates.

And oh god, the FOOD! Our plates each hold a serve of fish, crumbed in something yellow called polenta and topped with that fragrant herb we picked; a pile of carrots drizzled with butter and honey; crumbly, crunchy pieces of potato, which aren't shaped like chips but taste like them; and the cabbage and crinkly leaves fried up with butter, salt and honey, so that they're sweet and delicious.

Nothing could have prepared me for the exquisiteness of

vegetables and fish cooked just right and flavoured with smoke from a rocket stove. I eat far too fast, even though it's not polite, not caring that I could get food poisoning. I like to save the best for last when I eat, but I can't decide which flavour is best.

'Is it just you two,' I ask Marley, 'or do you have brothers and sisters? A dad?'

Robbie squints at my face and I can tell she hasn't understood. I've never seen my own facial expressions play out on someone else's face before, especially someone as sophisticated as Robbie. 'Can you translate?' I ask Marley.

'Actually, in the deaf community we'd say *interpret*, not *translate*,' he says.

'What's the difference?'

'We say *translate* for writing; that's fine. But for signing, *translate* is seen as simply exchanging the words of one language for another, while *interpret* means so much more than that. When you go from English to Auslan and vice versa, substituting signs for words often isn't enough.'

I frown. 'Can you give me an example?'

Marley stares at the ceiling for a moment, chewing his lip. 'Okay,' he says finally, 'if you say *kill two birds with one stone* and I translate that literally for Robbie, it will look like you are actually killing birds. So, I need to sign what you mean instead, which is that you are doing something a more efficient way.'

'Okay, but...wouldn't Robbie be familiar with expressions like that? If you translated it literally, wouldn't she therefore understand what I'd meant by it?'

'Maybe, sure. But Auslan is a very direct and literal language. If I did that, I wouldn't be being authentic to Auslan. I'd be doing a bad job. And while Rob's English is pretty good, lots of Deaf people don't know English well at all. So, basically, to say that an interpreter is merely translating is actually an insult. It's so much more than that.'

'Okay. Sorry! I didn't mean to insult you.'

Marley waves my apology away and winks at me.

'Why don't lots of Deaf people know English well?'

'Auslan is so different from English – the word order is different, the grammar and tenses are different…so if you're born Deaf and can't hear it, then it's really difficult to learn it all manually. How come your English is so good?'

I shrug. I've never thought my English is particularly good. 'I didn't go deaf until I was three, so I guess I could speak it already. Plus my mum's always on my case, correcting me.'

'There you go. You weren't born deaf.'

I take a breath and try my original question again. 'Can you interpret for me, please? Do you have brothers and sisters? A dad?'

Marley signs the question, and there's a moment of confusion as they both start to answer me at once. Robbie gestures for Marley to continue.

'I'm an only child,' he says while signing. 'My other mum, Van, died when I was younger.'

'Oh. That's awful.' I want to ask what happened, but that might be rude, so I stop. It feels like I keep putting my foot in it.

We're all silent for a little while.

'So, how did you come to be so well set up?' I ask eventually, thinking surely this topic cannot go awry, and Marley interprets again. On the floor under the table, his foot shifts to rest against mine. Did he do that deliberately?

Marley voices Robbie's signs. 'There are lots of people who live like this. They just hide it, like we do, behind a high fence.'

I'm concentrating on Marley's face, but I catch Robbie's hands moving in my peripheral vision, making the shape of a high wall.

Marley says, speaking for himself this time, signing at the same time, 'Robbie couldn't wait for the claps of sivissedation. She's spent her life preparing for it, and now it's here she's thrilled.'

Robbie swipes him, playful and indignant, and slams the side of her hand down on one palm.

'For the what?' I interrupt. Marley calls her *Robbie*, not *Mum*. Interesting.

'Collapse of civilisation,' he says, enunciating clearly.

Robbie signs fast for Marley, lips not moving at all, then waves her hands at him, insisting that he tell me. 'She says she always knew this day would come, but she hasn't been looking forward to it.' Robbie gestures to the outdoor kitchen, and Marley goes on: 'And she misses bread. Life isn't the same without bread.'

It's hard to keep my focus on Marley when I just want to watch Robbie sign – it's magnetising. And yet I also want her to disappear, so that he and I can turn those foot touches into leg touches and hand touches and everything else.

'We ran out of wheat,' Marley explains, 'and the farmer we buy it from has loads but can't afford to drive it into the city.'

'And the kitchen?' I ask, because it's definitely weird that Robbie and I cooked outside in the freezing cold, when I can now see there's another kitchen inside. The downstairs part of their house is just one room, with a kitchen with two stoves at one end, a table in the middle, and a cosy arrangement of couches at the other. It's not much bigger or warmer than the guesthouse, but it's *far* more appealing. There are plants in pots by the windows, a handmade striped rug on the floor, bags and coats on hooks, and bookshelves! Mum sold all our books once visis came along.

'The flue for the woodstove rusted through,' Marley says, pointing, gesturing and making the shape of the flue with his hands as he speaks to help me understand his words. 'If we light it, smoke fills the house. We ordered a new one, but it's taking forever. So, till we sort this, we have to cook outside.'

My plate's empty now, but Marley and Robbie are only halfway through their meals. I resist the urge to swipe some of Marley's fish.

'But you have two stoves,' I say. 'Is the other one electric?'

Robbie's fingers flash and Marley interprets. 'No, it's gas. But that's only for emergencies. For regular, everyday cooking we try to stick to fuel we can produce ourselves.'

Robbie signs something else to Marley, and he says, 'She's asking if our friend Nick said he could fix it without the part.' And then, to Robbie: 'Of course he could. But he's busy. He's trying to get his place up and running, especially his garden, so he can eat from it in spring.'

I drift off a bit, thinking of whoever Nick is and the garden he's making; of the intense beauty and wildness of Robbie's garden, and the exquisite meal. Like Nick, I need to set up my own system. But where? How? Our tiny patch of courtyard is exactly big enough for *one* of the garden beds in Robbie's box-room. There's the nature strip out the front, and the dead island down the middle of our street. But how would I protect them from tree vandals?

Robbie thumps her hand down on the table and I look up, startled. She's banging to get my attention, but there's no anger in her face.

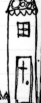

'You still want to learn to grow food?' she asks, both signing and mouthing the words. I don't need Marley to interpret that: I lipread it easily, and her signs are clear, her hands taking on the shape of plants emerging from the earth.

'Of course. But' – I gesture towards Robbie's garden – 'I don't think I could ever know enough to do this.'

Robbie shakes her head and signs something again, but I don't understand this time. I look at Marley.

'You don't start with this,' he interprets. 'I can break it down into simple steps to get you going. One thing at a time.'

'You would teach me?'

She nods. She turns to Marley and signs something fast.

Marley clears his throat. 'Rob's happy to teach you, but she doesn't have the patience for lipreading. You'd have to learn some sign language, even if it's just a few basics: how to fingerspell and a bunch of signs. Then if you help her in the garden, she'll show you what you need to know to start your own.'

Marley's signing while he talks, and even though I don't know most of the signs, it still makes it easier for me to lipread him, with him pointing to me and Robbie and the garden.

'Okay,' I say. But this doesn't actually feel okay at all. This whole sign language thing is mesmerising, but the thought of trying to memorise a few hundred thousand signs, on top of learning to garden, is more than a little daunting.

'Where do I go to learn sign language?' I ask.

'I'll teach you,' Marley offers.

Robbie's hands flash playfully and Marley blushes, but this time he doesn't interpret.

'I'm perfectly happy to teach you,' he says to me emphatically instead.

'What? Is something wrong?'

Marley swallows. 'Only deaf people are supposed to teach Auslan. But Robbie says because I'm a CODA, it's my language too.'

Robbie throws Marley an amused look, and I know there's more to it than that, but I don't press him.

'What can I do for you in return?' I ask. 'Or will you charge a fee for the lessons?'

Marley laughs. 'No, no. Keep your money. Come to the bike shop for your lessons; you can give me a hand while I teach you. Yes?'

I nod. So now I have a job in a bike shop, a language to acquire, and garden labour to do in exchange for education, while hearing people got to simply go to Angelo's free workshop then head home and grow food.

But I've also gained the perfect excuse to hang out with Marley...

Everyone's plates are empty now. Robbie slices our persimmons in half and we scoop out the flesh with a spoon. It's a rich orange jelly, breathtakingly sweet, its flavour delicate and foreign. I desperately want another but don't say so.

I help Marley with the dishes – a novelty, since at home we just dump our empty boxes into the bottom of the recon cupboard for Organicore to recycle, and before recon we always used a dishwasher. Marley washes, both hands in the sudsy water. I dry. Our arms bump, sending small electric shocks through my body. I'd like to lean over and rest my cheek against his shoulder, but I'm not brave enough.

Then it's time to go, and Marley volunteers to escort me home, which is just as well because I have no idea how to find the bike path. Robbie presses a small sheet of metal into my hand and shows me it's for the rocket stove. I remember a sign from earlier and place my fingers on my chin then bring them forward towards her.

Thank you.

Next thing we're riding, rolling down the hill of the bike path so fast that I'm flying. I gulp in great breaths of night air. My heart soars. Everything from this amazing evening whirls in my head. I feel like I've grown wings and Marley and Robbie have launched me into the night for my first flight.

Marley and I stop outside my gate. I think about inviting him in, but that would involve introducing him to Mum and showing him our dismal abode. I stare at him. Will we kiss? He shuffles from one foot to the other, awkward, then suddenly leans down to touch his lips quickly to my cheek.

'You might need this,' he says and hands me the heavy-duty bolt lock from his bike. Then he's gone.

I slide into bed without turning on the light, and my dreams are full of mixed-up, incoherent, beautiful images.

LIFE WITH WINGS

My body sings. I don't care that I'm at school. It was easy to get here, pumping the pedals on the bike Marley made me. I don't care that Taylor's not here. English and Science disappear as I dream of plants, without a hint of food-poisoning worry.

In Art I pull out my journal and it's me, paint and paper for a whole hour. I drip paint everywhere – rich greens and blues, the colours of Marley and me riding home late at night. I take one of Grandma's pieces of old sewing paper from my journal pocket, tear off pieces and scrunch them, gluing them down. I grab a palette knife and spread paint into a horizon, layering black, blue, green, smearing them together. I take the lid of a paint jar and spread it with white and press it against the page. It looks like the moon. Beautiful.

I can't believe a guy as gorgeous as Marley is interested in me. But he *is*. I feel it. And yet, how can that be? He doesn't even seem to mind that I'm deaf. It's almost as if…

he LIKES it?

WEDNESDAY JULY 22

It's been three days, and I can't hold out any longer – I have to see Marley again! I pull on my school uniform and unlock my bike. Then I practically inhale the second half of yesterday morning's Singapore Noodles, rubbery as usual, as I stand in the morning sunshine in the courtyard. I'd been planning to save them for lunch, or even brunch, but I couldn't resist – as usual. This constant hunger is really, really starting to do my head in. We received yet another half-cupboard from Organicore yesterday, the third in a row, and I've given up hoping that they'll deliver the other half next week.

I spot movement from the corner of my eye and catch the little boy, Tiger – no, Taggert – peeking out at me from behind the living room curtains. I wave, but he just stares back at me solemnly. I haven't caught sight of either of his parents even once since they moved in last week.

I wheel my bike up the driveway to the street and turn right instead of left, heading to Marley's bike shop, the cold air biting my fingers even through my gloves. I hope Mum doesn't catch me wagging. What's the point in going to school, though, when I could actually learn something useful instead?

I stop by the river to collect a bunch of twigs, for the rocket stove I'm going to build. I'd make one today but I can't exactly

do it during school hours with Mum breathing down my neck. I push the twigs into my backpack for later.

Next, thanks to my renewed interest in hygiene, I head back to High Street and stop at three shops looking for soap and washing powder. Mum and I are out of both, but it's sold out everywhere. Doesn't anyone make this stuff locally? Mum did a huge load of washing at a laundromat a week ago – it'd been two weeks since we'd moved into the guesthouse and lost access to our washing machine, and everything was dirty. But it cost so much, even on cold wash, that she's decided next time we'll have to handwash our clothes. How that's going to work with only cold water and no washing powder I just don't know.

By the time I've pedalled my bike up the hill to the bike shop, I'm much warmer. Marley is serving someone when I arrive – a red-haired guy with pitted but glowing skin and dirty clothes. Marley's face lights up when he sees me, and he throws me a grin. I plug my hearing aids in and grin back. He rents the red-haired guy a large three-wheeler, then two more customers ask for something and Marley says no – bikes for sale, I presume. He should put a sign on the door: *Bikes for rent only.*

Marley calls out something towards the back of the shop and a guy with a short dark-brown beard, flat hair scraped into a ponytail and warm black eyes emerges from the back room, wiping his hands on his jeans. He and Marley exchange a few words and he reluctantly takes Marley's place behind the counter. Marley grabs a bit of paper and writes 'Ryan' on it.

I start to speak but Marley gestures for me to stop. He shows me to clasp and rotate my palms; separate my hands, raise my index fingers and bring them together to meet each other; then point to Ryan. *Pleased to meet you.*

Ryan gives me the thumbs up, and Marley leads me down the back. We go outside into a concrete courtyard full of bike frames, squashed wheels, cracked bike seats with upholstery spilling from them, and dirty wheel pumps. I thought the shop was messy, but this is something else.

Marley clears some junk off a couple of plastic crates and offers me a seat. I wish I was wearing my jeans, not my school uniform – it's going to be impossible to keep it clean here. I dust off the crate with my hands and sit down.

Marley wriggles his fingers so that the tips seem to be kissing each other, then holds up one finger. 'Fingerspelling first,' I lipread.

'Okay,' I say.

He shakes his head, indicates his throat, and makes a hand movement as if he's turning off a tap. It's clear that he expects me to turn off my voice. He hasn't said a single word since I arrived.

Marley mimes writing in the air, first with his right hand, then with his left, then flips both hands out towards me in an inquisitive shrug, eyebrows raised: *Right-handed or left-handed?*

I hold up my right hand, and he nods. Then he waggles his own left hand. Hmm, okay then.

He touches the index finger of his left hand to his right thumb, and writes the letter *A* in the dust on the concrete. He touches the next finger along and shows me that it's *E*. Right, so we're doing the vowels. Five fingers, five vowels – only I'll use my right index finger, to point to my left thumb. I can do that.

I copy. Marley reaches over and takes my hands gently in his.

I startle at the heat from his fingers. For a moment I think he's abandoned the Auslan lesson, but then I realise he's shaping my fingers. I'm bending my left fingers back too far when I touch them with my index finger. He puts my fingers just where they need to be and withdraws his hands. Aww.

B, he shows me, and it does look a bit like a B. The *D* is a dead ringer. Unfortunately it's also easy to copy and Marley doesn't need to adjust my fingers again until we get to *S*, which I accidentally do with my index fingers instead of my little fingers. I toy with the idea of messing up more of the letters so he'll touch me again, but I don't want him to think I'm stupid.

Once we've done the numbers too, Marley graduates me to a sentence. It's much harder to make sense of the letters when they're not in alphabetical order. It takes me maybe twenty seconds, but then I have it. 'SORT THESE.'

I glance down at the rusted bucket Marley's indicating, which is overflowing with screws, nuts and other metal bits I can't identify.

I take the plunge and fingerspell a question. 'CAN I SWITCH BETWEEN WHICH HAND I USE?'

Hurrah, I've made another mistake. Marley takes my hands lightly and orients them towards me, rather than him. When making each letter I'd instinctively twisted my hands around so that those letter-shapes were facing towards Marley. But it seems I'm to hold my hands in front of me and fingerspell the letters as if I were my only audience. He will read the signs backwards. Do I imagine it, or does he squeeze my fingers slightly before he lets go?

To answer my question, Marley shakes his head. He mimes writing with his right hand again, only this time he's made his left hand a flat board and he's writing onto it. He points to me. Then he mimes writing with his left hand, using the right as a board, and points to himself. Okay, so the dominant hand does the most moving, with the non-dominant hand acting as a base – and I should be consistent.

Then Marley mimes holding a drink with his left hand, and shows me that even though his left is dominant and normally does the moving, he can cheat and switch to the right if the left hand is busy. Cool!

'YOU WANT ME TO SORT THESE INTO PILES?' I ask. It takes forever, and it's so awkward compared to how Marley and Robbie talk, fingers flying.

But Marley waits patiently and nods.

This is how the day continues – not a spoken word between us, me sorting, Marley dismantling derelict bikes and heaping their components into piles of wheels, handlebars and frames. Every now and then he drops a fistful of small bits into my bucket and we swap a few painstaking fingerspelled sentences. Unfortunately I can't think of any excuse to touch him, but the way he looks at me, intensely, right into my eyes, sets everything sparking between us anyway.

Between customers, Ryan joins us and fills my bucket too. Like Marley, he doesn't say a word to me, but I don't think he can sign. He's just the grunty type, maybe?

After a while, I realise I don't need my hearing aids anymore and slip them into my pocket. The relief is instant. It's more than just the lack of pressure in my ears. It's knowing that if Marley wants to talk to me, he'll touch my arm; that there is no expectation that I'll hear anything. I don't need to try to remember to scan the room every few minutes, just in case there's a whole bunch of people chanting *Pi-per, Pi-per*...Slowly my shoulders relax and I get into a zone.

Just after midday, Marley rests his hand lightly on my shoulder to get my attention. He mimes eating, which is a little awkward given I've polished off my food for the day already.

I follow him back inside, and we wash our hands at the sink behind the counter. There's no soap, though, and my fingers stay black. I twist around to check my school uniform but can't tell if the bike grease has smeared the back. Never again will I come here in this dress!

Marley and I perch behind the counter on rickety chairs and he takes a metal lunchbox from a shelf and opens it to reveal a hard-boiled egg and pile of cooked green leaves. He rummages around under the sink and produces an extra fork. Then he holds out the container and I realise we're supposed to share it.

I can't take his food! There's barely enough here for one person, let alone two.

But when I don't take any, Marley loads up a fork with a piece of egg and a small pile of the greens and holds it out to me. It feels too intimate to let him feed me, so I take the fork from him and let my fingers linger momentarily over his. Is he aware of it too, all this unnecessary touching we're doing? It's heavenly.

Marley eats some himself and his wristlet lights up – a message. He turns away to read it. Is he hiding something? I hope he doesn't have a girlfriend.

The egg and greens are delicious. I try to chew slowly, to make it last, and hope I don't get food poisoning – I got away with it the other night, but surely I'm tempting fate if I eat wild food too often.

Marley's busy writing back. My belly feels warm and good, and I'm so glad I came here instead of going to school.

When he turns back to me, I take a deep breath and spell, 'THAT YOUR GIRLFRIEND?'

Oh my god. How awkward can I get? But I *have* to know.

He shakes his head. 'I'M SINGLE. I SPLIT WITH MY GIRLFRIEND MONTHS AGO. YOU MUST HAVE A BOYFRIEND? OR GIRLFRIEND?'

Why would he think that? Of course I don't. It's not like there are great queues of guys – or girls for that matter – lining up to go out with the deaf girl. I shake my head, my face hot. Okay, we've put it out there. This flirting can get official. But I'm too embarrassed to take it further now, so I change the subject.

'IS THERE A SIGN FOR YOUR NAME?'

Marley nods. He shows me his left palm turned to the sky, his other hand bouncing in it twice, with his first two fingers making the shape of a V.

I copy him. 'HOW DOES THAT RELATE TO YOUR NAME?'

'IT DOESN'T. WHEN I WAS LITTLE I WAS ALWAYS BALANCING ON MY HEAD. EVEN IF I WAS IN A CHAIR, I'D BE UPSIDE DOWN. SO MY MUM GAVE ME THIS NAME SIGN.'

Marley makes his two fingers walk on his palm, and I get that they are supposed to be legs. Then he flips his hand upside down. The fingers I first saw as a V represent his two legs, up in the air. Clever.

'HOW DO YOU SIGN PIPER?' I ask.

Marley shrugs. 'YOU DON'T HAVE A NAME SIGN YET.'

'MAYBE YOU CAN MAKE ONE UP.'

Marley shows me the sign for *no*, forming a small O with his thumb and forefinger and shaking it.

'YOU CAN'T JUST MAKE UP A NAME SIGN. IT HAPPENS NATURALLY. AND THEY CAN ONLY BE GIVEN BY A DEAF PERSON.'

'WHAT DO YOU CALL A CHILD WHO DOESN'T HAVE ONE YET?'

'YOU FINGERSPELL THEIR NAME. OR SHORTEN TO INITIALS. BUT WHEN WE TALK TO SOMEONE IN AUSLAN, WE DON'T SAY THEIR NAME. WE JUST POINT.'

I can tell I'm not going to have a name sign any time soon, since I only know one deaf person.

'PMCB,' I sign, for *Piper McBride*. Marley fingerspells the last three letters back to me with a questioning look on his face, so I spell out my full name for him.

'DO YOU GET FOOD POISONING OFTEN?' I ask.

Marley laughs and holds up a single finger. Once! He mimes vomiting, then makes a dismissive gesture to show it wasn't that bad.

'I THINK THE GOVERNMENT SENDS JOURNALISTS TO HOSPITALS TO PUBLICISE EVERY SEVERE CASE.' It's a brain stretch to put together the individual letters of so many long words and make sense of what he's saying. 'THEY'RE TRYING TO GET US ALL HOOKED ON RECON.'

Once I've digested what he's said, I shoot back, 'I THOUGHT THEY WERE TRYING TO SAVE US FROM THE DANGERS OF UNBALANCED WILD FOOD.'

But even before I've finished spelling out the words, I'm thinking of everything Mum told me. Maybe the news makes food poisoning seem more common than it really is, just to get Organicore more money. But what about recon's health benefits?

'MORE LIKE CONTROL US THROUGH FORCED RELIANCE ON BIG CORPORATIONS VIA MASS MEDICATION, LACK OF KITCHENS IN WELFARE PACKAGES, PROPAGANDA IN EDUCATION...'

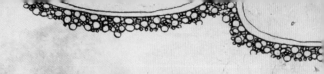

'RECON CURED CANCER! FIXED THE OBESITY EPIDEMIC!'

Marley squints at me, head to the side. 'I NEVER FIGURED YOU FOR A RECON GIRL.'

He seems disappointed. I know thirty-five per cent of the population still eats wild food, but it never occurred to me that some of those people might be philosophically *opposed* to recon. I mean, before the EDS and allergies and rallies started up recently.

I don't know what to say. There's no way I'm going to mention Mum now, or that until this week I haven't eaten wild food for years.

'YOU DON'T THINK IT'S GOOD, ABOUT THE CANCER AND OBESITY?' I ask instead. I know I'm being defensive, but I can't help it.

'YOU CAN BUY PILLS FOR THAT AT THE CHEMIST. GIVE PEOPLE FREE CHOICE, DON'T PUT DRUGS IN THEIR FOOD.'

'BUT THEN YOU MUST REMEMBER TO BUY A MILLION DIFFERENT PILLS FOR EVERYTHING, PAY A MILLION TIMES MORE, TAKE THEM DAILY. THIS IS A SIMPLE, CHEAPER SOLUTION FOR EVERYONE.'

'BUT NOT EVERYONE WANTS TO—'

Marley stops. We have a customer, and Ryan is out the back.

Have I ruined my chances with him, by being a *recon girl*? How can it be that he's not put off by my deafness but finds my eating choices a problem?

My wristlet buzzes.

▶ From: QuestTool – Content Approval Administration Office
In preparation for your interview on Friday, please complete the following security check.

While Marley serves the customer, I run through a series of prompts. Mother's maiden name? Father's date of birth? Are they joking? I can't count how many hours I've spent now answering inane questions for this job. Cesspool is a government initiative – why can't they just save everything about me in one place, scan through it, and then either approve me or deny me? This is ridiculous.

I fill in a bunch of the questions but can't get any further once they ask for my pre-Cesspool Medicare number. Who keeps track of that old stuff? I'll have to ask Mum.

Marley's still busy, so I message Taylor. 'Hey stranger! I got a job interview with Cesspool. Maybe you could apply. Then you can approve content, instead of spending all your time having sex with Beau...Oh, btw, now I know the alphabet in sign language.'

To my surprise, she answers right away. 'I like sex. It's probably more enjoyable than approving content.'

What! I was kidding. She really *did it* with him? I glance across at Marley, wondering if he'd expect sex. Would I want to? I haven't even told Taylor about him yet. I don't think I'm quite ready for sex. But just thinking about it sends a bolt of heat right through my body and something pulses in me.

I don't reply to Taylor, because Marley's done serving and is indicating for us to return to work out the back. Only we don't do as much work as we did this morning.

'PLAY TWENTY QUESTIONS?' he asks, after wrenching a damaged wheel off an old bike frame and giving me the resulting bolt. He squats in front of me.

I nod.

Marley drums his fingers against his nose, and I squint at him, puzzled. He fingerspells it. 'HOW OLD ARE YOU?'

'Sixteen,' I sign, and Marley corrects me, showing that I have to do it from my nose, because that turns it from *sixteen* into *sixteen years old*. It's very efficient – no wasting hand movements on separate words; you just do it from a different spot on your body and it adds to the meaning.

I drum my fingers against my nose to copy his question, but Marley's not satisfied with that. He shows me that I have to raise my eyebrows in a questioning way as well. It seems that's what you do in Auslan instead of signing a question mark.

'Nineteen,' he signs, and it gives me a little thrill to understand him. 'YOU'RE IN YEAR ELEVEN AT SCHOOL?'

I nod. 'I TAKE IT YOU'VE FINISHED SCHOOL?' I raise my eyebrows questioningly.

'NEVER STARTED. I WAS HOMESCHOOLED.'

'YOU NEVER WENT TO SCHOOL? EVEN ONCE? WHEN DID YOU FINISH?'

My eyebrows go up again, but this time Marley doesn't like it. He shows me that they're to go up when I'm asking a *yes* or *no* question. If I ask a question with a more in-depth answer required, my facial expression has to be different: I'm to lean forward, frown slightly, lower my eyebrows and squint thoughtfully. When Marley demonstrates this, it has the effect of making me feel like he cares immensely about my answer. It's nice.

'I NEVER OFFICIALLY FINISHED. JUST STARTED HELPING HERE. NOW I PRACTICALLY LIVE HERE! AND, NO, I NEVER WENT TO SCHOOL.'

If I moved my foot a bit, we'd be touching. I could do it. But I don't.

'SO, ROBBIE WAS YOUR TEACHER? DID YOU SIT DOWN EVERY DAY TO DO SCHOOLWORK?' I try to remember which way my eyebrows should go. Both are *yes* or *no* questions, so I belatedly raise them, ridiculously out of sync with the question, and Marley and I both laugh.

He shakes his head. 'I WAS UNSCHOOLED – I'D DO WHATEVER I FELT LIKE AND LEARNING HAPPENED ALONG THE WAY. BUT SOMETIMES ROB HAD A FIT OF CONSCIENCE AND MADE ME DO SOME BOOKWORK.'

'DO YOU MISS YOUR OTHER MUM?' Eyebrows up? Down? Argh, I can't remember. Marley gestures skywards for me and I quickly raise them.

Marley nods. 'YES. AND NO. I MEAN, I'M USED TO IT NOW. BUT SOMETIMES I WISH SHE COULD PUT ME TO BED LIKE SHE DID WHEN I WAS LITTLE. SHE USED TO LIE WITH ME UNTIL I FELL ASLEEP, TALKING IN THE DARK, TELLING ME STORIES. I WISH I HAD RECORDED THEM.' He smiles, sad and nostalgic.

'DID ROBBIE DO THAT FOR YOU, AFTER SHE DIED? OR NOT HER STYLE?' I raise my eyebrows, then realise I've asked both a *yes*-or-*no* question and an open-ended question, so I quickly frown. How does anyone remember to do this seamlessly?

'SHE TRIED. BUT I HAVE TO KEEP MY EYES OPEN TO WATCH HER TALK.'

Oh. Of course. I can't imagine finding it relaxing listening to anyone – my eyes are always open, my brain in overdrive, working to understand.

Marley sits on the ground and crosses his legs. I shift and casually let my foot rest against his thigh, pretending not to notice. 'ROBBIE GETS A BIT RESTLESS AND IMPATIENT,' he continues, 'SO I HAD TO GET THE HANG OF FALLING ASLEEP ON MY OWN. THAT WAS HARD.'

It takes full-on concentration for me to process the letters into words, but I realise something: these words are perfectly clear. There's no confusion, no uncertainty. There's no headache, either! It's wonderful.

'CAN YOU REMEMBER VAN'S STORIES?' There – my eyebrows rise in sync with my question! I will get this. I *will*.

'JUST SNIPPETS. I'M EVEN FORGETTING THE DETAILS OF HER FACE. I HATE THAT.' He blinks rapidly.

'YOU DO MISS HER.' I put my hand on his arm.

'WE'RE S'POSED TO TAKE TURNS WITH QUESTIONS. YOU COME FROM A NUCLEAR FAMILY?'

He shows me the signs for *mum*, *dad*, *brother* and *sister*. I have to withdraw my hand since it's kind of hard to hold the arm of someone who's signing. I can't tell if he liked my touch or not.

The afternoon disappears, with plenty more signing and not a lot more done on the bikes or the sorting. My uniform is filthy with dust and bike grease, but it's hard to care when my foot's touching Marley and we're laughing and overdoing our eyebrows and looking into each other's eyes.

Before I leave, Marley fingerspells, 'YOU ARE FREAKING AMAZING.'

Huh? I turn up my palms in confusion.

'I'VE NEVER SEEN ANYONE PICK UP AUSLAN SO FAST. IT USUALLY TAKES FOREVER TO LEARN TO READ FINGERSPELLING.'

'BUT I'M SO SLOW. READING YOUR WORDS IS HARD.'

'YES, BUT YOU CAN DO IT. MOST PEOPLE SIMPLY CANNOT. I SPELL THE SAME WORD OVER AND OVER AND THEY STILL DON'T GET IT.'

'OH,' I fingerspell. Then I add, 'Thank you,' using the sign I remember from the other night.

'I RECKON IT'S COS YOU'RE DEAF. DEAF PEOPLE ARE MEANT TO SIGN. THAT'S WHY IT COMES SO EASILY. AND YOU'RE SMART. THAT HELPS TOO.'

I beam at him. Then I offer to give back the bike, but Marley says to hang onto it for now. I don't ask twice.

Should I stand on tippy-toes and kiss him goodbye? My heart starts pounding again – why is it so hard for me to make a move? I just can't do it! But then it occurs to me that there's time, plenty of time, to let this grow all by itself, and that I don't have to force a thing – because here is this beautiful guy who has showered attention on me all day, and I'm smart enough to know he's *interested*. I can feel it.

Enjoy the ride, Piper. *Enjoy the ride.*

So, I do, literally as well as metaphorically. I kiss him quickly on the cheek, grab my bike and leave. I fly down hills, rolling through the back streets of Thornbury, my head whirling with every sign I've learned.

Bike – looks like your fingers pedalling.

WHY – raise thumb + forefinger & touch chest twice

WHAT – wave forefinger around questioningly.

FOOD – looks like putting a handful of food into mouth.

LUnch – like eating a sandwich.

Mum gives me permission to leave school early for my job interview, even though she's still furious. The school messaged asking where I was, at the end of the day when I was about five minutes from home. I arrived to find her freaking out, and guiltily tried to cover up by saying I'd been searching for soap and washing powder and got dirty falling off my bike. I still haven't told her anything about Marley and have this intense gut feeling that she wouldn't like the sign language thing at all.

In the school toilets, I change out of my wrecked uniform into a neat skirt and jacket, just like I promised Mum I would.

Cesspool's headquarters are uninspiring. I'm shown into a small grey windowless office lit with fluorescent lights. The interviewer is a middle-aged man with heavy bags under his eyes and a weary, slouched posture. He looks...*bored.*

I smile brightly and try to think of something to say, but it's not like I can say, *Nice office!* I take a seat opposite him and sit as straight as I can. 'Thank you for seeing me.'

He nods and speaks monotonously, like he's reciting a script. 'Thank you forrappiton tova QuestTool cont. Tday wiwaconseewer yagafe this roll. Thema important kwempees vistegret. Weendano weka rely on you wunnapassa tupple thevulsuv QuestTool.'

I nod.

He goes on, and despite my best efforts to concentrate, my eyes glaze, until he stops and I realise he's staring expectantly.

'I'm sorry, I didn't catch the question?'

He speaks louder, more clearly this time. 'If you come across conenta doesa meeta criteria, what will you do?'

'Umm... I will highlight the inappropriate words and pass them to my superior.'

I learned that much from the application process.

'Oneesa video?'

'Pardon?'

'And. If. It's. A. Video?'

'Oh. Ummm.' Damn. I was hoping to be the one to bring up the issue of videos. Maybe they could get someone else to do them. 'I note down the timecodes for the offending part.'

'Ennada think you will gewth poepry ortor marks?'

'What did you say?'

But his repeat is no clearer, and the man is losing patience. He glances at his wristlet to check my name and reads off it. 'Piper.' He looks at me. 'You have a... a...' He waves his hand around. 'Herry... Pedima...'

I've seen that before. *Hearing impediment.* Why can't he just say *deaf*? I sigh. I was hoping to luck out, get someone who speaks clearly.

'I'm deaf,' I say bluntly. Let's stop with the euphemisms. 'But I can still vet content!'

Sell yourself, Mum said this morning. I think of Marley telling me I'm smart.

'I'm sharp and pick up everything. I just can't hear. So, I was thinking you could get me to do the text-based stuff and give the videos to the hearing staff to check.'

115

He shakes his head. 'Eet dossawok like that. Connes automatically eleceta everyone gets a mex.'

'Did you say you have an automated system?'

He nods.

'Maybe we can change the system. Then it would work for lots of deaf people.'

But it's clear from his face that Cesspool is not an organisation that is interested in hiring lots of deaf people. 'Wekana mek a special system jestfa you.'

I pedal home slowly. My legs are weak – they need food. *I* need food. All those freaking hours I spent filling out questions! Why couldn't they have just written:

WE DO NOT ACCEPT DEAF PEOPLE SO DO NOT BOTHER APPLYING

Is there any job that will accept me, *ever*?

The hill on Smith Street is too much for me. I get off and push my bike listlessly. There are almost no cars on the road, but heaps of them are parked at the side. Some are abandoned; others have been pulled apart. I notice something new, too: there are people living in these cars. I see seats folded down, blankets and pillows. Some of them have actual people in them. A guy sees me looking and stares back, challenging me. I avert my eyes, but not before I've noticed something else: he's only wearing a T-shirt and jeans. I should have thought of this before – cars are warm! During the day, that is. I can make use of that heat!

I'm so dispirited, so empty and hungry, that I stop for a bit and lean against the wall of a shop to catch my breath.

I message Taylor. 'I didn't get the job. Can't say I blame them. Who wants to hire a deaf person?'

She messages me right back. 'Oh, babe. I'd hire you in an instant, deaf or not. I'm so sorry. I'm at Beau's place. Want to come hang with us?'

Aww. She's sweet. This is the warmest and most connected she's seemed in weeks. But Beau's place? I don't think I can handle yet another round of frustrating, confusing communication. I message back that Mum's waiting for me, though that's a lie.

The thought of telling Mum I failed this job interview isn't a prospect I relish. When I finally make it to our street, I can't bring myself to go inside. I sit in our car instead; I have a spare key. The warmth is exquisite. I try thinking of Marley to cheer me up, but even those good feelings seem to have deflated and I can't wrest them back.

I pull out my journal and sketch a girl being choked by red tape. *DEATH BY RED TAPE*, I write in large block letters, right over her body. I set up my paints and little water bottle on the dashboard then layer on colour, fast and loose, letting dirty water soak into the page, scratching back layers with the handle of my paintbrush and adding more before the ones beneath have even dried.

Venting my anger at the injustice of life…at my basic unacceptability…onto the page soothes me. The warmth loosens me, too.

It's not till the sun's gone down and I'm shivering and it's dinnertime that I finally pack up and trudge towards the guesthouse. It's not like Mum's been able to get another job herself – and she's probably got the best CV of anyone in Australia – but I still can't bear to tell her what a failure I am.

Finally it's the weekend and I can build my rocket stove! There's a jumbled, weed-covered mess of bricks stashed between our fence and the guesthouse. I picture Marley watching me as I work, hauling out bricks, breaking off the weeds, brushing them clean. I check the photo on my wristlet and stack bricks exactly as Robbie stacked hers, imaginary Marley nodding with approval, and I feel beautiful. Sexy, even. I insert the treasured piece of metal Robbie gave me.

'BETWEEN BRICKS,' I fingerspell to myself.

Mentally, I transform our courtyard. We could line the sides with huge plant boxes; hang pots from the fences, with trailing plants spilling from them; maybe grow a persimmon tree in a big pot by the guesthouse door? I need to see Robbie again, soon. I have so much to ask her.

I set a fire with the twigs I've collected and place a pot of water on top. Taggert is watching me through the bay window curtains with a serious look on his face. We left the curtains there for his family's privacy, but what about *our* privacy?

As soon as smoke starts billowing from my stove, smelling sweet and forest-y, Mum comes outside.

'Piper! What on earth are you doing? Is this safe?'

The fire's excited Taggert too; he's opened the curtains and dragged his mum to the window. It's the first time I've seen her since they moved in.

'Relax, Mum, I haven't turned into a pyromaniac – it's a stove. Look, you can use it for your morning coffee.'

'Where did you learn to do this?'

'Umm…school.' I feed twigs slowly into the fire, relishing the heat on my face and hands.

'Well, I'm glad they're teaching you something useful for those massive fees. Speaking of which, Piper, if I don't get a job soon we'll need to move you to Northcote High.'

I gape at her. School without Taylor? Besides, Mum's always looked down on free education.

'But you have the rent from the house now,' I say.

'That income is only a fraction of your school fees. The next instalment is due soon and I can't pay it,' Mum says simply.

Just then the back door of our house opens and out comes Taggert, pulling his mum behind him towards the fire.

'Sorry,' she says apologetically. Her face is thin and worn, her eyes dull. She's wearing weekend clothes – old trackpants and a thick slouchy jumper with a pair of furry slippers. Is this the same woman who efficiently stacked up the boxes last Thursday? I think it is.

Mum introduces me and Erin. Taggert stares at the fire, mesmerised.

'Don't touch it, it's hot,' Erin warns him. He doesn't respond.

'I'm using the fire to heat water,' I say, showing him. My hearing aid whistles, a sharp piercing sound directly into my ear. I push it firmly back in, and when the mould makes suction, the sound stops.

'Sorry,' Erin apologises again. 'He doesn't talk.' She speaks

clearly. If only she'd been the one interviewing me for that job at Cesspool.

'How are you settling in?' Mum asks. 'I haven't seen you all week.'

Erin faces Mum: '*Something something* had to stay there.'

'Sleeping in your car?!' Mum asks, shocked.

Erin nods.

'What?' I ask.

'Don't say *what*, Piper. It's not polite. Say *pardon*.'

I sigh. 'PARDON?' I wish Mum wouldn't do this in front of other people.

'Erin said she works in Oakleigh. It's too expensive to travel there and back each day, even on the train, so she's been leaving her car there and sleeping in it during the week.'

'Taggert's been missing me,' Erin says, squeezing him close to her. 'And I've missed him too.' He nestles back against her, eyes still glued to the fire.

I can't be bothered trying to follow their conversation after that, so I focus on the fire, feeding the twigs in slowly. Taggert reaches for them and I hand him one, showing him how to reduce the smoke by heating the end before pushing it all the way in.

He absorbs my instructions silently, applying them with care, and I feel like Grandma, who used to show me stuff like how to crush and soak acorns. She'd let me eat acorn cupcakes for afternoon tea on the platform she built in the oak tree at her farm.

Eventually the pot of water boils and I excuse myself to carry it inside. I strip naked and wash myself all over with a face cloth, dripping water onto the floor.

In the cold air, the warmth of the cloth is delicious. I scrub and scrub, a whole week's worth of grime falling away. Then I dip my HAIR into the HOT water and SWIRL it around.

I'm getting dressed when Mum comes in, sits in her chair and says something.

'Hang on.'

I point to my hearing aids, which are on the table. They're not waterproof, so I have to dry my hair first. I wrap the towel around my head, then slip them in. They squelch against the wet skin inside my ears.

'What did you say?'

'I've decided on the consequence for you wagging school on Wednesday.'

Oh. Fabulous.

'You can be the one to wash our sheets and towels by hand.'

'Mum! That's terrible parenting! You're supposed to apply consequences that relate to the crime.'

She slumps back in the chair. 'Well, what do you suggest, Piper?'

'Umm. I didn't get enough education, therefore I didn't get the job I applied for? See, the consequence has already occurred naturally.'

Mum sits up. 'Did you miss out on the job because you skipped school?'

'No! I'm just joking.'

'Well, what happened? Why won't you tell me?'

'I just didn't want to talk about it last night. It's same old, same old. Who would want to employ a deaf person? I think we can strike *approving Cesspool content* from my list of possible riveting careers.'

Mum sighs and slumps back down. This is her worst fear – that despite all her efforts at educating me to speak and behave properly, I might actually be unemployable.

I seem to have distracted her from the idea of punishing me for wagging, but I feel guilty, so I pull the pillowslip off my bed and drop it into the pot of still-warm water. Mum does the same with her pillowcases and we swish them around together. It's nice, companionable. Maybe she's forgiven me?

'How's *your* job search going?' I ask.

Mum scoffs. 'I am determined, *determined* to get my job with Organicore back. They need me.'

'Did you talk to Karen Kildare?'

'Yes. I told her that she's the PM, the most powerful woman in Australia. She doesn't *actually* have to do what the Organicore board tells her. She can tell *them* what to do. Such as employ me to fix the recon problems.'

'Will she?'

Mum shrugs. 'I don't know. She's so young. She's intimidated by them, especially Brent Marks. But people are sick! I told her she has to act!'

'I hope she does,' I say.

I can't say I blame her for feeling intimidated. I've met Brent Marks, the CEO, a handful of times. Once I took a deep breath and went up to him and suggested that he release recon art packs for kids – a box with the BioSpore, flavourings, texturisers and colours, and a kit of the rubber to make moulds. Then kids could design their own food. It would be so much fun. I reckon it would be a real hit. I'd put so much work into this idea, drawn up pictures of what the packaging would look like and everything. He chucked me on the chin and laughed and said to Bob Forsyth, Mum's colleague, who was standing beside him, 'She's so cute!'

I was not being *cute*! I was serious. Would he do that to Karen Kildare? Laugh at her suggestions?

Mum and I swish the pillowcases in silence for a bit, squeeze them out, and do my top sheet. Maybe I should tell her about Marley. But before I can figure out what to say, Mum says, 'I'm so pissed off with Brent. How could he fire me? I've given Organicore my *life*, and they ditch me like a dirty dishrag as soon as money's tight? I bet Brent still gets paid. I never thought they would betray me. I've been with them since the *start*.'

'I know. It's unbelievable.'

I start squeezing out the sheet and a huge puddle of water spills to the floor. Mum pulls her sheet off the bed and mops it up. I guess we're going to be here for ages, doing the sheets.

'I think you should look for a different job,' I say. 'Something that's nothing to do with Organicore.'

Mum sighs. 'I check the ads on Cesspool every day. There's not much going for high-tech food scientists. Karen Kildare said they're working on a rationing system. They'll need people to help roll it out, but that's a way off yet.'

Mum looks so flat. Clearly this idea doesn't inspire her.

'Will the rations include three meals a day?' I ask. 'When are they coming?'

Mum shrugs. 'She didn't go into detail.'

When the sheets are draped over the fences to dry, Mum rummages around in a box under her bed. 'Look! I saved these.' She holds up a couple of floppy rubber sacks.

'What's that?'

'What are *they*? Plural, Piper.'

'What are those weird flippy things? Dead fish? Or do I say *dead fishes*?'

Mum rolls her eyes at my insolence. 'The plural of *fish* is *fish*. They're hot water bottles!'

Oh. Wow. I remember using them at Grandma and Grandpa's place when I was little.

'We can heat water for them on your stove. I didn't know you could heat a whole pot of water with just a handful of twigs. I thought you needed *logs* for a fire.'

It feels good to be the knowledgeable one. 'I'll have to collect more twigs,' I say. 'Can we have our dinner early today?'

Mum relents, so we eat, and then I grab my bike and ride in search of shrubs with twigs to spare. When I find one at Fairfield Park I lie back on the grass and look at the sky. I think of a song Taylor taught me, by Synchronic Bleaks, 'Superficial Rising'. I reach for my wristlet to message her but stop myself. I have to get through the whole weekend without charging it. Instead, I fingerspell the entire lyrics of 'Superficial Rising'. I'm getting faster now, the signs rolling off my hands. Wait till Marley sees how much I've improved.

Thursday 6 AUGUST

Marley and I ride along the Merri Creek, wind whipping our hair and soft spray from the river peppering our legs. The path is busy with riders and pedestrians, carrying backpacks, pushing trolleys stolen from Allstar.

I really shouldn't be here. With Mum breathing down my neck, it's the first time I've dared wag school since the Wednesday before last. I did spend a couple of hours at the bike shop after school last week, but it's so much harder to flirt with a splitting headache, and Marley had a huge cargo trike to build, so we spent more time working than talking. My collection of signs is growing, though. Last time he said there was a place he wanted to show me once the trike was done. So, here I am, instead of school.

Marley turns off the bike path and I follow, pedalling hard to make the hill. Just when I think I'm going to faint from hunger, Marley stops and I pull up beside him, breathing hard, warm despite the crisp air.

We lock up our bikes and Marley casually takes my hand as he leads me around a corner. I glance sideways at him, trying to walk naturally, as if I hold hands with a beautiful boy every day.

Around the corner, in an ordinary, suburban Thornbury street with otherwise dead front yards and nature strips, is a giant vacant block with a huge, beautiful oak tree at its front, bare branches silhouetted magnificently against the sky. Why hasn't it been chopped down by vandals?

I realise that a platform has been built across its lower branches, around two metres up. Nailed to the trunk's base is a large hand-painted sign:

Beneath the tree sprawls a garden – a wilderness of green, plants clambering over each other. I recognise several plants from Robbie's garden.

Unfortunately, Marley has to let go of my hand to sign. He points to the garden. 'Guerrilla garden. Run by a group of my friends who share the food.'

Marley only has to fingerspell half the words, because I know the signs for *garden*, *friends* and *food*, and instead of using the little words, he simply points. Sign language is so economical.

There's movement on the platform, and I realise there's a guy tucked up there in a sleeping bag, reading a book. It's the red-haired guy Marley served at the bike shop. He and Marley talk for a bit but I can't follow the conversation. Marley does sign his side of it for my benefit, but I don't know enough Auslan yet to follow it when it's that fast.

Unlike Robbie's garden, this one isn't divided into rooms or spaces – it's just a sprawling mess of plants, none of which look particularly edible. I glance at Marley, hoping to catch a break in the conversation. I'm not wearing my hearing aids – I don't need them with Marley – so I can't hear whether the other guy is still talking or not. But Marley looks down at the path and indicates for me to follow him, and he doesn't seem to be talking or listening anymore.

'DOES HE LIVE HERE?' I fingerspell, indicating the guy on the platform.

Marley shakes his head and shows me the sign for *live*, which is two strokes above my breasts. He indicates that I can ask the question simply by pointing to the guy, signing *live*, and pointing to the ground. And, damn, I forgot that my eyebrows had to go up. There's so much to remember.

'They guard this place twenty-four seven, to protect it from tree vandals. Cam's on duty.'

There are a few new signs in there, which I pick up just from watching, and I'm thrilled to realise that reading the fingerspelling of Cam's name felt effortless to me. I try to commit the new signs to memory, which isn't easy to achieve while also maintaining the flow of the conversation.

'Are you part of this group?' I remember my eyebrows this time.

'No. Robbie grows my food. But my mates Cody and Oscar are.'

'HOW MANY PEOPLE RUN THIS?'

Marley shrugs. 'Maybe ten or twelve?'

We walk the paths, admiring the foliage. Maybe it's like Robbie's garden, where you have to know where to look and what to pull up to find the food.

'THERE'S ENOUGH FOOD FOR EVERYONE?' I ask.

Marley shows me the signs for *enough*, *everyone* and *for*. I repeat my question without fingerspelling a word.

'There's not enough to fill anyone right now. It's incredibly hard without grains.'

I touch plants as we pass them, rubbing their leaves between my fingers and inhaling deeply. Maybe I could join them? A little bit of wild food combined with our recon rations would make such a difference.

Marley and I are back at the tree now, and he gestures for me to climb a rope ladder suspended from the platform. At the top it's really homey, in a grungy way. There are candle stubs pressed into cherrygrog bottles, wax dripping down the sides, and some old cushions with stuffing exploding from them on a series of thin camping mattresses. Someone's woven a pretty disc from twigs and feathers, shaped like a spider's web, and hung it from one of the branches, along with a string of crystals and glass beads. It's pretty. Old paper books stand in a row inside a plastic crate.

One of the books, *Permaculture on the Loose*, is lying open next to Cam's sleeping bag. He's up now, lighting a fire in an old oil tin. It looks to me like another version of Robbie's rocket stove. He speaks to Marley, but I don't catch the words.

'Tea?' Marley asks and I nod.

Cam shimmies down the ladder, picks some grassy stalks, climbs back up and drops them into a kettle of water atop the oil-tin rocket stove. Marley sits next to me, close, his knee touching mine. The warmth of his body is delicious, and I glance at him and smile. Marley grins and winks back. I want to hold hands again, but not in front of Cam.

Cam says something to Marley. 'He's asking how Robbie is,' Marley tells me. He turns to Cam and signs while he speaks, and this time I can work out what he's saying, with a combination of lipreading and the signs I know. 'Mostly good, but she really misses bread!'

We sip the tea. It's warm and smells richly fragrant, but it has no flavour and only reminds me of how hungry I am. I wish Cam would give me a 'demonstration' of the food growing here.

I'm not sure if I should sign or speak, but given all the interpreting Marley's been doing it feels a bit weird to just open my mouth and talk normally, so I sign my question to Cam.

'DO YOU THINK...' I'm feel awkward asking, but I have to try. '...I COULD JOIN YOU? I DON'T KNOW HOW TO GROW FOOD, BUT I LEARN FAST.'

Marley voices for me and adds, 'She *does* learn fast!' He doesn't seem to mind interpreting.

But I don't need him to interpret Cam's *no*. His face is serious, firm. Marley signs as Cam continues: 'We don't have enough food for the members we already have.'

132

'FAIR ENOUGH.'

There's an uncomfortable silence. I probably shouldn't have asked.

'Has your family decided what to do about the farm?' Marley asks eventually. To me, he explains, 'They were growing BioSpore but Organicore won't pick it up now as their farm is too far from a train line. It's just rotting in the fields.'

Cam speaks and Marley interprets. 'Dad's thinking about putting in a crop of some kind of fuel.'

'Why not grow food?' I ask. I know all the signs for my question, which is immensely satisfying.

Marley signs, and I can't tell whether he's interpreting or speaking for himself this time. 'Because BioSpore wrecks the soil. We're still working out how to fix it. Fertiliser helps, but we can't transport it.' I'm glancing from Marley to Cam but still can't figure it out. 'A fuel crop might work but we haven't tested it.'

Mum never mentioned that about BioSpore and the soil. I wonder if she knows?

I drink more of my tea and check Marley and Cam's faces. I think there's a lull in the conversation, so I ask, 'WHO OWNS THIS LAND?'

Marley signs, and again it's not clear if it's him or Cam answering me. 'No one. I mean, the council, probably. There are heaps of guerrilla gardens around, if you know where to look.'

'THE COUNCIL ALLOWS THIS?'

Marley shakes his head and now it's clear it's him speaking. 'It's illegal to put anything on public land. People just do it anyway. So far, so good.'

An image flashes through my mind like a fire roaring tall: the dead island down the middle of our street, now a jungle of plants, with a vine-covered chook pen, some rabbits, a persimmon tree laden with fat orange fruit, and myself, digging out a pond…fish for dinner. The idea burns inside me, and I *know* I have to try this, even though it'll take months and months before there's any actual food. Where I'll find people to guard it, I have no idea. I picture myself sleeping outdoors, night after night, under the stars.

Okay, Mum would *never* allow me to sleep alone outside! Maybe I can persuade her to join me? She needs to eat too. But what about water?

'HOW DO YOU WATER THIS PLACE?' I ask.

Marley holds up a finger, and I realise that while I've drifted off, he and Cam have continued talking. Oops. I'm glad Mum's not here – she'd tick me off big-time.

When they're done talking, Cam gestures for me to look over the side of the platform. They've rigged up a tarp, which funnels water into an old plastic BioSpore barrel. Wow. I could do that.

On the fence of the house next door someone's painted, *Imagine if our military budget was spent on combating world hunger.* It's like the message at the bike shop, by Marley's friend. What was her name? Mafren Kilsy?

We leave soon after, parting ways once we reach our bikes. Marley has a booking to do another house-move by bike. We hug goodbye, a long, lingering hug, and the smell of him – smoke, the fragrant tea herb, and something musky and personal – gives me an adrenaline rush.

'Can you ask Robbie if I can get started with her soon?' I ask, using a mixture of signs and fingerspelling. Marley nods and promises to message me.

I've seen BioSpore barrels out the back of lots of restaurants in Northcote, so I ride back and weave through the side streets until I find one at an Italian restaurant. I knock on the back door, and eventually a stooped, frowning man with wrinkly skin opens it. 'Yes?' I lipread.

I don't want to put my hearing aids on, so I mime, indicating that my ears are no good. He smiles and pats my shoulder. I guess being obviously deaf has its advantages sometimes, though Mum would be mortified if she saw me doing this.

I mime tossing the BioSpore barrel into the skip next door and raise my eyebrows. *Is this rubbish?*

After a moment he gets me and nods.

I mime me carrying the barrel off, and he's right up for that, glad to be rid of it. I guess Organicore has scaled back their recycling program along with everything else.

I indicate to him that I'll be back in five, jump on my bike and ride to the bike shop. Ryan's there, and he lets me borrow a trike to haul the barrel home.

The old man at the restaurant kindly produces some rope and helps me tie the barrel to the back. He waves me off happily, and I have a sense that he feels good for having done something kind for the little deaf girl. People don't treat me like this when I speak.

I check three shops and can't get a tarp, but then I realise I can use the large plastic garbage bags in the cupboard under the sink at the guesthouse.

As I wheel the trike into the courtyard, Taggert appears

at the window and I wave. He lifts his hand tentatively, the smallest gesture, and then drops it again.

Mum comes outside, and I don't need my hearing aids to lipread her. 'Piper! The school just called. Where have you been?'

'Sparing myself a headache, that's where.'

'What? And what's this?' Mum turns to the trike, the BioSpore barrel strapped to the back. She speaks more, but it's nothing obvious and I don't catch it.

I indicate my ears, and Mum sees the lack of hearing aids. She throws her head back in exasperation, gives up trying to speak to me, and motions sharply for me to *PUT THEM ON*.

She has this idea that I should be wearing them twenty-four seven, with the only allowed breaks being when I'm asleep or washing myself. But Mum doesn't have to deal with the headaches, itchy ears, and the incessant blare of white noise.

I shove my hearing aids in and say, 'I'm making us a water tank.'

'We don't need a water tank! But you need an education, and I pay through the nose for that school! I expect you to go, *every single day*.'

'I'm going to grow us a food garden,' I say, but Mum's not impressed.

'I'm serious, Piper. There will be consequences for this.'

I have a feeling I won't get out of this as easily as last time – but I can't bring myself to care. No telling-off from Mum can erase the inspiration bubbling inside me, the excitement of starting right away by rigging up a water tank, and the exquisite fact that Marley held my hand today.

SUNDAY 9 AUGUST

Finally, I get to visit Robbie! Marley has to work, and I'm fretting about meeting her by myself – how will she know I've arrived, and what if we can't understand each other? But I needn't have worried: there's a little button by the gate that makes a light flash and a thing in Robbie's pocket buzz, and she lets me straight in, her eyes a warm pearl-grey, her smile vibrant, her hair a mess. She's pulled it into a ponytail but missed half of it, and she pushes it out of her eyes repeatedly as we talk.

She does the *how are you* sign and my hands are trembling as I reply. Following her, I try frantically to absorb, again, the details of her garden-rooms. She gestures to a weedy planter box in the box-room and mimes pulling up all the plants, then hands me a fork and mimes digging. There's no question about understanding her. I wish I could sign like that, with such efficient, precise hand movements.

I dig, but it's heavy work. I think I'm losing strength. I've definitely lost weight; my clothes are loose. I don't want Robbie to see how much I'm struggling, though, so I work the fork as hard as I can. Robbie does another bed and I watch her surreptitiously, copying her.

There are wriggling worms in the dirt. I get Robbie's attention and show her and she does the sign. *Worm.* She gives

me the thumbs up to show me these are a sign of magnificent soil.

I keep digging, and after a bit she interrupts me, pointing at my feet, ticking me off.

Don't stand on the garden bed.

I blush, glad I know the sign for *sorry*. But Robbie isn't finished. She gives a small performance: one finger becomes a worm, and when my giant boot comes down, it is gruesomely squished, its innards spraying everywhere.

It was a mistake! I said I was sorry!

But now Robbie's hands are plant roots, wriggling happily through the earth. When they reach the compacted section, they struggle and twist, the branches above the ground stunting in growth.

Robbie isn't telling me off. She's *teaching* me. Okay. This is the stuff I need to know. *Dig the ground, and then do not stand on it again, not even once.*

Once the beds are picked bald and forked over, we haul in some compost. Robbie's left hand is a plant and her right hand becomes its roots, gobbling happily at the compost – food for the plants.

Watching her, it seems there could be no other way to make a concept so clear. But I have no idea how to shape my hands elegantly the way she does, or make my fingers seem happy or miserable.

Robbie hands me a hose and I look at her in alarm – I thought hoses were banned. But Robbie sees my face and shows me a huge metal water tank hidden behind the bees. Her fingers are rain, water flowing into the tank, flowing out through the hose. Oh. Okay. You're still allowed to use a hose with water you collected yourself.

I pretend it's my future garden that I'm watering. The heady smell of damp earth rises, and I feel both calm and intoxicated at once.

We feed the weeds to the rabbits and chickens, Robbie picking out the favourites of each. The animals greet us enthusiastically and snatch up the greens.

Then Robbie shows me a glass cupboard set against the house. Inside are boxes and boxes of tiny plants.

'These,' she signs, using her visual theatre of drawings in the air, 'will be going into our newly prepared garden beds.' Her signs are so different from Marley's, which seem to relate more directly to English.

We collect eggs from the chook pen, an onion and some greens for lunch. There's a single spear of asparagus poking up from the earth by the path, and Robbie snaps it off crisply. I manage the fire in the rocket stove while Robbie boils the eggs and tosses the greens in butter and a red goo called sweet chilli sauce. It's delicious.

I bring up a photo of my rocket stove on my wristlet to show Robbie. She squints at it and suddenly grins. Then she straightens up and formally shakes my hand in congratulations.

Taking a deep breath, I attempt my first proper communication of the day. Resisting the urge to fingerspell, I mime myself cold, shivering. Then I show her me building the stove, lighting it, warmth cascading onto me. My fingers feel clumsy, oafish, compared to her swift, tight movements. Finally, I sign, 'Thank you!'

Robbie grins and takes a small bow.

I can't think how to do this next bit visually, so I revert to fingerspelling and signed words. 'I don't know where to start for my own garden. Maybe with some pots in my courtyard?'

She holds out her hand for my arm. It takes me a moment to realise she wants to see the photo again. She gestures to the image, shows me that the rocket stove is in shadow. Her hand makes the shape of the sun, and the other one becomes a plant hungrily absorbing energy from its rays. The courtyard is too shady.

With my hands, I draw an imaginary picture of our street and the island down the middle, miming myself planting seeds and the food growing tall and wild.

Robbie nods seriously. 'This is an important idea. You should do it,' she signs. She eats a couple of mouthfuls of egg and greens, then continues, 'You don't need to know a lot to start. I can tell you the first steps. If you begin now, you could be eating by midsummer.'

I have to concentrate hard to understand her, but it's not like lipreading – I'm not growing a headache.

'So…what's first?' I sign.

'Compost,' Robbie signs back, then she draws in the air exactly how I'm to build a pile from dead grass, green grass, water and leaves. Next, her hands make the shape of the little boxes in the glass cupboard on her verandah: 'You need to plant seeds.'

She shows me the compost breaking down, turning into dirt, food for the plants; the seeds growing up and up, until they're ready to be tucked into the new compost in a garden bed. The garden bed, of course, needs to be dug and watered.

It hasn't rained yet, so there's no water in my BioSpore tank. Hopefully the skies will decide to unleash some water in time.

this is an
impORtant
IDEa.

Robbie leads me to a large poster on the wall just inside the house, titled *Moon-planting Guide*. She points to 18 August and asks if I can come then, gesturing: 'I'll give you some seeds.'

'Why 18 August?' I sign.

'It's moon-planting day.'

I can't say I get what that means – we're meeting up in the daytime, so we're hardly going to be planting by the light of the moon – but whatever. I'll be here. Too bad it's a school day.

Robbie hands me a large hessian sack, raises her eyebrows and makes hand motions that look like the ocean.

I frown, confused. That can't be what she meant.

'BEACH,' she fingerspells.

Oh. I was right. I should have trusted that she knows how to make every single thing in the world crystal clear with her hands.

She mimes a plant growing underwater; me plucking it, washing it, and placing it in the compost pile; the seedlings gobbling it at twice the speed and growing twice as tall.

St Kilda beach is a long ride away. I hope I'll have the energy to get there. How does Robbie manage to do all this by herself?

All day at school I ignore what I'm supposed to be doing and draw and paint and plan. I paint Robbie. It's not a perfect likeness, but there's something about her serious energy, her strength, that comes through. I do this on a separate piece of paper, so that while she's drying I can work on other stuff in my journal. I make to-do lists for my garden. I remember the details for building the perfect compost pile. Under the desk, I fingerspell to myself. I'm getting faster.

▶ To: Taylor
Want to come over soon? It's been forever. I have a plan for my street. I'm going to grow FOOD!

After school, I borrow a trike from Marley and ride it through the back streets of Thornbury and Northcote. At the top of Northcote Hill, I find what I need: an imposing house with a freshly mown nature strip out the front. I grab handfuls of grass, which half-fill the sack Robbie gave me, then ride on, my newly sharpened eyes looking for more compost ingredients, until the sack is full.

I go home and dump the contents into a pile on the street island. It looks small and pathetic. Robbie said to aim for a whole cubic metre.

So I try Fairfield Park, and – YES! – it's thick with grass and weeds up to my knees. I suppose mower petrol isn't prioritised anymore. I use scissors to clip off fistfuls, and eventually I have a second sackful.

My legs ache on the second trip home. I'm exhausted to the core of my being. But I do as Robbie instructed, building the compost pile with layers of dead grass and leaves, green grass, and water. I fill our big pot with water inside then carry it out and sprinkle it over the top. It's hard to believe this will turn into rich black food for plants, but I already know nature is capable of magic.

HOW TO BUILD
A QUICK COMPOST PILE

1 Must be at least 1 cubic metre in size to become hot and break down quickly.

2 Build layers...

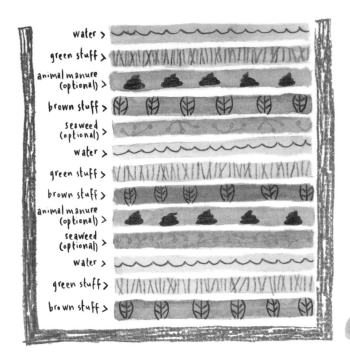

- water >
- green stuff >
- animal manure (optional) >
- brown stuff >
- seaweed (optional) >
- water >
- green stuff >
- brown stuff >
- animal manure (optional) >
- seaweed (optional) >
- water >
- green stuff >
- brown stuff >

3 Once a week, turn the pile, mixing up the ingredients.

green stuff (adds nitrogen) = fresh weeds, grass clippings
brown stuff (adds carbon) = dead leaves, hay, dry grass clippings
animal manure adds nutrients and helps it break down fast.
seaweed contains lots of minerals

FRIDAY 11 AUGUST

It's the weekend at last. I survey the island in our street, light-headed with hunger. There's no one about except an older man I've seen before, who nods as he waddles past. The ground seems hard. I hope I can dig this. I picture the garden from Sprouted Earth superimposed on top: soft black dirt, lush green plants, droplets of water sparkling on leaves. I can almost smell it.

I'm going to do this!

The next step for my compost is to turn it inside out by flipping the contents into a new pile next to it, so I make a start. The first few handfuls are fine, but I'm stunned to find the middle is hot – really hot, little strands of ash streaking the grass. How this alchemy works, I cannot fathom. Wishing I had a fork, I grab a big armload, toss it into the new pile, and watch as little blisters form on my palms. Ow. I try using my feet to kick the pile, but that just makes a mess. Damn.

In the end I kick the pile into a thin layer on the ground, which cools it pretty quickly. Then I reassemble it into a new pile. My hands are burning. I blow on them, but it doesn't help. I imagine Robbie standing beside me, giving me a theatrical pat on the back. She'd be pleased that I worked it out in the end.

I head inside, waving to Taggert on the way. He waves back with just his fingertips.

SUNDAY 15 AUGUST

I spend Sunday down by the river, looking for more sticks for my rocket stove and doodling in my journal as the water rushes past. I probably spend more time daydreaming than drawing, though, as my hands are still burning and holding the pen hurts.

When I get home in the early evening, Mum's waiting for me, wound up tight like a spring. She's chosen our recon already, and the packages sit on our little marble table alongside two fresh glasses of water. She presses the heat buttons as soon as I walk in and sits back, excitement radiating, so sparkly I can almost see it. It's *weird*.

'What?' I ask, putting in my hearing aids.

Mum doesn't even correct my speech. 'Organicore rang. They want me back!'

I rush over to her and throw my arms around her neck. 'Mum, that's wonderful!' Looking at her closely now, though, I think she might be a bit nervous.

She takes a deep breath. 'The job's in Sydney.'

My arms fall to my side.

'They are giving us a nice apartment to live in. And a full subscription of recon.'

They *are*? 'Mum?' I croak. 'Have you said yes to this already?'

She ducks her head. 'Maybe.'

Oh god, no. NO. NO. NO.

What about Marley?

What about my food paradise?

Who will teach me to garden? And sign?

I can't give up Auslan now. I can't.

This is not happening. It can't be. Mum puts her hands on my shoulders and sits me down. She hands me a glass of water, and my hands are shaking.

'Take a deep breath, Piper. This could be an incredible new beginning. We'll enrol you in a good school, nice and close, so you don't have to ride so far. We'll have money again. And it's all happening in two weeks!'

Two *weeks*? I put the water down and slump back in my chair. I finally find my voice. 'I can't move to Sydney, Mum. It's out of the question.'

And that is the truth. I would rather live in this dingy place. But I know Mum – there's no stopping her. A sick, sinking feeling seeps over me. What say do I have in this?

'They'll pay our electricity bill too,' Mum says. 'And water. They've booked us seats on the overnight train up there. Look, I know it's hard for you to imagine leaving Taylor, but it's an opportunity for us to fix our lives.'

'Taylor? She's already...'

Left me. I can't tell Mum that. She'd want to know why else I need to stay. Though maybe it's better if I just tell her...not the sign language thing, but about Marley, Robbie and the garden. I open my mouth, but the words don't come out.

'They want you to fix the recon problems?' I ask instead.

'It's management, not research. Organicore is establishing a new rail network to transport recon. I'll be looking at that and other strategies to get their deliveries back on track.'

'What about the sick people?'

'At least I'll have my foot in the door. They sold the research labs and Melbourne headquarters to raise funds for the rail project – that's why this job is based in Sydney. Once deliveries are running smoothly and there's money again, I'm sure they'll put me back on research.'

'They should recall recon until it's safe! Not deliver more of it!'

'We have food shortages, Piper. Recon is essential. It helps more people than it harms!'

'People need to know about this! People should have free choice!' I'm shouting now. I can't seem to help it.

Mum holds up her palm, as if it will somehow pacify me. It doesn't.

'FOR THE FIRST TIME IN MY LIFE I'VE FOUND SOMETHING I WANT TO DO AND YOU JUST RIP IT OUT FROM UNDER MY FEET!'

My arm, out of control, swings wildly and the food crashes to the floor. *Stop it, Piper. Stop it!* But I can't stop.

NO WAY AM I MOVING TO SYDNEY! YOU CAN'T MAKE ME!

I kick out and the table topples to the side, smashing glass and sending water flying across the floor.

Mum grabs me in a vice-like grip. 'You need to calm down, Piper. NOW. The neighbours can probably hear you!'

I wrestle against her, but she's stronger than me. I don't care if Taggert hears. Or Archie. Her embrace is soothing, though, and I let her lead me carefully around the glass to my bed.

I curl up tight, hugging my pillow. Mum sits beside me, stroking my forehead.

'What is it you've found that you want to do?' she asks.

The gentleness of her words unleashes a tide of tears. I sob, hiccupping, and try to explain. 'There's...this boy I like. And...and...I think he likes me. I met his...his mum. And... she's...teaching me to grow food. I have this vision...I'm gonna grow our street. Food plants everywhere, down the middle.'

I don't say about the signing. I know there's no hope of Mum understanding that.

'Piper,' Mum says, gentle but firm, pushing my hair back from my eyes, 'it's not healthy to run your life around guys. We women, we need to be independent, do our own thing. We can get you the stuff to grow some food up there, if that's what you want to do.'

She doesn't get it. Not at all. How can I explain the miracle of it, that there's actually a guy out there who would want to be with *me*, despite having to put up with my deafness; in fact, that for some bizarre reason this seems to be something he *likes*?

How can I explain the magic of standing in Robbie's garden and understanding that food and nature and immense beauty are all entwined and can wrap themselves around me and carry my soul to the sky? That it transcends me from concrete and grey and plastic?

That in this sky-place, I understand everything – there's a captivating language that unfolds with our hands, expressive and theatrical?

That it's not about a guy.

It's about how to LIVE.

I refuse to go to school, and Mum doesn't push me. I light a fire in the rocket stove and sit beside it with my journal. I want to draw Sprouted Earth, but I'm exhausted. I need to do something easy today. I pull out one of Grandma's pieces of paper and paint it yellow.

Taggert comes out and watches. I draw circles on a sheet of plastic and cut them out with a Stanley knife. Taggert touches the wet paint and presses tiny dots of yellow onto his arm. Then he reaches for the Stanley knife, but I hold it away from him.

'It's sharp. Don't touch.'

He accepts this and watches patiently while I cut. I try to cut away the emptiness I feel inside me, but of course cutting just makes the hole bigger.

A shadow falls over us. I glance up and it's Archie, an anxious look on his face, his mouth moving.

'What?'

'He bithra you?'

I shake my head. 'It's fine. He's not bothering me.'

It's easy being with Taggert. I like that he doesn't speak.

Archie retreats. Taggert watches, riveted, while I spray black dots through my newly cut stencil onto the yellow paper. My hands shake slightly. I feel like I've been through the washing machine – small and vulnerable and wrung out.

As I lift the stencil, revealing the dots, Taggert puts his hand over his mouth in delight. He seems oblivious to my mood. He wants me to spray the stencil onto his arm, but I won't. I take a spare sheet of plastic and spray that instead, giving it to him. He holds it like it's the most precious thing he's ever owned.

When it's dry, I take out scissors and slice my stencilled painting into pieces. Taggert is horrified and tries to stop me.

'No, it's good,' I tell him. 'They're to collage into my journal.' I show him the book, the other pieces of collage I've done, and he turns the pages like it's a picture book, fingering everything slowly. He lets me cut up the painting after that.

The water on the rocket stove boils and I pour some into my hot water bottle, which I tuck under my jumper. The heat is comforting, but nothing can fix this gaping void inside me.

Mum can't force me to go to Sydney! She can't.

▶ To: Taylor
Yeah, so I don't know if you got my last message. But apparently the plan has changed. It seems Yours Truly is moving to Sydney. In two weeks. My life is over.

▶ From: Taylor
Pipes! No! Why?! You can't move to Sydney! I will miss you too much.

▶ To: Taylor
Really? I didn't think you'd notice.

That was mean. I wish I could unsend it. But I don't even message her back to say sorry. Instead, I head for the bike shop. For Marley.

'What's wrong?' he signs as soon as I wheel my bike through the door.

I try to smile, but I can't. Marley takes my hand and leads me out into the courtyard. I nod to Ryan on the way past.

'What happened?' Marley asks when we're outside.

'Mum says we're moving to Sydney in two weeks,' I sign back.

Marley shakes his head, his eyes widening as the implications of this sink in. He puts his hand on my shoulder, pulls me close. I rest my head on his chest and breathe in the exquisite mix of bike oil, coffee, musk and smoke. I snake my hands around his waist and we hold each other for several minutes. He's solid and warm, like I'm holding the earth.

But then he stirs, and I feel his chest vibrating. He's talking. I look up and Ryan is behind me, gesturing towards the shop.

'Sorry,' Marley signs to me. 'Someone's here to see me.'

He follows Ryan inside and I take a deep breath. I need to pull myself together. I grab my journal out of my bag and traipse after them into the shop. I'll draw while Marley serves customers – that always calms me. I flip it open to the first empty page, and glance up.

There's a beautiful girl with an open, vibrant face talking to Marley. I've seen her before. Where? The food-growing workshop! I remember her skirts – long and scruffy and layered over each other. She and Marley know each other? I suppose it makes sense, since Marley said the teacher, Angelo, was a mate of his.

Her hair is clean and shiny, hanging halfway down her back in soft waves, almost the same brown as her skin, and she's wearing a tight little orange jumper onto which she's sewn a collection of mismatched vintage buttons. The skirts are different today, blue instead of brown, and there's a patch stitched to the side of her outer skirt on which someone's written with texta *Imagine…*

I glance at the wall. It's the same handwriting. *Imagine if the GDP was replaced with a contentment index.* Is this Mafren Kilsy? She looks…like a girl version of Marley, I realise with alarm. The perfect mix of scruffy and clean, of effervescence and earth.

He's smiling at her, talking emphatically, with enthusiasm, showing her the bike he's been working on. I was so self-absorbed when I arrived that I didn't even notice the battery he's rigged up to it.

They know each other well – there's a comfortableness to the way they stand and look at each other. I wish I was wearing my hearing aids. Maybe I'd understand them. But they're out the back in my bag. I'm about to go and grab them when Marley spots me and introduces me.

'KELSEY,' he fingerspells. I was right. Except about the spelling. And what I'd thought was her first name. *Mafren. My friend?* Oh!

'She runs Transition Towns. And she's a member of Sprouted Earth.'

Kelsey gives me a warm smile and appraises me curiously. There's something in her eyes – she's taken aback to see me here with Marley. She throws Marley a look, raising one eyebrow, challenging him.

I don't catch her words, but Marley interprets them. Even though I don't know all the signs, with the ones I do know and lipreading, I understand him clearly: 'She says she doesn't run Transition Towns. At least, she's trying not to. The group is supposed to run itself. Her job is to make herself obsolete.'

Now that I know the context, I lipread Kelsey's answer easily. 'I've been trying to make myself obsolete for five years now.'

Marley interprets her words, and I don't stop him. Is she old enough for that? I look at her closely. I guess she could be twenty-five?

'What's Transition Towns?' I sign, tucking my journal under my arm to free up my hands, and Marley voices my words.

I'm kind of liking this, that she might see me as being like Robbie, an exotic Deaf person who signs and doesn't speak at all.

Kelsey hoists herself onto the counter and makes herself comfortable. Marley signs her words as she speaks, which is slow since he has to fingerspell several of the words at a speed I can take in. He doesn't seem to mind. 'It's a movement where groups of people aim to transition to living without so much reliance on petrol, oil and electricity.' She's been waiting while I catch up, and now continues, with Marley signing: 'It started in the UK. A whole town planted out every bit of open space with food and bought water tanks and solar panels while they were still cheap.'

Kelsey and Marley both laugh, but I don't know what the joke is because Marley hasn't signed it yet.

'They're probably plump and living the good life now,' he signs. Oh. That's the joke. But Marley and Kelsey aren't laughing anymore so I just nod.

'Transition Towns has become really popular recently,' Kelsey continues. 'We have heaps of new members.'

'What does it mean to be a member of Sprouted Earth? Do you spend lots of time working there, in the garden?'

I wait while Marley repeats my question. Kelsey shrugs. 'A few hours a week, and I sleep there now and then.'

I'm about to ask exactly how much food she gets, but she glances at my journal. 'What's that?'

I take it from under my arm, but then my hands are full and I can't sign, so I put it on the counter. I touch my chest and fingerspell, 'JOURNAL.'

'May I?'

I nod and she opens it, right on the page of Robbie. Marley's mouth falls open. 'Did you do this?'

I nod.

'It looks exactly like her!'

'Who is it?' Kelsey asks, and even though I understand her, Marley signs her question. I wish there was some way to telepathically convey to him which bits need interpreting and which don't.

'My mum.'

Kelsey stares at Marley in astonishment. There's something going on here. Even though Kelsey and Marley know each other well, Kelsey hasn't met Robbie. And she seems affronted that *I* have.

Marley's cheeks turn pink. They exchange a look I don't understand, then both turn back to my journal. Kelsey turns back a few pages and I'm mortified when she stops at the one of Marley in the bike shop. She holds it up against him, marvelling at the likeness.

'She says you're very talented. And you are! Do you draw *everything*?'

My face is burning. My huge crush on him couldn't be more clearly spelled out. 'Yes. Most days.'

I reach over and turn the pages hastily to something more neutral. I stop at the one about how to make compost. This captures Kelsey's attention, and she pores over it carefully. Finally, she looks up and speaks seriously.

Marley signs, 'She wants to make a poster of this. It would be a great reference for everyone in Transition Towns. It's perfect. So good!'

'Oh. Um. Okay. Sure.'

Kelsey holds up her wristlet and checks it's okay with me that she takes a photo. I nod. She's really inspired by this, excited. She flips another page and there's the 'Death by Red Tape' painting. She gets it immediately and laughs, jabbing her finger onto the page with emphasis. It's something she relates to.

'You are jelly, Piper. This should be on every wall in Melbourne!'

When Marley interprets, I get the missing word. *Genius.*

She turns to Marley and says something about the bike with the battery.

'I'm making her a battery charger,' he explains to me. 'Pedal the bike and it charges it up.' To her, he says, 'Sorry it's not working yet. Hopefully tomorrow.'

I'm glad for the opportunity to stare at them, unabashed, while they talk. Is there something more than just friendship here? If there is, why on earth would Marley pick *me* rather than her? She's older, gorgeous, and clearly moves in the same world that he does. I bet she's no recon girl.

But he *hasn't* exactly picked me, I realise. Is this why things haven't progressed?

Before she leaves, Kelsey says, 'Your language is beautiful. How do I sign *beautiful*?'

I haven't a clue, but Marley supplies the sign, a kind of wiping of the chin, and I copy. Kelsey doesn't realise it's the first time I've ever done it. She slides her hand over her chin, but I see she's got it wrong because she doesn't finish with a closed fist.

'You'll have to teach me one day,' she says to me. 'I've always wanted to learn sign language.'

After she's gone, I giggle. 'She thinks I can actually sign.'

'You can,' Marley insists, serious, 'even if your vocab is a bit limited. She can't tell the difference between fingerspelling and proper signs, so it all looks fluent to her.'

We turn our attention to the bike Marley's working on. He gets me to pedal while he tries rigging up different combinations of wire between a small black box and the battery. It's not working and he's not sure why.

'I haven't done this before,' he tells me. And then, with worried eyes: 'So, are you really going to Sydney?'

'I don't want to. But Mum's got a job there, and she lost her job here.' I don't mention her name, or that she works with Organicore. Then he'd know I really am the recon girl.

'You're sixteen. You're allowed to make your own choices. Just because she goes doesn't mean *you* have to.'

This hadn't occurred to me. I try to picture it – me living alone in the guesthouse, no Mum to come home to. The image is bleak and it scares me. 'I'm not sure I'm ready to live alone.'

I want him to say, *Come and live with me and Robbie!* But of course he doesn't. He says, 'You need a plan. Either you go and you make plans for how you're going to cope, or you decide to stay and you set yourself up.'

Marley disconnects the black box from the charger and opens the lid. I watch him, thinking about it. Planning to go is out of the question. Planning to stay... well, setting myself up is the only thing I want to do. I think of the lists in my journal, all the stuff I have to do to get my garden growing. The next step is to get seeds from Robbie, and tomorrow is moon-planting day. Could I do it like that? One step at a time?

'Pedal,' Marley instructs me, and I do. He's pleased. Something is working now. He smiles and we look into each other's eyes for a few beats longer than we need to.

I help Marley for a few hours and then ride home. When I go inside I ignore Mum. I don't even put on my hearing aids. I get a drink, turning on the tap hard. I can see she's trying to get my attention, probably to tell me not to waste water, but when she comes over, I close my eyes, point to my empty ears to show her there's no point in talking to me, and turn away. If she's yelling, I can't hear her.

I grab my evening recon and take it to my bed. While I eat, I hunch over my wristlet and message Taylor.

▶ To: Taylor
I'm sorry. I know I was mean. I know you'll miss me. I just... I don't know what to say. It's hard not seeing you at school every day. I don't have to move to Sydney to miss you. Don't you worry about your future? Aren't your parents freaking out? Do they even know where you are? Maybe you should call them, huh?

I press *send*. Out of the corner of my eye I see Mum waving her hands around, but I refuse to look.

After five minutes, Taylor messages me back.

▶ From: Taylor
I love you, Piper. It's all okay. Sorry, I know I'm a terrible friend right now. I just have a lot going on, and it's kind of a bad time to talk about it. I'll message you later.

YEAH.
Sure you will.

TUESDAY AUGUST 18

Early the next morning, I'm out on the street about to leave for Robbie's when the Organicore truck turns slowly into our street. Long mechanical arms drop off each new cupboard and retrieve the empty ones we've left in our front yards, lifting them high above the fence tops.

I rush back to check our cupboard. Please, please let there be a full delivery this week! But when I touch my thumb to the sensor, the door swings open and this time there's not even half. I count the boxes and sink to my knees in disappointment. Mum's going to say we're only allowed one a day now.

I grab a box at random and rip it open, not even waiting for it to heat. *Indian Butter Chicken*, the box says. I devour the contents so quickly I hardly taste them. It feels good in my belly, though. My head clears a bit. I dump the empty box in the bottom of the cupboard and head for Merri Creek.

I know Mum's mad that I'm wagging again, just as she'll be mad about me eating dinner for breakfast, but there's only so much she can do when I refuse to look at her or communicate in any way. What's the point of school when I have real stuff to learn? I know it's immature of me but I'm glad to be pissing Mum off.

See, you can't make me do what I don't want to do.

When I get to Robbie's it turns out she wants me to help her kill a chicken before we plant by the moon. Inside the chook pen, she scoops one up and holds it under her arm, upside down. Signing one-handed, she shows me how this makes the blood go to its head, and that for the chicken this is like being in a placid dream.

We head into the pond-arbour room – Robbie shows me that she doesn't want the other chickens to see what we're about to do. She hands me the chook, and tells me to grip it really, really tightly.

I'm getting tougher these days, so I watch as Robbie takes a knife from her leather pouch and slices it cleanly across the chook's throat, holding its head back so that blood drips to the ground.

Suddenly the chook starts convulsing, wings flapping violently. I lose my grip and it thrashes to the ground. I watch in horror as it flails about, blood spraying everywhere. Robbie tries to catch it, but she can't. Eventually it slows and lies limp in a pool of its own blood.

Robbie's face is spattered with blood, her hands dripping with it, and I feel a fine wet spray all over my skin. I take a deep breath.

That was HORRIFIC.

'Sorry,' Robbie signs. 'I should've told you how strong they are.'

'No matter what you told me, I don't think I could have held that.' Where does she get all her strength from? 'You hurt it,' I add. Surely there's a less barbaric way to kill a chicken?

But Robbie shakes her head. 'It's reflex. From the moment I slit its throat, it can't feel anything.'

The rocket stove is already heating water, and Robbie scoops us each a bowl of it before she holds the chook by the feet and dips it into the pot. She shows me that the hot water makes it easy to pluck its feathers. She's right – most of them come off easily in my hand, though I have to pull harder to get out the tail and wing feathers.

Finally, the chook lies naked on the chopping board, and Robbie hands me a bar of soap.

'How do you have any soap left?' I ask. I do a little mime of me entering a shop, looking for soap, and giving up in frustration.

Robbie smiles at my effort, and signs herself making soap from chicken fat and ash from the rocket stove. It sounds disgusting, but it's obviously more of nature's magical alchemy because this soap is the real thing – it even smells of lavender.

The chicken gizzards – mixed with too many herbs to count, onion, butter, salt and pepper – turns out to be the best meal I've eaten in my life. I learn the signs for *heart* and *testicles*, and that you need to fingerspell *liver*, as I hold up each skerrick of meat.

There must be some nutrients I really need in this, because my nausea disappears and my body says *gimme-gimme-gimme*, and I swear it's not just because I'm starving. Maybe Mum missed something in Nutrium Sustate, despite all her careful work.

I don't know how to ask my next question visually, so I fingerspell most of it. 'How do you remember so much about plants? When to sow each one, and where in the garden to put it?'

'I learned by doing. A little bit at a time. But if you want a head start, I have a great book you can borrow.'

Robbie goes into the house and returns with a heavy book, *Identifying Local Plants*, which she hands to me. I flip it open to a page about milk thistle. The book says it's a weed that grows all over Melbourne, and that the stem, leaves and flowers can be eaten raw or cooked.

'You can eat weeds?' I ask Robbie. 'I thought they were all poisonous!'

The picture in the book looks familiar. I'm sure I've seen this plant around.

After lunch, Robbie leads me to the glass cupboard outside the kitchen and shows me how to move tiny seedlings into a bigger box, where they'll grow for a while before they're ready for the open, wild world.

We work together, each using a knife to transplant the seedlings. I copy Robbie carefully, ignoring the stinging of my blisters. Then we top up the original box with soil, and Robbie sprinkles some seeds into my palm.

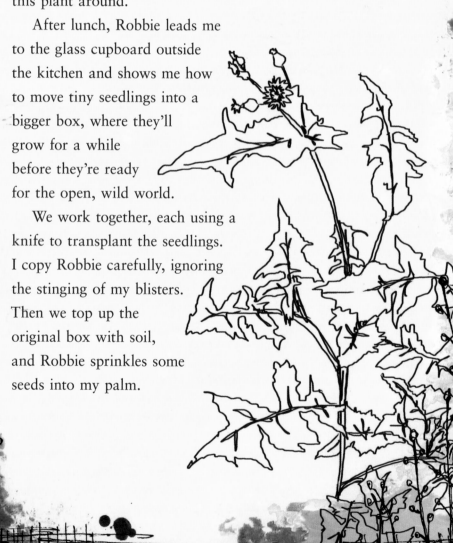

She demonstrates poking tiny holes in the soil, two finger-widths apart, and dropping a single seed into each hole.

'Why is this called moon-planting?' I ask.

I don't fully follow her answer. She makes the shape of the moon in the sky, something about it affecting the tides in the ocean – and how at the same time as the tide comes in, so it does within a seed, which affects its germination.

It seems a little farfetched to me. 'Do you actually believe this?'

She shrugs. 'If you follow the moon calendar for when to do your garden jobs, you end up with a nice flow of tasks. Everything gets done, but not too much in a day. If the plants really do grow better with tidal help, that's a bonus. Works for me, whether I believe or not.'

'How do you know whether to put a plant in one of your garden boxes, or in a wild area? Or—'

Robbie shakes her head, slides her fingers down her cheek, then smoothly forms a shaking fist. That last bit is a sign I know: *finish*. I frown, and she fingerspells the meaning: *It doesn't matter*. An entire phrase in one sign.

She shows me that I should follow a much simpler method for my garden, drawing a mandala in the air, with six round garden beds and water in the middle – a pond, I presume.

I'm to build a compost pile on one bed, then a week later turn it onto the next bed. Robbie makes like she's digging into the first bed, the soil made soft by the compost, and mimes trying to dig in the beds that have not yet had a compost pile sit on them: rock hard.

I can do this.

Make a Mandala Garden

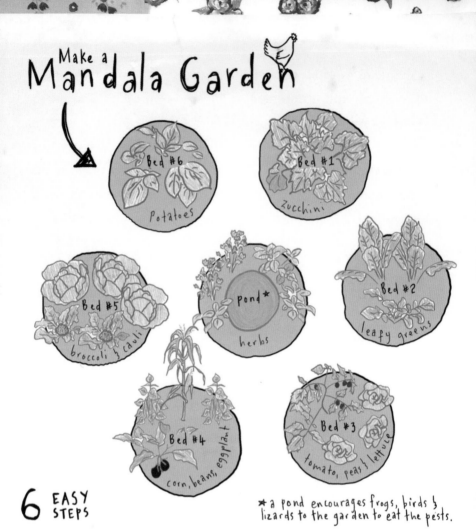

Bed #6 Potatoes

Bed #1 zucchini

Bed #5 broccoli & cauli

Pond ⭐ herbs

Bed #2 leafy greens

Bed #4 corn, beans, eggplant

Bed #3 tomato, peas & lettuce

6 EASY STEPS

⭐ a pond encourages frogs, birds & lizards to the garden to eat the pests.

1. Build a compost pile on site of Bed #1. Water pile to help soften soil underneath. The heat of the pile kills any weeds.

2. A week later, turn the pile and transfer it to site of Bed #2. With compost now removed from Bed #1, dig over the bed.

3. Another week later, repeat Step 2 by transferring the compost pile from Bed #2 to Bed #3, and dig over Bed #2.

4. Once the compost on Bed #3 has broken down, spread the compost over Beds #1, 2 & 3 and dig Bed #3. These beds are now ready to plant. Follow the suggested diagram above.

5. On the site of Bed #4, build a 2nd compost pile and repeat the above Steps for Beds #4, 5 & 6.

6. Once a bed has been harvested, fence chooks onto the area to eat the weeds, fertilise the earth with manure and scratch over the soil. When the chooks have done their job, the bed is ready for more compost and planting!

A shadow falls over us and we look up. Marley! I'm struck by the incredible realisation that Robbie didn't hear him either. It's always me who's the last to know, but not here. Robbie, so knowledgeable and sophisticated, cannot hear him either.

He leans down to kiss her on the cheek and gives me a quick, perfunctory kiss on my temple. I hope Robbie got all that chicken blood off. I want to throw my arms around him but not with Robbie here watching.

'How are you?' Robbie signs, and I can see the affection in her eyes. 'Want some chicken?'

Marley nods. 'I have to get back to the shop.' He looks at me. 'But I knew you'd be here, and I wanted to give you this.'

He pulls a roll of plastic out of his bag and unravels it. There's the compost page from my journal, printed large onto a poster! At the bottom, in tiny, typed text, it says: *Artwork copyright Piper McBride.*

Wow. It looks so … official!

'You did *this*?' Robbie asks, incredulous.

I nod.

'I love it!' To Marley, she asks, 'Can I have one? I can show it to …' But she's signing too fast; I miss who she wants to show.

'I'll ask Kelsey. She had heaps printed.'

'You should make one about how to kill a chicken,' Robbie says to me.

I mime myself drawing a poster with the chicken thrashing on the ground and blood spattering all over the page.

Robbie laughs. 'Not like that!'

She redraws the poster with a nice neat kill, then washes her hands and goes to make lunch for Marley. He sits on the verandah and watches as I drop the last few seeds into their holes.

'You could make a whole series of posters,' he suggests. 'They'd be really popular with Transition Towns.'

'I'll get drawing.'

He grins, then his face becomes serious. 'Have you made a plan? About Sydney, I mean? Do you think you might stay?'

I wipe my hands on my jeans and sigh. 'I don't feel old enough to…live independently.' *Hint hint!* But I know it's unrealistic to hope he'll invite me, a girl he hardly knows, to live with him.

'When exactly are you going?'

'Next Sunday. But I can't imagine it really happening.'

In my mind, I see myself getting onto the train with Mum. The doors close, and my life's over.

Marley puts an arm across my shoulder and I lean in. My body goes soft as I inhale the now-familiar smell of bike-grease and boy. I could sit like this forever. His finger strokes my shoulder, tiny circular movements. But all too soon the food is ready, and I have to resist the urge to swipe morsels from Marley's plate. Next thing, he's gone.

As I leave too, Robbie gives me some seeds of my own and a small bag of compost. Then she reaches into her leather pouch, pulls out some potatoes, and tucks them into my pockets with a grin.

On my ride home, I see that someone has sprayed a stencil onto the side wall of a terrace house showing the Organicore logo wrapped around Karen Kildare's face. It's clever – the likeness is unmistakeable.

I stop and stare. Do others know too, about Karen Kildare being Organicore's front?

I emerge from the bike path onto High Street and next thing, taped to a concrete post between two shops, is my poster about how to make compost! Wow, Kelsey doesn't mess around. I can't believe it's my work.

Mindful that today is just the right day for moon-planting, as soon as I get home I hunt around for little boxes to tip the compost into. I can't find any, so I sneak the recon box from the recycling section of the cupboard, and prick holes into the bottom with my Stanley knife. In my peripheral vision I can see Mum watching me, raising her hands to protest, or maybe to ask what I'm doing, but I ignore her.

I press the compost into the box and make a diamond pattern of holes as I was taught. I drop one seed into each hole and carefully tuck them in, closing the dirt over them. I sprinkle on a cupful of water. Now to wait. And wait.

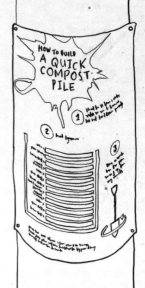

It's been almost a week and my seeds have been hiding. But today, finally, I see tiny shoots of green against the dirt. There are no leaves, just miniscule sticks. I might have missed them if I wasn't watching so closely for progress.

I don't have the strength to keep fighting with Mum – she can always outlast me. She's stopped trying to argue and simply does kind little gestures, like handing me recon and making my bed for me. This morning I pull on my school uniform for the first time in a week and sullenly accept a cup of warm tea. I can't believe she figured out how to use the rocket stove herself. I suppose she's been watching me.

I go to school, but it's a weird, dissociative experience and feels so pointless compared to what I've been learning lately. The only good thing that happens is on my ride home, when I discover a clump of the weed I saw in Robbie's book – milk thistle – growing between the cracks in some bluestones. Although what if there's another plant that looks like milk thistle but actually kills you…?

I get off my bike and crouch down, peering at it closely. It's *exactly* like the picture. I break off a leaf and gingerly lick the milky sap. It's bitter but not too bad. I chew the rest of the leaf. Hopefully if it's poisonous this will only be enough to make me sick, not kill me. I gather up a large handful and slip it into my backpack.

When I get home, I instantly regret having gone to school because I see Mum's put my absence to good use. The entire contents of the guesthouse, except for the furniture, have been packed into boxes lining one wall. Without our clutter, it's even bleaker than before.

'Where's my art stuff?' I yell.

Mum steels herself and says something. There are heavy rings under her eyes. The roots of her hair show a thick line of grey. I hadn't realised she'd become so thin.

'What?' I say.

'Put your hearing aids in!'

I contemplate ignoring her, but I want to know where my art stuff is, so I jam them into my ears and eye her warily.

'Second-top box from the left.'

She could have just pointed. Auslan is so much more efficient than English.

I rip open the box and my art stuff spills across the floor.

'I use this stuff *every single day*! You can't pack it!' I kneel and arrange it all back into my desk drawers.

Mum's talking, and reluctantly I turn my eyes to her. 'What?'

'It's rude to say *what*. Pardon.'

I stare at her defiantly and say nothing.

Eventually she sighs, and I know I've won. 'Our stuff is getting picked up by the coras tomorrow. We can only take one case on the train. So, use the case for what you need until we go.'

Mum points to a case she's left at the foot of my bed. I presume *coras* means *couriers*.

'My art stuff is staying in my desk until we go.' Did I really say that? *Until we go*? I think of Marley's arm around me.

'Well, if you have too much stuff for that case, whatever doesn't fit will be left behind.'

I pick out my favourite, most-used art supplies and put them in my backpack along with my journal. I don't trust Mum not to repack them.

Tuesday
25 AUGUST

I toss and turn all night and wake long before dawn. Five days until Sydney. Mum's still sleeping, her mouth open, one arm flung wide.

The good news is that I don't appear to have died from milk-thistle poisoning.

I get out of bed to check my seedlings. I've been bringing them inside every night so they don't get too cold, since I don't have a glass cupboard like Robbie's. One of them is starting to open, a tiny unfurling of leaf. I take the box outside – maybe the morning sun will inspire its leaves to open further?

I open the door and…it's raining! I race around the side of the guesthouse in my pyjamas, droplets sprinkling my face. Water slides from the guesthouse roof onto my garbage bag and down into the BioSpore barrel I've rigged up. It works! I peer over the top and see that it's nearly half full of water. It must have been raining for hours. This is a great start for my garden. I set the box of seedlings on the fence, so my babies can have a big drink.

I can't stop thinking about Sydney. *You have to make a plan, Piper.* The only logical option is to do as I'm told, go with Mum. And yet how can I abandon all I've started here?

I shake my head. I'll just keep building my garden. Mum will see I'm serious – that this has to be part of my new life up there, at least. But how will I communicate with Robbie from Sydney, ask her questions? She doesn't have a wristlet, nor a visi.

I light a fire in the rocket stove, and while the water heats I scrub Robbie's potatoes.

Mum emerges in her pyjamas, drawn by the smoke. She's holding a thick folder of research notes. I glance at our house but it's too early for Taggert to be at the window yet.

Mum waves her hand in front of my face and I look up. 'I said what are these? Are you wearing your hearing aids?'

I don't want to put in my hearing aids yet. But Mum keeps talking and gesticulating at me, and the effort of trying to understand her is too much, so I skulk inside and grab them.

'What are you cooking?' Mum asks as soon as I've switched them on.

'Potatoes.'

'Where did you get them?'

I shrug. 'Umm…I found them. In the weeds by the Merri Creek.' I've never been a good liar.

'They could be anything! How can you possibly know they're safe to eat?'

'It's fine. I identified them.' Inspired, I grab Robbie's plant identification book, praying to god there will, indeed, be a listing for potatoes.

Mum asks something else, but I'm looking at the book so I miss her question, running my finger down the index column for *P*. There is! I flip to the right page. There's a beautiful drawing of a potato plant.

Mum touches my arm and waits until I look at her face. 'Did the leaves look like this?'

174

potato /pəˈteɪtoʊ/, *n., pl.* -toes. **1.** the edible tuber (**white potato** or **Irish potato**) of a cultivated plant, *Solanum tuberosum.* **2.** the plant itself. **3.**→**sweet potato.** [Sp. *patata* white potato, var. of *batata* sweet potato, from Haitian]

'Yes! That's how I found them.'

Mum frowns, unconvinced.

When I think the potatoes are ready, I throw in the milk thistle and take the pot off the heat, like I've seen Robbie do. Greens don't take long to cook. I rinse out more of the recon boxes that are waiting to be recycled, and serve up our meals – one for me, one for Mum.

She's peppering me with questions – I catch the words *poisonous* and *book* – but I can't look at her and cook at the same time, so I pretend I don't notice she's talking.

Mum stares dubiously at her breakfast while I tuck in. The taste is disappointing after Robbie's food; the butter, salt and honey make a huge difference. But still, the potato is hearty and floury, and the milk thistle slippery and smooth, the perfect balance despite the bitterness.

'They won't kill you, Mum,' I say. 'I tasted them both last night and I'm still here.' Well, that's a lie – I only tasted the milkweed, but I trust Robbie completely.

Eventually she takes a bite and chews slowly. Mum never complains, but she must be as hungry as I am.

'Do you think there are more of these by the creek?' she asks eventually.

I shrug.

'What are you growing?' she asks, gesturing towards my seedlings.

The rain has eased, so I take her over to them and point. 'These ones are cauliflower and broccoli; this row is rocket. There should be carrots and tomatoes in these gaps. They haven't come up yet.'

'You know we can only take a case on the train, Piper. You won't be able to bring these.' She checks her wristlet. 'You need to get to school.'

I exhale heavily. 'What's the *point*? You're dragging me to a new school in Sydney. Let me off until then.'

'Piper, I logged you as sick last week, to let you get used to the idea. But you need to go back now.'

I scowl darkly, any semblance of positivity I was feeling now well and truly gone. I go inside to change into my uniform, but it's filthy.

'I need you to wash this,' I say as I unlock my bike.

She looks up from her notes. 'That's something you can do yourself, Piper. I'm busy.'

'With what? You don't have a job yet.' I know I'm being a brat, but I don't care.

'Any minute the courier will arrive to pick up our boxes. And I'm making a testing plan for the recon. I have an idea for a set of spesive tests that should highlight exactly where the problem is.'

'What kind of tests?'

'Inexpensive. Cheap. Organicore won't be able to turn down this proposal. I'm going to convince them to put me back on research. I can probably oversee that *and* manage the railway project.' Mum checks the time on her wristlet again. 'Piper – *school!*'

I sigh and get my bike.

The compost needs turning this afternoon, but I can't face burning my hands again. The guesthouse looks barren and bleak with just our cases and furniture, but luckily I convinced Mum we'd need to keep out the pot and serving spoon for the rocket stove, in case I find more potatoes.

I grab the serving spoon and my pillow case and head onto the street. I'm using them to scoop handfuls of compost into a new pile when the older guy who walks slowly up and down our street stops in front of me, his eyeballs working furiously. His mouth is going too, but my hearing aids are on my desk next to my bed.

I waggle my forefinger, the sign for *what*, even though I know he won't understand me. Faintly disapproving, he speaks again, but his mouth barely opens. The possibilities include *It's a beautiful day* – but he doesn't have that nice-weather-appreciating air about him – or perhaps *Get that pile of weeds off my street*. Maybe? I point to my ears, and make a gesture with my hands that indicate that they're kaput. He gives a slight nod. His eyes are puffy, and thick red veins spider across his face. His belly protrudes over his jeans and his hair is white-grey where he's not bald. He takes his slow, resigned walk off to a house nearly opposite mine. Some minutes later the man waddles back, holding a garden fork. Wow! To show him how handy the fork is, I take it and start hauling weeds with it right away, but he frowns and shakes his head. Then he grabs the fork from me, rolls up his sleeves, and turns the pile for me. Only he's not getting all the outside bits into the middle, and I don't think Robbie would be entirely happy. I grab the misplaced weeds using my pillow case as a glove and toss them onto the top of the pile. How did this happen? It's ... nice?

Now we need water. I head back down my driveway, and using Mum's wine glass, I scoop some from my barrel into our cooking pot. From the bay window, Taggert watches. I wave, and he waves back.

When I return to water the compost pile, the man is still standing beside it, watching me and nodding. A shadow falls over us and there's Marley! He's the perfect mix of gorgeous and industrial cool, with his re-made bike and enormous leather saddlebags and hair hanging over his eyes.

Marley gives me the usual kiss on the cheek and I store up the smell of him, and the scratch of his stubble, to remember later. I introduce him to the man, and it's a little awkward since I don't know his name. Marley holds out his hand and they shake, exchanging a few words. 'HALIM,' Marley fingerspells for my benefit.

'PIPER,' I fingerspell back, and Marley interprets my name for Halim.

'Robbie will be impressed,' Marley signs, surveying our work. I presume he's using his voice at the same time, because Halim seems to understand him. Marley takes a photo with his wristlet, and Archie and Taggert emerge from my house.

Archie speaks to me, but I don't catch a word – his moustache and beard obscure his mouth completely.

Marley interprets. 'He said the little boy wants to watch. Would it be okay to keep an eye on him?'

I'm about to say *sure* to Archie, but I stop myself. I've spent all afternoon miming to Halim. If he knew I could just speak normally, would he think I was ridiculous for having put him through such a convoluted method of communication?

Instead I nod and sign, 'All right,' which Marley voices for me, and I wonder if Archie thinks this is bizarre, given that last time I saw him I spoke with my voice. But he's busy kneeling in front of Taggert, giving him instructions, I think. If he's weirded out by the communication, it doesn't show on his face.

He goes back inside and Taggert stands close to me, holding the side of my jeans with one hand. I do another round of introductions for his benefit. We finish off the compost pile as a group, which is immensely satisfying, and just as we put the last bits on, Marley takes a photo of us all. Then Taggert takes one of me and Marley, and now it's my favourite photo *ever*.

Halim returns his fork to his house and lumbers back. Then Taggert wants to go down the driveway of our place. Marley and I follow, Halim tagging behind us.

Proudly, Taggert shows Marley and Halim the rocket stove and pulls at my sleeve, so I indulge him by setting a fire. We can all drink tea; I have some dandelion leaves to try, which I spotted on my way to school this morning with help from the plant identification book. I appear to have survived the taste test I did at the time.

Mum comes out of the guesthouse, a little startled to find company. I go to introduce her, but the words freeze in my throat. Do I speak or sign? If I thought it was awkward with Archie, that's nothing compared to this! Mum doesn't even know I *can* sign! I can't sign in front of her, but what will Marley think if I speak instead? Will he be disappointed in me? Why did I let Taggert lead us down here? We should have stayed on the street!

I hesitate so long that we're all left just staring at each other. Marley does a double take, and I see recognition flash over his face.

Yes, Marley, my mum is Irene McBride.

But Marley collects himself quickly and breaks the ice by leaning across, holding out his hand to Mum, and saying, 'Marley.'

Mum says, 'Irene.'

I clasp my fists together, making the sign for *friends*, which I hope to Mum just looks like a random gesture, and half-croak, half-whisper, 'My friends.'

If anyone notices my bizarre behaviour, they don't let on. Mum goes back inside and she *still* doesn't know I can sign, and Halim still doesn't know I can speak properly, and somehow I've got myself mixed up in a twisted web of lies.

I don't know which is the PROPER me.

Taggert reaches for another twig to add to the fire and I show him to count to ten before he pushes it in. I don't want him burning up all our fuel at once.

I break the dandelion leaves into the water. They're limp and soggy after sitting in my pocket all day.

I pour a cup of tea for Mum and carry it inside. I hope there's some nutrition in this, because I'm definitely not into the bitter flavour. When I return, Marley catches my eye, and signs something I don't recognise. His hands are spread wide, as if holding an invisible beach ball, which he rocks up and down twice. His mouth gives no clue. He seems to be saying *bah bah* or maybe *pa-pa*.

'What?' I sign. Mum would tell me to ask for clarification in a more polite way, but I've seen both Marley and Robbie sign this and they never seem to think it's rude.

'I would never have guessed Irene McBride is your mum! But now I do see the resemblance.' Marley gestures to my face. I thought he might make the association between her and me being a recon girl, but he doesn't mention it.

I hand some tea to Halim and Marley. 'What was that sign you did before?' I ask Marley, miming holding a beach ball.

He repeats the sign, and again his mouth moves: *pa-pa*. 'It means strange or weird,' he tells me. 'But in Auslan that sign has its own lip pattern. Pa-pa.'

'IS IT PAPA OR BABA?' I fingerspell.

Marley laughs. 'No one can ever agree. And it doesn't matter, because we don't say it out loud anyway. Just make the shape with your mouth.'

I copy the sign. 'Pa-pa,' I mouth, rocking my invisible beach ball.

Halim does the sign too, and I gather he says something because Marley turns towards him. His lips barely move, and I raise my eyebrows at Marley, who obligingly interprets: 'He thought it was *pa-pa* too, when he realised Irene McBride was living right across the road.'

I shrug. I guess to me, my mum will never be anything other than a normal person.

Once the tea is gone, Marley says he has to get back to the shop. He gives me a sweet kiss on the cheek which he holds just a fraction longer than necessary, and heads off, Halim plodding in his wake. Marley still doesn't seem horrified that I am practically the daughter of his nemesis, Organicore. Thank god.

Mum waves her hand in front of my face. 'Ten minutes to go.'

NO!

It's D-day. Well, D-night. Train to Sydney. I can't believe how quickly the days have disappeared. Where's my plan? I'm really going. The guesthouse is stark and unloved, beds stripped bare. I didn't even say goodbye to Taylor – just received a handful of messages as she had 'too much going on' to actually find the time to meet up.

I pull my case up to the door and test dragging it while balancing my recon box of seedlings in my other hand. There are little pairs of heart-shaped leaves sprouted everywhere and they are so cute, but Mum was right. This is not practical.

What should I do with them? I can't just leave them to die. On a whim, I hurry over the road and set them down on Halim's front verandah. A thankyou for the fork, and the help. My compost pile sits abandoned on the island in the middle of the road. Maybe Halim will make use of it?

When I get back, Mum's already in the driveway, my case and backpack next to hers, tapping her feet impatiently. I haven't seen her so bright or vibrant in months.

'Think of it as an adventure, Piper,' she says, squeezing my arm. I hoist my backpack on and swallow hard to suppress my tears.

We catch the tram to Southern Cross Station, and I can't believe the station is jam-packed given the price of the tickets, but I guess flying is no longer an option and people will always need to travel. It's spooky here at night with almost all the lights out despite it being thick with travellers.

I take a last toilet trip, leaving Mum standing on the platform waiting for the boarding call, guarding our cases. As soon as I turn away from her, the tears start rolling down my cheeks.

I went to the bike shop yesterday to say goodbye to Marley and return the bike he made me. There didn't seem to be any point in trying to kiss him. His energy was flat, kind of distant. His way of protecting himself from my departure?

I sit in the toilet cubicle, filled with regret. I should have kissed him. All my nerves seem so silly now. What do nerves matter when I probably won't see him again in…forever? I hunch forward and hug my backpack. When those train doors close, they'll be closing on everything that matters.

Everything.

I realise what I have to do. Marley's right. I'm sixteen. I'm old enough to be independent.

Grow up, Piper.

You can't rely on your mum FOREVER.

Let Mum have the adventure she needs, and I will have the life *I* need – even if it doesn't have Mum in it.

I should have made this plan while there was still time. I think of Mum standing on the platform, waiting for me. It's five minutes until the train goes. She'll be antsy now, worried about me taking so long.

I could go back, tell her I'm not coming, kiss her farewell and wave her off. But I know Mum. There'd be a huge scene. There's not a single chance in hell she'll accept my decision and calmly roll off towards Sydney.

I know it's spineless of me. But my feet make their decision of their own accord. I leave the toilet and push and shove my way through the crowds until I find myself on Spencer Street, the station behind me. Mum will have to start her new life without me.

As I walk, instead of feeling light and free with my escape, all I can think of is Mum.

Go back! Piper, go BACK!

But it's too late. The train will have gone now. How could I do this to Mum? I am sick with guilt, but even so, my feet don't turn around to retrace my steps. My wristlet vibrates. And again. Without looking, I reach down and turn it off. I can't deal with this right now.

I walk and walk, my hips finding a comforting, rocking rhythm. By the time I arrive home, an hour or two later, I am both calm and numb.

I don't have a key to the guesthouse, and Mum took my spare key to the car too. I look at the window but can't bring myself to break it. No way could I afford to repair the glass. I wonder if Marley knows how to pick a lock. Or if Mum will send the key down from Sydney.

I fetch my seedlings back from Halim's verandah and give them a sprinkling of water from the BioSpore barrel. The windows are dark in the house. I slump down next to the rocket stove. What now?

It's way past dinnertime and I'm starving. Mum and I were going to eat our recon on the train. At least she'll get two boxes to herself now. Where should I go? Where will I sleep?

Is it too presumptuous to visit Marley and Robbie? Marley visited me, didn't he? He never gave any reason or excuse for it. I'll just tell him the truth – that I completely failed at making a plan, but I've finally figured out it's time for me to start living independently. And then I'll stand on tippy-toes and kiss him, because what do I have to lose?

Why am I so scared of letting him know how I really feel?

I grab my backpack and walk along Westgarth Street until I hit the Merri Creek. I pass another of my compost posters, taped to a power pole, but tonight I'm too distracted to stop and admire it. I wish I had my bike.

On reflex, I check my wristlet. It's weird to see the screen black. I know Mum will be trying to video me and I still can't face dealing with her, so I force my hand down and my eyes back to the street.

I trudge along Merri Creek, the air biting my cheeks, my stomach growling with hunger. Maybe Marley will give me a late dinner. It takes an hour, maybe more, to walk to his place. When I turn into his street I see him right away, at the front gate, his bike leaning against the wall. He's working the key in the lock. Yes!

I'm about to run to him – I'll throw myself into his arms! – when I realise he's not alone. There's someone else there, a vague shape in the darkness. I stop short and squint, straining to see clearly. Long layered skirts come into focus, and cascades of honey hair. Kelsey.

She reaches a slender arm to his neck and offers him her lips. There's a pause, and then Marley leans into them, and it's no chaste peck like he's given me. Their lips slide against each other. Marley abandons the lock and wraps both arms around her waist, pulling her tight against his body. Stunned, I stare, motionless.

Eventually, eventually, their kiss ends and Marley pulls Kelsey through the gate. As she disappears, her head tips back – she's laughing.

I sink down, my backpack suddenly unbearably heavy, my feet aching, nausea rising even though I haven't eaten in forever. Now what? Where will I sleep? I think of the platform at Sprouted Earth, but I can't face the possibility of rejection.

I don't care about food anymore. I just need to rest, and I don't have the energy to walk all the way home again. The cold from the concrete path rises up into my bones. What did they sleep on in the old days, before mattresses? Straw, I think?

I force myself off the concrete and retreat to the creek, my breath coming in short, sharp gasps. My hands shaking, I rummage in my backpack and retrieve my Stanley knife. It takes a while, but eventually I have an armload of cut grass to use instead of straw. I make myself a nest a little way from the path, half under a bush, where I hope no one, namely Marley and Kelsey, will see me if out for an early-morning ride.

I curl into a ball, tight against the cold, and try to sleep. But the kiss replays itself in my mind, over and over: the soft flick of Kelsey's tongue – which I didn't actually see; the curve of Marley's neck as he brought himself close to her, which I *did* see.

He didn't waste any time, did he? Or were he and Kelsey seeing each other all along? But he told me he didn't have a girlfriend. Did he lie? Or is this something new?

I replay our whole relationship. Maybe I imagined the flirting, the chemistry between us. Did he always see me as just a friend? But I remember sitting with his arm around me, the intense way we stared into each other's eyes. You don't do that with an ordinary friend.

Eventually I fall asleep, Marley and Kelsey twisting through my dreams, and when I open my eyes it's light and something is moving, clambering over the bush above me. A possum?

An image comes to my mind of swinging it hard by the tail, head smashing into the trunk of a tree. I shiver. No way can I do that. But I'm starving, and I can practically smell the sizzling chicken Robbie cooked us – surely possum would be rich and hearty too? The possum's tail flicks down briefly. I could grab it, but I don't. Then it's gone.

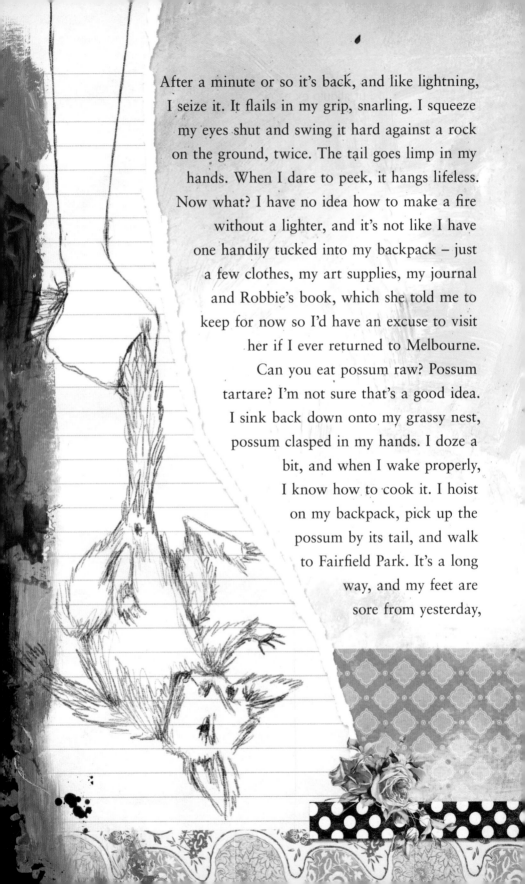

After a minute or so it's back, and like lightning,
I seize it. It flails in my grip, snarling. I squeeze
my eyes shut and swing it hard against a rock
on the ground, twice. The tail goes limp in my
hands. When I dare to peek, it hangs lifeless.
Now what? I have no idea how to make a fire
without a lighter, and it's not like I have
one handily tucked into my backpack – just
a few clothes, my art supplies, my journal
and Robbie's book, which she told me to
keep for now so I'd have an excuse to visit
her if I ever returned to Melbourne.
Can you eat possum raw? Possum
tartare? I'm not sure that's a good idea.
I sink back down onto my grassy nest,
possum clasped in my hands. I doze a
bit, and when I wake properly,
I know how to cook it. I hoist
on my backpack, pick up the
possum by its tail, and walk
to Fairfield Park. It's a long
way, and my feet are
sore from yesterday,

but at least the movement warms me, and the prospect of a meat meal cheers me no end. I hope the barbeque still works. I'm not sure if they power it with gas or what.

Despite the release of BBQ recon, which comes with little plastic tongs and an authentic burned flavour and even sizzles when you press the button to heat it, Australians are still addicted to barbeques, and Organicore hasn't figured out a way around that. The last time Taylor and I went to Fairfield Park together, the barbeque still heated up when we switched it on.

By the time I've made it there, the sun is high in the sky and the park is deserted. I set to work on the possum, skinning it with my Stanley knife. The blade is too short and flexible to cut the meat into pieces, though, so I lay the possum on its side on the barbeque, and once some of its flesh is cooked, I bite straight into it.

The meat is hot, greasy enough to be satisfying, and tastes incredible, even without salt. I lay the possum on its other side to cook some more.

I picture Marley with me, watching, cooking, eating, but shake my head to clear it. I have to break this habit of imagining him with me. It hurts too much.

I eat until I'm stuffed full, and that's less than half the possum. With Marley banned from my mind, and Robbie too by association, I wish Mum was here to share it with me, to discover how utterly amazing wild food can be, even if it isn't perfectly balanced. I picture her alone and lonely in a barren flat in Newtown, her case open beside her bed, mine zipped closed by the door. She's hurt, maybe angry, maybe crying,

about how I abandoned her – and I left why? For Marley? Oh god, what have I done?

But it wasn't just for Marley. It was for my garden. I try to picture going ahead with that, no Marley in the picture...Can I still see Robbie? He seems to be the central link to *everything*. I shake my head to clear it again. Don't think about Marley. Don't think about Mum, either. Just be here and now, with the sun shining warm, belly satiated.

Now what? I need to let Mum know I'm all right. I turn on my wristlet, and sure enough, it's flooded with messages from her. There are so many I'm not sure where to start.

A fly settles on my possum and I wave it away, but it only buzzes around and lands again. I pick up the possum and wrap it in its own skin. I'm still holding it when I glance up and see that I am surrounded by police on bikes. There are maybe six or seven of them, and they're all wearing dirty navy-blue uniforms with heavy black boots and broad sunhats. It's hard to tell the women from the men.

The one in front of me, a guy, looks at me with concern. He has broad shoulders and rough red skin, but his pale-blue eyes are kind. He's speaking, but I can't hear his words without my hearing aids on. From his body language I'd guess he's asking if I'm okay.

I indicate my ears, doing the kaput gesture that was so effective with Halim, and he nods. He knows this already. On his wristlet he writes, 'Are you hurt?'

I shake my head. They're enclosing me now. One of them reaches out and takes the possum from my hands. As she unwraps the skin and sees what it is, the energy changes. She asks something, and the guy types it for me. 'Do you realise that possums are an endangered species?'

I blink. I'm so shocked at the sudden invasion of police that it's hard to think about the possum. Why are there so many of them? I shake my head.

The energy of the police changes again. They're brisker, harsher now, faces blank, exchanging words rapidly. I wish I could understand them. Where are my hearing aids? I think I zipped them into a pocket in my bag. I cast around for it, but one of the cops is holding it and has unzipped it, emptying my journal and art supplies onto the barbeque.

I reach out to grab them – I don't want meat juice on my journal – but I'm interrupted as the first cop holds out his wristlet with another question. 'Do you know your mum is looking for you?'

I nod. I type on my wristlet, 'I'm sorry. I ran off.'

The police are losing interest. Three of them are already halfway across the park with their bikes by the time I've finished typing. The one holding the possum speaks briskly to the guy communicating with me and makes out that she's going to leave. I touch her arm to get her attention and hold out my hands for the possum. I almost say, *Give that back*, but it would feel weird to suddenly speak when we've been communicating in writing.

I don't have time to write anything to her, though, because she gives me a look that says, *Are you out of your mind?* and packs the possum into a plastic saddlebag on the side of her bike. She doesn't glance my way again, and my possum disappears with her. Damn! I should have eaten the whole thing, no matter how full I was. Will someone else eat it? It hardly seems fair, given that it was me who caught and skinned it.

There are just two cops left now, the broad-shouldered guy and an older woman with a heavily lined face and disapproving grey eyes. The guy holds out his wristlet again. 'We'll escort you home.'

'Can I have my possum back, please?' I type.

He shakes his head, face blank, eyes not so kind now. He indicates for me to get my bag, and I snatch up my journal and wipe the meat juice onto my jeans. I repack my backpack and hoist it onto my back.

The walk home is tense, to say the least. They appear to know where I live. It only takes fifteen minutes and we're at the bottom of the driveway. Taggert's glued to the bay window, eyes wide at the sight of the police.

The guesthouse door is open, and the bleak emptiness inside is gone. Our beds are made up, my case sitting neatly on the end of mine, while Mum's belongings are hanging again on her nails. And there's Mum herself, sitting in one of our blue velvet chairs, shaking. Her hair hangs in lank strands, and her eyes and cheeks are hollowed out, grey. She stands as soon as she sees me and takes me into her arms, squeezing so hard my bones creak. Tears stream down her face.

It's not until the police have gone and I've put my hearing aids in that she starts shouting.

'FOR GOD'S SAKE, PIPER, WHAT WERE YOU THINKING? I JUST NEEDED ONE MESSAGE, *ONE MESSAGE* THAT TOLD ME YOU WERE ALL RIGHT.'

I stand meekly, absorbing the full force of her rage. 'I thought you were in Syd—'

'SYDNEY?! I THOUGHT YOU'D BEEN KIDNAPPED!

Did you *actually* think I'd just get on the train and GO WITHOUT YOU?'

'Well, yes...'

Mum wrings her hands. She wrenches at her hair. 'You are so naïve, Piper.'

'I'm sorry.'

'Do you have *any idea* what I have been through? When you didn't come back, I had that train delayed for *a whole hour* while the police searched it. They kept saying you'd run away, and I told them there was no way you would do that. It wasn't until I said you were deaf that they took me seriously.'

'What, they think deaf teenagers don't run away?'

Mum rolls her eyes. 'They think deaf people are like five-year-olds who cannot survive without a grown-up to hold their hand.'

She gives me a look – a look that says, *This is something you know, and I know, and the rest of the world doesn't know* – and it makes me want to cry. This is why I can't live without her – because I'm not connected to anyone else like that. And I'm SO GLAD she's here and not in Sydney, even if she's furious with me.

'I might have used it,' Mum admits, 'to convince them that you needed looking for.'

'Is that why there were so many of them?'

'They put out a massive search party, at my insistence. All through the station, all around the city, around our home. They're not happy with you, Piper, for wasting so much police time and resources.'

I sink down onto my bed. 'I'm sorry. I'll go to Sydney; I won't run off again. I'll pay you back for both our tickets.'

This sets Mum off again. 'SYDNEY?' she explodes. 'AS IF!!' She's so mad that she hammers her fist against the wall. I can hear her shouting but not the words. Eventually she turns back my way and I think she's screaming, 'WHAT JOB IN SYDNEY?'

Have I misheard her? 'Your job?' I ask, tentatively.

She leans towards me and enunciates clearly. 'BOB FORSYTH'S JOB! They gave it to him when I missed the train. THERE IS NO JOB IN SYDNEY ANYMORE.'

Mum collapses onto her bed, sobbing.

Stricken with guilt, I watch for a while, then slink over and lay my hands across her back. 'I'm so sorry. I never thought…'

Mum cries loudly, and maybe she shouts but I can't hear the difference with her face buried in her arms. I hold her, for what feels like hours, and eventually she goes still and her breathing slows and I think she might be asleep.

MONDAY 7
september

I never thought I'd miss school, but with Taylor still MIA and visiting the bike shop out of the question, there's nowhere else to go to get away from Mum's cold, angry energy as she slumps in bed all day. She unenrolled me from Mary Magdalene's before the Sydney move, and since she can't pay the next set of fees, they won't let me back in. She's enrolled me at Northcote High instead, but there's a few days' waiting period before they'll let me start. How I'll figure out where I'm supposed to be at a new school, and how I'll begin the daunting process of making friends, is totally beyond me. Dread sits heavy in my stomach.

I messaged Taylor to fill her in on Sydney, the possum, the cops...and that I have a broken heart. It's been a week, and she hasn't even replied. I stay in bed, trying to ignore my hunger. I can't survive on one recon meal a day! I distract myself any way I can, even by checking out the news on my wristlet, which I never usually do. It doesn't exactly help.

Food and Fuel Crisis Meetings

Meetings between federal, state and local governments continue in private, with no statements made to the media yet about proposed plans. Sources hint rations may be on the cards, forcing equitable distribution of imported and local foods currently being snapped up by wealthy buyers before they hit the shelves. Whether citizens will still be required to pay market prices for rations or will receive handouts is uncertain. At a media conference last night, Karen Kildare stated, 'We remain committed to finding the best way forward for Australians in this new climate.'

My wristlet buzzes. It's Taylor! Finally.

▶ From: Taylor
Who broke your heart? Are you going to JAIL? Save some possum for me? I know I've been horrible – let's get together. This Saturday afternoon? I'm SO GLAD you haven't disappeared off to Sydney and need to make the most of having you here!

▶ To: Taylor
Yes! Saturday afternoon! It's a date. Come over? I want to show you the garden I'm making. I'll tell you all then.

▶ From: Marley

Hey, Piper... How's Sydney? I should have said before you left that there are Deaf organisations in every state – you could look up the one in Sydney and make contact. Maybe you can find out about sign language classes or meet the Deaf community? It's so quiet without you here.

▶ To: Marley

We didn't go. I realise now I should have planned to stay. Sixteen is old enough to live independently, but I didn't realise until it was too late, and the short version of that particular story is that I caused Mum to lose her job and now we're staying.

▶ From: Marley

What the hell? I'm intrigued now. Surely your mum can get her job back?

He *wants* Mum to get her job back? Can't he at least *pretend* to be happy I'm staying? There's no invitation to go to the bike shop. No mention of Kelsey, either. I glare at my wristlet.

I don't feel like messaging anymore, so I flip my journal open to a page with a background I started when I was using up some leftover paint on my palette and hesitate. Then, on a whim, I sketch a tree. I'm thinking of Grandma's oak tree again. The first draft looks ridiculous, so I rub it out and look up an image of an oak tree in Robbie's book. Copying slowly,

I draw in branches, scribbling quickly to shape the knobs on the trunk. But when it comes to drawing acorns, I stop. There are no acorns here. Instead, I draw blocks of textured concrete hanging from the tree – lots of them. Words form in my mind as I sketch, and by the time the concrete blocks are filled in, I know what I want to say:

GROW FOOD NOT CONCRETE

I'm distracted when Mum suddenly hauls herself out of bed and goes outside. Peeking through the window, I see her talking animatedly on her wristlet. It's the most normal she's looked all week. I work on shading the block letters in my journal until something soft lands on my back. Mum's jumper. I look up.

'That was Bob Forsyth. He's taking my cheap research proposal to the board. I suggested I could work for him remotely, and he's not sure there's enough work, but if there is he'll prioritise me. So I can get started on my proposal.'

'Mum, that's great.' Since she seems to be in a better state, I decide to broach the Northcote High problem. 'About school, do you think I could have a break, just until all this…is over? Until life goes back to normal? Then I could go back to Mary Mag.'

I suddenly realise that for the past three months I've had this feeling of *waiting* about me. All the stress of living in the guesthouse, and cars and public transport and electricity and *everything* being far too expensive or impossible to get…I'm just waiting for it all to be over.

A look of pain clouds Mum's face. She comes to sit beside me on the bed. 'Piper, I don't think this *is* going to be over. The days of cheap oil are probably behind us forever. And even if this job comes through with Bob, I still won't have enough for Mary Magdalene.'

I don't reply. I just stare at her.

Eventually Mum says, 'One way or another, you need an education. So, Northcote High it is.'

I think again of trying to fit in without Taylor; of trying to make friends and keep up with what I'm supposed to be doing.

I swallow and say, 'I'm sixteen. I'm old enough to leave school. You can't make me go.'

And that's it for our harmony. Mum says something under her breath that I don't catch. She looks...bitter.

'What did you say?'

She shakes her head.

'Tell me!'

'I said I think you have just established that I can't make you go anywhere anymore.' The disappointment in her face is sharp. She stands and pulls out a folder of her notes.

'Mum,' I say, wanting to make it all okay, but she doesn't look at me again.

I go outside to check on my seedlings. Thank god for my garden – one positive thing to focus on. My seedlings are about ready to be transplanted to a bigger box. I make one by cutting open a few recon boxes and taping them together then set to work, transplanting. Handling seedlings, looking at tiny green growing things, soothes me, and the guilt I feel fades into the background slightly.

When I wake and switch my wristlet on, it buzzes right away.

INFRINGEMENT NOTICE
TO THE ADDRESSED

FROM:	Victorian State Police
OFFICIAL NOTIFICATION TO:	Piper McBride
OFFENCE(S):	Wasting Police Time Harming of Threatened Species without Licence
PENALTY:	**$2000 fine** payable before 21 October

If you wish to contest this matter, you may apply before
21 October.

If you do not pay the fine by the due date, you will be summoned
to the Magistrate's Court.

PAY THE FINE HERE

Oh god. No *way* can I come up with two thousand dollars.
A thin layer of sweat forms on my upper lip. Who knew
eating a possum was an offence – why didn't they teach
us this in school? What happens if I have to go to court?
I'm under eighteen. They can't do anything too terrible to
me … can they?

What that cop said about the possum being endangered suddenly really hits me. The idea that soon there won't be any more possums, just like what happened with the fish, makes me feel sick. What if the possum I ate was the very last one? I'd thought there were heaps of them. Hunger is turning me into a person I don't recognise. What would Marley say if he knew?

Get out of my head, Marley!

I haven't answered his last message, but I miss hanging out at the bike shop and I'm going insane without a bike. Mum hasn't mentioned the issue of school again and I've spent my days fussing over my seedlings, using Halim's fork to dig garden beds in the middle of our street, and hauling around my sack to collect compost materials, twigs for the rocket stove, and weeds. I'm an expert on edible weeds now.

I'm so glad Taylor's coming over today.

I'm angry with her, but more than anything, I miss her. Maybe she'll have a brilliant idea about how to raise that insane amount of money. I pull on my jeans. I was so resentful about only getting half a recon through the day, but now there's nothing until dinnertime and I'd do anything for a half-box.

'Mum, look.' She's sitting by the rocket stove, sipping dandelion tea and working on her notes. I hold out my wristlet and show her the infringement notice.

She stares at me flatly. 'What will you do about this?'

My stomach drops. 'I don't know,' I say in a small voice. 'Do you have any ideas?'

'No, Piper, I don't. And since you've declared you're above

the legal age for an education, I don't feel obliged to educate you further on this matter.' Her voice and eyes are cold.

I don't know how to get back in her good books. I miss her. 'Can I have some tea?'

Although the dandelions taste bitter, my body keeps asking for more. There must be some nutrition in there that I need. Robbie's book says weeds are excellent at mining nutrients from the soil. Without looking up, Mum hands me the pot of greenish water, limp leaves floating in it. It's warm, not hot, so I tip a large mouthful down my throat.

'Any news from Bob Forsyth?' I ask, trying again.

She looks up. 'Bob went to the board, but they said no to my proposal. They can't fund it right now. Had I been there, I'm sure I could have talked them into it.'

'Can you get work with Bob?'

Mum shrugs. 'He still doesn't know. He's yet to see a budget. He's trying to get some deliveries back on track by train rather than truck, but there's no big-picture plan yet.'

Taggert emerges from the house. I hand him a twig and he pokes it slowly into the rocket stove, just as I've taught him.

'Maybe you could offer to make a plan for deliveries?' I say to Mum. 'You're good at planning.'

'I know, but you can't plan when you don't know the scope.'

'Have you tried Karen Kildare? Maybe she knows? Maybe she can delegate this to you?'

'She hasn't got back to me. I try her every day.'

Mum turns back to her folder. I'm dismissed.

'Want to go to the street?' I ask Taggert.

He nods and puts his hand in mine, even though we're nowhere near the road. I dump my hearing aids inside, and tap on the kitchen window of the house to indicate that I have Taggert with me. Archie gives me the thumbs up and waves me to the door, where he hands me Taggert's bucket and spade. The blinds are drawn over the bedroom windows; Erin is still asleep. I doubt Taggert would be hanging out with me if not.

Halim's on the street already, and when he sees me he lifts a finger and heads off slowly to fetch the fork. I survey my work: The first compost pile's been turned twice, leaving two round, softer patches of dirt that I've dug over. The second pile is ready for turning. It won't be long until I have a whole mandala of six garden beds. I have a few more weeks until my seedlings are big enough to plant out here.

What am I going to do about the fine?

I shake my head to clear it. Halim reappears and watches while I spread the compost, which now looks like dirt, back over the two beds I've dug. Taggert scoops compost with his plastic spade, and when he steps onto the garden bed I grab his wrist to stop him. Miming, just as Robbie did with me, I show him he must never stand on a garden bed. I hope Halim's paying attention too. Taggert gets it right away and carefully steps around the edges.

Next thing, I push my fork into the compost and catch sight of something wriggling. A worm! Taggert's as excited as I am. He picks it up gently, but it slithers between his fingers.

I finish digging over the third bed, spread the compost back over it, and set to work on the middle area where I'm going to make a pond, but the ground is hard and it's heavy going. I need to eat.

An elegant woman with a sleek black bob appears, carrying a spade and walking like a dancer. Halim says something to her, but she has more manners than him and turns to greet me.

'I'm…' I miss the rest. She holds out her hand.

I shake it, and instead of nodding and saying 'Piper', I point to my ears and indicate my deafness.

Unfazed, she writes her name in the air with her index finger, but I can't make it out. I mime writing in the dirt, which she does. *Connie Sato.*

She opens her mouth enough to enunciate clearly without exaggerating ridiculously. 'How big would you like the pond?'

Surprised, I show her with my hands. She sets to work, professionally excavating the ground to make a smooth, shallow bowl, clearly experienced at this.

'You know it's leega to make gardis on pubbic land? Aren't you worried about tree vandals?' It's easy to figure out her words from the context. *Illegal to make gardens on public land.*

I channel Robbie and mime plants growing, and me eating their food. Then I become a security guard. I'm not sure how to show this so I stand like a soldier, salute, and mime myself shooting someone who sneaks in to steal food. It's an exaggeration, sure, but it gets the message across.

'Security isst cheap.'

I point to myself.

Connie holds up ten fingers and flashes them twice, then holds up four, then seven. She's quick at this. *24/7?* she's asking.

I use my finger to write in the dirt, because I don't know how to mime what I want to say next. 'I'll need help.'

She crouches and writes beneath my words: 'I'll help. For food. My partner too.'

She talks to Halim, and I suspect he might be a part of the arrangement now too. Taggert crouches beside me and uses his finger to make squiggles in the dirt. He looks up at me expectantly and I give him the thumbs up, which satisfies him.

Connie writes again: 'At my last house I planted vegies on the nature strip and the council made me clear it.'

'Surely they won't *now*?' I write.

She shrugs. She's not optimistic.

I wonder how much food we'll get, and if it can stretch to feed so many of us. Robbie and Marley have a huge garden and even they're still hungry. But I need help, with tools as well as security.

In the dirt, I write a list of jobs that need doing, such as collecting compost materials and carrying water, getting another BioSpore barrel for water, going to St Kilda beach to get seaweed, and figuring out what to line the pond with. I indicate that we could share the jobs.

Connie reads the list carefully and volunteers for the pond lining. Then she runs her finger down the whole list and indicates she's up for anything.

She adds, 'Make a security roster.'

Taggert runs his finger down the list too, smearing the words, nodding seriously. I grin. Things are looking up.

My wristlet buzzes.

▶ From: Taylor
So sorry, Pipes, something's come up. Will message real soon to make another date.

My smile fades. I could reply...but really, what is there to say?

TUESDAY 22 SEPT

A week and a half later, I can't stand it any longer – I go to visit Robbie. Uninvited. When she opens the gate and sees me, her eyes widen in surprise. Since she doesn't have a wristlet, I couldn't message ahead. I'm so glad she's here, that I didn't walk all this way for nothing. I admit I timed it to arrive just before lunch. The scent of her garden hits me – herbs and leaves and dirt and water and something earthy – and I inhale deeply, soaking in the magic.

Is Marley here?

For god's sake, get out of my head! It doesn't matter whether he's here or not. I'm here to see Robbie.

But still I scan the garden behind her, checking for him. Robbie takes me into her arms and gives me a tight hug. She's smiling, deep crinkles around her eyes, happy to see me. She signs something I don't catch, but I recognise the sign for *Sydney*, which Marley taught me. Your fingers become the Sydney Harbour Bridge.

So Marley didn't tell her. I shake my head. 'WE'RE NOT GOING AFTER ALL,' I fingerspell.

'Why?' Robbie's eyebrows furrow. It has the effect of making me feel she's deeply interested in my answer, even though I know it's just the standard sign language technique for asking open-ended questions. She gives my arm a squeeze and throws me a quick, delighted smile.

I hesitate. I don't want to tell Robbie what a brat I was to Mum. 'THERE ARE PROBLEMS WITH HER JOB.' That much is true.

Robbie looks at me closely. 'Are you okay?' she asks. She pokes two fingers into her neck. I frown, not understanding the sign, and she fingerspells it for me. 'DISAPPOINTED?'

I use a mixture of signs, mime, drawing in the air and fingerspelling to reply. 'No. I'm glad to stay. I can keep making my garden. I'm stressed because…I ate a possum and the cops caught me. Now I have to pay a two-thousand-dollar fine in one month and I don't know how.'

Robbie takes my arm and escorts me through the garden to the outdoor kitchen. She's cooking already. There's green stuff and onions in the frypan and it smells heavenly. 'Eating a possum is not a good idea,' she signs. 'There are so few left.' But she doesn't seem upset with me. Just thoughtful. 'Do you have a job? Maybe they will let you have a plan to pay it off more slowly.'

I shake my head and tell her about the mortifying interview with Cesspool. 'What kind of jobs can Deaf people do?'

She indicates for me to fetch an extra egg from the chook pen. Yes! She's going to feed me. When I hand it to her, she cracks two eggs into the pan and signs, 'It's not easy. I studied for four years to become a pharmacist, but even though I graduated with good marks, the board wouldn't give me a licence because I'm Deaf. So be careful of that trap. They'll tell you that you can do anything until it's crunch time, and then you've wasted years of your life.'

'What did you do when you couldn't get your licence?'

'I fought. But no luck. I worked for a Deaf organisation for a while. They always hire Deaf staff. The pay is pretty low, though, and these days you need to be fluent in sign before they'll take you. Allstar had an inclusive policy' – I have to interrupt Robbie here for a fingerspelling repeat of *inclusive* – 'and hired deaf people to haul boxes, but there's new management now' – and again here for a *management* repeat – 'and the deaf employees are being laid off. They "can't afford" to pay for the interpreter. If you're lucky you can get an apprenticeship to become a tradie, but you need to find someone who is prepared to take you on.'

I'm glad Mum's not here. To have my dismal career prospects laid out so starkly could possibly be the end of her. Is school 'preparing me' for a career I'll never be able to have? Maybe Mum needs to hear that. I ask Robbie if she still works for the deaf organisation.

She shakes her head, gesturing to the garden before us. 'I can work for money to buy food, or work to grow food. Growing food is more satisfying.'

She serves the eggs and greens into two bowls. We sit with our legs over the edge of the verandah, and I try my hardest not to scoff it down. It's exquisite – hot and fragrant and hearty in a way recon never is.

'Don't you need money to buy stuff like water tanks and gas and solar panels?'

Robbie nods. 'I get asked to consult these days, to help people design their gardens, and that brings in enough to cover the basics. Marley earns money now, too.'

'How do you communicate with your clients?'

'Pen and paper. They want to know how to make a garden like mine, so that gives them patience.'

Well, that's hardly going to help me come up with two grand by the twenty-first of October.

On the far side of the garden, there's a rustle of movement. Robbie and I watch. We can't see the gate from here, but after a few moments, Marley emerges from the arbour by the pond. I freeze.

When he spots me, his face lights up. He hurries over and throws his arms around me in a long hug. 'I've missed you,' he signs, and I catch the new sign, *miss*, which goes from cheek to cheek. He stands close to me, closer than you'd expect. I'm starting to see how I got the wrong idea. The scent of him settles over me, and my stomach butterflies. It's not easy to get over this boy.

'Do you want lunch?' Robbie asks.

Marley nods, and she gathers our bowls and heads back to the rocket stove. Marley sits himself beside me, so close I can feel the heat from his body. How can he have missed me when he's been busy with his new girlfriend? I presume that's the reason he hasn't asked me to come to the shop.

'So, what's new?' I ask, testing him.

'Ryan got a bunch of broken bike bits from the tip, enough to build several more bikes – to sell, not rent. So I've been doing that.'

His eyes are intense, sparkly, focused on me.

I nod, silent. I don't want to hear about bikes.

He takes a deep breath and his face reddens. 'You remember Kelsey, who runs—'

'I know who Kelsey is.'

'We kind of…got together.'

So he knew. He knew how I felt about him, or he wouldn't be so awkward now. Have I been so transparent?

My face heats, and I force a smile. 'That's great. She's so…nice. I'm happy for you.'

There's an uncomfortable pause, both of us nodding and trying to smile.

Finally Marley signs, 'Did you hear about Sprouted Earth?'

'No. What about it?'

'The council slapped a clean-up notice on it. They have two months to return it to bare land or the council will sue them. It's a fire hazard, apparently.'

My mouth drops open. 'In times like these?'

Does the island on my street belong to the council too? Or to us, the people who live there? Will we be told to return it to bare dirt and tree stumps? I can't afford another fine.

'We have the big corporations to thank.' Marley has to spell *corporations* twice, but I get it on the second go.

'What do you mean?'

'As soon as the Kildare government was elected, Organicore practically took over, all recon this and recon that. Suddenly health and safety laws for real food were impossibly strict, all the feeds saturated with food-poisoning stories.'

So people *do* know. I think of the graffiti I saw, of Karen Kildare's face with the Organicore logo. I suppose it's obvious. Somehow, though, I find myself defending her.

'Karen Kildare *is* progressive – she supports the recon welfare program with inexpensive housing options and so on...' I have to fingerspell most of this, but Marley supplies some of the signs, and I learn *support* and *welfare*.

'Yes, and once someone moves into an apartment without a kitchen, they lose the option to eat real food. Where's their free choice gone? It's just another way to get people addicted to recon.'

I frown. I never thought of it that way. I wonder if this has occurred to Mum.

'Surely *now* the authorities can see that it's sensible, practical, to let people grow food, though?' I ask.

'Piper, they're only interested in how much profit Organicore makes. Even if we're starving, it's still in their best financial interests to make it as difficult as possible for us to grow real food.'

I think of Karen Kildare, her worries about people's health. I think of Organicore struggling to meet deliveries. 'I don't think Karen Kildare would be opposed to us growing food. Maybe she doesn't know about this.' But even if she did, could she really do anything about it?

Marley looks at me oddly. 'How would you know? Have you met her?'

I nod. 'Mum worked with her sometimes. Before she lost her job.' He's sitting so close that if I moved slightly, our legs would touch. Before, I've scooted against him, casually allowing the connection to happen. But today I keep my knees back, tight to my body.

'Kelsey's starting a protest group. They'll lobby the government to allow food production on public land, as part of the solution to the food crisis.'

'That must be great – a project with your new girlfriend.' I can't believe I just said that! I sound so bitter.

But Marley just sighs. 'I feel like an imposter. I've known the Transition Towns people for ages, but never been this intensely involved with their events. I keep worrying I'll do something wrong.'

'What do you mean?'

'Well, like the other day I saw this guy I hadn't seen in ages, and I really like him so I gave him a hug. In the Deaf community, that's fine. Deaf guys hug each other all the time. But try that in the hearing world and everyone thinks you're gay. Which obviously doesn't matter, but it's not how it's done normally. I feel like I have to watch myself the whole time, so I don't slip up. I usually spend my time with deaf people and other CODA kids.'

'What else is different about the deaf community?'

'I think more in terms of what's different about the *hearing* community. For example, we say it like it is. If something looks ugly, we say that – or if something doesn't work or fit, we say exactly how. Hearing people are so convoluted – you have to work out whether it's okay to say something bluntly or not, and if you suspect it isn't okay, then you have to come up with a polite workaround, like saying that something is nearly perfect, it's just great, except for this tiny little bit here which almost fits but just needs a bit of tweaking. Jesus! Why can't we just spit it out! And that's what I mean: being with Kelsey, I have to keep that part of my brain switched on, to make sure I say or do it right. I can't quite relax.'

'But surely you can tell her about the cultural differences, just like you're telling me?'

Marley ponders this for a bit. 'You're *interested* in the deaf thing,' he says, finally. 'Kelsey doesn't even get that there's something to be interested in. She thinks sign language is beautiful but she doesn't remember any of the signs I show her or use them to communicate with…'

I don't recognise the last sign. 'What's that?' I ask, attempting to copy. I cross my first two fingers and touch them to the little finger of my opposite hand with a swinging motion.

'ROBBIE,' Marley fingerspells. 'It's her name sign.'

'Why is that her name sign?'

Robbie rejoins us, handing Marley a bowl of egg and greens. He thanks her, a small casual gesture. I could watch them sign with each other forever. I want to see how it's done naturally, which is different to when they make it all clear and sharp for me. Marley signs to her, 'Tell Piper how you got your name sign.'

Robbie mimes herself as a little girl. 'My family lived in the country, but there was no deaf school there, so I had to go to school in the city. I boarded there through the week. My room was the last one down the end of the hall.'

I frown, confused. 'How does that make the name sign?'

Marley holds up his two fingers crossed and signs, 'This is R, using the American alphabet.' He makes a chopping motion with his right hand onto the little finger of his left hand. 'That's the sign for last. Now combine the two.' This time he chops his left hand with the American R, rather than just a flat right hand. 'The last room down the hall. So, R-last.'

'It's a very boring name sign,' Robbie tells me, but nothing about her is boring to me.

I wonder if I will ever be given a name sign. I push the thought away and turn to Marley, who's digging into his food. 'Is there any chance I could borrow a bike again?' I ask.

'Of course! Sorry, I forgot you didn't have one or I'd have offered. Just come by the shop.'

I let go of my resolve and put my hand on his arm. He throws me a small smile, and the heat from his body floods mine. He might have a new girlfriend, but the chemistry between us is as strong as ever. *What the hell is he doing with her?*

I'm waking up when Mum grasps my shoulders. She's talking frantically and pushes my hearing aids into my hands. Blearily, I jab them into my ears and her voice blasts into focus.

'Quick, get up! Karen Kildare is coming!'

Surely I heard her wrong. But I can't think of another phrase that looks the same as *Karen Kildare*. 'Karen Kildare? Why?'

'She's in the area and will call in very briefly in about ten minutes. You can't be here, Piper.'

'I live here!'

Mum sighs impatiently. 'Don't do this to me. She'll be more open if our meeting is confidential.'

'I won't be able to hear her anyway.'

Mum grabs my wrists and hauls me upright. 'Get dressed! Go outside!'

I pull on my clothes while Mum whirs around me, making my bed, straightening everything. I can't believe she's letting Karen Kildare see where we live. Then again, maybe it will inspire her to give Mum a job. Maybe then Mum will offer to help me with my fine.

Soon enough, Karen Kildare steps elegantly down the driveway, flanked by two soldiers wearing military uniforms, broad camouflage hats and large guns. If they want to blend in around the city then surely they should wear grey fake-concrete vests and helmets made of beige brick. Stripes of white up their chest, like lines down the middle of a road. This would make a good painting. *The uniform of the future.*

While they look like they're fresh from the jungle, Karen Kildare herself appears to have just stepped off the catwalk, in a pale-yellow skirt suit and a white shirt with a high ruffled neck. Her high heels are made of the same fabric as the suit. Everything is spotlessly clean, including her honey-gold hair, which frames her face in a lovely soft bob. The sun shines around her like a halo.

Mum gives me the sideways evil-eye – *get out of here* – but I'm mesmerised. Maybe I can talk to Karen Kildare about Sprouted Earth. She shakes Mum's hand and turns to me.

Mum obliges. 'You may remember my daughter, Piper?'

Karen Kildare extends her hand to mine, her skin cool, soft and smooth.

'Would you like a cup of tea?' I ask her.

Mum eyeballs me with alarm, but Karen Kildare says, 'Thank you, Piper, but I won't be able to stay that long.' She speaks clearly, formally, and it's easy to understand her.

Mum ushers her to my blue velvet chair and they sit facing each other over the tiny marble table. The soldiers wait, one outside the door, one inside, their faces blank. 'Tea?' I ask the one on the inside, but she shakes her head, a barely perceptible movement.

I go outside and water my seedlings. Some of them are halfway up my finger already and have sprouted jagged leaves to replace the baby hearts they started with. Curiosity about Karen Kildare gets the better of me, though. I head back inside and lounge on my bed, journal open. They're deep in conversation, and Mum glares at me, but my presence doesn't seem to inhibit Karen Kildare. Keeping my head down, I slide my eyes sideways. She's in profile from here, but I can lipread from the side, to an extent.

Mum says, 'Are the rations going to be recon or wild food?'

Karen Kildare's answer is detailed and not so clear. I catch the words *Allstar* and *Organicore* and *provider bids*. She gestures brightly towards Mum and says something that could be *job for you*. Mum is pleased, so I probably got that right.

After a bit Mum asks another question, something about *proposal* and *sick kids*, and Karen Kildare's energy changes. She shakes her head and raises her palms in a gesture of frustration. Something something something *government* something something *budgets depleted* something something...Mum glares at me again and jerks her eyeballs towards the door.

I have a flash of guilt, remembering how I ruined her job prospects for Sydney. I don't want to mess up anything for her this time. I stand, intending to walk out the door, but instead my feet carry me over to the two of them. I'm too scared to look at Mum now. Karen Kildare looks up at me with a polite smile.

'Sorry to interrupt,' I say to her. 'I'm going. I just wanted to suggest that maybe one way to help the food crisis is to encourage people to grow food on public land.'

'Of course,' Karen Kildare says, polite but not really engaged.

'It's just that current legislation—'

'Piper!' Mum says.

What's the quickest way to say this? 'My friends were ordered to clean up their garden—'

Mum's on her feet now, almost shouting: 'The Prime

Minister of Australia has bigger things to think about than your friends' garden!'

I glance at Karen Kildare. Her face remains blank and she doesn't contradict Mum, doesn't ask to know more. She looks so…*young*. She can't be more than twenty-five or so. Mum takes my shoulders and forcibly ushers me out. 'Sorry,' I hear her say.

Damn. I handled that all wrong. I should have finished what I was saying about the legislation. Karen Kildare may well not know what the rules are for gardens on public land. Marley would have known what to say. Kelsey would have probably whipped out an eloquent speech on the spot.

Get out of my head!

Frustrated, I traipse up to the street. There's a large black car with darkened windows parked across the top of our driveway. Beyond that, there's a woman bent over my pond, smearing it with a thick grey paste. Her hair is shaved and she has impressive, hulking muscles. She glances up to reveal round black eyes with really long lashes, and plump lips. I soak in her features while trying not to stare too obviously – my fingers are itching to paint her.

I gesture towards the pond and shrug questioningly as I approach her. She wipes her hand on her jeans and holds it out to me, and while we shake, she speaks. I'm wearing my hearing aids and I hear her voice but can't make out her words. I frown and indicate my ears. She says her name slowly and clearly: 'Sowa.'

'Zoe?' I write in the dirt.

She nods. She writes 'Piper?' and I nod. She writes 'Connie' and mimes putting her arm around someone, a loving smile.

Zoe

So she's Connie's partner. 'Concrete,' she writes, and points to the grey paste.

Halim comes over and speaks to me, but I can't understand a word. He gestures towards my house. I shrug.

He keeps talking. Doesn't he get it? I can't hear him! But he continues, no mime, no nothing, and I keep shrugging.

Eventually Zoe writes 'PM?' in the dirt.

Oh. I suppose Karen Kildare's arrival wasn't exactly discreet, given it was in an actual car and included two sidekicks from the jungle. I nod, but what am I supposed to say? Does he expect me to outline the reason for her visit? Zoe gives me a warm smile and shakes her head slightly, an acknowledgement of Halim's inappropriate line of questioning.

She gets back to work and I'm about to ask if I should help – anything to avoid more of this fruitless communication with Halim – when Connie appears with a couple of sacks and a rake. She bends over, graceful and smooth, and kisses Zoe on the back of the neck, before taking a small stick and writing her question for me: 'Where do you want to be when you guard the garden?'

I pull off my jumper and tie it around my waist. Finally, spring has made it to Melbourne! I point to the end of the street – from there you can look in one direction and see the whole garden. If I'm sitting at a table with a bunch of people, I always try to sit near the end so I can see who's talking just by looking one way. Otherwise it's like watching tennis, only you never get to actually *see* the ball.

I take the stick and draw out my vision for the entire street, which involves several more mandalas of garden beds, fruit trees, a tool shed, chickens, rabbits, a large fish pond and a dedicated compost pile. Connie takes a photo with her wristlet and gestures to Halim to take a look.

Erin and Taggert cross the road, and Erin asks if I mind him joining us. He has his plastic bucket and spade ready to go. I give them both the thumbs up and show Taggert the concrete lining for the pond. I mime the pond without concrete lining, us pouring in water, and the water draining away. Then I mime Zoe smearing on the concrete, and this time the water fills the pond instead of disappearing. Taggert is excited about this and wants to fetch water right away. Zoe says something to him and he settles down to wait for the concrete to dry. Erin grins and leaves us to it.

Everyone looks up and I follow their gaze. Karen Kildare and her soldiers climb into the black car and it drives away. I keep my eyes firmly turned away from Halim and make like it has nothing to do with me. I hope Mum has a job now.

Once Zoe has finished lining the pond, Connie speaks to her and I can tell she's giving instructions, gesturing towards the area designated for the guard station. Zoe nods and retreats to their house, which is about five doors along on the same side of the street as mine.

Connie writes in the dirt, 'I've always wanted to learn to sign. Maybe you can teach me some?'

I show her the alphabet, and she's fingerspelling it back to me when Zoe returns carrying a mismatched selection of fake-wood posts, with notches already cut in them and rusted nails poking out everywhere. I watch as she works, efficiently pulling out nails, digging a hole for each post, and getting me to hold them in place while she fills back the dirt, Taggert helping by adding tiny scoops with his shovel.

By late afternoon, there is a frame for our security platform, and Connie and Halim have collected sacks full of grass from Fairfield Park and built us a compost pile for the second mandala of garden beds. The first mandala is ready for my seedlings – six large round beds of soft black dirt. The seedlings just need to grow a little more before they can be planted out.

It's becoming cooler now so I return Taggert to Erin and settle in the car, pulling out my journal, some thick plastic sheeting and my Stanley knife, thinking that 'The Uniform of the Future' would look particularly good as a stencil. The car is practically my art studio now. But then I have a new idea. I look up a photo of Karen Kildare on Cesspool and place a piece of thin paper over my wristlet. I can just make her out through the paper. I trace the outline of her features, then draw in her body as a puppet, strings descending from a giant hand. To show just who is in control, I trace the Organicore logo onto the sleeve of the hand. It strikes me how ironic it is that their logo shows a sprouting seed – the very thing they are stopping us from doing. I suppose it's their way of pretending they're selling us the real deal. Karen Kildare's face is somehow a perfect likeness, even though her features are just blobs of black.

I've sketched out the design onto a new plastic sheet and am starting to cut the stencil when I glance up and see the silhouettes of four people in the fading light – guys, maybe in their late teens or early twenties, each wearing black jackets with the hoods pulled up – file onto the island in the middle of my street. I freeze. They lift a pair of enormous saws and begin hacking into the stumps on our island. Tree vandals! They each saw off a round disc, maybe twenty centimetres

thick. Is it really worth the risk for such a small piece of wood? Penalties for tree vandalism are severe – much worse than possum-slaughter. They must be really desperate.

I recall Mum shaking her head sadly the morning our street was first vandalised and all the trees stolen. 'When the last tree has gone,' she said, 'civilisation will die.'

These last two weeks I've been doodling, drawing and painting in my journal, but there's been nothing to write. Nothing has changed. Mum doesn't have a job – Karen Kildare promised her she'd be manager for the Darebin area once rationing begins, but it hasn't materialised yet. I don't have a job either, so I haven't saved a *cent* towards my fine and it's due in under a fortnight.

IMPOSSIBLE.

I did drop by the bike shop to pick up the bike Marley agreed to lend me, but I couldn't quite bring myself to message him in advance, and he wasn't there, so Ryan found the bike for me. Taylor hasn't messaged me in forever. Every day when I wake I give myself a little kick, trying to force myself to take on Northcote High, but I can't face it. It would be so different if I knew there were other deaf people there, some people who could sign. But what are the chances of that?

Mum's so disappointed in me. She's so sure she knows what's best for me, and I hate letting her down. But I keep thinking of what Robbie says – maybe school is just there to prepare me for a career I'll never be able to have. Thank god for

Robbie – I visit as much as I can and soak in the beauty of her garden, which soothes my soul and reminds me there *is* magic in this world. I need to keep going, keep planting, digging and growing, even if Mum doesn't approve.

Which is why I'm on the street on a Friday afternoon, transplanting the last of my seedlings. Using an old kitchen knife Robbie gave me, I cut carefully around the root of a zucchini plant, lift it from the recon box, and tuck it into the soil. I nod to Taggert and he uses his little plastic watering can to sprinkle it with water. It's hard to believe that something so small will become an enormous plant, but Robbie warned me to leave at least half a metre between zucchini seedlings and even more between the pumpkins.

I stand back and look at my garden. There are six round beds of black soil, with small green seedlings tucked at intervals throughout. There's water in the pond and herbs around it – tiny bits of fragrant plant Robbie dug from her garden, with little bits of root attached. She promised they'll grow into significant bushes.

As it grows dark, I settle on the newly finished security platform with my journal, pillow and doona, ready to watch over my plants until morning – the very first security shift. Tomorrow it will be Connie's turn. The next night it will be Halim's, and so on.

I check my wristlet, looking for something to read, even if it's just the news. Its charge has been lasting a lot longer since I stopped messaging Taylor and Marley all the time and started communicating only with the people right in front of my face.

Food and Fuel Crisis Strategy Announced

Following weeks of intensive meetings between local, state and federal governments, Karen Kildare today made an impassioned statement about plans to assist Australians. Rations are coming. The military is being commissioned to take over farms, fuel depots, railways and transportation animals in order to collect and distribute food and fuel equitably. Karen Kildare urges Australians to keep calm in the face of changes that may feel challenging but are for the greater good. Support our military to support us.

watch speech

I blink. *The military?* Equitable rations sound good, though. How will it work? Will people who can't pay still receive some? Will they mix recon with real food, and encourage people to do what I'm doing, grow their own food? Or hold their line about wild food being dangerous? Or will the Organicore board use this to force absolutely everybody to switch to recon?

Mum emerges from the driveway and stands in front of me.

'Mum, they announced rations! When does your job start?'

Mum shrugs. 'I just messaged Karen. Let's have dinner.'

'Can you bring our recon out? I'm watching the plants.'

Mum glances around. 'What will you do at bedtime?'

'Sleep here.'

'You're joking! You can't sleep on the street! It's not safe.'

'It's the only way to keep my plants safe.'

'Piper, *you* are far more important than the plants.'

'These plants will become our food, Mum. Someone's got to watch them, or they could be stolen, just like the trees.'

She purses her lips but fetches our recon. We eat it together on the platform, and although she doesn't say much, Mum sits with me until late. When she's rubbing her eyes, I tell her firmly to go inside. 'I'll yell out, loud, if anything happens. I'll be fine.'

'I don't like leaving you out here by yourself.'

'I'm not really by myself. Connie, Zoe and Halim will all hear me and come out too if I yell. And I've slept outside before. It's no different to the night we were supposed to go to Sydney.'

Mum slumps, beaten. She goes inside and I shiver. It's creepy as hell out here by myself.

The night drags endlessly. It's too dark to work in my journal. Around two in the morning my eyes close, even though I'm sitting up. There's a sound. I get a huge fright and jump, but I can't see anything. Argh! I don't know how long I slept for. Maybe the sound was a car going past in Westgarth Street? I'm not used to hearing anything at night. It's weird to have my hearing aids in, but I don't dare to take them out. I rub my itching ears, rub my eyes, pinch my cheeks. My eyes are closing again.

In the end the only way to stay awake is to get up every hour and walk around the garden, which feels kind of mystical. I see the stars, tiny speckles shimmering in a raspberry-black sky. I breathe deeply and inhale the darkness, which fills me with calm. I can do this.

I LiKE it.

MONDAY 12 OCTOBER

I spread grease over the pedal threads and wind them onto the bike frame. I caved and messaged Marley; he replied right away, and he has me building bikes now. I keep checking the time on my wristlet. Surely we can eat soon? Finally Marley nudges me and we go inside. He rummages under the counter and hands me a metal container. He packed me my own lunch!

Inside the container is a boiled egg atop a mash of red stuff. 'What's that?' I sign. I don't even have to think about the correct hand movements now – they just roll off my fingers.

'Rabbit and tomato stew.'

'One of your rabbits?' I picture them in their tower of cages, doe-eyed, white and downy. Even after the possum and chickens, the thought of killing rabbits makes my stomach turn. How can you do that to something so sweet? But once the stew's flavour and grease hits my tongue, I stop thinking about rabbits.

'I was thinking,' says Marley, 'you're getting the hang of this bike thing now and don't really need me for signing. What if you build your own bikes and sell them here? You'd need to do a tip run with me to collect bike parts. Ryan's happy for you to give thirty per cent of whatever you make to the shop, same as I do.'

A job? Wow.

A real paying job. I can't believe it. And I don't need to be able to hear a word to do this. Cesspool should have put 'bike building' on its list of suggested careers for me.

I throw my arms around Marley in excitement. He pulls me close and we embrace for a moment, then I force myself back, lest he think I'm flirting with him. I'm just happy.

Nine days until my fine's due. I wonder if I can come up with two thousand dollars from bike sales before then. Not likely. But maybe they'll agree to a payment plan – give them something each time I sell a bike – like Robbie suggested?

'Can we do a tip run tomorrow?' I ask.

Marley shrugs. 'Should be fine.'

I think of Taylor, toying with the idea of inviting her to build bikes with me, but in truth I can't really see it. Unlike me, she's never been very interested in working with her hands.

Marley glances up and I follow his gaze. Robbie is wheeling her bike into the shop. She does an eloquent performance with her hands, depicting herself pedalling along, a nail inserting itself in her front wheel, and the tyre hissing out air before deflating miserably. How can she make it appear that a tyre has emotion? She hugs me warmly, and when I show her a photo of my garden she grins, gives me the thumbs up, and pats my back with exaggerated enthusiasm. Marley helps her remove the tyre and sets her up at the counter with a puncture-repair kit.

Kelsey shows up next, her honey-coloured hair and skin

radiant. Her energy's so big it takes up the whole shop, and her fragrance fills the air around us – apples and soap. Even though it's not a warm day, she's wearing a tight little orange singlet with her long skirts, along with three necklaces. Half her hair is piled elegantly on top of her head, while the other half cascades down her back in shiny ripples. She greets Robbie with enthusiasm, kisses Marley wetly on the lips right in front of me, and grabs me for a tight embrace as though we're best friends. No wonder Marley picked her. It's like the sun has come out.

She speaks to me and Marley interprets. 'Do you have your journal here? Have you done any new artworks?'

I fetch it to show her, flattered by her interest. Robbie leaves the counter and comes to look too. Kelsey's mouth drops open when she sees Karen Kildare as Organicore's puppet. 'How did you get it to look exactly like her?'

I mime tracing a photo.

'Isn't that cheating?' Marley signs, and for a moment I think it's his words, but then I realise he's interpreting for Kelsey.

I shrug. 'I don't think so. Tracing is just a tool to help me get down what I want to say.'

Robbie raises both hands in the air and shakes them, and I frown, confused. 'What's that sign?'

'It's how Deaf people clap,' Robbie replies. 'Deaf people can't hear the clapping, but we can all see raised hands like this.' Marley interprets this for Kelsey, who raises her own hands in an imitation of Robbie.

Robbie nudges me. 'I think your name sign should be…' She holds her left hand flat as if it's a page in my journal, and makes a drawing motion with her right hand, her fingers shaped in a skewed V with her thumb inserted between them.

233

'Why this handshape?' I ask, copying the skewed *V* with the thumb.

'That's *P* in the American alphabet.'

'Why not use *our* alphabet?'

Robbie shrugs. 'For some reason lots of names and words are formed with the American alphabet. Besides, if I tried to do the Auslan *P* using just my right hand, it would only have half the shape, and so it wouldn't be a *P*.'

Marley grins. 'I can't believe you have a name sign already! And such a good one, too.'

My face spreads into a wide, happy smile. There's nothing boring about my name sign. It's about my art. I love it. 'Thank you,' I sign to Robbie.

I'm not sure if Marley has voiced this exchange for Kelsey's benefit, but either way she's still glued to my journal. She's found 'Grow Food Not Concrete' and she raises her hands and shakes them vigorously – clapping – then talks emphatically. Marley signs for her, and I wonder if he minds, but he doesn't seem bothered.

'You should make a stencil version of this and spray it onto walls all over Melbourne! In fact, maybe I could use it to help encourage more people to grow food on public land. If more people grow food, we think that might convince the councils to legalise it. Would you mind if I stole the words as Sprouted Earth's slogan? It's just so good! Could you make us a poster?'

I hadn't thought of redoing my drawings as stencils – what a great idea. I could turn 'Death by Red Tape' into one too.

'Sure,' I sign.

A guy I've seen before comes into the shop and it takes me a moment to place him – Cam, from Sprouted Earth. He launches into conversation with Kelsey and Marley. Robbie's back at the counter, head down, cleaning around the hole in her wheel's tube, ready to patch it.

Marley sees me looking and signs, 'Cam's just telling us his farm has been occupied by the army. There are soldiers everywhere, telling them what to do.'

I look at Cam, shocked, wanting to see whether he's adopted the *support our military to support us* attitude suggested by Karen Kildare, and if not to give him some sign of commiseration, but he's looking at Kelsey and doesn't see me trying to communicate.

Marley nudges me. 'I need to finish that bike. It'll be picked up later today.'

We leave Kelsey and Cam to it, retreating to the back of the room, and I ditch my bike to help Marley, holding while he tightens a bolt. A customer enters: an older guy with craggy skin and a salt-and-pepper beard. He sees Robbie at the counter, assumes she's staff and asks her a question, but Robbie's oblivious. Kelsey interjects, saying something to him, and the guy looks taken aback. He puts his hand on his heart in sorrow, his mouth moving constantly. I wish I was wearing my hearing aids. He speaks to Robbie, who continues to ignore him, and Kelsey responds.

Suddenly Marley slams the spanner onto the floor and stands up. He's mad. He stomps on the floor, sending vibrations through the shop, and Robbie looks up.

'Kelsey!' Marley signs, heated. 'You can't speak for Robbie!'

'What did she say?' Robbie signs, and at the same time Kelsey speaks. Her mouth is open in surprise, a little indignant.

Marley holds his palm up to Kelsey. *Wait.* To Robbie, he signs, 'This guy is heartbroken that you can't hear the beautiful music playing right now. He advises you to get a bio-engineered ear.'

Robbie rolls her eyes and scoffs. She's not taking it seriously.

'Kelsey said she doesn't think you can afford one right now.' Going by Marley's expression, this is an appalling thing for Kelsey to have said, though people have suggested the same thing to me a million times.

Robbie raises her eyebrows and signs something too quick for me to catch. I look at Marley, wondering if I'll catch his interpretation to the customer, but I don't: something about how she won't get one because she's fisofacla posed.

The customer speaks, impassioned. 'But then she will never get to hear beautiful music,' Marley interprets for Robbie.

Kelsey speaks and Marley glances at her with irritation. He signs her words too, though clearly he doesn't like what she's said. 'Or the rain. I love lying in bed listening to the rain. It's so soothing.'

I've never heard the rain, beyond an irritating underlay of white noise, and I can't say it feels like my life is impoverished without it. Music is not something I think about much, though one of my favourite memories of Grandpa is him singing to me when I was little. I never understood the words but I liked the way he held me and the rise and fall of his voice, his chest reverberating against my cheek. That was soothing.

Robbie pulls herself up tall and signs slightly sarcastically, overly slow and clear, which makes it easy for me to understand. 'Do you really think you are the first person ever to suggest this to me? That now you have had this brilliant idea I will go home and book in the surgery? I was thinking that you should get your wristlet implanted.' Marley interprets for her.

The guy looks down at his wristlet, clearly considering the idea. He answers her seriously, oblivious to her sarcasm. I wonder if Marley got that through in his voice when he interpreted Robbie's words. 'I don't want my wristlet implanted,' Marley signs for him. 'My mate got his done and it became badly infected. Very painful.'

Robbie throws up her hands and slams the side of one hand down on the palm of the other. I glance at Marley and lipread him easily this time. 'Precisely,' he says, his face sharp and pointed.

The guy frowns, confused. Marley changes the subject by asking how he can help, serves the customer and returns to me. He's in a mood, handling the bike parts roughly, clenching the tools too tight.

Cam and Kelsey talk for a while longer, then make to leave. When Kelsey leans down to kiss Marley goodbye, he turns his face slightly so that she kisses his cheek, not his lips. If she notices, Kelsey doesn't give any indication. She squeezes my wrist and says something about the poster, but Marley doesn't interpret. I give her the thumbs up and indicate that I'll message her when it's done.

Late afternoon, a guy comes through the door who Marley greets warmly in sign language. He's maybe thirty-something, has shaved off all his hair, and wears loose, dirty jeans and a tight green T-shirt revealing large muscles.

'This is Justin,' Marley says to me. 'He's deaf.' To Justin he spells my name, shows my new name sign, then says, 'Piper is deaf too.'

I feel a bit weird about that. I never, ever tell anyone I'm deaf. Obviously they figure it out anyway most of the time, but the longer I can postpone that moment, the more they get used to talking to me normally; otherwise most people immediately overdo the way they speak to me, and I hate it.

But Justin's face lights up, and he turns to me in delight. 'Piper? I haven't met you before. Where did you grow up?'

'Here, in Melbourne,' I sign back.

He frowns, confused. 'Which school?'

'MARY MAGDALENE,' I fingerspell.

'I didn't know there were Deaf there?'

I shake my head. 'Just me.'

He hooks his fingers and circles them in front of his mouth. I thought it was the sign for *lipread*, but Justin is mouthing something else.

'ORAL,' Marley fingerspells. His bad mood seems to have evaporated.

I frown, confused.

'If you grow up oral,' Marley explains, 'it means you didn't sign, you had to lipread.'

'Oh. Yes, that's me.'

Justin gives me a sympathetic smile. 'But you are learning to sign now.'

I nod. 'Marley's teaching me.'

This pleases Justin and he gives Marley a high five.

'If you ever want to meet other Deaf, just message me. I'll take you to the Deaf club. I grew up oral too, so I know what it's like.'

We swap contact details, though I admit I can't really picture myself going out with a guy in his thirties. How do I know I can trust him? Is he trying to pick me up?

After Justin has enquired about buying a bike and been told there's a long waiting list, he and Marley hug and he leaves.

'He seemed to move very fast,' I sign to Marley, 'inviting me out, wanting to know about my background.'

'No!' Marley's surprised. 'It's not like that. He's gay. That's normal in the deaf community. If you meet another deaf person, you always ask for their life story, starting with where they grew up and what school they went to. He was just concerned that you're so isolated because you've grown up oral.'

'Isolated?' I copy his sign, a single finger moving in small upright circles. It's not as if I haven't been around people.

'Isolated from people who sign.'

He's talking as if I've been denied my birthright. As if being deaf is such an important part of my identity that I need to spend time with other deaf people. I thought that deafness was meant to be like having freckles – something that fades into the background so you don't really notice it after a bit. Do people with freckles seek to spend time with other freckled people? 'Does it matter?' I ask.

'That's for you to tell me. But I'd have thought it'd be kind of hard for you – you know, making friends, understanding what's going on, trying to fit into a world you can't hear. With other deaf people you'd have a shared experience, and a shared language you can all access easily.'

If I'm honest, this is *exactly* the reason I've been avoiding Northcote High. It's also part of what thrills me about spending time with Robbie: Not being the only one oblivious to what's happening around me, or confused by it. Knowing there's no chance she'll try to speak to me – that if she wants to communicate, it will happen visually. Not being the only one with limited career opportunities, and getting to share the frustration of that with her.

239

'If you go anywhere in Australia, and you see people signing, you can just go up to them and tell them you're deaf, and they'll be your friends, instantly. If you sign in public, other deaf people will come up to you and do what Justin did. Inviting you out, that's normal.'

Wow. I kind of like that.

On the way home I stop at the police station, intending to ask if I can pay off my fine in instalments. I'll explain that there's a waiting list of people who want bikes, which sell for good money, even if I do have to use some of it to pay for ridiculously expensive new parts. I'll be able to pay off the fine eventually, assuming I can get enough free parts from the tip. But the queue at the station snakes out the door and halfway down the street. I remember trying to report my stolen bike stolen, and wonder how they found the time to fine me when they don't have anywhere near the resources they need to manage the public's claims. I suppose because Mum was so forceful in getting their attention. Sigh.

I reply to the message about the charges against me instead, explaining my genuine desire to pay and how I've just now got a job, asking whether they'll grant me permission to pay in instalments.

'Mum!' I call, jamming in my hearing aids as I barrel through the door of the guesthouse. 'I got a job!'

She lowers her wristlet. 'Doing what?'

'Building bikes! I'm going to collect pieces of old bikes from the tip, put them together, and build new ones. Well, new-old ones. And sell them!'

She's startled. 'Don't you need some training to do that? You couldn't even sort out the handlebar of your last bike. Sorry, I don't mean to be discouraging.'

'I'm learning! Marley's teaching me. I know how to do most parts now.'

'Marley? The boy who came here?'

I nod. 'But he's just a friend. Forget all that about me liking him. The important bit is that I've found a way to pay off that fine!'

'Two thousand dollars before the twenty-first of October?' I'm surprised she remembers the date. 'What's the rate of pay?' Mum opens her wristlet, ready to calculate how many hours I'll have to do.

'There's no hourly rate. I just build the bikes and sell them and keep seventy per cent of the proceeds.'

'PRO-cedes.'

'What?'

'For the noun, you say PRO-cedes, not pro-CEEDS.'

'Oh. Ok. PRO-cedes. Really? PRO-ceedings?'

'No, that's different. You say pro-CEED-ings.'

I sigh. It's hard to remember subtle differences between versions of words like this. 'Does it really matter, Mum?'

'Piper, it does! If you don't pronounce words correctly, people will think you're stupid, uneducated. They won't respect you.'

That's another thing that would be nice about hanging out with deaf people. They'd never care how words are pronounced. I doubt they'd judge me for that.

'So, what do the bikes sell for?' Mum insists.

'It depends how good the parts are, and what features it has. But maybe three or four hundred? Thirty per cent goes to the shop.' Can't Mum just be happy I have a job? Happy that *I'm* happy?

She does the calculations on her wristlet. 'You'll need to sell around eight bikes. Is it realistic to build and sell that many in nine days? A bike a day?'

I shake my head. 'No way. It takes Marley and me a couple of days to build one, and I'm much slower if I do it by myself. But I messaged the police to ask if I can pay off the fine more slowly.'

'Good luck with that,' Mum says. She nods, thoughtful. 'I know you've missed the first month of school, but it's not too late to enrol you at Northcote High. Bike-building is great, but it's hardly a career.'

'If I'm at school I won't be able to build bikes! How will I pay off the fine?'

'After school, on weekends. Piper, it's *so important* you get an education.'

My chest tightens and my excitement evaporates. 'Mum! Lay off it. If bike-building is all I ever do for a career, that would be awesome as far as I'm concerned.'

She purses her lips, unhappy. Always unhappy. I change the subject.

'How about work for *you*? Any word yet on when the rationing starts and whether you'll still get to be the Darebin manager?'

Mum shrugs. 'They're still working out the system. It's a while off, I think.'

There's a skinny old guy hunched over the pond in my garden, a pile of broken old-fashioned plates beside him. He's smearing goo round the pond edge and pressing pieces of plate into it: mosaic. He's done about a quarter, and the tiles' jagged edges and rush of patterns speak to me – a small handmade voice in a monolith of machine-made guttering and tarmac.

'Sorry, sorry,' he says when he sees me, then another rush of words I don't catch since he's looking down, gesturing to the mosaic. His white hair is wispy, his skin deeply lined.

I wait till he glances back up and sign, 'I'm Piper.' I hold out my hand, but his is smeared in goo. He shrugs sheepishly.

'This is beautiful,' I sign, half whisper-speaking, my face showing an exaggerated appreciation for its loveliness.

'Umga, opa doma, sowa sedakadoo this.'

I frown and shrug. 'What?' I write in the dirt with my finger.

He gets me right away, and copies my method to reply. 'I'm Gary. I hope you don't mind…Zoe said I could do this.'

I give him the thumbs up. 'I love it,' I sign.

'I can kind of hear you, you know,' he writes. 'You speak really well.'

I squint at him. This is not me speaking *well*. I can speak so normally that people don't realise I'm deaf, though I do often get asked where I'm from. And yet, with my weird

tiny-bit-of-whispering voice he tells me I'm speaking well! I'm not sure what to say. I stretch my lips in a fake smile, as if he's complimented rather than patronised me.

Next he writes a question people I've just met often ask. 'Were you born deaf?'

I shake my head, sighing inside. 'I became deaf when I was three. No one knows why.'

'Have you considered being fitted with a bio-engineered ear?'

I remember Robbie's curt answer to the same question: *Do you think now you have had this brilliant idea I will go home and book in the surgery?* But I can't bring myself to say that. Gary's just contributed something beautiful to my garden. I can't be rude to him.

'The bio-engineered ear won't help me because my ears are fine. The nerves connecting my ears to my brain died, so I'd need a nerve graft inside my brain.'

I hate talking about personal medical stuff with people I don't know. I need to figure out a better way to answer this.

I turn and look at the rest of my garden, and Gary goes back to his mosaic. There are tiny weeds sprouting between my seedlings. I crouch down and pluck them out carefully. The seedlings are growing already, with new leaves, more substantial after only one week.

I check my wristlet – there's nothing from the Victorian State Police. Do they even read their messages? I've been working on collecting parts and building bikes every day for this past week, and I've made two, which will be picked up the day after tomorrow. Once I've been paid I'll have a quarter of the money, but the fine is due that same day! Is it possible the police will be too busy to do anything about it if I just don't pay?

I ride home from the shop, my wristlet practically burning a hole in my arm now that I have just under five hundred dollars in my account. I've decided I'll go back to the police station, wait in their never-ending queue and try to insist on a payment plan in person. But this time I'll ask Mum to come with me.

I'm on Westgarth Street when I see the compost poster I did for Kelsey, blown up huge and stuck to a wall. I smile. Why should Organicore and Allstar get to dominate everything, day after day? Now a little piece of my voice is in the world too, and I think the world is partly mine now.

I take a deep breath as I approach home. Will Mum even agree to go with—

Where's the car?!

I scan up and down the street. It's not here.

Where's my art stuff??

I race down the driveway, fine forgotten, fumbling in my pocket for my hearing aids. 'Mum? Where's the car?'

She comes to the door of the guesthouse and waits while I put in my hearing aids. 'I sold it,' she says. 'I can't believe I paid over thirty thousand for it and they could barely give me two back, but there you go. Someone will use it for parts, or a place to sleep.'

'WHERE's my art stuff?'

'Don't worry, it's on your bed.'

Thank god. I breathe again. 'Why did you sell it? I liked sitting out there.'

'To pay your fine. You can pay me back as you sell the bikes.'

I stare at her in shock. Then, slowly, relief starts to seep through my body. The next thing I know, I'm crying.

'Mum! You're the best!' I throw my arms around her and am alarmed to feel how skinny she's become – nothing but bones. 'Thank you, thank you, thank you! I promise I'll pay you as fast as I possibly can.'

She hugs me back.

'And Piper,' she goes on, a strange expression on her face, 'I've been thinking. I want so much for you to get an education. But you've made it perfectly clear that you're making your own decisions now. You're sixteen, it's legal for you to leave school. As long as you have a job instead, then, well... you have my support. These aren't normal times. But I still hope you'll decide to go back to school next year.'

I'm not just crying a little bit now – I'm absolutely bawling my eyes out. Mum starts up too, and suddenly we're clinging to each other, tears pouring. I hadn't realised just how much her anger had been weighing on me – about Sydney... about school... all mixed in with the dread of being unable to pay that impossible fine. Suddenly, though, things are okay again, even if she is still disappointed in my decision about school. I'm going to work so hard, and pay her back so quickly she won't believe it. And then I'll be able to start contributing financially, and she'll be glad I made this decision.

I've borrowed a bike with a large box-tray at the back and am rattling it through the back streets of Brunswick. There are soldiers everywhere, dressed in their ridiculous jungle outfits. I'm tempted to stop, pull out my journal, and sketch up my recommended new uniform style for them. But they're scary. They carry huge black guns and scan everyone with blank eyes.

Three soldiers supervise the tram stop on the corner of Lygon Street and Glenlyon Road. A tram has stopped, and I stop too, waiting for it to pass before I cross the road. There's a crowd of people, mostly dressed in business suits, trying to board the tram, but the soldiers bar them.

A man standing next to me turns and says something. I'm not wearing my hearing aids, so I raise my palms questioningly and tap my ears to show I'm deaf. He faces me and enunciates more clearly. 'Yavta avana fishal pass to travel onth tram now.'

'Did you say *official pass*?' I sign, mouthing the words a bit and probably making a little sound.

I assume it's too noisy for him to hear me, as he leans in close, puts his ear to my mouth and says, 'What?'

'Official pass?' I repeat, a bit louder now, not sure how loud to talk to be heard above the street noise, and not wanting it to be so loud that he instantly forgets I'm deaf. I sign at the same time, even though I know he can't understand me and isn't even looking.

He frowns at me in confusion, but I don't need him to confirm it because now I see the soldiers checking the wristlets of would-be travellers. Most of them lack the required credentials, whatever they are. Isn't this overkill for public transport? It's hard to picture that the soldiers are 'helping', given that most of these people now can't get to work. I smile at the man and thank him, even though our communication has not exactly been effective, then wheel my bike through the crowd of frustrated people and cross the road.

Next, I ride past a woman walking a cow. She's holding a gun, looking around warily, and I stop to stare until she glares at me and I pedal away hastily. I don't like the look of that gun, but what a great idea for city milk: if you don't have a paddock, walk the cow to let it feed! I wonder where I could get a cow, and how much they cost. But when would I have the time to walk it? I'm already feeling guilty about taking the afternoon off from bike-building to collect chickens. Maybe I could suggest Mum take up cow-walking, since this rations job is taking forever to begin, but I have a feeling it wouldn't appeal.

It doesn't take long to find Ben's place, following Robbie's directions. Ben, who I've never met before, sells chickens. I knock but there's no answer, so eventually I lock my bike inside his front fence and make my way down the side.

There's a huge backyard, with a totally different style of food production to Robbie's: plastic crates sitting over plants to protect them; half plastic bottles settled around seedlings as clever miniature greenhouses; an old rusting bathtub sprouting a sea of green, and vine-covered rubbish everywhere. The back half

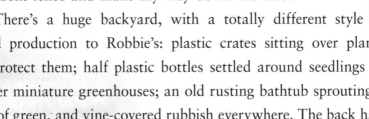

of the yard is divided into several fenced chicken runs containing different types of chickens: large black, white and brown ones; prettily feathered and delicately speckled smaller ones; and tiny chicks sporting a strange mix of soft down and proper feathers.

A hand touches my arm and I turn towards a tanned guy with long dreads and several tattoos running down his arm. He's probably thirty or so, dirty feet bare beneath a pair of filthy cut-off jeans.

'Sorry!' I sign. I mime knocking, waiting, coming down the side looking for him.

He shrugs. His face is kind, and he doesn't seem particularly bothered to find a strange girl in his garden. That I'm deaf and signing doesn't even make him blink. Maybe he's used to it, since he knows Robbie.

I point to the chickens and rub my fingers together in a gesture that says *money*, even though the Auslan sign for *money* is actually totally different.

He understands immediately. 'You want to buy chickens?' Given the context, it's pretty easy to understand him.

I nod.

'How many?'

I hold up ten fingers.

He asks something I don't catch. I try to figure out what else he'd need to know, furrowing my brows and raising my palms questioningly.

He chews his lip and looks at the sky for a moment. Then he places his fists on his shoulders, flaps his elbows and squats down, before reaching between his legs to pick up an imaginary egg and hold it out towards me. Next, he steps to the side to become another chicken, then becomes a person, reaching down to break this chicken's neck and miming eating it. He shrugs and looks at me questioningly.

Eating them versus eating their eggs? I want to do both. Isn't that what chickens are for?

Seeing my confusion, Ben (well, I presume he's Ben) steps inside one of the pens and indicates a huge chook. This one, he shows me, produces lots of eggs but doesn't taste so good.

Now I get it! I mime that I want both.

Ben nods and goes into the pen with the little chicks. He mimes that these will produce several eggs, but not as many as the huge chook. The meat is good – he chomps his jaw appreciatively.

I point to the pretty white chickens with black spots, but Ben shakes his head, twiddling his thumbs to show them taking their time to lay very small eggs and having almost no meat on their bones. I want to ask what they're for then, but can't think how to mime it. As if he's read my mind, Ben squats in the dirt, looking admiringly at one of these chickens, nodding with pleasure. She's there to be beautiful. Ben is better at this than I am!

The beautiful chickens are also three times the price of the others. I negotiated a loan extension with Mum to invest in a flock of chickens: ten little chicks it is! I transfer the money to Ben on my wristlet, and he loads them into a plastic crate for me, then scoops one out and hands it to me. Even though it's ugly, with a strange mix of feathers, it's warm and its heart beats so strongly that it vibrates in my palms. Tiny bead-like eyes flicker back and forth between me and Ben. How will I ever kill something so sweet?

When I ride into our street, slow and careful to make the trip gentle for the chicks, Halim's on duty, and Zoe's hammering stakes into the ground and tying chicken wire to them – a home for our new babies. She looks strong and tough in her sleeveless flannel shirt. Gary's mosaic is finished and glitters in the sunlight.

Zoe and Halim crouch over the chickens, and Archie brings Taggert out to join us. Taggert, of course, wants to hold them, so I hoist him inside the new pen to ensure there are no escapees. Zoe, Halim and I hand each chick to him to gently set down on the ground in there. The chicks huddle together, tight against the fence. They don't look too sure about this.

Archie disappears, returning with a huge plastic packing box from their move. He cuts a doorway in it with a Stanley knife, and Halim fetches rocks from his front yard to weigh down our new chook house. It's not very sophisticated, but I doubt the chooks will care.

Zoe taps my arm and writes in the dirt, 'I'll build something better later.'

I give her the thumbs up.

I'm grinning as my wristlet buzzes. Marley!

▶ From: Marley
Sprouted Earth was bulldozed by the council yesterday afternoon. This morning, the oak tree's gone too. Tree vandals.

It's as if a brick has hit my stomach. Then I feel the sickness slowly transforming into white-hot rage. Who would do such a thing to a beautiful tree that took hundreds of years to grow?

Marley sends through a photo. The stump sits slightly raised in a sea of dirt. Tears stream down my face like rain.

I'm pedalling up Smith Street, returning from an unsuccessful hunt for compost grass in Fitzroy, and I'm busting. I duck into Foxy's, a rather chic café, which is crowded even though they're currently only serving tea and coffee without milk in the dark. I push my way through all the mums with prams to the back courtyard bathroom, hoping nobody notices that I'm not going to buy anything.

Mission accomplished, I wait at the concrete trough to wash my hands, behind a girl with mahogany hair cut in an abrupt Karen-Kildare-style bob who's splashing her face with water. She turns and I startle: it's *Taylor*! What happened to her long brown hair?! Her eyes are rimmed red. She does a double take when she sees me.

'Piper? Oh my god, I didn't recognise you. You're so thin!' She takes my hands and pulls them towards her, my arms stretched out between us.

I look down at myself. Taylor's face is rounded, her arms slightly plump, while my arms are just skin on bone. I'm shocked.

Taylor pulls me in for a hug, and I hold her tight. She smells strange in a fake, posh way – like the perfume department in David Jones. 'I'm so glad to see you,' she says, releasing me. 'I've missed you, Pipes.'

'How can you say you *miss me*? You don't make any time to see me! Even when I was moving to Sydney, you couldn't so much as squeeze in a goodbye!' I'm trying hard not to cry. I drop my head and fossick around in my bag for my hearing aids. I lipread Taylor fine, but it's so much easier when I hear her voice too. I put them in and white noise slams me.

Taylor leans back against the sink and rubs her hands over her face. At first I don't think she'll answer me, but then she drops her hands and mumbles something, looking downwards.

'What?' I ask and realise I'm signing at the same time.

Taylor glances at my finger, confused, but she speaks more clearly this time, and I can lipread her: 'I said, it's complicated. Beau's kind of moody. It's not easy to go out and do the stuff I used to do.'

I frown. This isn't what I was expecting. 'Is...is he manipulating you? He won't *let* you go out?'

Taylor shakes her head, twirling some hair around her index finger. 'He just likes it when I'm around. And I have to be ready to go out with him at a moment's notice.'

I flick off my hearing aids. There's no point subjecting myself to the blare of the café if I can't hear her words. 'That's controlling. That's a red flag, Tay.'

'No, it's not. He's not. He's just…well, maybe a bit. But it's my own fault, I choose it. I like hanging out with him too. I've got this. I'm fine.'

'So fine you can't even see your best friend? Or is it that you don't *want* to see me?'

Taylor sinks her face back into her hands, and if she answers, I can't tell. So now I realise that things haven't been easy for her either – but surely it's worth standing up to Beau for *me*?

Eventually Taylor lifts her face again, her eyes weary. Are they red from rubbing, or has she been crying? She doesn't say anything, and hurt sits heavy in my stomach. I could never have imagined being relegated to last priority in my best friend's life like this.

I swallow. It's clear nothing's about to change, and that she doesn't want to talk more about Beau, so I change the subject. 'What have you been eating? How come you aren't thin too?' Just a few months ago this would have been an insulting question, but everything seems different now.

'That's the thing. Beau has plenty of food. It's a good reason to keep him happy.'

'But *how*? It's not like you can buy it in shops.'

'Beau has…knichas.'

'What? Connections? The black market?'

Taylor shrugs. 'Maybe.' She glances at her wristlet and springs forward. 'I have to go. He's waiting for me.'

I try to take her hand, but with a kiss to my cheek she's gone.

If I had to choose between food and my best friend, which would I pick? My hunger gnaws at me. I'd like to say my best friend, but I can see it's not that simple.

MONDAY 2 NOVEMBER

Two days later, I discover huge orange stickers plastered all over the chook house, security platform and even the rocks around our little garden pond.

CITY COUNCIL NOTICE OF PRIVATE PROPERTY ON COUNCIL LAND

In accordance with Section IV, 34b, this property has been **MARKED AS UNCLAIMED LITTER**. If not removed by **31 DECEMBER**, the City Council reserves the right to forcibly remove and destroy this item.

OWNERS MAY FACE LITTERING FINES. MAXIUMUM PENALTY $8,590.

I feel numb as I survey the garden. The mandala's beds are now a vibrant mass of green, with tiny yellow flowers sprouting between the zucchini and cucumber leaves, and white flowers that look like little butterflies scattered along the pea vines. The chickens are larger, their down now replaced with proper feathers. Zoe's crouched beside their plastic chook pen, at work building them a more permanent home from upcycled planks of fake wood. My head throbs suddenly, and I realise I haven't had a headache in ages.

Zoe sees me and writes in the dirt, 'I explained it's a community garden. They just said they're doing their job, and to take it up with the council.'

Was this all for <u>NOTHING</u>?

Will we get to eat ANYTHING before they destroy it all?

Zoe puts a strong arm around me. She's speaking, but of course I can't understand her without seeing her face. I shrug and she lets me go and writes in the dirt again. 'I bet it's just hot air.'

I think of Sprouted Earth and I'm not so sure. Why is the council putting resources into this when there's a food and fuel crisis to solve? Surely they can see that we need other food sources?

I was headed to the bike shop, but I'm too upset. I go back inside instead, putting my hearing aids in. 'Mum, the council is going to destroy our garden!' I show her a photo of one of the orange stickers. 'Is this Organicore's doing?'

Mum's up to her elbows in cold water, washing our sheets. Her T-shirt is dirty, and her hair hangs limp and unwashed. I've never seen her look so unkempt. She shakes her hands dry, takes my wrist with ice-cold fingers and squints at my wristlet. 'That law was made years ago. Surely it's a normal part of the council's work, to keep our streets free of litter?'

'It's not litter, Mum!' I shout. 'It's a community garden!'

'Sorry. I didn't mean it like that. I know you've been working hard out there. But it is public land.'

'Doesn't that mean it belongs to the public? Can't we use it how we want to? Mum, can you suggest to the Organicore board that since they can't meet demand right now, they get behind some laws that will make it easier for us to produce our own food?'

Mum sighs and puts her hands back into the pot, swirling and rubbing the sheet against itself. 'Bob Forsyth just called. You remember he got my job when we didn't make it to Sydney? Well, he says the job is a joke. He hasn't been paid, or received anything like enough recon. The apartment is a dump and the electricity has been disconnected. He says Organicore knew they couldn't afford him and basically tricked him to work for free. I think Organicore has bigger things to worry about than council littering laws right now. I'm not sure the company is going to make it.'

'Lucky we didn't go to Sydney then.'

Mum raises an eyebrow at me. 'Yes, perhaps it is lucky,' she says drily. But I can tell she's not about to thank me for the change of plan.

Since the orange stickers appeared on Monday, the neighbours and I have made sure there's always someone in our garden. What if they decide to come early and bulldoze the lot? Today it's my turn, with Taggert 'assisting' me, and we're giving the garden a drink. He tugs at my arm and I look up to see a boy a bit younger than me walking… a goat! On a lead! I remember the woman with the cow. People are finding clever solutions to their hunger.

Taggert and I settle on the security platform with some of my art stuff. There are a couple of cushions up here now, and a candle stub. It's homely. Taggert draws a bunch of red scribbles inside a rough circle, and I sit thinking about what Mum said – that the council sees our garden as rubbish. If we put up my educational compost poster, and they read it, might they come to understand that this place is actually valuable?

I pull a folded copy of the poster from my journal and deliberate over where to put it, settling in the end for gluing it to a board cut from a plastic box, which I tie to the chicken-wire fence, Taggert holding it in place. Once it's up we stand back to admire our work. It makes the whole garden look more professional. I think that maybe if we add a bit more art, it will make the place look loved and cared for, so next I spray our favourite stencils onto several more plastic boxes and attach them to the chook fence and the security platform.

Halim comes out and nods, as though we require his approval. Archie comes to fetch Taggert, who makes him admire our work too, and Gary emerges from a house down the far end of the street and ducks his head awkwardly when I tell him again how much I love his pond mosaic.

I feel a slight rumbling under my feet, like when a tram goes past, and everyone turns towards Westgarth Street. There are six horses pulling what looks like the tray of a truck, loaded high with something secured beneath a tarp and crisscrossed ropes. Behind the truck walk several soldiers. The sight is so astonishing that we all traipse to the end of our street to get a better view, where we find the street lined with other people like us, staring.

Archie says something and Gary writes on his wristlet to interpret. 'He thinks it might be rations. They're setting up in the town hall up on High Street.'

A woman in her late twenties wearing a neat high-necked suit, with short curly hair and warm dark eyes, rolls up to us in a wheelchair. She's cleaner than the rest of us, though her shirt has small stains on the ruffles and the cuffs are grubby. She seems to know Halim, who introduces her to Archie and Gary, and gestures to me. The woman does a double take, wheels her chair around and holds out her hand for me to shake. Her mouth moves and she stares at me intensely, but I don't catch her words.

'That's Amber,' Gary types. 'She's been wanting to meet the person who started our garden. She says it would make a good story.'

Amber takes Gary's lead and taps away on her own wristlet. She's the fastest one-handed typist I've ever seen. 'I work for News Melbourne. I was wondering if I could interview you?'

I shrug, surprised, then meet her eye and nod.

'Now?' she types.

I hesitate. I'm not wearing my hearing aids. I could go and get them, but she seems unfazed by my deafness, and I figure we can find a way to accommodate my inability to hear and the fact that she probably thinks I can't speak. I give her the thumbs up and she gestures for me to go in front of her, pointing to a house a few doors up from Halim's. As we pass the garden, she stops and points to the orange stickers, shaking her head.

'I don't think our garden will be here much longer,' I type on my wristlet.

'That's why I want to interview you. I've seen you all out here, working together. The council should be encouraging this! They might be reluctant to go against a positive story from News Melbourne.' Amber rolls her chair up the rim of concrete onto the island and stops in front of my compost poster. 'Is this your work?'

I nod and she gives me an emphatic thumbs up. 'I thought you couldn't publish anything on Cesspool that goes against government policy,' I say, tripping on the gutter as I do so. That's what I get for typing while walking, but I manage to right myself.

Amber nods. 'It's bloody annoying having to find ways around their censorship! It's a fine line, but I think I know how to get this through. We'll make it a human interest story, about you inspiring the community with a solution to the food crisis.'

'If you want to blog freely, why not just post on the old internet?' I ask.

'Then I'd lose my job at News Melbourne.'

She leads me to the front door of her very ordinary-looking old Edwardian terrace house, front steps replaced by a ramp. When I step inside, though, I see the whole place has been gutted. There are unsheltered wires everywhere, the room is lit like daylight with bright fluorescent lights, and one side of the house is filled entirely with technical equipment – two huge visi-screens side by side, speakers rigged in each corner, a bench littered with microphones, video cameras and styluses. News Melbourne must pay well.

She gestures for me to grab a stool and place it in front of one of the visis, then hands me a portable keyboard. 'I'm going to record my questions with my voice, then I'll type them for you, okay? You can type your answers, and I'll get someone else to read them up for the audio-feeds.'

I nod, suddenly intimidated. What if I don't know what to say?

But it turns out I'm a bit of a natural. I tell her all about how my desire for food slowly morphed into a community garden for our street. How it's beautiful now, a little oasis in the city. How it started when I attended the Transition Towns workshop, then met Robbie, and how next thing I was making compost and it all grew from there. (I don't mention my complete emotional meltdown at the workshop – or the fact that I first tried looking up food-growing on Cesspool and failed.)

Amber soaks it all in, giving what looks like a professional laugh every now and again, just like she's on a live video feed. 'I think a great many people out there are with you, Piper, on wanting to grow their own food. So, peeps, Piper is quite the artist, and as well as creating a beautiful garden, she's done an incredible series of drawings showing the techniques she used to create it.' To me, she asks, 'Can we include your compost poster? I think our audience would be very interested to see it.'

'Of course.'

'Well, I think we're good to go. Thank you, Piper.'

'But we didn't get to the orange stickers...?'

'Don't worry. We'll get everyone to fall in love with you and the concept, then we'll make a heartbreaking announcement that the council has decided to dismantle your garden. It will get a reaction. Trust me.'

MONDAY 9 NOVEMBER

Arriving home from the bike shop after work, I discover a woman with a huge camera crouched in the middle of the island, snapping close-ups of our plants. Taggart watches from our driveway, holding his little plastic watering can.

The woman sees me and straightens. 'Piper?'

I nod, wary. Is she from the council? Documenting our trespass? Taggert waves to me, and I check both ways for cars (a fairly pointless exercise these days) and gesture for him to join me.

The photographer types on her wristlet: 'I'm from News Melbourne. Amber asked me to get some photos to go with your story. Would you mind?'

I touch my hair. It's filthy. So are my clothes. But the photographer indicates she doesn't want me to change a thing. She has Taggert stand a little closer to me and takes lots of shots of us, first with his watering can, then up close with the chickens and squatting among the plants in the mandala beds. She asks Taggert a question, but he doesn't reply, and when she looks at me I just shrug.

I try to see the garden as the photographer must see it. It looks loved and inviting. The herbs' leaves around the pond now mostly cover the dirt. We've started a second mandala garden bed on the other side of the chook pen, two piles of compost currently working their magic to soften the ground. The chickens are bigger, pecking happily at the ground. The security platform is now home to a thin camping mattress and a sleeping bag, as well as recon boxes holding our next batch of seedlings.

I peer into the pond, wondering if any tadpoles have hatched. Robbie said they might, but I can't see any yet. Even without live creatures, though, the pond adds a magical air to the place, and that's not lost on the photographer, who snaps several shots of me leaning over the water.

The photographer makes her exit, and I sag. All this will be gone come the new year. And then what will I have left?

Working at the bike shop must have really taken it out of me yesterday, as I'm so weary this morning I can't drag myself out of bed. If I could just eat a huge meal…recharge.

I'll go to the shop this afternoon, I tell myself.

I'm still lying in bed, listless, when Mum stands over me and gestures for me to put on my hearing aids. I feel too tired to process any sound, but obligingly shove them into my ears.

'I'm going to the rush centre in High Street – I'm starting work tomorrow. I want to check it out.'

'Going where?'

'RATIONS CENTRE.'

So the rumours were true! 'When are we getting rations?'

'The centre opens tomorrow. I'll be managing the queues.' Mum looks brighter than I've seen her in ages.

'I thought you were going to manage the whole place?'

'Apparently not,' she says drily, 'but at least it's a job.'

'That's great, Mum,' I say. 'I can't believe it – we'll have recon delivered today *and* rations tomorrow.'

'Organicore isn't delivering today. They're contracted to provide recon as part of the rations instead.'

My newfound energy drains out of me.

When Mum's gone I ditch my hearing aids and check the recon cupboard, but there are only empty boxes inside awaiting recycling. I don't even have weeds for a tea.

I flop onto my belly, and my mind wanders to Taylor. I want to message her, but don't want to be just another pressure on her – Beau tugging her one way, me the other. How can I be supportive, kind? My gut tells me I should be worried – I think again of her red-rimmed eyes. But she was gone so quickly, and given she basically denied there was a problem, what can I do? Maybe just stay in touch…

I snap a photo of my milk thistle and send it to her. 'Weird fact: this weed tastes surprisingly good with potato.'

The light above me flashes on and off. Huh? I glance at the door, which is slightly ajar, with a hand snaking through the gap. I know that hand – gold skin, pale hairs. Marley!

What an awesome way to get my attention! It's so respectful. Mum or Taylor have always just walked right in if I don't hear them knock. I've never known for sure if I have privacy.

Forgetting my exhaustion, I jump up. It *is* Marley. But his eyes are swollen, his shoulders stooped. I hold out my arms to him and he almost falls into them. I inhale deeply and lay my cheek against his hair, breaking my own rules.

'What's wrong?' I sign when he shifts away from me. I take his hand and lead him inside. He's never seen inside the guesthouse before. It's not cosy and lovely like his place, but I don't care. I'm just glad Mum's not home.

'I broke up with Kelsey,' he signs.

I stare at him, unable to suppress a beautiful bubble of gladness from rising in my chest. I keep my face serious. 'Why?'

'I gave up.' Tears squeeze out of his eyes, and he makes no effort to wipe them away. 'I thought I could do it – be someone I'm not, you know. A hearing person. A normal person.' He glances around, spots my bed, and sits down. 'She's nice. She's lovely. But she doesn't *get* me.' Marley picks up my journal and absently runs his finger over some doodles I drew earlier.

'Did you two have a fight?' I ask, sitting next to him.

Marley shakes his head. 'This morning she asked how Robbie and I fight, if we can't yell at each other.'

'What's wrong with that?'

'Fighting in Auslan is the same as fighting in English! It's not some glorious spectacle to ponder over with excitement! I told her it was over.'

I can't help but feel sorry for Kelsey. What if I ask him some question about deafness and he responds by ending our friendship? But on another level, I get what he means. I remember Gary telling me how well I spoke. I knew he only meant to compliment me, but there was something underneath it, something I couldn't quite put my finger on, that made me deeply uncomfortable. Something about knowing I can't trust hearing people to give me an honest assessment of my voice? Not that I care. But there's a divide there. An 'us and them'. And Kelsey asked her question from the other side of this divide.

'How'd she take it?' I ask.

'She was upset. But, you know, it felt like she was going through the motions. I don't think she was really that into me. She didn't say she'd dedicate herself to understanding my cultural background and getting that we're just normal people, fights and all.'

Marley flips a few pages in my journal and lands on the self-portrait I did ages ago. He holds it up against me. 'This is amazing! How do you get it to look just like you?'

I shrug. 'Practice. I did that one in front of the mirror.'

He turns a clump of pages and there's him and me eating rabbit stew. My face hots up. I feel exposed.

He looks at it for a long time. Eventually, he meets my eye and signs, 'I thought I had a one-way crush on you...'

Breathe, Piper...

'But if you had a crush on me, why did you get together with Kelsey?'

'You went to Sydney! Or, at least, I thought you did. I would never have got together with her if I'd known you were staying.'

I can't help remembering he didn't waste any time after I'd left. 'What made you think the crush was one-way?' I ask.

'I knew you didn't want to go to Sydney. But it was all about learning to grow food and sign language. I didn't think you were bothered about leaving *me*.'

Emboldened now, I reach out and place my fingers on his wrist. He takes my hand, holds it a moment in both of his, then lets go so he can sign.

'I also didn't think it would be wise to be with a deaf person. I thought I needed to get away from the deaf world, stop rubbing my face in all the ignorance deaf people cop, the things I can't change. I thought having a hearing girlfriend would give me that.'

'Just let me clarify this. You had a crush on me, but you don't want to be with me because I'm deaf?'

'I guess...yeah...Only that was before. Now I realise the deaf world is inside me. I can't get away from it. I need to embrace it.'

Well...where does that leave *me*?

Marley flips to another page, and there's the little slip of paper where he wrote his name the first time we met. He runs his finger over it.

'You must spend hours on this. Hours. How do you find the time, as well as building community gardens on your street and rocket stoves and bikes, and working with Rob and all that?'

'It's how I relax before I go to sleep. Some days I write, but mostly I just go back over pages I've already written on, or pages I haven't written on yet, and draw, doodle, add paint. I don't have to think. I just play around and see what works. It's kind of random.'

'You have talent, Piper. This whole book is an artwork in itself.' He stops and points at the word *deaf* on my fingerspelling chart. 'That should have a capital *D*.'

'What do you mean?'

'If you spell *deaf* with a lowercase *d*, it just means that your ears don't work. But Robbie, she's Deaf with a capital *D*, to show that she's not just unable to hear, but that she belongs to the Deaf community and uses Auslan. It's a cultural thing, using the word as a proper noun. When we talk about Greek culture or Italian culture, we start them with capital letters too.'

Can I be considered *Deaf* yet? One day, maybe…

Marley spends ages with my journal, looking at every picture, recognising people and places, and it's the best feeling in the world to be so approved of. That's partly why I like him so much – because he has this way of making me feel so good about myself. Well, when he's not calling me a recon girl, which he hasn't done again. He makes me feel like a real artist.

Eventually I take the book from him. 'Sorry, but I have to know,' I sign. 'Do you *still* have a crush on me?'

'How could I not? You're just…*gorgeous*.'

'Does the fact that I'm Deaf mean you don't want to act on that crush?'

'The fact that you're Deaf makes me want to act on that crush even more.'

I drop my journal and reach for him. He slides his arms around my waist and pulls me close, so that I'm sitting pressed against his chest. I lift my head and Marley's lips find mine, at first the lightest touch, grazing my skin exquisitely. I don't think I've ever felt so close, so connected to another person, so understood, as in this moment. I bite down on his lip gently, sucking, and then we're kissing properly and it's beyond anything I could have imagined. My body is transformed to liquid, a complete surrender. I pull up his T-shirt and my singlet and kneel astride him so that our bellies are bare against each other. His tongue is hot and rough in my mouth. I suck and he sucks back. Time disappears. It's his body and mine, his mouth and mine, sliding together. I pull him tightly against me, crushing my breasts. My nipples tingle.

Then the floor vibrates, Marley stiffens, and I jump. Mum is standing just inside the door of the guesthouse!

I spring off Marley and pull down my top. He wipes his mouth and runs his fingers through his hair.

Mum just stares at us both, eyebrows raised, jaw tight. We stare back. My voice box is paralysed.

'Hello,' Mum says eventually.

I scratch around on my desk until my fingers meet with my hearing aids, shoving them in quickly.

'Umm, hi,' Marley croaks.

They both look at me. Marley hasn't heard me speak since the day at the bike shop when he started teaching me to sign, months ago.

It's not a big deal.

But it is. I'm going against everything I've started to become.

I take a deep breath. 'Mum, do you remember Marley?' My voice sounds hollow, the pitch strange, a bit wrong.

'Yes, I remember. Hello, Marley. Piper...?'

'Marley is my... *friend.*'

'So I see.' She puts down her bag and draws a deep breath. 'I'm making some hot water. Would you two like some?'

'Thanks,' Marley says, so I nod too, although I can't think of anything worse than sitting around drinking hot water with my mum and my... can I call him my *boyfriend* now?

Mum goes outside to light the rocket stove and Marley sinks his head into his hands. 'God... sorry.'

'It's not your fault. I didn't think she'd be home for ages.' Or maybe it has been ages. I check my wristlet, and it's early afternoon. I'm even hungrier than before.

We join Mum by the rocket stove and sip the hot water.

'Where do you go to school, Marley? Or have you finished?' she asks, polite.

'I was homeschooled.'

Mum frowns. 'You didn't go to school at all?'

'No.'

'But what about maths, science...?'

'My mum taught me.'

Mum does not look approving.

'Don't worry, I know that *A*-squared plus *B*-squared equals *C*-squared and how to use cos, sin and tan. And I know all the elements in the periodic table. I've read Shakespeare, too.'

This seems to reassure Mum, who apparently doesn't realise that Mary Magdalene failed to get these 'essentials' through to me. 'Do you live around here? Will your mum be queueing up for rations tomorrow? I might see her.'

'The rations are going to be recon, right?'

'There's not enough recon to fully fill out the ration packs, and they've sourced some wild food, so there'll be a mix.'

'My mum might be interested in the real food. But she wouldn't touch recon if you paid her.'

Mum's shocked. 'Recon is nutritionally—'

'Mum!' I cut her off. I can't let her spout the benefits of recon to Marley, of all people. It's mortifying, the way she assumes he is ignorant, with no idea he is politically passionate about big corporations and their power over the food chain. It's actually *Mum* who is ignorant. 'Marley and I need to go. I'm on security watch tonight.'

I'm actually wondering if I can get out of my shift, swap it with someone else – because then we could go back to Marley's place, and surely he and Robbie would give me dinner.

'Are you doing security watch too?' Mum asks Marley.

'Uhh, err.' He glances at me. 'Yes, I thought I would.'

Okay, that will work too...

Even better, as we're leaving, Mum opens her bag and takes out a box of recon. She hands it to me. 'You'll have to share it. They gave me one for each of us ahead of tomorrow's rollout.'

I take it with a grateful smile.

Connie's on the street with Taggert and Gary. 'CAN YOU WATCH THE GARDEN? WE WANT TO GO AND COLLECT CHOOK FOOD,' she fingerspells to me, her hand movements delicate as a dancer.

I nod, pulling off my hearing aids and putting them in my pocket. 'You don't have to do security with me,' I sign to Marley once they've gone.

He reaches out and tucks a strand of hair behind my ear. The gesture is exquisitely affectionate. 'I'd like to.'

I get him to help me water the plants, then we settle on the security platform and I press the button on the recon. 'Want half?' I ask.

Marley shakes his head. 'Nahh. I've never eaten recon in my life, and I'm not breaking my record now.'

I can't believe anyone would turn down food right now. It seems such an odd achievement to be proud of, especially when he clearly doesn't have enough to eat either.

'I don't have anything else to give you. There's nothing big enough in the garden...'

Marley shakes his head. 'S'okay.'

'Do you mind if I...?'

He shakes his head, and I shovel in mouthfuls of steaming hot roast pork, apples and carrot – not a meal I'd ever have chosen before, but it's delicious. Energy floods my veins, clearing my head.

Marley leans over with curiosity and inhales the steam. He makes a face. 'That doesn't smell anything like real roast pork.'

I've no idea what real roast pork smells like, so I shrug. 'I don't care.' I know I'm being a bit defensive.

He regards me carefully for a bit, then lets it go.

Once I've finished eating, Marley pulls me down so my head rests on his lap. We stay like that for hours, watching the garden and signing, then fingerspelling on each other's fingers when it eventually becomes too dark to see.

Everything feels right: my full belly, Marley and me snuggled up together... I can't believe it's real.

Marley leaves at dawn. I sleep until afternoon then wait for Mum to come home with rations rather than going to work. I need to EAT the minute she arrives. So, I draw in my journal, tend to my plants, message Marley, and help Connie make a new security roster – but still no Mum. I check the news.

NNEWSMELBOURNE

Ration Centres Chaos

Queues for the first packages of taxpayer-funded rations are blocks long, with fights breaking out among some citizens who've waited all day. Efforts to prioritise the elderly and families, and designated collection dates for specific streets, have been met with anger by those not listed immediately.

Australians will receive a packet of wheat, beans or lentils; powdered milk, tea and coffee; sugar and salt; butter or oil; eggs; and an Organicore package. To speed up the rollout, Organicore packs contain BioSpore plus a flavoured sachet of Nutrium Sustate powder for a do-it-yourself meal-preparation approach. The company has been unable to move sufficient volume of BioSpore to its state processing plants to provide ready-made meals as per their contract. Instead, farms are packaging BioSpore and transporting it direct to rations centres.

Still no Mum.

▶ To: Taylor
   Tay, I got together with Marley!!!

No reply.

It's almost ten pm when Mum finally walks through the door, the lines around her eyes made so much heavier by all the weight she's lost. She's wearing a baggy black T-shirt with *RATIONS STAFF* printed on it in white block letters, so unlike her usual tailored outfits that I almost don't recognise her. I throw my arms around her. 'Are you okay?'

Mum raises an eyebrow and hands me her bag. She knows I'm after the food.

Inside is a disappointingly small plastic-wrapped package stamped with a 2. Rations for two people. I rip it open and survey the contents. The eggs are full-size, but there are only two of them. Two eggs for a whole week! There's a plastic packet of what looks like hard red lollies. 'What's this?' I ask.

Mum sinks onto her bed and peels off her shoes and stockings. 'Kidney beans.'

'Do we have to cook them?'

'Yes – they need to be boiled. Heaven knows what all the people without kitchens are supposed to do. I couldn't get a straight answer about that all day.'

I hope they're filling, because there's only a handful here. The packets of milk powder, tea, sugar and salt seem small too, and I'm not sure how much they'll fill us up – maybe they're just there to make everything taste better. The recon packet looks promising, though. The box is a decent size – half a shoe box – and I'm excited about mixing my own recon. I hope they've taken the fat-destroyers out of this batch.

'Vide that ito seven days,' Mum says.

'What?' I ask, looking up. 'I mean, what did you say?'

'You'll need to divide the contents into seven, so we don't eat too much all at once.'

'Okay. I'll make us recon for dinner.'

'I'll make us tea,' Mum says. 'How I'm craving tea with milk.'

I've never tasted real tea – just weeds steeped in water.

'There's no coffee, though,' she goes on. 'And where's the butter? I thought we were getting either butter or oil too?'

I check through the box but there's nothing more.

'Honestly, I'm not surprised,' Mum says. 'It was like a bomb had gone off in there.'

I sit outside with Mum while she makes a fire and puts water on to boil. Carefully, I slice one-seventh of the BioSpore from the block and slide the white quivering mass into a small pot, since we don't have a mixing bowl. The flavouring sachet is labelled *Barbeque Flavour, with Nutrium Sustate* – so much for tailoring vitamins to the individual. Hmm. I can't quite visualise what this meal is supposed to be.

There are no instructions for what to do with this. I cut today's portion of BioSpore into four small gelatinous blocks and sprinkle them with the powder, then hold the pot out to Mum. She looks at it dubiously and eventually takes a piece. We each bite into it. It's...*revolting*. The flavouring powder is far too strong, and the BioSpore has absolutely no flavour at all. I chew and chew – it's like eating soft rubber.

Mum waggles her fingers to get me to look at her. 'Maybe it needs to be mashed? So the flavour is better integrated?'

I try that with the rest of my piece, but it's useless: squashed chunks of rubber covered with intense salty-sweet flavouring powder is no better.

'Do you think I should try cooking them?' I ask. 'Maybe they need to be cooked to get that authentic old-fashioned burned barbeque flavour?'

Mum shrugs.

I wait until the water's boiled for the tea, then swap it for the little pot with the other two pieces of powdered BioSpore, hoping it will fry, like little chops or something. Instead, the BioSpore melts into a transparent whiteish liquid with clumps of flavouring powder floating in it. I show Mum, who makes a face of alarm.

'How did they do it in the lab?' I ask.

She shakes her head. 'I never saw. I just focused on the Nutrium Sustate.'

'Now what?'

'Hmm. I suppose...we drink it?'

I pour it into two cups. I try tipping mine down quickly, but it's so disgusting that I gag. 'Urgh!!' Thick, hot, tacky goo sticks to the roof of my mouth and the sides of my throat. I swallow hard, but it doesn't disappear. Instead, a clump of flavouring-powder lodges itself onto one of my tonsils, burning me, my coughing unable to dislodge it.

Mum's having a similar experience, it seems, as she coughs and sputters too. She mixes up tea for us and hands me a cup. At first I can't taste it, but gradually it melts the BioSpore covering my tongue and washes it down, and then there's just sweet, milky tea…and it's delicious. The best thing I've ever drunk!

I sit down and blink at Mum, shocked. This was not how I envisaged the rations. I type 'How to prepare BioSpore rations' into my wristlet, but nothing comes up.

'Let's cook the beans,' Mum suggests.

I put them in a pot of water on the rocket stove, and we chat and drink tea while they boil. 'So it was chaos at the rations centre?' I ask.

'Beyond chaos. I stayed so late, but eventually all the staff had to leave, and everyone who was still in the queue was crying and begging us to stay, just dispense one more meal… I felt so mean.'

'Was it satisfying handing over the rations? The people who *did* get some must have been happy?'

Mum shakes her head. 'I wasn't dispensing. I was just on crowd control, checking people were in the right queue.'

Wow. I can't picture Mum in such an ordinary job. 'Did people recognise you?'

'Yes. Every second person was asking me questions, like I had some authority to change things. But I don't.'

I poke the beans with a fork, but they're still rock hard.

'You know, I think Organicore knew all along that they were sinking,' Mum says, and she might be talking more to herself than me. 'They could have paid us all and closed gracefully, paid out their shareholders. But instead they've lied to us to get us to work for free, squeezing that last bit of profit out of us, knowing they'll never be able to pay us.' She drains her tea.

I indicate our half-drunk cups of BioSpore. 'It doesn't seem like they're any closer to getting their act together.'

'The board collected all that money from the Australian government for rations, and they still couldn't give us actual recon. Just the unprocessed ingredients. That's a crime! I trusted them. Piper, I gave them my life. And in return, they've thrown me onto the street. I could have helped save them...if they'd just let me.'

'Mum, you need to accept that they've shafted you. Why would a big corporation that prioritises profit start prioritising people now?'

I sound like Marley. I like it.

'Hmm. I suppose. Are the beans ready yet?'

I check them again, but they're still hard pebbles. Mum and I sit up for another half-hour, until all the twigs for the stove are gone and the flame dies. The beans are slightly softer. Experimentally, I test one between my teeth. There's a thin coating of powdery stuff, like potatoes, around the edges, but inside it's like a rock. Nup, I'm definitely not eating that. I spit it out.

'These are going to take hours to cook,' I say. 'Where will we get the fuel?'

Mum shakes her head. Neither of us can face another go at the BioSpore, which has turned back into rubber in the bottom of our cups, so we go to bed as hungry as ever.

On my way to visit Robbie and Marley, I notice the bushes along the Merri Creek are getting smaller, with few dead twigs left under any of my favourites. I snap off some small branches instead, even though green wood doesn't burn so well. It's late afternoon and the bike path is packed with cyclists and families walking together. On the other side of the path a man is crouched under a different bush, collecting twigs so fine they're almost just dry grass.

'Did you get rations?' I ask Robbie when she opens the gate.

She grins, her eyes sparkly. 'We've got bread!' she signs.

'They gave you *bread*?'

She shakes her head, miming opening the rations packet, discovering the recon components and tossing them aside in disgust. Then she sees a packet of wheat, and her fingers jump up and down in her palm in excitement. She kisses the imaginary wheat packet, rips it open, and sets to work – grinding the grain, kneading, waiting while it rises. Finally, she bakes it, and the smell is heavenly. 'Come and taste it,' she signs, grabbing my wrist and leading me to the outdoor kitchen.

The loaf, wrapped in a tea towel, is dense and deep-brown, not the fluffy white I was expecting. Robbie cuts a thick slice, spreads it with butter and something dark from a jar, and hands it to me. And it's perfect: rich and heavy, the butter creamy and the other stuff tangy and sweet. My head clears.

'What's this?' I ask, pointing to the jar.

'Chutney.' She mimes making it in summer and putting away the jars for later when food is tight. 'Did you get wheat?' she asks me.

I shake my head. 'KIDNEY BEANS.' I mime our disappointing experience last night, doing my best to infuse it with the same level of emotion Robbie did.

'You need to soak the beans in water first. Then they'll be much faster to cook. Raw beans can make you really sick.'

Why doesn't it say that on the packet? We could have saved all those twigs! I hope biting a bean wasn't enough to infect me. I mime trying to read the non-existent words on the packet, and Robbie laughs.

'You can also grind them and make bean cakes.' Robbie gestures for me to follow. She hands me a small but heavy stone bowl with a rounded stone stick, and shows me how I should use them to crush the beans.

A pair of arms slides around my waist and I twist my head around in surprise. Marley! He kisses my cheek and pulls me close against him. Again I'm flooded with a feeling of rightness. How I wish I could stay here with these two. Robbie knows how to do everything, the flow of food is consistent, and the beauty is intense.

Once I've finished my bread and Marley has downed a slice too, he asks if he can steal me away. 'Come and see my room.'

He takes my hand and leads me upstairs. His room is tiny, set into the roof so you can't even stand upright, except in the middle. But it's homey, even though it's filled with stuff like an electric guitar and big black speaker boxes and a visi-screen that's bigger than I'd have expected for this little cottagey house.

He also has a double bed, which triggers the unpleasant image of him and Kelsey in it together. Marley sits down on it, and I sit beside him. 'When did you get a double bed?' I ask.

'I've always had one. This is where my other mum, Van, lay to tell me stories while I was falling asleep.' Marley gestures to the side closest to the window.

'Do you think about her a lot?' I ask.

Sadness crosses his face. 'Less as time goes by.' He swallows hard. 'I wish I could hear her voice. Or ask her questions. There are so many questions I should have asked her.'

'Like what?'

'Why she wanted to have me. She was really against over-population, so it seems strange she'd want a child. And yet it was hardly an accident!'

I touch his shoulder gently. 'Why not ask Robbie?'

'I have, but she just says Van wanted nothing more than to have me, and that she was so happy when she got pregnant with me.'

'How old were you when she died?'

'Ten.' Marley's eyes are shiny. He rubs them fiercely and says, 'Let's talk about something else, okay?'

'Okay.' Damn. I wanted to ask what happened. 'Umm...How many girlfriends have you had?' I ask.

'I dunno. I've never counted. First I was with Matilda, when I was seven and she was six.'

I put my hands on my hips. 'That doesn't count. I mean *real* girlfriends.'

'She *was* a real girlfriend! We kissed!' Marley puckered up tightly and pecked the air. 'What about you? How many have you had?'

I know he means boyfriends, but I deliberately misunderstand him. 'My only girlfriend has been Taylor, my bestie. Only she's not really my bestie anymore.'

'Why, what happened?'

I shrug. 'I'm worried about her. I think her boyfriend is stopping her from doing what she wants. He seems to keep her on a tight leash.'

'That's not healthy.'

'I know. He seems to be loaded. He has heaps of food, and I wonder if he's using that to get her to do what he wants.'

'How can anyone have heaps of food right now? That sounds seriously dodgy.'

'Yeah. I don't know what's going on with that.' I hesitate, feeling unsure, but then press on. 'She seems to have totally ditched me. And I know I should just be worried about what she's caught up in, but I can't help feeling really hurt. Why aren't I important enough to her to stand up to him? I can't imagine letting any guy come between me and her.' I feel better as soon as I've said it.

Marley purses his lips. 'Ouch. Have you told her how you feel?'

'Sort of. But I just felt like I was pulling her in one direction while he was pulling her in another. I don't want to be part of the problem.'

'Yeah. Sometimes I think we have to accept the ebb and flow of friendships. They don't always last forever.'

I know he's right. But it still doesn't feel right to just forget about Taylor, leave her behind me.

I run my hands through my hair thoughtfully, and Marley copies me, his fingers tangling in it. He catches my eye and the mood changes when he pulls it gently, teasing.

'You evaded my question before,' he says. He pushes me down onto the bed, leaning over me.

I twist to free my hands. 'What question? I would never do that!'

'How many boyfriends have you had?'

Oh. That. I'm surprised he even needs to ask. 'A big fat none. It's not like I've had boys queueing up to get with the Deaf girl.'

'*What?!*'

I shrug.

'Are you saying that because you're Deaf, no boy would want you?'

'Well, maybe, yeah.'

Marley sits up again. It's hard to sign while we're both lying down. 'I don't know what planet you're on, but being Deaf does not make you *any* less desirable. In fact, it makes you seem amazing, clever and alluring. You can *lipread*, for god's sake. Mystical talents abound!'

I blink and sit up too. 'Well, you didn't see it like that at first. You said yourself you didn't want to be with me because I'm Deaf.'

'Not because being Deaf makes you unsexy. Because I'm a twisted mess of confusing emotions that I needed to work out.

It took everything I had to try to convince myself that I wasn't madly in lust with you. Trust me, I'm not the only guy who'll feel this way.'

My mouth falls open at this, but before I can reply Marley wrestles me back down and we're kissing, his breath hot in my mouth, flavoured with bread and chutney and something else I can't quite place. I close my eyes and lose myself in the softness of his lips and tongue. His hands slide up my back, and it feels as though he's holding not just my body but my soul too. I tangle my legs around his, squeezing him tight to me, pressing my face into his neck and scratching my fingers down his chest over his shirt, then back up under it.

His skin against mine is electric, tingling. I inch his shirt up until it's bunched around his armpits, and when he pulls it off I take mine off too, so we're both just wearing jeans, except I have my bra on.

We hold each other, our lips grazing together, his eyes a direct line into mine, until Marley leans over and switches off the light. After that all communication is body language, except when I turn on my wristlet to message Mum. 'I'm staying at Taylor's tonight.'

SUNDAY 15 NOVEMBER

As soon as I get home, Mum hands me a package. I hot up when I see the contents: a tiny pill that will protect me from pregnancy and sexually transmitted diseases for three months.

As soon as I've put my hearing aids in, Mum starts. 'Don't ever lie to me again!'

'Mum! I didn't...' I stop. I've never been a good liar.

'You haven't seen Taylor in months, and all of a sudden, just after you get a boyfriend, you're *sleeping* at her place?'

I slump. 'We didn't have sex.'

'And I'm not encouraging you to. Take it slowly. But swallow that. I don't want you pregnant. And don't lie to me again.'

'Okay. I won't.'

She gives me a look – a good, long, hard one – and hugs me. I hug her back. Then she turns away, fiddling with her wristlet. There's a blare of disjointed white noise: her news feeds.

I pull out my journal. Soon after, Mum tosses an empty recon box at me. She's excited. 'Piper! You nivatol me!'

I fumble my hearing aids back in. 'Pardon?'

She holds out her wristlet. It frames a photo of me and the pond, the colours even more vibrant than in real life. You can see every detail of my skin, and tangled, greasy hair, and yet somehow in the photo I look striking and compelling.

I switch on my wristlet and tap through to the news.

McBride's Daughter Rejects Recon in Bid to Solve Food Crisis

Piper, the sixteen-year-old deaf daughter of former Organicore scientist Irene McBride, has turned her back on manufactured meals and is taking her chances growing wild food. In a move that's proven popular with her neighbours, Piper's created a thriving community garden on the nature strip down the middle of her Northcote street, which she expects will provide an abundance of vegetables, eggs and meat for the community.

Piper, an artist whose work you may be familiar with from posters across the city, has designed and created an appealing space, bringing together isolated community members. Neighbours contribute tools and skills to support her vision, and take turns protecting the garden from potential vandalism.

'We didn't know each other before Piper started this,' says neighbour Connie Sato, 'but we've found food production can be a pleasure.'

The garden is an exciting model demonstrating how communities can work together to address the food crisis while adding beauty to our streets and strengthening human connections. Piper encourages News Melbourne followers to contact a group called Transition Towns to learn more. 'The first step is to make compost,' she advises.

If Piper can do it, anyone can – and, in fact, only blocks away a copycat garden is being created by another local, inspired by Piper. Her inability to hear has not prevented her from creating a little oasis in the city.

Breaking news: McBride's Garden Scheduled for Demolition. In a heartbreaking move, as we prepare this story for the feeds, the local council has classified Piper McBride's community garden as 'litter' and insists it be removed. What do you think?

share your views

There are more photos, all stunning: Taggert, close-ups of the chooks, my compost poster.

'What's this about rejecting recon?' Mum asks.

I shrug. 'I never said that. Though maybe I will reject it now, after trying home-prepared BioSpore!'

'Hmm. I guess it's a sensationalist way to hook in readers.' Mum looks me over, her eyes narrowed. She seems…approving. 'You've done a good thing, Piper.'

Did she need to read about it in the feeds to get that? She's seen me out there day after day, but she's thought I've just been faffing around with a pile of weeds and a bunch of dropouts. I guess I have been, and I *am* a dropout – but Amber makes it sound glamorous.

'Maybe now you'll forgive me for not going to school?'

Mum shakes her head. 'I still think you're making a mistake there, Piper. But it's *your* life. I can't stop you.'

Mum's so stubborn – she will never change her mind. But will the council, with all this publicity?

My wristlet buzzes. It's Madison, from school. I haven't thought of her in ages. 'Seems you are on to bigger and better things. Way to go, girl!'

I raise an eyebrow. She never spoke like that to me at school. I like her casual, friendly tone, and it strikes me as a pity that I never knew she talked like this back at school. In fact, the whole school thing suddenly seems unbearably sad. How different things might have been if I'd understood my classmates and had been able to have actual friendships with them.

My wristlet buzzes again. It's Alice, my art teacher. 'So exciting to read what you're up to! I hope you're keeping up with your journal. Drop in some time and show it to me.'

The next message is from Taylor. 'Pipes, you're famous! And now you have a boyfriend called Marley?!! We have so much to talk about. Sorry I had to rush off the other day. I can't wait to hear it all, truly.'

I blink hard, then fire back: 'Yep, can't believe I have an actual boyfriend. You sound...different. Is everything okay?'

To my astonishment, she answers right away. 'How'd you *know*? Beau and I had a fight. He was in a mood, driving dangerously – I think he wanted to scare me. So I got out of the car, and he drove off! Arsehole.'

Driving – his own car?! 'Where are you? I can meet you.'

'Footscray. Thanks, but I'm walking. Almost home. He'll calm down and get over this, don't worry.'

'I'm worried about *you*. What kind of boyfriend dumps you in Footscray? Not cool. And what do you mean by dangerous driving?'

'You know, going fast, slamming on the brakes, doing skids. I hate it when he does that. But it's only when he's mad, and he didn't dump me, Piper – I got out. So that's my fault.'

'Today wasn't a one-off?' This is bad. Can't Taylor see that? 'I get having food is awesome, but...' I start cautiously.

'I know, I know. It's complicated, though. Not easy to extricate myself.'

'But you *want* to? Leave him?'

'Argh. I have to go – I'm home.'

'Taylor, don't go in! I can help you sort things out. Come over! Or let me come to you.'

'It's just not that simple. Pipes, I need to go deal with this. Love you.' She signs off with a kiss, and once again she's gone.

I sigh shakily, feeling a little sick. I miss her so much, and now I'm even more worried than I was before. I consider telling Mum, but…what could she do? Taylor didn't ask anything about Marley, either. It's unbelievable that I have my first boyfriend, and I haven't even told her how it happened.

My wristlet continues to buzz intermittently all afternoon – everyone I've known seems to have something to say. I watch the feeds too, as people log their dismay that my garden will be demolished. Amber adds another update saying that News Melbourne will be seeking commentary from the council.

I show the update to Mum, and she rewards me with a cup of milky, sugary tea. We've worked out we can have two cups each a day. We ate the eggs on Thursday, beans on Friday, and Mum, it seems, polished off the last of the beans without me when I didn't come home last night. There's nothing left now but the BioSpore, and it's dinnertime…

I open the packet again and look at it doubtfully. It's meant to be full of calories. Calories = energy, right? I carve off a slab and try eating it plain, no flavouring powder, no heating, no nothing. I might as well be eating a rubbery brick, and have to chew and chew, which is gross, but it doesn't actually taste bad. It's just…an effort. And it does make a difference – I feel the calories hit my bloodstream.

I hand a slice to Mum. 'I think this is the only way we're going to get energy right now. Next time you get rations, try to get a pack with wheat in it. We can make bread.'

'You can't tell what you've got till you open the pack,' Mum says. 'And it's not like I have a say. They just hand me my package, same as everyone else.'

I'm not used to Mum being the same as everyone else. I'm not used to any of this.

293

MONDAY 16 November

Councils Open Kitchens to Aid Rations Struggles

Australians have not embraced their ration packages, which the government modelled on an adapted version of those supplied during World War II. Recipients report confusion about what the ingredients are and how to prepare them, with lack of fuel and long cook times being the most common complaints, particularly from those in kitchenless apartments. Local councils are responding by setting up kitchens with volunteers to cook legumes and grains in bulk, capitalising on fuel efficiency. Australians will be able to present the legume or grain portion of their rations at their local kitchen and receive an equivalent quantity of cooked food in return.

kitchen locations   volunteer

Northcote Town Hall is mad – people everywhere, so many queues. I touch the arm of an older woman with a friendly face and sign to her, trying to make it as visual as possible, showing her I'm looking for the council kitchen queue. Her face lights up in recognition, but she doesn't point me to a queue – she talks instead, and nothing fits. I put in my hearing aids and am assaulted with such an intense blare of white noise that I immediately turn them off. No way can I distinguish a single voice in the midst of all that. She's still talking. I catch the word *feeds*.

Could it be she saw the article about me? I watch her face carefully and, yes, there are words that fit. *Inspiring… garden…community…* There's a question on her face.

'Yes, that's me,' I sign.

Her next words are clear: 'I knew it!' She hugs me, then points me to a queue snaking right up High Street.

A few others recognise me outside, including a girl aged around eleven. On one side she has dirty blonde hair falling past her shoulder, and on the other a shaved patch and large scar where I'm guessing a bionic ear has been implanted.

'PIPER?' she fingerspells.

Her signs are different from Robbie's and Marley's, her movements small and swift, hard to decipher. But, concentrating hard, I figure she's telling me something about seeing the story

295

on her wristlet, realising I was Deaf, and doing a huge double take, reading the rest of the story with great interest. She gestures for me to join her at the back of the queue.

'My name's Selike,' she signs, and I have to get her to fingerspell her name twice. She shows me her name sign, her palm sweeping across her face in the same line as her hair. I show her mine.

'Why's that your name sign?' she asks, copying the sign.

I tell her it's because I love drawing, and she gets it immediately.

'Did you grow up in Melbourne?' she asks.

I nod.

'I haven't seen you around. Where did you go to school?'

I explain that I grew up oral, glad to know the right terminology, and that I've only just learned to sign. I remember the protocol of the Deaf community and obligingly ask where she went to school. Within fifteen minutes we've exchanged our entire life stories in superficial terms, and she tells me I should come to the Deaf club.

'Do you know Justin?' I ask, remembering the guy at the bike shop who invited me to go to the Deaf club with him.

The girl nods. She uses her hands to describe him – big muscles, shaved head, and for an instant she becomes him, standing with exactly his confident, broad-shouldered posture. 'He's friends with my dad. I've known him my whole life.'

Two hours in the queue disappear fast, and I realise Marley was right when he said that I'll always have instant friends in the Deaf community. I just have to sign in public, and they'll make themselves known to me.

Finally we get to the table at the front, and an exhausted-looking guy with thick dark curly hair fanning out from under his cap asks me a question. I frown, uncertain.

Selike touches my elbow. 'You need to give him your rations.'

I fish them out of my bag and give them to him – this week we got lentils, not wheat. While Selike hands hers over, I snap a discreet photo of her and send it to Marley. 'Do you know her? She's Deaf.'

He messages back right away. 'Yes. Selike. Her whole family's Deaf. Robbie used to babysit her mum when she was a teenager. I still remember the day Selike was born.'

Selike and I wait while the man serves our food into containers. 'Does the bionic ear work?' I ask her.

'I understand more with it. But it doesn't make me hearing,' she signs, and lays her palm briefly over the scar. 'It still hurts. It feels weird in my head.'

The man hands us each three plastic containers with the labels *dhal, chilli* and *wheat porridge*. Wow. I thought I'd just get cooked lentils, but apparently all the rations are combined and everyone is served the same meal selection. It's hot and I want to get this home to Mum as quickly as possible. She should be finished her shift by now.

I say a hasty goodbye to Selike and pedal hard to get home. Mum's thrilled about the still-warm dhal, which is creamy and delicious and slides down my throat thickly, warming my belly. I taste the chilli, a sophisticated thing they've done with the kidney beans and some kind of flavouring, and the beans are soft as flour as they melt in my mouth. Incredible. The porridge is sweet, and after a single mouthful Mum sets it aside and says we can have some for breakfast.

Filled with dhal and chilli, my limbs feel warm, open and heavy. 'So, how was your shift at work?' I ask.

Mum shrugs. 'Long. Slow. Gives me lots of time to think.'

'About what?'

'Organicore seems to be on its last legs. If…*when* they fold…food's future will be wild again. Which is hintly unsafe.'

'Which is what?'

'INHERENTLY UNSAFE.'

'Well, not really. We've been eating wild food for thousands of years, right? Marley's only had food poisoning once, and it wasn't serious. You don't think those food-poisoning stories are just a scare tactic?'

'Of course they're a scare tactic! But that's not what I meant. Nutritional deficiencies are a major problem. Parents trying to get their kids to eat the right stuff is a nightmare. Maybe I could remake Nutrium Sustate into a basic single nutrition supplement people could take daily with wild food. I'll put in the fat-destroyers, cancer zappers, virus preventers, everything. Complete nutrition and medication in a pill. Or maybe in a lolly. The kids would eat that.'

'You'd better omit the fat-destroyers! But won't a pill cause the same problems as recon? Making people sick?' I ask.

Mum nods. 'I need to get a lab, sort that out, then do *thorough* follow-up tests. This time I won't let anyone bulldoze me into releasing it before we have the long-term results.'

'But a lab costs money…'

Mum nods. 'I think Karen Kildare will be interested in this. We just need to wait for Organicore to go right under. In the meantime, I'm putting together a proposal.'

Of course she is. Mum's mind is far too busy to ever settle as a queue manager. I suppose that's how she became Organicore's head scientist in the first place.

I'm at the bike shop, trying to find a wheel the right size for the bike I'm building, when Marley wheels a trike through the front door, his skin glistening with sweat. He's been helping someone move house.

'Cam messaged me. Transition Towns is organising a rally,' he signs, and I have to get him to fingerspell the last word, as I've never seen it before. Clever – it looks like a person holding up a sign at a protest march.

'What for?'

'To protest the closure of Sprouted Earth. And they're hoping to legalise food-growing on public land. It's in three weeks.'

I suddenly feel a bit embarrassed. I've been miserable about the orange stickers all over my garden, but it never occurred to me to do something large-scale to protest against it.

'They're wondering if you can design a poster promoting it?'

'Sure,' I say, flattered.

I show Marley the bike I'm working on, asking if we have any wheels the right size, and he points me in the right direction. My mind whirs with poster ideas. I remember Kelsey suggesting I turn my 'Grow Food Not Concrete' drawing into a poster for her. I never did get around to it. I can adapt it now, adding the rally details.

As soon as the wheel is affixed, I snap a photo of the drawing and send it to Cam, finding him in a list of Marley's friends.

'Something like this for the rally?' I ask. I hope he answers today, because I'm inspired to do this tonight.

But when I'm finally done with the bike, there's still no reply. I show Marley my message and ask if Cam usually responds quickly.

'Oh, that's perfect for the rally. But, yeah, I think Cesspool deletes any messages along those lines?'

Really? I test this out by shooting Marley a message: 'Looking forward to the rally.'

We wait, watching Marley's wristlet, but he's right – nothing comes through. I try a couple more times. Still nothing.

Marley sends me a message saying, 'I'll meet you at Fed Square on 19th Dec.' My wristlet buzzes right away as it lands. But when he tries the same message with the words *gathering* or *rally* added, they don't arrive.

Wow. I had no idea we were being censored like this. I'm suddenly glad I didn't get the job vetting content at Cesspool. I'd have become part of the great machine of oppression. Then again, maybe I could have let some rallies slip through.

I stew angrily for the whole ride home. Is that why they took over the internet? I'm appalled at my own naïvete; at how I believed Organicore and the government were working for our greater good. I pull out my journal as soon as I get home – I want to vent onto the page, but I'm not sure how to express it.

I start by drawing myself in profile, then pasting words from Grandma's old books and magazines coming out of my mouth. I find a picture of a large pair of scissors, cut around them and glue them in so it looks like the words are being sliced off as they leave my mouth. I peel off a few words and re-glue them sideways, as if they've just been snipped and are falling to the ground. *DON'T DELETE MY VOICE*, I write.

Yes! That says it.

Kelsey is having a party to promote the rally. It's in her garage – her family car's in pieces on the front lawn, so presumably the garage is no longer needed – and Marley has somehow convinced me that it's a good idea for us to go together. I haven't seen Kelsey since she and Marley split up, and I'm not at all sure about being here.

'It's just a meeting to organise the rally,' Marley reassures me. 'Only Kelsey never does *meetings*, because that would be too boring.'

We push through a throng of people, Marley leading the way, clasping my hand tightly in his, pressed against the small of his back. I love being with him, knowing that people see us together. When he spots Kelsey and waves to her, I squeeze his fingers, nervous.

She makes her way to us and grins, throwing her arms around Marley. If she's upset about the break-up, it doesn't show at all. She turns to me just as warmly. 'Piper! You're famous!' Marley supplies the sign for *famous*: thumb to forehead and fingers splayed out, which I see is made from the signs *know* and *all*. Known to all. I like how Auslan can be so sensible, literal.

I shake my head and shrug, not sure what to say. As usual she's vibrantly beautiful, an old-fashioned green peasant blouse leaving her golden shoulders bare and glowing.

302

'No, really,' she says, and Marley interprets her words. 'My wristlet hasn't stopped buzzing. We have so many new Transition Town members I'll have to throw another party just to welcome them all!'

I can actually lipread about half of what she says, but it's so nice not having to strain to figure out the confusing bits, with Marley interpreting. If only there was some way to convey to him which words I missed.

'Did you know your story's been picked up by Everything Australia and...'

But I don't catch the names of the other feeds running my story, because someone's grabbed Marley and he's not interpreting anymore.

I shrug, happy to let that be the end of the conversation, but Kelsey wants to say more.

'Woodoo consata spikking at the rally? Well, signing. Weaver. You know.'

I consider putting my hearing aids in, but there are too many people here; they'll be useless. I shrug and turn my palms up, and mime typing on my wristlet.

Kelsey gets the message and types on hers. But before I've even read it, I work out what she said. *Would you consider speaking at the rally?* I check her wristlet and I'm right.

I stare at her, aghast. It's one thing to do a school presentation with no one paying attention, but to stand up in *public* and *speak*?!

'Ask Robbie,' I type back. 'She knows way more about food growing than I do. So does Cam. Can't he speak?'

'He's going to. But what you're doing is something special. It's not a bunch of radical Transition Towners trespassing on public land – you have ordinary people, neighbours, a mix of young and old, and you're transforming *your* street, which belongs to all of you. You show that food in public spaces is for everyone, not just activists. And…you being Irene McBride's daughter…that makes it extra strong.'

'I'll think about it.' To get off the subject, I open my wristlet photos and flick through to the adaptations I made from my 'Grow Food Not Concrete' sketch. 'I tried to message this idea to Cam, but it didn't get through,' I type.

Kelsey raises her hands and shakes them. She's evidently remembered how Deaf people clap. 'I love it!' she types. 'We had the same problem with messages. Then we made a Cesspool info-centre about the event, without using any protest-type keywords…but it was denied. Just like any info-centres about growing real food are denied. We have to get the message out, though, so we'll print and paste up posters instead.' She leans over and takes a photo of my photo using her wristlet. 'We can't let them silence us.'

I let her know I agree by showing her a photo of my 'Don't Delete My Voice' artwork.

'Oh my god, I love this too!' she types. 'It's perfect. Do you mind if I steal it too? It's just…*so good!* And I want to make censorship a key issue at the rally.'

'I'm planning to make a stencil of it,' I type.

'Maybe we can spray it onto placards for the rally? You should definitely spray that onto walls, too – fill Melbourne with this message. It concerns everyone. It's incredible.'

I nod and glance around, looking for Marley. He's halfway across the room, laughing with a bunch of guys. 'I'm sorry. You know, about Marley.'

Kelsey laughs and types, 'S'all right, darling. He's hot as, and a really nice guy. But I prefer them without a truckload of emotional baggage. You can have him.'

That shocks me – that she can dispose of him as if he's some little boy who's annoyed her by crying too much. That she can see him so differently to how I do. Am I just young and naïve? Or is Kelsey callous?

I drift through the crowd until I land at Marley's side. He's talking to Cam and Angelo, the teacher from the food-growing workshop. He puts his arm around me, then withdraws it to interpret. 'We're talking about Cam's family farm.'

'What's happening with it?' I sign to Cam, to be polite. I check Marley's voicing my words, and lipread as he repeats them.

Cam speaks and Marley signs. 'It's been occupied by the military. They call my parents their *employees*, but really they're now slaves, working crazy hours to harvest and load the BioSpore, with no pay in sight.'

'They need to get out,' Marley signs, shifting his shoulders to show that it's Angelo talking now.

'They can't,' Cam retorts. 'They're worried they'll lose the farm altogether if they leave. And where would they live?'

Angelo says something else, and this time Marley doesn't interpret. He seems kind of tense, his jaw locked tight. 'I'm just gonna grab a drink,' he signs, and disappears. The conversation rolls on around me, and I can't follow it, so I drift off again.

I spot Robbie across the room signing emphatically to a man about her age, who's answering with a mix of awkward fingerspelling and mime. Robbie tips back her head in polished laughter, seamlessly fitting in. An older woman dives between them, grabbing Robbie for an exuberant hug, and Robbie launches into a story. She's drawing in the air, adding dramatic flourishes using her face and hands, while the group around her stands gripped, laughing, putting their hands to their mouths in horror. I realise that to these people, Robbie is not some Deaf person to be pitied, to feel sorry for. She's an asset, her communication striking and magnetic, drawing people towards her with intrigue and flair.

Just then, everyone in the room freezes momentarily, then turns towards the front of the garage. Kelsey stands on a plastic crate, tapping a microphone. Next to her, on another crate, stands a man dressed formally in a suit. I slip my hearing aids from my pocket and slide them into my ears – with everyone quiet, I stand a chance. But Kelsey holds the microphone close to her mouth, blocking her lips.

As she speaks, the man beside her begins working his hands. It takes several moments for me to realise that he's an interpreter – not like Marley, who just helps with communication, but a real, professional interpreter. I follow his gaze and see that he's signing directly to Robbie. I don't think he has any idea that there's another Deaf person in the room.

I don't understand a single sign except *thank you*. Is he even using Auslan? When he fingerspells, he does it so fast that I can't catch the individual letters of a single word. How is this comprehensible to anyone? Unlike Robbie's expressive face, his hardly moves.

I shift my eyes back to Kelsey. She's moved the microphone back a bit. 'Not easy,' she says, then turns her head towards the people on the other side of the room, so that I lose my line of sight again. I feel the familiar stirrings of a headache, and a sudden wave of despair washes over me.

I will never, *ever* belong.

Robbie can use Auslan to captivate an entire room. She's alluring and glamorous, and she communicates stories so clearly that even people who don't sign can understand her. But my signing is like a child's, pinned to awkward, literal lexicons and laboured spelling. I'll never be able to do what Robbie does. *Never.*

I cast my gaze through the crowd for Marley, but my eyes blur and my throat chokes tight. I have to get out of here before I embarrass myself the way I did at the food-growing workshop, which suddenly feels like it was only yesterday. I put my head down and push through the crowd.

What's wrong with me? I never cried about being Deaf before this year. But suddenly I can't take it in my stride anymore and everything's upside down.

I'm outside, in a garden. It's too dark to make out more than shadowy outlines, but one of them looks like a person, so I turn the other way. I lose my balance and almost fall over, cursing the fact that while other people use their middle ear to balance, I have to use my eyes. Not easy when it's dark. I anchor my feet widely apart to steady myself. I resist the urge to spread my arms wide too.

A hand closes around my wrist. Marley! I extract my hand and sign, 'What are you doing out here?'

He signs something back, but I can't make it out in the dark. I swivel us both so a thin glimmer of light from the garage falls on him, and he tries again: 'Why aren't you watching the speeches? They're being interpreted.'

I shake my head, blinking hard to smother the tears, but one escapes. I rub at it hastily. 'Because I can't understand him. The only interpreter I understand is you!'

Marley stands stock-still for a moment. Then he lets loose a barrage of signs, and I take that back about being able to understand him. I pull him closer to the garage door, so he's in a wider beam of light.

'What?'

'That is *exactly* the problem!' He's upset. Very. Him too! What just happened? His jaw works hard, Adam's apple bobbing up and down, his eyes too shiny. 'I can't do this! I can't. I can't be the only person you understand. I can't go to a party with you and spend the whole night interpreting!'

'I never asked you to interpret!'

'No, but you stood there all innocent, not taking charge to get Kelsey to communicate clearly with you. You just waited, and how could I do nothing, knowing it was all going over your head? You just left it for me to fill in the gaps.'

'I did not! I fully expected to come to this party and understand nothing and no one. Because that's how it's always been. Other people don't worry about filling in gaps for me, so I just don't understand!'

One of the things that's drawn me to him is the way he doesn't accept that as good enough. He always seems to believe in my right to understand and participate, even though I'm not sure I believe in it myself. It seems too good to be true. And now I see that it *is*, because Marley is signing big, angry.

'You assumed I'd interpret for you! You liked it! And the minute you can't follow everything, you're out here sulking.'

'That's rubbish!' I slam my hands together, furious. Though if I'm honest, he's right. And maybe that's why I'm so upset about not understanding Interpreter Man. One taste of inclusion, that incredible, unknown feeling of being able to participate, and I can't bear to go backwards. 'I have never once in my life asked anyone to interpret for me! When you interpreted, YOU chose to do that!'

Marley takes a step backwards, hands in the air in a gesture of surrender. 'This is why I knew I couldn't be with you! I should have listened to myself. I knew it. I'm not your keeper, and I don't want to spend my life being responsible for you!'

With that he's gone, disappeared into the darkness.

I feel sick. My hands tremble. Kelsey's words come back to me: *I prefer them without truckloads of emotional baggage.*

But, to be fair, I have as much emotional baggage as he does; I'm out here crying and upset too. Tears snake down my cheeks as I mount my bike, and they drip onto my shoulders as I ride home. Is it over already? Two and a half sweet weeks with the love of my life, and it's gone, just because I let him interpret for me?

My dreams are a horrible mishmash of Kelsey's words and Marley's.

Would you consider speaking at the rally? I can't do this.

I KNEW I COULDN'T BE WITH YOU.

I prefer them without truckloads of EMOTIONAL BAGGAGE.

I don't want to spend my life RESPONSIBLE for you.

When I open my eyes, and Marley and I being over hits me again, all I want to do is cry, but I blink hard and push it away. I picture myself speaking at the rally, but that just makes me feel even worse. I put my hearing aids in and sit up. 'Mum?'

She's in bed too, surrounded by folders and plastic sheets covered with diagrams, working on her proposal. 'Mmm?'

'Could you speak at our rally? About how we need to let people grow food on public land?'

'What would I know about that?'

I think of Kelsey saying my speech would be extra strong because I'm Irene McBride's daughter. Well, it would be even stronger to have Irene McBride herself speak.

'You could talk about the dangers of recon, warn people it hasn't been properly tested. About food-poisoning stories being sensationalised to scare people into eating recon. Say you've realised the future is wild food, and we need land to grow it on.'

'That would break my confidentiality.'

'So? They're going under. Surely it's more important to let people know the truth?'

'I could be sent to prison! Absolutely not.'

'Can you ask Karen Kildare if she'll come to the rally? We need her to understand the importance of change. Whenever we try to promote it on Cesspool, or through messages, it gets deleted, so it's not like we can send her a message to invite her.'

Mum blinks. 'I can barely get Karen Kildare to talk with me about *my* project. She's very busy. It's not easy being the prime minister through a major crisis.'

'This will help *ease* the crisis!' I want to throw myself into her arms. Cry, and tell her about Marley. But she'd want to know what the problem is, and I can't tell her about signing, the interpreting. She wouldn't understand. 'Umm…*did* you talk to Karen Kildare about your proposal?'

Mum nods. 'She likes the idea. But for later, once the food-and-fuel crisis is under control. In the meantime, I'm putting together the details. I want to have a budget for her, so that as soon as the money's available she can route it into this.'

I lie back against the pillows. Marley's angry face appears in my mind. *I am not your keeper…* I shake my head to clear it.

I wish I could talk to Taylor. I know I can message her, but this is cry-on-your-shoulder-in-person stuff. The loneliness of being without her hits me again, stronger than ever.

I push that away too, get up and pull on my clothes. I wonder if it's still okay to go to the bike shop, now Marley has broken up with me. He and Kelsey are still friends, so presumably he

and I can be friends too. But I can't face the thought of seeing him today. I'll work in the garden instead. That'll distract me.

It's so beautiful on the street now, with waist-high green growth, masses of yellow, white and purple flowers, and flickering water in the pond. I pluck a handful of weeds, inhaling deeply, trying to calm myself, and toss them into the chook pen. The chickens scramble over in a rush, fighting for the weeds, all larger now, with fully grown white feathers and tiny red combs at the tops of their heads. I check the nesting box Zoe built onto the side of the chook house, but there are no eggs yet.

The tomato plants are tied to metal stakes, an offering from Gary, who had them in his garage. Some branches have grown too long, trailing towards the ground, so I grab some string and set to work tying them up to the stakes.

Zoe taps my shoulder. She's with Amber, Halim and Taggert. I didn't see them arrive. 'I THIEGHT I COULD BOILD A TOOL SHID,' she fingerspells, so slowly that it's hard to keep my eyes on her hands. Wow. Connie must have taught her, because I didn't.

'IS THERE ANY POINT?' I ask, gesturing to the orange stickers. I've been feeling more optimistic after the reaction to Amber's article. Today, though, everything just feels hopeless again.

But Zoe can't read back my fingerspelling. I contemplate writing in the dirt, but she'll get faster if I make her practise. I spell my sentence three more times. She says the letters aloud, and Amber helps turn them into words. Gary sees us together and joins us. I throw him a smile between letters.

Then they all turn and smile politely at someone behind me. My mother.

I wave at her lamely, instead of greeting her as normal.

She's frowning. 'Piper, what are you doing?'

I know she means, *What's with all this hand stuff?*

When I don't answer, Zoe says, veeeeeery slowwwly, finger-spelling at the same time, 'WE'RE WIRKING OUT WHIT TO BOILD NEXT FOR THE GARDIN.' I still have my hearing aids in from earlier, and her voice is strange, embarrassingly drawn out. I wish she'd talk normally, ditch the signing.

'I'M ZOE,' she goes on, spelling her name carefully without mouthing the words or using her voice at all. It's clear she wants Mum to see what an effort she's made to learn to communicate with me.

Taggert lifts his hands and spells 'TAGGERT', though Mum already knows his name. Someone must have taught him to fingerspell too. I didn't even know he could spell yet! This is really taking off.

Mum stares around at us all, one eyebrow raised, then she swallows and says, 'Well, this is nice. Is this some kind of sign language club?' Her eyes bore into me.

I can't answer her, because then Zoe and Taggert, Halim, Amber and Gary will hear me. They'll wonder why I've forced them through such complicated, stilted communication when we could have been talking normally to each other all this time. Gary will find out that when I 'speak well', that's not even half of it.

I freeze.

Zoe says, fingerspelling along with her slow, slow voice, 'WE'RE JIST MEKING SURE PEPER IS ONCLUDED.'

My cheeks burn. My throat's so tight I might gag. I resist the urge to fan my face. I just want to bolt.

I make a snap decision. Mum will have to deal with it. I'll treat her like she's anyone else I just met. Defiant, I lift my fingers and sign, 'We're trying to decide whether to build a tool shed.'

No one understands me.

Mum's eyes widen and she stares at my hands.

No! I had it all wrong. I shouldn't have signed. She'll be so disappointed in me. And she's going to blow my cover, for sure. She'll ask me when I learned sign language, and everyone will know not only that I *could* lipread them if I chose to but also that I can't sign fluently to save my life.

I turn and run for the guesthouse, throwing myself onto my bed. Mum trails in after me, bewildered.

I feel like I've been ripped in half. Half One has to be a perfectly *normal* person. Half Two is Deaf and signs and doesn't speak; people meet Half Two in the middle when it comes to communication. But I can't introduce them to each other, because one of them is lying, and I can't figure out which one.

'Is this some world-class secret you've been keeping from me?' Mum asks.

I shake my head. 'I just…learned some sign language from Marley, and I like it.'

'But Marley's not deaf. Is he?'

'No, his mum's Deaf. Robbie.'

'Is she the one you've been learning gardening from?'

I nod.

'So all those people on the street, who

you've made friends with, think you can't speak – is that right?'

'Yes.'

'But Piper, *why?* You speak so well! Aren't you proud of your voice? Of how well you communicate? No one would even know you were deaf if you didn't tell them.'

'That's exactly the problem, Mum! When no one knows I'm deaf, they don't tell me what's going on! No one knows how much I'm struggling to understand, how left out I am. I'm so sick of the headaches...'

'What do you mean? What do the headaches have to do with this?'

'I finally worked out why I have them. From lipreading! When people sign to me, I don't get a headache.'

'But you always still lipread outside of school – during your holidays – and you don't get headaches during the holidays.'

'School is concentrated lipreading, all day!'

Mum's not convinced. She stares at me, her eyes flashing. 'What will they think? That I didn't bother to raise you properly? That I didn't care enough about you to get you speech therapy, or make sure you could cope in the real world?'

She sinks down into one of the blue velvet chairs, the one I normally sit in. 'It's mortifying, Piper. I gave you everything, *my EVERYTHING*, to make sure you have the skills you have today. You can't just throw it all away!'

'I'm not throwing anything—' But I can't speak anymore, because I'm crying. Mum's crying too, tears streaming down her face. 'You...you could...' I hiccup, my words stuttering, 'learn to...*sign.*'

Mum cries even more. 'I'm told talena...' There's more but I miss it, because Mum's face is in her hands.

'What?'

It takes two more goes for me to get her words. *Too old to learn a new language.*

'It's easy.' I want to tell her how visual it is, how quickly I picked it up, and that she's so smart she'll learn it with no problems, but I'm still crying too much to get my words out.

Mum sobs, '...too inept to communicate with my own daughter?'

I go to her and sit on her knee, wrapping my arms around her neck. 'Sorry,' I say, wishing I could make it all better. But I'm not prepared to give up signing and promise to be the 'normal' daughter she wants me to be. I'm not.

We cry and cry, and she holds onto me too. Eventually I extricate myself to set a fire in the rocket stove and make us some milky, sugary tea.

It doesn't help. All day, I'm restless. I unload myself in my journal, but even that makes no difference. I need to feel connected with someone, and there's no one. No Marley, no Taylor...Mum so upset and disappointed in me. I'm too embarrassed to go back to the street after running off the way I did.

By the time night's fallen, I've cut the final pieces out of my 'Don't Delete My Voice' stencil and decided to road-test it – and not in my garden this time. I pack a can of spray-paint, some rags and heavy-duty tape into my backpack, and tie my folder of stencils to my bike. I hear Mum saying something, but I pull off my hearing aids and pretend I can't hear her. I get on my bike and ride into the moonlight.

At first I head towards Brunswick, but then I change my mind. It's the council I'm mad at – who needs to pay attention.

So I ride to Northcote Town Hall. The kitchen is closed and the crowds have dispersed. There's no one around. On a fence outside, over the road from the hall, someone has painted:

NON-CONFORMITY MAY BE DISTURBINGLY LIBERATING

I love it.

A few people ride past me, rolling down High Street. There are no cars, no soldiers, no police, no people walking. Just cyclists. I pull out my 'Don't Delete My Voice' stencil and tape it to the footpath. Quickly, checking around me before I begin, I spray over it.

I don't even look at the image I've created until I've cleaned the stencil and hidden it away in its folder again. It's great: crisp and clear, black against the pale-grey path. It's my most complicated stencil yet, and I'm in love with it. A surge of adrenaline courses through me. This *is* liberating!

I cross the road and stand in the square, which sits between the council offices and the town hall. This time using a stencil version I made of my 'Grow Food Not Concrete' rally poster, I spray a path all the way to the front door of the council offices. I don't even stop between sprays to clean the stencil, or to check around me. *Spray, lift, move it along a bit, tape, spray again* ... I'm so absorbed in what I'm doing, the beautiful line of my art, that my horrible day melts away behind me.

At the front door, I try to wipe the stencil clean but the rag sticks – the layers of paint I've sprayed have become tacky. I set it aside to dry fully and pull out the 'Don't Delete My Voice' stencil again. I tape it right to the council office's glass sliding door, and I'm mid-spray when both my wrists are grabbed from behind. I jump and paint spurts, uncontrolled, beyond the stencil, onto the glass. The can flies from my hand. I twist around, trying to see who has me.

Police.

Oh god. What was I thinking?

But that was the point. I *wasn't* thinking. I needed a break.

The police officer holds me firmly against the door, my arms pinned high, and I feel his breath on my neck. He's talking. I need to let him know I'm Deaf, but I can't move my hands, and my hearing aids are in my pocket, hidden. I wriggle my fingers experimentally and he tightens his grip.

I twist my head even further around. It's hard to see his face properly in the dark, but this is not an officer I have encountered before. He's enormous, with beefy muscles and rough-looking skin. Beyond him I see another officer, her gun drawn, pointing at me.

What the hell? It's not like I'm an armed, dangerous criminal!

Maybe I should just speak with my voice? But no, something tells me they'll be more lenient if they see my Deafness.

I quit struggling and wait. The policeman puts his head close to mine and says something, his face harsh. He's asking a question. He repeats it, but I can't lipread

anything. I try again to move my hands, then mouth some words, maybe making a slight croaking sound with my throat, but I can't hear myself.

Suddenly he loosens his grip and lets go, standing back slightly, his arms out as if ready to catch a wild animal. I immediately pat my ears, a gesture that usually seems to effectively communicate that I'm Deaf.

He frowns. Nope. I figure that if I sign something, anything, even if he doesn't understand me, then he'll get that I'm Deaf. 'Sorry,' I sign. 'I just wanted to promote a rally…'

He has it now. 'Oh!' His face changes dramatically, features softening, though he's still intimidating.

The woman officer drops her gun and comes closer. 'Can you lipread?' she asks.

I lipread her question perfectly, because it's so obvious. But I stare at her blankly. She asks the question again, pointing to her lips, and I shrug. They speak to each other, then the man points to the other side of the square. He takes my arm.

I reach for my bag and the stencils on the door and ground. The woman hands me my backpack but holds up her arms in a large X to block my access to the stencils. She uses her wristlet to take several photos, then puts on gloves and gathers them up herself, along with the rag and the can of spray-paint, holding them carefully away from herself.

The man steers me down the street, around the corner, and next thing we're at the police station. Despite the late hour and the quietness of High Street, the station is busy, with a queue of people waiting for attention. They all turn to stare at me as the officers escort me inside. I drop my eyes, embarrassed.

I'm placed in a small room with a table, four chairs, and

nothing else. The only light comes in from the hallway. The officer lets go of me and takes my bag, emptying the contents onto the table, but there's nothing much in there, just a few pens and a handful of dandelion leaves. I left my journal at home. He holds out his hand, wanting something, and I shrug, confused. He points to my wristlet. Oh.

I unstrap it and hand it to him. Then he's gone, closing the door behind him so that the only light is a thin line shining in from under the door.

I wait and wait. I go to the door and try it, but it's locked. Eventually I lie down on the floor and shut my eyes, but I'm instantly accosted with unpleasant images. The officer's rough skin looming, too close. Marley: *I'm not your keeper.* Kelsey: *Will you speak at the rally?* Mum: *What will they think of me? That I am too inept…?*

I can't tell if it's half an hour or several hours later, but eventually the door opens and a dim light flickers on. The officer with rough skin shows in an elegant Asian woman with sleek long hair, dressed professionally in a black high-necked suit. I sit up and rub my eyes.

'Hi,' she signs in the light coming in from the hallway. 'Are you Deaf?'

I nod from my spot on the floor.

'Can you sign? Do you understand me?'

I nod again.

'I'm here to interpret for you. My name's Abbey Lee.' She signs clearly and gives me a warm, reassuring smile.

The officer says something to her.

She signs as she speaks her answer to him. 'You need to ask *her* the question.' She gestures towards me.

The officer turns to me and says something. 'What's your name?' Abbey signs.

'PIPER,' I fingerspell. I show her my name sign.

She relays my name to the officer, omitting any mention of my name sign, and he types it on his wristlet.

He asks her another question. Abbey points to me and waits.

After a moment he gets it and repeats the question, this time addressing it to me. 'I'd like to know your last name,' she signs.

'MCBRIDE.'

Abbey's eyes widen in recognition, but she doesn't comment. I give my address and date of birth too, as required, and the officer abruptly leaves the room.

'I haven't met you before,' Abbey signs when we're alone, her face pleasant. 'Where are you from?' She doesn't seem bothered by the idea that I'm potentially a criminal. She pulls out a chair from the table and sits on it.

'Melbourne. But I grew up oral. I'm only just learning to sign now.'

'When did you start to learn?'

'A few months ago.' I tell her about meeting Marley at the bike shop, and learning Auslan in order to take gardening lessons from Robbie. It feels weird sitting on the floor, so I join her at the table.

'You sign very well for someone who's only just started!'

'It's a pity I didn't learn when I was a kid. I'll never be fluent.'

Abbey shakes her head. 'You will be. I didn't learn until I was twenty.'

Really? She seems so...*fluent*.

'Give it two or three years.'

'By fluent, do you mean I'll be able to watch a Deaf person or interpreter signing full-tilt with no facial expression and actually understand them? Even if I arrive in the middle of the conversation?' I'm thinking of Interpreter Man at Kelsey's party.

Abbey laughs. 'It can be pretty hard to make sense of a signed conversation if you start in the middle, since when we're talking about people and places we give them a location in the air, then just point to them after that. So you wouldn't know what's being pointed to. But if *you* are having the conversation, then yes, I reckon you'd understand them, no problem.'

'I saw an interpreter who fingerspelled so fast I couldn't see a single letter.'

'When you get the hang of it, you don't need to see letters. You see the pattern of the fingers, and you come to know it.' Abbey does something with her fingers, which I'd barely have recognised as fingerspelling if I hadn't already seen Robbie and Marley talk to each other like that. 'SHOES,' she spells next, clearly. Then she shows me how the quick movement is made by brushing past each letter.

I copy her. It's not neat and flowing like she does it, but I can see where this is going.

'I can't read the letters of that word either,' Abbey says, 'but I know it means *shoes*. Even Deaf people, when they spell a word for the first time in a conversation, spell it slowly, and they only do the quick messy version once you know what they're talking about. That's another reason you can't dive into a conversation in the middle – you'll have missed important clarifying information.'

Oh. Why didn't Robbie tell me this? Why didn't Marley?

'Anyway,' she continues, 'half the Deaf community don't learn to sign until they're adults.'

I blink in surprise. 'Really?'

'Most people get fitted with a cochlear implant, or these days the bio-engineered ear. But in their late teens, early twenties, I know a lot of people who take off their cochlear implants and chuck them out, choosing to use Auslan instead.

'Anyway...' Abbey glances towards the door, 'are you okay? They were embarrassed about your arrest.'

'What do you mean?'

'They thought you were ignoring them when they told you to turn around. So they pulled out their guns...'

She stops as a new officer comes into the room. Her black hair is pulled tightly into a bun, a thin halo of dark frizz surrounding her face, and her shoulders are broad, intimidating.

She pulls out a seat at the table and sits beside Abbey, her thick round lips set together with a look of satisfaction.

'Piper McBride, you are being charged with two counts of vandalism of public property.' She waits while Abbey signs. Abbey is slow and careful, checking I've understood each word. 'You have the right to remain silent, and you have the right to a legal representative. Do you have a lawyer you can call?'

I shake my head. 'Can I message my mum?' I feel sick at the thought of telling her what I've done now, but she'll know what to do. I glance at the officer.

'You're allowed to make one phone call. No messaging.'

'I can't call my mum. I can't hear her! We always message each other. Please can I have my wristlet back, just quickly, so I can tell her where I am?'

'No wristlets. You may make one call.'

Abbey holds up her hand. 'Can I suggest…I can interpret a call to Piper's mother.'

The officer nods.

She hands me a device I don't recognise. I stare at it, confused. Abbey takes it from me and asks for Mum's Cesspool contact details. She enters them and holds the device up to her head. It's an old-fashioned mobile phone! I haven't seen one of these in years.

Abbey presses a few more buttons and sets it on the table between us. 'Hello?' she signs.

I'm not sure what to do. I can't talk to Mum like this! Abbey gestures for me to say something.

'Umm. Hi, Mum, it's Piper,' I sign, feeling awkward. I lipread Abbey as she voices my words. She adds, 'I'm speaking through an interpreter.'

Thank god. I never thought of saying that. Mum must be confused as hell.

'I'm at the police station,' I sign. 'I've been arrested. Can you come?'

The officer interrupts and says something. 'You can have visitors tomorrow,' Abbey signs.

'Umm. Not now. I mean, can you come tomorrow. Mum, do we have a lawyer?'

Abbey listens for a bit and then signs, 'Yes, but we can't afford a lawyer right now. She'll need legal aid. What has Piper done? Who is this on the phone?'

I glance at the officer and remember, from a million movies, my right to remain silent. 'I'll explain tomorrow,' I sign.

The officer gestures to Abbey to end the conversation and

she clicks off the phone. I spend the next while filling in forms for legal aid, and having my fingers and eyes scanned and my photo taken, with Abbey helping me, explaining the terms I don't understand. Finally I'm shown to a different room, a small concrete cell with several vinyl mattresses on the floor. One is empty and has a blanket folded on one end. The others are covered with the sleeping forms of women: blobs of hair and blanket. One stirs but no one wakes up. It must be way, way past midnight.

Abbey says goodbye. I don't want her to go. She shakes my hand and gives it a warm squeeze before leaving with the officer. Thank god I'm Deaf – imagine trying to do that all on my own. At least she was friendly and kind.

Wow. I've never been glad to be Deaf before.

I wonder if Abbey could be my friend? Maybe I could get some signing lessons from her. But I don't have her contact details.

I lie on the empty mattress, pull up the blanket, and wait for morning. I imagine Marley's arms around me, comforting me, but push the thought away. He's not my boyfriend anymore.

SUNDAY 29 NOVEMBER

I wish I had my journal with me. My arm feels naked without my wristlet. The woman on the mattress nearest to me wakes and sits up, but she doesn't look at me. She's hunched over, tattered long fluorescent-green hair hanging over her face, a thick band of white roots at her scalp. The skin on her arms hangs off the bones, crusty with scabs around her elbow. I look away.

The wall is painted a peeling pale-mint green, and I lie back and imagine what I'd draw on it: me, alone, everyone important to me tiny specks in the distance. I'd draw a birdcage placed over me, a romanticised version of this cell. I'm tempted to take out a pen from my backpack and draw directly onto the wall, pour out my heart.

Instead I wait. And wait.

And forbid myself from thinking about Marley, Kelsey, Taylor, Mum's unhappiness about me signing, the rally...

I have no idea what time it is when the door opens and the satisfied-looking officer gestures for me to follow her. I grab my backpack and she leads me back to the interview room. I'm astonished to see Mum sitting inside, beside a well-dressed man in his early thirties. Mum's face is firm and tight – she's in professional mode. I want to throw myself into her arms, but she eyes me with a steely gaze and I resist. The officer indicates for me to sit opposite Mum.

The man stands and signs, 'My name's Jacob. I'm here to interpret for you.' His signs are swift, tight, polished little movements. It takes me a moment to figure out what he said.

I glance at Mum, unsure whether to speak with my voice or sign. If I speak with my voice, will the officer think I lied last night, when I relied on the interpreter? Will Mum think I'm destroying my chances of getting out of this if I sign rather than speak? My gut tells me they'll be more lenient if I sign. *You'll just have to suck it up, Mum.*

I nod to the interpreter and sit down, fumbling in my pocket for my hearing aids. Everyone waits. Then Mum speaks to the officer, and even though I understand her perfectly, Jacob interprets for her. 'What charge do you have against my daughter?' I'm not sure whether to look at Mum or Jacob – it seems polite to look at the interpreter, but I'm not used to how he signs and it's easier to lipread Mum. I try darting my eyes back and forwards between them.

The officer speaks and I don't understand her, so this time I just watch Jacob, and I'm glad he's here. 'Two counts of vandalism of public property,' he signs.

'Vandalism? What did she do?'

The officer pulls a printed photograph out of his folder – and I can't help feeling slightly thrilled to see all my stencils in a pathway to the door of the town hall.

Mum takes the photo and squints at it, frowning. 'Piper was promoting a rally – is that correct?'

The officer shrugs. 'Something like that.'

'Are you aware that organising a rally is a legal activity, and that all efforts to invite people to attend are being censored on QuestTool?' I stare at her in surprise. 'Piper was left with no choice but to use public means to get the word out. Her right to freedom of speech is being denied.'

The officer speaks and Jacob signs, but it's too fast for me to understand. I do the sign for *again* as surreptitiously as possible, and then the sign for *slow*. Mum throws me a confused look, then quickly irons her face back to professional tightness.

'Sorry,' Jacob signs. He says something to Mum and the officer, and they wait while he catches me up. I have to ask for several repeats, but eventually he gets how slowly he needs to go for me. 'That's for a judge to decide at trial. In the meantime, Piper will need to wait for a bail hearing.'

Bail hearing. We don't have money for bail. Will they remember the possum? Will it hurt my chances now? What if they keep me here for *years*? My heart drops, terrified.

'...she's a minor?' Mum says. I miss the start because I'm darting my eyes around trying to figure out who to look at.

Jacob signs the officer's reply, something about sixteen being the age of *something* and *something* accountable for my actions. He's going too fast again, and I'm too embarrassed to ask him for yet another repeat. He has none of Abbey's warmth and kindness – his manner is detached, remote.

They talk for a few more minutes and I only catch some of the words. *Lawyer. Legal aid. Weekend. When will it be?* I give up trying to follow. I feel too shocked to concentrate properly, and Mum seems to have this in hand.

The officer stands and signals that the meeting is over.

'Mum,' I sign. Jacob voices for me. I can hear him. It's weird.

Mum's mouth drops open at the sudden intimacy of being called *Mum* by a stranger. Jacob gestures towards me to indicate that his words are actually mine. Mum blinks and looks at me, raising an eyebrow in masked exasperation.

'Can you contact Kelsey for me?' I continue. 'Tell her what happened, and that I can't speak at the rally if I'm still here in a fortnight?' Jacob interprets, and the officer waits by the door, impatient.

'Who's Kelsey?' Mum says to Jacob. She glances at the officer, who is drumming her feet. 'Scrap that. What's her contact?'

I supply Kelsey's Cesspool address, and Mum thanks Jacob curtly. I'm not sure she realises it was *me* talking. The officer indicates that Mum and Jacob are to head down the hall, then he leads me back to the cell. I realise I have no idea when the bail hearing is, how long I will be here or what's happening next, and now Jacob has gone. I fight a rising sense of panic. I should have been more switched-on.

Back in the cell, another woman is awake now. Her boots are unlaced, and one heel flaps off. Hoping she doesn't speak to me, I curl up on my bed and face the wall. I need something to think about – something pleasant. Anything to take my mind away from the terror forming in my belly over the idea that I could be in jail for a *long, long* time.

My garden.

I recall each plant, unfurling leaves of green, tiny flickers of an insect in the pond that could be mosquito larvae or tadpoles. I wonder when the vegetables will be ready to eat. Maybe I should try Kelsey's way, and throw a party for the street to celebrate our first harvest. I could rebuild my rocket stove on the street. We could cook one of the chickens...

Monday November 30

The day lasts forever. It's punctuated once with a welcome bowl of hot, delicious food that I recognise from the council kitchen. I make it last for as long as I can. Thank god they're feeding us. Still, is this going to be my life now? Head down, avoiding eye contact, my entire history (or rather, herstory) playing out in my mind while I flop listlessly on a sticky vinyl mattress? Other women come and go, but I keep my face turned away, too full of despair to try to communicate with anybody.

The door opens and it's an officer I haven't seen before. He makes an announcement I can't hear. We all stare at him. He's thin, and his blue uniform has faded to a dark grey. He says it again. And again. I think I lipread my name. *Piper McBride?* I raise my hand slightly and he looks at me. 'McBride?'

I nod, and he indicates for me to come.

Along with several women from another cell, I'm loaded into the tray of a ute. The cab's been cut off and it's pulled by four horses. We lurch down High Street, Hoddle Street and into Victoria Parade, and eventually stop outside the courthouse in the city. I wish someone would tell me what's happening.

We're herded through court security, where we're patted down and dusted for drugs, before we're eventually locked into a small room with real wood panelling on the walls. It seems tree vandals have not tapped into this particular source of bounty. I clutch my backpack tightly, wishing again that I could work on my journal. Instead, I wait and wait.

Hours later, the faded officer reappears and leads me to a private room. I can't contain my excitement when I see Abbey. I grin, so relieved to at last have someone I can connect with. I want to hug her, but she's standing beside a stocky old man with a beefy face and unruly white hair. His suit is rumpled and he's looking at his wristlet. He mumbles something. Abbey frowns and signs, 'I can't hear him. He's your lawyer.'

'What's going on?' I ask.

'This is your bail hearing. The lawyer is from legal aid and will represent you. We only have a few minutes before we start. He'll probably have some questions for you.'

I look up at him and he's tapping furiously at his wristlet.

'I'm Piper McBride,' I sign, and Abbey voices my words.

He glances up briefly. 'Nick Brown,' Abbey signs.

She raises an eyebrow at me, acknowledging his abruptness. Then she signs, 'Announcement. We need to go in now. Stand when the judge enters and leaves.'

I follow them out of the room. The officer is waiting outside. He positions himself tightly beside me and we enter a courtroom – a small hall with green carpet, long wooden benches to sit on, and more of the opulent wood panelling on the walls. There's a high bench at the front and huddled groups of people on the long benches. Some, like me, look dishevelled and dazed, wearing rumpled, unwashed clothes. Others are dressed more formally.

I scan through the faces and there's Mum! She's sitting near the front, her head swivelling as she looks for me. She seems less tense today and shoots me an encouraging smile. I show her the panic in my eyes and she gives a reassuring grimace.

'Can I sit with her?' I sign to Abbey.

She relays the question to the police officer, who says no, I'm to sit with him. We're still making our way along the bench when everyone stands. The judge enters, an older woman with her hair pulled back tightly and an old-fashioned sharp black suit. She sits behind the high bench and everyone else sits too. The police officer, lawyer and I take our seats and Abbey stands at the end of the row, facing me.

The judge calls other cases. Abbey interprets, but I don't understand – too many names and long words fingerspelled. Suddenly Abbey sharpens and signs, 'Victoria Police versus McBride.'

My lawyer and a well-dressed woman stand before the judge. The exchange is so fast I don't catch it properly. *Graffiti, vandalism, public property, minor, only sixteen, lives with her mother, first offence, fifteen-hundred dollars.*

The judge bangs her gavel. The police officer and lawyer lead me out into the foyer, and Mum hurries after us. She grabs me in a tight hug, her eyes shiny with tears.

'I don't have the money, Piper,' she says, desperate. The officer indicates that she needs to go now, and tells the lawyer that he has five minutes. Mum steps back, panic in her face.

I try giving her a brave smile as they lead me away. Once we've turned the corner, I sign to Abbey, 'What just happened?'

'Your bail has been set at fifteen hundred dollars. It can be paid at the registry office. Otherwise, you will be held on remand at the Melbourne Custody Centre until your trial.'

'When will that be?'

Abbey shakes her head. 'They didn't discuss that.'

What if it's months away? My heart sinks, nausea rising. Why, why wasn't I more careful? How will I cope with jail?

THURSDAY
DECEMBER 3

Day Four at Melbourne Custody Centre...It's so crowded here that there are fold-out beds in the hallway and recreation room. Mine is in a corner under a large visi-screen. Every half an hour or so, someone approaches to try to turn it on, sometimes hitting it or kicking my bed in frustration when they realise there's no power.

I'm making a routine: Sleep as late as I possibly can. Stretch on my bed. Walk circles in the small concrete yard. Try not to think about food. Lie on my belly on my mattress and draw with my finger.

I'm doing an imaginary drawing of the tool shed Zoe should build when a hand grabs my shoulder. I jerk up in alarm, but it's just a security guard. He indicates for me to get my things and follow him.

He ushers me to a small office, where he hands me my wristlet. I blink, dazed. What's going on? He speaks but I don't understand him. I follow him out of the room, and suddenly we're in a reception area.

Kelsey and Marley stand together, waiting for me.

Have they got back together?

When they see me, their faces light up. I glance at the security guard but his face is blank. Am I free?! I'm not sure.

I run to them anyway, and they take me into their arms in a tight, three-person hug.

I thought Marley didn't care about me. But here he is. 'Are you okay?' he signs after releasing me.

The security guard sees him signing and speaks to him. Marley glances at the guard with irritation, but he interprets. 'He says, *Tell her she needs to sign for the conditions of her release.*'

I want to slap the guard for being so presumptuous. But I also want to slap Marley – he could have told the guard he's not here to interpret. Hastily I go to the desk and press my thumb against the visi in all the required places. Then Marley, Kelsey and I are free to go.

'Did you pay my bail?' I sign to them outside, incredulous. Marley voices my question for Kelsey.

She nods, enthusiastic, and lets out a torrent of words. 'The Transition Towns members all got together – everyone contributed something, to raise it.'

My mouth drops open. *What? Why?* Then I abruptly close it and hold up both my hands. 'Marley, stop,' I sign. 'Don't interpret. Kelsey and me, we can write to each other.' I press the button to turn on my wristlet, but the battery is flat. I shake it in frustration, but of course that doesn't help.

'It's okay,' Marley signs. 'I'm happy to interpret right now. I just don't want to be *obliged*.'

I eye him warily. I don't trust this. What if he suddenly changes his mind and feels obliged?

'Well, you have to stop the instant you've had enough, then. Kelsey and I will find a way.'

Marley nods. They unbolt their bikes from a bike rack and we walk together, the two of them wheeling their bikes.

'Why on earth did everyone at Transition Towns pay for *my* bail?!' I ask.

Kelsey talks and Marley signs. 'You were promoting the rally, which I'd asked you to do. It's my fault. It's not fair that you were scapegoated.'

'It wasn't your fault! I was careless. I got absorbed in what I was doing and forgot to watch for the cops. I'll pay it back, I promise. I just need to finish paying off my debt to my mum first.'

Kelsey shakes her head. 'People put the money towards a cause they believe in. You took the fall for all of us. We're going to talk about this at the rally – how our freedom of speech is blocked. You can work this into your talk, too.'

I take a deep breath. No way will I get out of speaking at the rally now. I owe them.

Marley says, speaking for himself now, 'I love the line of stencils you painted, right up to the council doors. It's the perfect spot, with so many people queueing there every day.'

I didn't think of that. I just wanted to get my message through to the council. But of course – it must be awesome advertising!

'Did you see the feeds?' he goes on. I'm not clear if it's Marley or Kelsey who said this. Maybe Kelsey, because she holds up her wristlet to me.

McBride's Daughter Arrested

Piper McBride, the sixteen-year-old daughter of Irene McBride, has been arrested. McBride junior, creator of a popular inner-city community garden, was charged not for 'littering' the street, but for vandalism of public property. Transition Towns leader Kelsey Maine claims Piper was legitimately attempting to promote a gathering they have been unable to advertise using traditional means. Victoria Police, however, report that McBride was on a destructive graffiti rampage. A judge will settle the question when McBride goes to trial. Watch News Melbourne for updates.

Oh god. Everyone knows.

Kelsey taps for more information, and I see the article was written by Amber Lawrence. 'The woman on your street!' Kelsey says. 'I asked if she could do a story in our favour, but everything she writes is censored. This was the best she could do.'

I wish she hadn't written anything at all. I'm mortified to think of all my neighbours, friends and old schoolmates picturing me on a 'destructive rampage'. And what will this do to Mum's reputation?

Kelsey nudges me. 'I'm sorry but I've gotta go now.'

I give her a tight hug. She may have been the big-mouth who spoke to Amber, but she also got me free. I still can't believe it. She high fives Marley and rides off. No hug. No kiss. I guess they aren't together.

Marley and I stare at each other awkwardly. I want to melt against his chest, but he's standing back, slightly stiff. And yet he's here. He must care about me at least a little.

'I'm sorry,' I say. 'About the other night. I never meant to upset you. Don't ever interpret for me if you don't want to.'

He nods. 'S'okay. I kind of overreacted. I guess I need to work out where I stand on all this stuff. It's not your fault.'

I put my hand tentatively on his arm, finger the golden hairs. 'So…do you want to…continue where we left off?' I ask.

Marley chews his lip. 'I do and I don't…I don't know…I think I need to sort myself out first.'

I close my eyes briefly. I want to persuade him, lure him. But that would be pressuring him to do something he doesn't want, and he'd just get mad at me again later. He's right. He does have to work himself out.

'Because I'm Deaf,' I say. I knew it.

'No, Piper. Not because you're Deaf. Because I can't figure out how to navigate the Deaf world and the hearing world and to what extent I want to be part of each, and how much I want to help and how much I want to watch the people I love being excluded. I can't win, you know.'

I take his hand and squeeze it briefly. 'I need to go and tell Mum I'm out,' I say. 'Do you want to come with me?'

Marley shakes his head. 'I'd better get back to the bike shop.'

'I'll see you there tomorrow?'

I hold my breath, but he nods. Thank god.

We hug a bit stiffly and ride side by side until the town hall. Now to find Mum. I hope she saved up my rations. I'm starving.

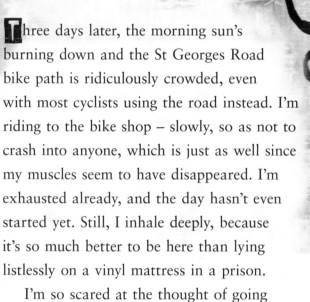

Three days later, the morning sun's burning down and the St Georges Road bike path is ridiculously crowded, even with most cyclists using the road instead. I'm riding to the bike shop – slowly, so as not to crash into anyone, which is just as well since my muscles seem to have disappeared. I'm exhausted already, and the day hasn't even started yet. Still, I inhale deeply, because it's so much better to be here than lying listlessly on a vinyl mattress in a prison.

I'm so scared at the thought of going back to jail if they find me guilty at my trial, whenever that may be. I half-hope Transition Towns might raise money for a good lawyer, who could get me off based on my right to freedom of speech, but that's probably wishful thinking.

My wristlet buzzes. It's Taylor and I pull over. She sent me a sweet message when I let her know I was out of jail, but nothing since. Typical. Now she's messaged me the link to an article.

339

Ringleader of Major Tree Vandal Gang Arrested

Police believe they've caught the ringleader and several other members of a large gang of tree vandals during today's early-morning raid of two Fitzroy homes and a warehouse. Officers of the Tree Crimes Squad, working with Australian Federal Police, received an anonymous tip-off leading to the discovery of wood from a large oak tree believed to have been stolen from Thornbury. A search of the warehouse also revealed traces of rare timber from the now defunct Botanical Gardens in Melbourne, suggesting that this gang has been operational for several years and may be behind the mass removal of trees that led to the closure of the gardens. Beau Williams, 28, thought to be the ringleader, and his co-accused faced a Melbourne court today and were refused bail.

Oh my god. *Beau!* That absolute creep.

I shoot a message straight back: '*TAYLOR, your* Beau? That tree was the centre of my friends' incredible garden, Sprouted Earth. They're a part of Transition Towns, who're organising the rally I got arrested for promoting. Everyone's still DEVASTATED about it. Were you involved???'

'Of course not. I didn't have a say in what Beau did. I'm kind of in shock – I mean, I knew he was up to dodgy stuff, but I can't believe he's in *jail*. I'm just... rethinking everything.'

'Rethinking being with him?'

'Yeah. Everything is suddenly a lot less complicated without him here. Maybe I *can* leave him…But it feels a bit mean to break up with him just when he got arrested.'

'Do what's right for YOU. How would you like it if someone stayed with you just because they felt sorry for you?'

'How are you always so wise? I'm going to pack my stuff and go back to my parents'. My god, they are sooooo mad at me.'

'Tay, they'll probably just be glad to have you back. Like me.'

I think about turning around and riding to Beau's place, offering to help her move, but in truth I'm still stinging from the way she dropped me. If she really leaves Beau then maybe she'll build space back into her life for me. In the meantime, I have bikes to build. Wearily, I climb back onto my bike and force myself to pedal on.

It feels like forever since I've spent time with Robbie. When she opens the gate and sees me, she grins and hugs me.

'Thank god you got bail!' she signs, and I learn a new sign – *thank god*, a single, swift movement that starts as a *thank you* and morphs into the sign for *god*. Clever. 'Did they treat you all right in jail? Are you okay?'

I nod. 'I'm fine. What are you doing? Can I help?'

Robbie takes my arm and leads me to the animal pens, which she's raking out. The sun burns down on us as we work. I covered my plants with sheets this morning, to protect them.

'When do you think we'll be able to start eating?' I ask her, holding out my wristlet with a photo of my garden.

Robbie studies the photo carefully. 'Some of it's ready. Pick those peas right away. The lettuce and rocket – take a few outer leaves.' She fans her face with her hat. 'I reckon you'll get your first decent meal around...'

I don't recognise her last sign, her middle finger touching the palm of her opposite hand. 'What's this?' I ask, copying it.

'SOLSTICE. SUMMER SOLSTICE.'

'When's that?'

'21 DEC.'

Oh, that's only a week away! I picture everyone gathered on our street in a Kelsey-style party. I'll invite Robbie, because she taught me how to do it all. How I'd love to serve everything all delicious, the way Robbie does. The things she adds to her vegetables – the butter, oil, salt or honey – make the difference between bitter slimy greens like the weeds from near the river versus a proper, satisfying meal.

'How do you have salt, oil and all the extra stuff to make food taste so good, when you can't get it in the shops?' I ask.

Robbie leads me to a brick shed behind the house, entering a combination on a padlock on the door to let us in. The cool inside is exquisite. Once my eyes adjust to the gloom, I make out shelves and shelves of jars and buckets. Everything is neatly labelled.

'How did you ... Why ...' I can't work out the right question to ask. Why does Robbie ration her eggs when she has so much food stashed away? Why are she and Marley always hungry too, even if they do eat way more than I do? There's so much here, *so much!*

'I get this food direct from farmers, and sometimes I buy from the Transition Towns co-op. We get about one chance a year to buy each thing, except for the butter, which I get from a friend with a cow once a month. Then I preserve it in jars or store it in buckets. I have to make it last, so I ration it carefully.'

'Is it too late for me to do something like this? Now that petrol is too ...'

Robbie shakes her head. 'Join the co-op. And start saving. When you have the opportunity to buy food, you want to buy a whole year's worth, and that can be expensive. I mean, per meal it's cheap – way cheaper than a recon subscription – but when the time comes, you need to be ready to hand over several hundred dollars.'

I gulp. I have to sell one more bike and then Mum will be all paid off. Now I know what I'm going to do with the money I earn after that. Unless I'm locked in jail ... I'm still waiting on a date for the trial. Or unless my garden is entirely destroyed by the council on New Year's Eve.

'How did you know to save up all this food?' I ask.

Robbie shrugs. 'It's just a cheap, healthy and efficient way to eat – I've done it for years. I like supporting small farmers instead of those monoliths ruining our soil with BioSpore.'

I can't meet Robbie's eyes after that, thinking of how excited Mum was when farmers began switching over to BioSpore crops, and how our whole life has been centred around Organicore's success. Marley has surely told her who my mum is. I disengage and browse through her shelves. Robbie leaves me to it, closing the door carefully behind her to keep the heat out.

Some time later the door opens again and Marley stands silhouetted against the light. I pull him inside and quickly shut the door to keep it cool. His skin against mine is electric, and abruptly I drop my hands and step back. We stare at each other, awkward, even though we just saw each other yesterday at the bike shop. But at the shop he's all business now, so I keep my head down and work. Now he's staring at me intensely.

'I just wanted to say…' he signs, and then doesn't say anything.

I wait.

'Umm…about working myself out…I guess…it's not really possible.'

Despite the heat, my belly goes cold inside.

'I mean, it's not possible to work myself out. There's no easy answer to how a CODA fits into the Deaf world or the hearing world. So I'm just going to muddle along and hope I can figure things out as I go.'

I frown, confused.

'Umm…would you like to muddle along with me?'

My eyes widen. 'Are you suggesting we get back together?'

'Yeah. If you want to, of course. Maybe you don't. I wouldn't blame you.'

'Of course I want to! But…what about the interpreting thing?'

'I'm sorry. I was completely unfair to you. I know that now.'

'But what about in the future? I think you shouldn't interpret for me, ever. I'll survive. I've survived every day of my life so far, and no one interpreted for me before I met you.'

'Then how did you participate? Socially, I mean?'

'I didn't. I've only ever had one friend anyway. It works when it's just the two of us.'

My eyes hot up and I blink to try to stop the tears. I remember playing a game of dolls with the other girls in Year One when suddenly they ran away and I didn't know why. Later, one of them said, 'You broke the rules!' I didn't even know there *were* rules, much less what they were. I remember school camp, everyone playing Chinese whispers and me laughing with the rest of them, even though I couldn't play unless I started the whisper.

I take Marley's hand and use his fingers to wipe my tears. 'I think I need to learn to change things myself – to ask people to repeat themselves and communicate ways I can understand.'

Marley nods. 'I'm still happy to interpret sometimes. I just need to be able to stop when I've had enough, or when it's preventing me from participating.'

'Do we have a deal, then?' I ask, holding out my right hand.

Marley takes it and we shake.

'One more thing,' I say. 'If something goes wrong and it feels like it's not working, rather than picking a huge fight with me and ending it all, how about you *talk* to me so we can see if we can work it out?'

'Yeah. Sorry about that.'

Gingerly, I slide my hands into the sweat beneath his singlet and rest my head against his chest, inhaling as deeply as I can. He gathers me tight against him, fingers tangling through my hair, cradling my head softly, as though it's so delicate it might break. I stand on tiptoe, reaching for his mouth. His stubble grazes my skin, setting off small electric shocks. There's tenderness in his mouth, and urgency too.

When we finally go inside, Robbie's cooked dinner – a huge pancake thing called a frittata, loaded with eggs and vegies and butter and salt. It's rich and hearty and heavy in my stomach.

'Have you worked out what to say in your speech at the rally?' Marley asks as we eat.

'Yes, but it's impossible. I can't do it,' I sign, my mouth full.

'Why not?' Robbie asks.

'If I speak at the rally, all those people who think I can't speak will know I've been lying to them all this time.'

'So sign.' Robbie crosses her arms and nods: to her, it's a foregone conclusion.

'I can't sign my speech. My mum would die!'

'Hold on.' Marley holds up his hands. 'You're not lying to people when you sign to them. You're Deaf. It's within your rights to use your own language!'

'But it's *not* my language! My signing is so amateurish.'

Robbie leans forward. 'My parents don't like that I sign either. It's part of growing up. You can't always please your mum. You have to do what's right for *you*. So, ask yourself honestly, do *you* want to sign it or voice it? Don't worry about it being fluent. If you plan your speech in advance, I can help you to make sure it looks good. What do *you* want?'

I close my eyes briefly. An image flashes before me of Robbie at the party – glamorous, holding everyone captivated, standing with poise and grace. Could I be like her? Could I make a crowd think that I, too, am a person of mystery, possessor of a magical, extraordinary language that ebbs and weaves with your fingers, shoulders and face?

'I want to sign it.'

347

'Practise it plenty, and no one will notice or care that you are new to this,' Robbie assures me.

'What if someone asks me a question? I'll have no idea what they're saying.'

'We'll get an interpreter – someone who specialises in interpreting for oral Deaf and new signers. There are plenty around.'

'I know someone,' I suggest, 'but I don't have her contact details: Abbey Lee.'

'Abbey's great,' Robbie says. 'I'll ask her. She's always up for a good cause.'

'Can you show me how to sign the way you do?' I ask. 'With drawings in the air?'

'Of course. What do you plan to say?'

I bring up some notes I've been making on my wristlet and run her through the start. When I get to a bit about how beautiful Robbie's garden is, she stops me. 'Slow down. Be as you were in that very moment, and show us everything you felt.'

I do as she asks, but that means I just stand there looking around, because how can anyone know the wonder and amazement that happened inside me that day?

Robbie shakes her head and demonstrates. I watch everything play out on her face. 'Tilt your head back, look up high, see the trees; show awe on your face while you draw them with your fingers. Add a flourish here, to show their magnificence, their grandeur.'

Then Robbie's fingers become the vines, climbing up the trees, tangling across the branches, and she shows me that my face must now radiate peace and serenity. It's visual poetry.

'Everyone will fall in love with you,' Marley says.

'And with the idea of gardening and growing food,' Robbie says.

And now I understand that Robbie's true talent is her mastery of the fall-in-love moment.

It takes hours for Robbie to walk me through every bit of my speech. We add in little visual touches that even people who don't know Auslan will understand, such as using the sign for *house*, which looks just like a house, instead of the sign for *home*, which is your hand making an unintuitive little hump.

She makes me lay out everything properly: the pond can't be here and then later replaced by a house in the same spot, unless I've wiped the air clean. After some deliberation, we put Robbie's garden on my right, and I'm to remember to angle my shoulders that way when I talk about it. My own garden is central, right in front of me. Fairfield Park is in the distance, so I'm to lean my shoulders forward when referencing that. Who would have thought sign language is all about where your shoulders go? How does anyone make up this kind of theatre-signing on the spot? But Robbie does it.

Later, once the kitchen is all cleaned up and I'm stretched across Marley's bed feeling lazy from the heat, I ask him to play something for me on the guitar.

'You'd be able to hear me?'

'With my hearing aids. Without them I hear nothing, though if you plugged in the speaker and turned it up loud I might feel the vibrations, and to me that's just the same as hearing it, because I can't really tell where vibrations end and sounds begin.'

I put on my hearing aids and Marley sits on a ledge in front of the window with his guitar. The music washes over me, and though I couldn't say whether the song is happy or sad, romantic or cruel, to me it feels beautiful and it takes me away, outside of myself, the oppressive heat. My worries begin to drift off, floating, distant.

'What's it called?' I ask when he puts down the guitar.

'*All About You.*'

I shrug. I never know popular music.

'By Synchronic Bleaks. It's one of their hits.'

'Will you sign it for me?'

Marley sings and signs, and by the second time through I'm signing with him. I haven't learned a new song in ages, since if I play something on my wristlet it's just white noise. But watching Marley's fingers strum, his mouth as he sings, I get a sense of the music. Add in sign language, and suddenly I understand the rhythm, the energy, the flourish-y bits. It's beautiful – a lyrical dance that turns my insides to soup. By the time we finish, I have such a handle on the song that when Marley plays it on his guitar again I can lipread it, hear it to an extent, and sign along, music deep in my body. Taylor and Mum get sick of songs before I've reached this point of understanding.

Marley opens the window and there's a slight breeze – such a relief. I slide onto the window ledge behind him and wrap my arms around his waist while he plays another song, the breeze cooling my back, my head on his shoulder, absorbing the vibrations his chest makes when he sings. By the time the song ends, I'm kissing the nape of his neck, my fingers under his T-shirt, skating across his belly, which is slick with sweat. The guitar slides to the floor and then it's just us on the window ledge, mouths and fingers everywhere.

I sit in bed with my speech notes, running through them for what must be the hundredth time. My hands still stutter awkwardly while I remember the location of each subject and try to sync up the right facial expressions and shoulder positions.

Mum comes in from the rocket stove and places a tiny bowl of reheated porridge on the desk next to me. I put my hearing aids in. 'What are you doing?' she asks once they're in.

I scoff some porridge. Delicious. 'Practising my speech for the rally.'

'What do you mean?' Mum furrows her eyebrows, confused. 'You don't mean you're planning to sign it?'

I nod, squirming.

'What?! Why?'

'Because...' Suddenly words evade me. I think of Robbie, sophisticated and glamorous, but can't convey this to Mum.

Mum sits on my bed. 'Listen, Piper, this is not a good idea. You don't want people feeling sorry for you. You have such a nice voice. I'll help you work on projecting it strongly. Don't embarrass yourself like this.'

'Mum! I'm not going to be embarrassed by signing in public. That's *you*. Meanwhile, it will make food-growing feel accessible to everyone, even people with disabilities.'

'How does waving your arms around and pretending you

can't speak make food-growing accessible?! Do you know what those speech therapy lessons COST ?'

'Mum, you were rich! What does the money matter?'

'I was not rich when you were little. I worked hard for every cent, and before your father left I threw half of it away on his ridiculous art ventures. It wasn't easy. Remember that teacher's aide you had when you started primary school? She cost the earth, and the government only picked up half the tab!'

'Why didn't I learn sign language when I was little? Why didn't you?'

'I considered that at length, I really did. But I felt you'd use it as a crutch; that it wouldn't help you in the real world. You'd do so much better learning to lipread and communicate normally. I didn't want people teasing you for being different.'

I sigh. 'Mum, I'd rather be *different* and understand what's going on. I *am* different, there's no changing that, even if you try to cover it up with hearing aids and perfect speech. This is how I'm going to do it. I'm sorry – I really am.'

Mum's wristlet lights up and she snaps to attention. 'It's Karen Kildare!' She turns away, but I can see her in profile and still make sense of her words. 'Yes … Mmmm … Absolutely … I'm on board with that … When, do you think? … And the budget? … What if we make it part of the rations program? … Yes … I understand … Of course I'll develop a different formula, though it won't be needed if Organicore goes under … It would be better for the public if we start sooner rather than later …'

I gather they're talking about Mum's proposal for Nutrium Sustate to supplement wild food.

The conversation goes on for a while, then Mum's posture changes. 'Karen, before you go … what do you think about this freedom-of-speech business?...Of course you are, but it may be worth focusing on – there seems to be quite a growing movement...Are you aware there's a rally?...Well, it would show that you represent the younger generation...There's a lot of passion. It wouldn't be wise to lose them...No, no, they're wanting to grow food on public land, and remove censorship around advertising rallies, that's all...QuestTool *does* suppress a lot...There must be a way to open it up a bit while keeping it safe; just cut the pornography and truly inappropriate content...I think Organicore's fighting a losing battle, Karen. You have more power than you think...Yes, yes, of course. Lovely to talk with you. Do consider the rally – I think it would be a strong statement. You too. Bye, now.'

I grab Mum's arm, excited. 'Do you think she'll come?'

Mum shrugs. 'There's a good chance. She liked what I said about keeping the younger generations on board.'

'Thank you! Thank you for asking her.' I wrap my arms around her in a tight hug.

Mum lets me hold her for a bit, then disengages herself. 'I'd better get to work.' She busies herself, pulling on her queue-manager T-shirt and brushing her teeth.

I feel too self-conscious to keep practising my speech while she's here, so I pull out my journal instead and flip through the pages. Some look unfinished. I scrutinise one of them: it's a bit empty. I doodle in some flowers, and the page springs to life. There. That's better.

I faff around more, adding things here and there, then get sidetracked reading past entries. I find the word *deaf* and realise it should be *Deaf* with a capital *D*. I change it with a fine-liner pen, then flip back to the start and fix all the relevant ones.

Taggert and I hit the garden early, before the day hots up and turns the plants limp. The garden is incredible. There are stalks of corn nearly as tall as me, and tomato plants up to my waist; when I touch them, their tangy fragrance wafts around me. Enormous zucchini leaves fight for sunshine, crawling across the garden, and a pumpkin vine spills right out of the mandala garden and onto the road itself. The mosaic around the pond is barely visible, buried in a mass of green. We pick a small bowl of lettuce, rocket and peas. Watching my face carefully, Taggert reaches his fingers into the bowl and picks out a single pea. Slowly, allowing plenty of time for me to stop him, he brings it to his mouth and bites into it deliberately. His whole face spreads into a grin while he chews.

I eat one too. It's like candy, only better – sweet, with a floury-ness set to fill my stomach. Though of course a single pea can't do that. This is way better than any wild greens, as there's no bitterness.

Taggert reaches for another and I shake my head. 'We have to share them,' I sign. I mime us dividing the bowl evenly between our neighbours.

Taggert and I go to each house in turn. 'Hey,' Zoe says, rubbing her hand over her shaved head as she opens the front door. She's wearing only a T-shirt and undies.

Taggert holds up the bowl. 'Connie!' she yells, and after a few moments Connie appears wrapped in a sheet. I've never seen her hair mussed up before. I give them each a tiny piece of torn lettuce, one pea, and a rocket leaf.

They eat my offering slowly, appreciatively, and then give Taggert a high five. 'THANKS FOR BRIAKFAST,' Zoe says, fingerspelling it for me, still super slow.

'It's just a tiny taste,' I sign, taking care to make my signs really visually obvious. 'I think we should have our first proper meal on the summer solstice – a party to celebrate. What do you reckon?' I fingerspell *summer solstice* too, like Robbie did for me, then mime everyone coming together, and remember Robbie's advice about showing everything on my face. I draw a bowl of food in the air and show awe and heaven on my face as I pretend to eat from it. Connie and Zoe both give me the thumbs up. They understood me! And they like this idea!

We deliver greens to Halim, Gary and Amber, inviting them all to the solstice party, then go back to our place to share with Archie, Erin and Mum. Mum bites into her pea and chews appreciatively. 'It *does* taste good,' she says. 'I hope you can harvest all this before the council comes.'

And just like that, my buoyant mood deflates again.

SATURDAY 19 December

It's rally day. Am I really and truly going to stand up in front of a million people and give a speech? Oh my god, I feel sick. But I'm going to do it, because this is the person I want to be – someone who fights for change. Please, please let this make a difference. Then even if I'm sent to jail, at least I will know my garden is thriving and growing without me.

I walk into the big open public area at Federation Square with Marley and Kelsey, my head held high with a confidence I don't yet feel. We make for the stage, where people are setting up microphones and speakers. The square is already filling with people. I've never been to a rally before, but I've seen them on the news: hordes of people, passionately chanting, feisty, angry. This is nothing like that. The people of Melbourne look emaciated. They're hollow-eyed and listless, but with a determination about them. They've bothered to show up. They carry banners and placards saying things like *Grow Wild, Grow Free* and *Free Land = Free Food*.

Marley cups his hand over my cheek, gently turning me towards him. 'Piper, are you okay?'

'I'm fine,' I reply. That's a lie. But I shake my head to clear my nerves and give him a big smile.

On the far side of the stage I see a flurry of people in fancy clean suits and Cam hopping around awkwardly, greeting them, his red hair glinting in the sunshine. In the midst of them, I catch a glimpse of Karen Kildare. She came!

I point her out to Kelsey, who jumps up and down excitedly. 'Stay here,' she mouths to me firmly, and she hurries around the stage towards them.

Someone taps me on the shoulder; it's Robbie. She points behind me, smiles and waves. 'ABBEY LEE,' she fingerspells.

I turn and there's Abbey, her dark hair glossy against the jacket of her grey skirt-suit, which is in the same style as the one I've borrowed from a friend of Kelsey's. Abbey gives me a quick, friendly hug and signs, 'I didn't get your speech notes.'

I frown. 'I sent them. Oh! Cesspool probably censored them.'

'Okay. Quickly, tell me what you're going to say in your speech, so I can do the best possible job of voicing for you.'

I run her through it, keeping my signs as small and unobtrusive as possible so as not to attract attention, but even so, I see several people staring at me.

Abbey's eyes widen, and she puts her hand on my arm to still me. 'The speeches are starting.' We're only halfway through. 'Don't worry, I'll wing it.' I give her the thumbs up.

I look up at the stage and there's Kelsey with a microphone. Beside her is Interpreter Man from the party. My heart sinks. I'll never understand anything now.

Kelsey begins, and Interpreter Man's hands whir into action, but sure enough the signs don't make sense to me. I nudge Abbey. 'Do you think…is it too much to ask? Could you interpret this for me? Because I can't understand that man.'

She gives a sympathetic smile. 'He's a CODA. Lots of people find him hard to understand.' Then she adjusts her position so she's standing between me and the stage, and assumes the same facial expression as Kelsey.

'…Why should one person take the fall for us all?' Abbey signs, and I glance at Kelsey. 'Those charges need to be cleared, and Cesspool regulations need to be adjusted. The government has no right to block our communication.' I have to ask Abbey for a couple of repeats, as I don't know the signs for the longer words. *Regulations. Government.* She fingerspells slowly and clearly.

'Sorry, I missed a bit,' she signs next. 'I'll have to summarise. Kelsey's talking about food now. Public spaces are just that: public. We all have the right to use and access them, and now with the food and fuel crises, it's critical that we can utilise public land for food production…'

A guy I don't know taps my shoulder, leans close and says something in my ear. I lean back, trying to see his face. Abbey steps forward and indicates he should say it to her, not me. 'You're on next,' she signs. 'Please come and stand at the side of the stage.'

I follow them both to the edge of the stage. My heart pounds and my stomach churns. I can't believe I'm going to do this. Abbey signs a few more of Kelsey's words, but I stop her. 'I need to concentrate now.'

Kelsey walks offstage and hands me the microphone. A small river of sweat trails down my back, inside my jacket, and I wipe my palms on my borrowed skirt. I'm not sure what to do with the microphone, because I'm not going to speak into it, and while holding it I can't sign, so I stand there stupidly until Abbey takes it and steps graciously aside. She gestures, and I walk to the middle of the stage.

I stare out at the crowd. The whole place is packed. I can't see the ground at all, just a sea of faces, banners and placards. A little way back, to the left, a familiar child catches my eye, hoisted on the shoulders of a man. Taggert! Next to him are Zoe and Connie, Halim, Gary and Amber. Is Mum here? I scan the faces, but I can't see her.

I stare blankly, while the whole crowd looks at me. Suddenly my eyes find Robbie's. She's at the front, her face raised expectantly. She holds up her hands, prompting me with the first few signs of my speech.

As soon as I start, I'm fine. I introduce myself to the crowd and show them my name sign. My signs roll automatically off my fingers, my eyebrows and shoulders doing their thing obediently. I show myself falling in love the moment I saw Robbie's garden, and the magic that such beauty can also provide food. My fingers draw the barren, empty strip of tree stumps and dead grass down the middle of our street, my face bleak and depressed. My hands show the compost pile rising as I dump load after load of collected grass and leaves onto it, and then I become the neighbours, my face curious, perplexed as I approach.

More confident now, I feel myself projecting Robbie, a sparkle in my eyes, the emotion I'm portraying larger than life. I show myself overwhelmed by all the things I need to learn to grow a beautiful garden, and Robbie breaking down the instructions into finger-sized steps. I show my hands blistering from the hot compost, and Halim handing me his fork. 'You just get started and the people and tools will come...'

There's a ripple, and the crowd cheers. At the front, Robbie raises her hands into the air and shakes them, and the people around her do the same – the Deaf version of clapping. I grin at them, delighted.

Encouraged, I show myself doing a double take in shock when I see the orange stickers from the council: a knife in my heart. My fingers shape the beautiful ramble of greens, the pecking of the chickens, the reflection in the pond, and then a huge bulldozer driving in to flatten it all.

The crowd roars, angry, fists in the air. I continue, but Abbey holds up a hand for me to wait. When the crowd finally settles down, she nods at me. I mime sitting at a visi, typing, inviting people to the rally, and Cesspool blocking it. My shock and disappointment registers on my face, over the top. There's more roaring from the crowd. I wait. Then I show myself spray-painting my 'Grow Food Not Concrete' poster on a wall on the street, and everyone cheers. I exaggerate my arrest, me obliviously spraying, hearing nothing, while police gather around me, guns drawn. The crowd is outraged on my behalf. I finally get to my point. 'We need freedom of speech.' The crowd goes wild.

In front of me, Robbie signs, 'Teach them the signs for *freedom of speech.*'

'Let me show you how to sign that,' I say. I place my thumbs on my chest, span my fingers, and wriggle them as I fly my hands in front of me. *Free.* The crowd copies me, a huge sea of flying hands stretching as far back as I can see. My heart catches, exhilarated.

Robbie feeds me the sign for *speech* – I hold my palm outwards, next to my mouth, and move it out in front of me in two firm strokes. The crowd copies. We all do it together again. *Free speech!*

They turn it into a chant, and I join them, and we repeat it, over and over.

Abbey indicates for me to take a bow. I do, and the crowd roars, hands high in the air, copying Robbie and the Deaf people around her. Trembling, I walk from the stage. I can hardly breathe. Wow. Who could have guessed they'd respond like that?

Marley envelopes me in his arms as soon as I step down. 'You were amazing! AMAZING! You are going to be the next Future Girl. Move over, Adhya Vasi – Piper has the future of food in her hands.'

On the stage, Karen Kildare takes my place. Abbey joins me, and Interpreter Man steps onto the stage. 'Can you interpret?' I ask Abbey.

The crowd quietens right down as Karen Kildare greets everyone. 'I have an important announcement to make,' Abbey signs, her face the exact expression of Karen's. 'Last night, Organicore filed for bankruptcy.'

A murmur runs through the crowd as everyone turns to each other, shocked. My mouth drops open. Where's Mum? Does she know this?

Karen Kildare continues: 'This means we need to make radical changes in order for Australia to produce enough food. As you know, we also face severe fuel shortages, which impact our production capacity. I see before me Australians offering up a valuable solution – that of individuals growing food on public land – and I take your voices seriously. I will consider what legislative changes I can propose to assist with this. In the meantime, I can confirm that any pending removal orders of existing community gardens will be cancelled.'

She has to pause for a moment then, as the crowd reacts, cheering wildly. I cheer with them. My garden! Thank god!

'I also hear your request for freedom of speech,' Karen Kildare continues, 'and I acknowledge that there have been issues in this regard. I will be addressing these in the coming months.'

Abbey's face changes. 'Someone from the audience yelled, *Are you able to do that now Organicore is dead?*'

From the side of the stage, I see Karen Kildare's face tighten. 'I am not at liberty to discuss that,' Abbey signs.

Someone else yells, 'What are you doing about electricity and transport?'

'There are no easy solutions. Perhaps the answer lies with us becoming less dependent on electricity and travel. I thank you for bringing these important issues to my attention.'

With that, Karen Kildare nods her head in a small bow. The crowd claps heartily, satisfied, though I notice it's not the enthusiastic roar they gave for me. She leaves the stage and I find myself standing right beside her.

'Piper,' she says, extending her hand. We shake. How can her fingers be so cool and dry after addressing such a massive audience? I wish I had her poise. Abbey shifts to stand beside her. 'Your speech was impressive,' Abbey signs for Karen Kildare. 'It touched me, and clearly touched many others. I understand you have charges against you relating to your lack of freedom of speech. In confidence, I can tell you I've already ensured that anybody charged for protesting about this particular matter will be having their cases automatically dismissed – including you. It is possible you'll be compensated for any time you spent incarcerated.'

My mouth drops open.

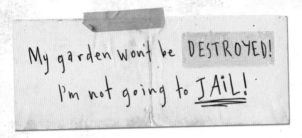

My garden won't be DESTROYED!
I'm not going to JAIL!

'Thank you,' I sign, and Abbey leans in close to Karen Kildare to relay my answer.

Two men in suits appear and usher Karen Kildare away. I feel hands on my shoulder and turn – it's Robbie. 'I'm so proud of you!' She hugs me tight.

As soon as she's finished, Kelsey hugs me too, then gives me a high five and very emphatic thumbs up. 'That couldn't have gone better!' Abbey signs, Kelsey's excitement on her face.

Next, the group of people who were with Robbie surround me, questions flying on their hands.

'Where did you grow up?'

'Why I haven't met you before?'

'What school did you go to?'

Robbie must see how dazed I am, because she signs, 'Enough! I'll bring her to the Deaf club!'

She hustles them off, and now there are strangers all around me, giving me the thumbs up. I hope I don't faint. Their faces swim around me. I need to sit down.

Then a hand slides across my shoulder. Marley. I sink my head against his neck, and just like Karen Kildare's bodyguards did for her, he ushers me away.

I've rebuilt my rocket stove on the island in the middle of our street. Connie lights a fire and positions herself elegantly in front of it: self-appointed fire manager. I plonk a pot of water on top, in preparation for chicken-plucking. But first Taggert and I need to harvest our crops – Taggert trying to pick everything regardless of whether it's ready or not; me grabbing his hands before he kills anything and directing him towards something ripe. He cradles each cauliflower, zucchini, broccoli and tomato as though it's a beloved doll as he delivers them to his dad, who's brought out a table and assumed the role of chef. Archie is clearly trained in wild-food preparation, and neat piles of vegetables mount up in front of him. Zoe and Erin sit together shelling peas and washing vegetables in one of Taggert's plastic buckets.

Halim appears wearing a shirt that's almost clean, and Gary has donned a tie for the occasion. Amber wheels out of her house with a small black box on her lap; she places it next to the rocket stove and taps a few buttons on her wristlet. I point to the box and turn up my palms questioningly, my eyebrows furrowed.

'It's a speaker. For music,' she types on her wristlet. 'What's your favourite song? I'll put it on.'

I type on my wristlet, 'I don't listen to a lot of music.' I indicate my ears.

'Oh, of course! I'm so stupid. I forgot.' Amber hits herself on the head, embarrassed.

'It's okay. I do actually like *Superficial Rising*, by Synchronic Bleaks.'

The music obviously starts, as everyone glances up and grooves to it slightly, rocking their heads in sync. I can't tell if it's 'Superficial Rising' or not as I'm not wearing my hearing aids. Then I forget all about that, as Robbie and Marley pedal onto our street, sweaty and flushed, hauling goodies in bulging saddlebags. Robbie hands me a bottle of pink stuff with red spots floating in it – sweet chilli sauce, one of her secret ingredients to make wild food taste amazing – and I throw my arms around her and kiss her cheek as she laughs.

Once I've let her go, Marley slides his arms around me from behind, and when I twist my face towards him he kisses me softly on the lips and gives me a little block of something wrapped in waxed paper. It's butter – another thing that turns an ordinary meal of greens into something delicious and satisfying. He also produces a small container of salt, a jar of Robbie's tomato sauce, salad dressing and a loaf of bread. We are definitely feasting tonight!

I give Robbie a tour of my garden and she walks slowly, stroking plant leaves, inspecting the dirt, inhaling deeply over my herb bed, and rippling the pond water through her fingers. She straightens and gives me an approving nod. 'This is good. Very good. It's beautiful and productive. Once the other garden beds are producing, you should get regular meals for all of you.

365

Through summer, these will grow you mountains.' She gestures to the tomatoes, zucchini and pumpkin vines.

I introduce Robbie around and she's polite and gracious, and I make a mental note along the lines of, *This is how a real Deaf person does hearing people*, though it's not really that different to how I do it. Zoe starts with her super-slow signing, and if Robbie is impatient, it doesn't show. Instead she sits down on one of the folding seats Halim has brought out and applies a face of rapt concentration to Zoe's fingers.

I leave her to it and grab Marley. 'Help me kill a chicken?'

'I just washed!' he protests. But he comes with me to the chicken coop, so I know he's not too fussed. He cups his hands around my face, turning it towards his and peering closely into my eyes. Then he signs, 'Is this the same girl who wouldn't even watch me kill a fish five months ago?'

'I've clearly matured,' I sign back haughtily. 'I'm now a properly murderous being. Look at what you and Robbie have done to me.'

Once I've sliced its neck and the chicken stops thrashing, Marley holds it casually by the feet with one hand and tenderly wipes a smear of blood from my cheek with the other. It strikes me that killing together is a kind of intimacy.

As we deliver the chicken to Archie for plucking and cooking, I get a message from Taylor: 'Want to hang out?'

I message her straight back, Marley stroking my neck as I type. 'Yes! Come over! We're having a solstice party on my street right now, with lots of food.'

Then I head inside, where Mum's hunched over her wristlet. She at least tried to pretend that she was fine with me appearing on every visi-screen in Australia giving my speech in sign language, but things have been pretty weird between us since then. I put my hearing aids in, run some water into the sink and use a cloth to scrub the chicken blood from my face and arms.

'The party's started,' I say. 'Come out with me.'

'I won't sit and eat with a group of people who think I'm so inept I can't even communicate with my own daughter,' she snaps back.

'Robbie's there,' I say. 'Marley's mum. You can meet her.' The logistics of how that's going to work evade me, but I decide that Mum's issue with my signing is NOT MY PROBLEM, and that this is a perfectly acceptable stance because my Deafness [IS] my problem and I have to deal with it every single day.

Mum sighs. 'Okay...I'll come.' She stands in front of the mirror and adjusts her hair.

I change into a dress I haven't worn since last year, and by that time Mum's all spiffed up and lets me lead her onto the street. A really, *really* good smell wafts from Archie's pot, and I squeeze Mum's arm as she inhales deeply. 'Wow,' she says. 'Icawata eeta.'

'What did you say?' I can hear Amber's music now that I have my hearing aids in, but it's just a jumbled blare and I can't hear Mum over it. I squint and move so I'm directly in front of her.

'Icawata eeta.'

'You...what?' I speak softly, signing at the same time, in the hope that it's not obvious I'm voicing to Mum. I wish Amber would turn down the music.

'I...CAN'T...WAIT...TO...EAT...THAT!' Mum shouts.

I hold up my finger to her. *Hang on.* I tap Amber and point

to the black box, making a motion like I'm turning a dial down. There's no dial on this box, but she fiddles with her wristlet for a bit and the music fades to a soft, irritating background burble. I want her to turn it right off, but I suppose this is a good compromise. 'Thank you,' I sign.

Zoe and Connie hold Robbie captive as they practise their sign language. I interrupt. 'Robbie, this is my mum, Irene. She's been looking forward to meeting you,' I sign. I turn to Mum and flush as I use my fingers instead of my voice, though I mouth the words clearly, with the teensiest bit of sound in the hope she'll understand me. 'Mum, this is Robbie. She has the most amazing garden and taught me how to do all this.'

Mum turns to Robbie and says, enunciating only slightly more clearly than usual, 'Pleased to meet you.'

When Robbie signs her reply, there's an awkward pause. Finally Mum says, 'I'm sorry. I don't know sign language.'

Marley's watching us. He hurries over. 'I can interpret,' he signs.

'You don't have to!' I sign back, but he waves me off.

'I want to.'

So Marley interprets and Mum says formally, 'So, Robbie, what do you do?'

'This,' Robbie signs, gesturing around. 'I grow food. I prefer that to working a different job in order to earn money to pay for food.'

Mum frowns as she digests this idea and quickly moves on to another topic. 'Does Marley have any brothers and sisters?'

'No. Van, his other mother, and I felt that we should be attempting not to increase the world's population.'

I'm not sure Mum's ever considered this concept before. She looks a little taken aback, but she spreads her face into her professional smile and says, 'I see. And where do you live?'

'Preston.' Robbie takes the conversation in hand. 'Don't you think Piper has done the most magnificent job out here? You must be *so* proud of her achievements! Not just locally and within the community, but lobbying for a better Australia.' Robbie ruffles my hair affectionately. 'I think she's found her calling.'

Mum stares at me in surprise. This appears to be another new concept for her. I want to add:

Yes, the question is no longer WHAT I'M GOING TO DO but what YOU'RE going to do, Mum.

But that would be mean. It strikes me as ironic that when Mum lost her own career and stopped trying to force one on me, I found my way.

I glance up and there's Taylor, hanging back on the footpath watching us, her mahogany bob sparkling clean, her cheeks round and healthy. She's much more dressed up than anyone else here, in a classy short pale-blue lace dress with matching pale-blue platform shoes and a small silver purse.

I hurry over and throw my arms around her. 'I'm so, *so* glad you came,' I whisper. I don't want anyone to see me talking with my voice, but I haven't introduced Taylor to this signing thing yet. I lead her down the far end of the street, away from the party. We need to talk.

We sit next to each other in the gutter. I clear my throat and use my voice again. 'That tree...I still can't believe it was *Beau* who took it.'

Taylor arcs up. 'I told you, Piper – I didn't know the details of what he was up to. He just had me wait in the car during all his secretive meetings. He wanted to keep me close, but he didn't trust me, not as anything other than his lookout.'

Heat rises inside me. I can't just accept this, pretend I'm fine with it. 'You were complicit!' I insist. 'You knew something was up, but you didn't question it or try to stop it – just acted dumb and benefited from the profits.'

She slumps, and I can see I've hit a nerve. 'I...okay...you're right. And I'm sorry. I've seen all the comments on Cesspool – I had no idea how much people cared about the trees he was stealing. God. I was so naïve. But I didn't feel like I had anywhere else to go. You were right, though – my parents *are* happy to have me home, now they're done screaming at me and grounding me until forever. And you know what, I feel kind of...free. All that stuff Beau was doing, the anger and the threats, was wrong. I just couldn't see it properly.'

'Did you actually tell him you've broken up with him?' I ask, softening.

'I went to visit him, and yeah, I told him. He cried. He said I was the love of his life. I said that if he truly loved me, he'd think about what's best for *me*. Making me an accessory to crime, stopping me from seeing people I love and doing the things I enjoy – that's not love.' Taylor glances down the street, and I follow her eyes. Marley is still interpreting for Mum and Robbie. 'Is that Marley? Are you going to drop me for him now?'

I frown in confusion. 'Yes, that's him. But no! I won't drop you for him. *You* dropped *me*!'

'You refused to come out with me, hang out with my friends,' Taylor says. 'It was like everything had to be with you alone. You wanted to own me – not so different from Beau.'

'No! That's not true!' But even as I'm saying it, I know she has a point and I put my head in my hands. This is not going how I'd hoped. 'I'm sorry,' I say. 'I didn't mean to pull you away. I just…I don't know how to communicate in groups of people who don't sign.'

'I saw you signing on the news. When did you learn to do that? You always said you didn't need sign language.'

'I realise now that it was *Mum* who always said I didn't need to sign. I never knew how relaxing it was to have a conversation with people without needing to lipread.'

'Fair enough,' Taylor says. I can still feel the wall between us.

'I found that if I don't speak, it works better, because people are more likely to communicate in ways I can actually understand.'

She raises an eyebrow at me.

'So, with all my neighbours down there, I don't speak. I just sign, and we all communicate in different ways. Some of them sign and fingerspell – not very well. Or they write in the dirt. Or type on their wristlet…whatever works. Maybe I should try that with your friends too.'

Taylor's intrigued rather than appalled. 'Really? You never use your voice with them *at all*? And it works?'

'Come and see.' I stand and hold out my hand. She puts her hand in mine and lets me lead her back to the group. We head for Marley and I sign, 'This is Taylor.'

He smiles warmly and signs, 'Pleased to meet you.'

'Taylor can't sign, so can you use your voice?' I sign. It feels unfair to ask when I'm not using *my* voice, but I'm not sure how to navigate all of this. It would be so much easier to keep the people I voice with separate from the people I sign with, but that's probably impossible.

'How do you know Piper?' Marley signs, this time using his voice too.

'We went to school together, since we were this big.' Taylor's hand hovers at hip level. 'How come you know how to do this so well?' She wriggles her hands together in front of her chest, a mock imitation of sign language.

'I'm a CODA – Child of Deaf Adult. My mum is Deaf,' Marley replies.

'Wow. Is it hard to learn?'

He shakes his head. 'You just learn the alphabet and take it from there.'

'Will you show me?'

'No, I won't – but Piper might!'

I lead Taylor through the alphabet, both of us giggling. If only Mum could be like this, as if it's no big deal. I glance across and see that she's still sitting with Robbie, even though Marley is no longer there interpreting for her. I hope she's coping all right.

Zoe catches my eye and waves us all over. Dinner's ready! She gives each of us a bowl of chicken-and-vegie stew. Erin adds half a slice of buttered bread per person. I hand a bowl each to Mum and Robbie, then sit near them on the ground, gesturing for Taylor and Marley to join me. We all inhale deeply and sigh.

The stew is incredible, the vegies cut large enough that when you bite into each one, you can taste its own individual, fresh, sunshine-y flavour. The sauce blends through everything beautifully, sweet, tangy-sour and greasy with butter. Archie really does know his stuff.

Taylor nudges me and indicates the stew with her eyes. 'YUM,' she fingerspells, and I'm thrilled to see her diving into this and making an effort. Not bad for a complete beginner!

I show her the sign for *delicious*, kissing my index finger and ending with my thumb up – a combination of the signs for *taste* and *good*. She copies me and laughs, doing the sign with a dramatic flourish.

Putting down her bowl, she concentrates hard to remember the right letters. 'WI SHOILD HAVE DINE THIS YEARS AGO! OT'S FUN.'

And as I lean sideways and tuck my head onto Marley's shoulder, chewing the last of my bread with my eyes closed, I have to agree.

THE END.

DEAR READER,

As an oral deaf child who couldn't sign, like Piper, I found myself ill-equipped to ask for inclusion and for my needs as a deaf person to be met. I was too busy trying to pass as hearing – as 'normal'.

If you are a hearing reader, I hope that reading about Piper's experience gives you some insight into what it can be like to be d/Deaf, and an understanding of what a huge difference it can make if you demonstrate inclusive, thoughtful behaviour. If you are d/Deaf, I hope that you can relate to some of Piper's experiences, and that seeing them written down makes it easier for you to explain your own experiences to other people. I hope it also helps you to build a sense of entitlement to ask for access.

The United Nations made a resolution in 1975 asserting that disabled people (and thus d/Deaf people) have the same right as fellow citizens to enjoy a decent, full life; that we are entitled to measures designed to enable us to become as self-reliant as possible, and entitled to have our needs taken into consideration at all stages of economic and social planning. In other words, we are entitled to ask for and expect the same access as a hearing person or able-bodied person would receive.

Here are some ideas to keep in mind when it comes to relating to d/Deaf people:

it is not my GOAL to be 'NORMAL'

Share the burden of communication. Don't expect us to do all the work, especially when it comes to lipreading. Remember that many of us have been conditioned, like Piper, to carry this burden alone, without assistance. If a person communicates with you using sign language and you can't sign, don't expect them to lipread you. Try mime or writing instead.

Remember to include us. That means being aware of important sounds/audio information and relaying them to us, and communicating in a way that we can understand. Some small examples include: if the phone is ringing, rather than just going to answer it, let us know that the phone is ringing and that is why you're walking away in the middle of a conversation; if the speeches are starting, let us know; if something important is happening in the world, tell us about it; if there's an announcement, let us know what it says. Tell us the nicknames you use for people, and what's going to happen next, and where we're going, because this is the kind of stuff hearing people pick up by overhearing, but that we miss. If there is a Deaf person present and you can sign, always do so, even if you are talking with another hearing person and you think the Deaf person isn't looking. Like hearing people, we glean so much about the world and dynamics of our social groups by being able to glance up and understand snippets of what people say to each other.

Don't ask us overly personal questions or propose medical interventions that might 'fix' us. Many of us are sick of answering questions like 'Were you born deaf?' and 'Why don't you get a cochlear implant?' and 'Can you lipread?' It's none of your business.

Don't tell us your assessment of our skills. We don't need to hear your opinion about how well we speak, how well we lipread, how well we sign, or how much we can or can't hear. Chances are, we have a much better handle on our own skills than you do.

Think about what it means to be d/Deaf, so that you don't shove a microphone at us when we are about to go onstage to sign a speech, nor expect us to look at something you are pointing at while lipreading you. At the same time, don't assume to know a d/Deaf person's experience without asking – we may still enjoy music, and we may still do things you assume are impossible for d/Deaf people.

Don't patronise us, nor assume that we are stupid. Treat us as intelligent. We can be just as cunning, savvy, cheeky and interesting as hearing people. In this story, the police mounted a huge search party for Piper because they assumed a deaf teenager would not be able to survive in the real world. This matches my experience of peoples' assumptions about me.

Remember that we are more than the label, DEAF. When I first meet people, I often feel that they see me as a Deaf person first, and it comes as a surprise to them that there is so much more to me. Piper, too, is d/Deaf, but her capacity for problem-solving and inadvertent leadership is far more interesting, as is her courage to jump in and try new things. When you meet a person who is d/Deaf or has a disability, try to find out who we are beyond that label.

If there is a person in your life who uses sign language, make the effort to learn. As a child, I never knew how relaxing communication could be – it was always a stressful, challenging experience. It was not until I learned to sign that I understood the fun of socialising. By the same token, if you have a deaf child, even if they have fantastic speech and lipread well, encourage everyone in the family to learn to sign, so that your child can sometimes have a break from the intense pressure of trying to pass as hearing. Meet us on our turf. It's fun, too. You'll find free Auslan instruction videos on my website, www.asphyxia.com.au.

If you are a parent of a deaf child, it may be your goal for them to grow up to be as normal as possible. Remember that this can create a huge pressure on us. While some people who are d/Deaf or have a disability do put a high value on 'passing as normal', many of us would rather take a different approach: that of accepting that we are different and asking for our needs to be met. Teach your child how to recognise their specific needs and how to adjust their world to suit them. This means believing in our entitlement to access and developing the confidence to ask for it. It means allowing us to sometimes choose to be in a signing-only space so that we can relax and know that our d/Deafness is accommodated. It means using technology for things like flashing-light doorbells, text message communication and other visual cues, rather than expecting a child to wear hearing aids so that they can function in an unadapted world.

Don't throw things at us to get our attention. Instead, try flashing the lights on and off, waving your arms, stomping on the floor, banging on the table, or simply coming over to tap us on the arm. Don't be shy to touch us on the arm to get our attention, but never tap us on the head or other parts of our bodies – that's rude and feels invasive.

Thanks for reading. If you'd like to know more about Deafness, or find out about my other books, please meet me online at www.asphyxia.com.au.

Asphyxia

ART JOURNAL IDEAS

+ Flip through and randomly paint backgrounds, experimenting with colour and textures.

+ Collage pieces of paper over parts of your backgrounds, noting which colours and patterns look best against various pages. Add complimentary strips of patterned paper, stickytape or washi tape. You may wish to leave space for writing.

+ Experiment with making your own collage papers by painting and drawing patterns on paper. Dots and stripes of various thicknesses and spacing, flowers and geometric shapes work well.

+ Collage in words that appeal to you – snipped from magazines or newspapers, printed out or hand-lettered.

+ Add drawings and paintings of images that express what is happening for you – print from the internet if need be.

+ Keep your book with you through the day and doodle randomly over the top of everything to fill bits of dead time.

+ Stick in photos of things you make, things that inspire you, important events, yourself and the people you love.

+ When you have an idea, jot it down in your journal, along with a sketch, instructions or related images.

+ Write your goals, to do lists, plans and calendar in your journal. Let it function as your organiser as well as an art play space.

+ Add a pocket and use it to collect bits of paper, notes and junk from your everyday life, until you are ready to glue them in.

+ Write your feelings. Getting down your deepest, darkest and most difficult feelings has been shown to improve health, grades and even result in more job opportunities!